"How wonderful," Tas cried. "I'll fly just like the draconians!"

Palin shouted out in horror. He lunged, tried to grasp hold of the kender's shirttail, and missed.

With a cry of glee, Tasslehoff spread his arms like a bird and leaped straight off the final stair. He plunged downward and disappeared into the smoke.

The DRAGONLANCE® Saga

Read these books by Margaret Weis and Tracy Hickman

Dragons of Autumn Twilight
Dragons of Winter Night
Dragons of Spring Dawning

Time of the Twins
War of the Twins
Test of the Twins

The Second Generation

Dragons of Summer Flame

Dragons of a Fallen Sun
Dragons of a Lost Star
Dragons of a Vanished Moon
(June 2002)

. . . and more than one hundred other DRAGONLANCE novels and anthologies by dozens of authors.

THE WAR OF SOULS

VOLUME TWO

DRAGONS OF A LOST STAR

Margaret Weis & Tracy Hickman

DRAGONS OF A LOST STAR
©2002 Wizards of the Coast, Inc.

Cover art by Matt Stawicki
Map by Dennis Kauth
First Printing: April 2001
First paperback edition: March 2002
Library of Congress Catalog Card Number: 00-190770

9 8 7 6 5 4

ISBN: 978-0-7869-2706-7
620-88549-001-EN

U.S., CANADA,	EUROPEAN HEADQUARTERS
ASIA, PACIFIC, & LATIN AMERICA	Hasbro UK Ltd.
Wizards of the Coast, Inc.	Caswell Way
P.O. Box 707	Newport, Gwent NP9 0YH
Renton, WA 98057-0707	GREAT BRITAIN
+1-800-324-6496	Save this address for your records

Visit our web site at **www.wizards.com/dragonlance**

Dedication

To Laura Hickman

For her help, encouragement, and support over the years,
we dedicate this book with much love.

—*Margaret Weis and Tracy Hickman*

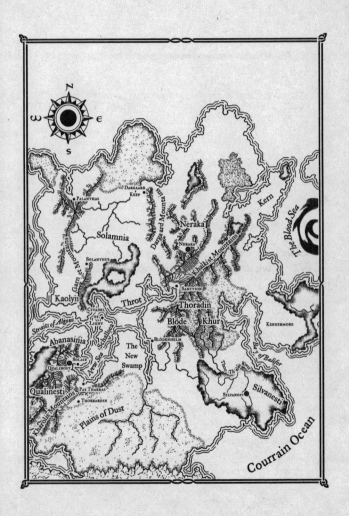

1

An Accounting Nightmare

orham Targonne was having a bad day. His accounts would not balance. The difference in the totals was paltry, a matter of a few steel. He could have made it up with the spare change from his purse. But Targonne liked things to be neat, orderly. His rows of figures should add up. There should be no discrepancies. Yet here he was. He had the various accounts of moneys coming into the knights' coffers. He had the various accounts of moneys going out of the Knights' coffers, and there was a difference of twenty-seven steel, fourteen silver, and five coppers. Had it been a major sum, he might have suspected embezzlement. As it was, he was certain that some minor functionary had made a simple miscalculation. Targonne would have to go back through all the accounts, redo the calculations, track down the error.

An uninformed observer, seeing Morham Targonne seated at his desk, his fingers black with ink, his head bent over his accounts, would have said that he was looking on a loyal and dedicated clerk. The uninformed observer would have been wrong. Morham Targonne was the leader of the Dark Knights of Neraka and thereby, since the Dark Knights were in control of several major nations on the continent of Ansalon, Morham Targonne held the power of life and death over millions of people. Yet here he was, working into the night, looking with the diligence of the stodgiest clerk for twenty-seven steel, fourteen silver, and five coppers.

But although he was concentrating on his work to the extent that he had skipped supper to continue his perusal of the accounts, Lord Targonne was not absorbed in his work to the exclusion of all else. He had the ability to focus a part of his mental powers on a task and, at the same time, to be keenly alert, aware of what was going on around him. His mind was a desk constructed of innumerable compartments into which he sorted and slotted every occurrence, no matter how minor, placed it in its proper hole, available for his use at some later time.

Targonne knew, for example, when his aide left to go to his own supper, knew precisely how long the man was away from his desk, knew when he returned. Knowing approximately how long it would take a man to eat his supper, Targonne was able to say that his aide had not lingered over his tarbean tea but had returned to his work with alacrity. Targonne would remember this in the aide's favor someday, setting that against the opposite column in which he posted minor infractions of duty.

The aide was staying at work late this night. He would stay until Targonne discovered the twenty-seven steel, fourteen silver, and five coppers, even if they were both awake until the sun's rays crept through Targonne's freshly cleaned window. The aide had his own work to keep him occupied—Targonne saw to that. If there was one thing he hated, it was to see a man idling. The two worked late into the night, the aide sitting at a desk outside the office, trying to see by lamplight as he stifled his yawns, and Targonne sitting inside his sparsely furnished office, head bent over his bookkeeping, whispering the numbers to himself as he wrote them, a habit of his of which he was completely unconscious.

The aide was himself slipping toward unconsciousness when, fortunately for him, a loud commotion in the courtyard outside the fortress of the Dark Knights startled him from a brief nap.

A blast of wind set the window panes rattling. Voices shouted out harshly in irritation or warning. Booted feet came running. The aide left his desk and went to see what was happening at the same time as Targonne's voice called from his office, demanding to know what was going on and who in the Abyss was making all this blasted racket.

The aide returned almost immediately.

"My lord, a dragonrider has arrived from—"

"What does the fool mean, landing in the courtyard?"

Hearing the noise, Targonne had actually left his accounting long enough to turn to look out his window. He was infuriated to see the large blue dragon flapping about his courtyard. The large blue looked infuriated herself, for she had been forced to alight in an area that was much too small and cramped for her bulk. She had just missed a guard tower with her wing. Her tail had taken out a small portion of the battlements. Other than that, she had managed to land safely and now squatted in the courtyard, her wings folded tight at her sides, her tail twitching. She was hungry and thirsty. There were no dragon stables close by nor any sign that she was going to have anything to eat or drink anytime soon. She glared balefully at Targonne through the window, as though she blamed him for her troubles.

"My lord," said the aide, "the rider comes from Sil-vanesti—"

"My lord!" The dragonrider, a tall man, stood behind the aide, loomed over him. "Forgive the disruption, but I bring news of such dire urgency and importance that I felt I had to inform you immediately."

"Silvanesti." Targonne snorted. Returning to his desk, he continued writing. "Has the shield fallen?" he asked sarcastically.

"Yes, my lord!" The dragonrider gasped, out of breath.

Targonne dropped his pen. Lifting his head, he stared at the messenger in astonishment. "What? How?"

"The young officer named Mina—" The dragonrider was forced to interrupt himself with a fit of coughing. "Might I have something to drink, my lord? I have swallowed a vast quantity of dust between here and Silvanesti."

Targonne made a motion with his hand, and his aide left to fetch ale. While they waited, Targonne invited the rider to be seated and rest himself.

"Order your thoughts," Targonne instructed, and as the Knight did just that, Targonne used his powers as a mentalist to probe the Knight's mind, to eavesdrop on those thoughts, see what the Knight had seen, hear what the Knight had heard.

The images bombarded Targonne. For the first time in his career, he found himself at a loss to know what to think. Too much was happening too fast for him to comprehend. What was overwhelmingly clear to Morham Targonne was that too much of it was happening without his knowledge and outside his control. He was so disturbed by this that he actually for the moment forgot the twenty-seven steel, fourteen silver, and five coppers, although he wasn't so rattled but that he made a note to himself when he closed his books as to where he left off in his calculations.

The aide returned with a mug of cold ale. The Knight drank deeply and, by that time, Targonne had managed to compose himself to listen with every appearance of outward calm. Inside, he was seething.

"Tell me everything," Targonne instructed.

The Knight complied.

"My lord, the young Knight officer known as Mina was able, as we reported to you earlier, to penetrate the magical shield that had been raised around Silvanesti—"

"But not lower the shield," Targonne interrupted, seeking clarification.

"No, my lord. In fact, she used the shield to fend off pursuing ogres, who were unable to break the enchantment. Mina led her small force of Knights and foot soldiers into Silvanesti with the apparent design of attacking the capital, Silvanost."

Targonne sniffed in derision.

"They were intercepted by a large force of elves and were handily defeated. Mina was captured during the battle and made prisoner. The elves planned to execute her the following morning. However, just prior to her execution, Mina attacked the green dragon Cyan Bloodbane, who had, as you were no doubt aware, my lord, been masquerading as an elf."

Targonne had not known that, nor did he see how he should have known it, since not even he could have seen through the cursed magical shield the elves had raised over their land. He made no comment, however. He never minded appearing omniscient.

"Her attack forced Cyan to reveal to the elves the fact that he was a dragon. The elves were terrified. Cyan would have slaughtered thousands of them, but this Mina roused the elven army and ordered them to attack the green dragon."

"Help me understand the situation," said Targonne, who was starting to feel an aching behind his right temple.

"One of our own officers rallied the army of our most bitter enemy, who in turn slew one of the mightiest of our green dragons?"

"Yes, my lord," said the Knight. "You see, my lord, as it turned out, it was the dragon Cyan Bloodbane who had raised the magical shield that had been keeping our armies out of Silvanesti. The shield, as it turns out, was killing the elves."

"Ah," said Targonne and rubbed his temple with a forefinger. He hadn't known that either. But he might have been able to deduce it, had he given it much thought. The green dragon Cyan Bloodbane, terrified of Malystryx, vengeful toward the elves, built a shield that protected him from one enemy and helped destroy another. Ingenious. Flawed, but ingenious. "Proceed."

The Knight hesitated. "What happened after that is rather confused, my lord. General Dogah had received your orders to halt his march to Sanction and proceed instead to Silvanesti."

Targonne had given no such orders, but he had already observed Dogah's march from the Knight's mental processes and let this comment pass unremarked. He would deal with that later.

"General Dogah arrived to find the shield prohibited him from entering. He was furious, thinking he'd been sent on a kender's errand. The land around the shield is a terrible place, my lord, filled with dead trees and animal corpses. The air is fetid and foul to breathe. The men were upset, claiming the place was haunted and that we ourselves would die from being so near it, when, suddenly, with the rising of the sun, the shield shattered. I was with General Dogah, and I saw it with my own eyes."

"Describe it," Targonne ordered, eyeing the man intently.

"I have been thinking about how to do so, my lord. Once when I was a child, I stepped on an ice-covered pond. The ice beneath my feet began to crack. The cracks spread across the ice with a snapping sound, then the ice gave way, and I plunged into the black water. This was much the same. I saw the shield shimmering like ice in the sunshine, and then it seemed to me that I saw a million, million infinitesimal cracks, as thin as the strands of a cobweb, spread across the shield with lightning speed. There was a shivering, tinkling sound as of a thousand glass goblets crashing onto a stone floor, and the shield was gone.

"We could not believe our senses. At first, General Dogah dared not enter the shield, fearing a cunning elven trap. Perhaps, he said, we shall march across and the shield will crash down behind us, and we will end up facing an army of ten thousand elves, yet have nowhere to go. Suddenly there appeared among us, as if by magic, one of Mina's Knights. Through the power of the One God, he came to tell us that the shield had indeed fallen, brought down by the elven king himself, Silvanoshei, son of Alhana—"

"Yes, yes," said Targonne impatiently. "I know the whelp's pedigree. Dogah believed this chit, and he and his troops crossed the border."

"Yes, my lord. General Dogah ordered me to take my blue dragon and fly back to report to you that he is now marching on Silvanost, the capital."

"What of the ten-thousand-man elven army?" Targonne asked dryly.

"As to the army, my lord, they have not attacked us. According to Mina, the king, Silvanoshei, has told them that Mina has come to save the Silvanesti nation in the name of the One God. I must say, my lord, that the elves are in pitiable condition. When our advance troops entered an elven fishing village near the shield, we observed that most of the elves were sick or dying from the cursed magic of the shield. We thought to slay the wretches, but Mina forbade it. She performed miracles of healing on the dying elves and restored them to life. When we left, the elves were singing her praises and blessing the One God and vowing to worship this god in Mina's name.

"Yet not all elves trust her. Mina warned us that we might be attacked by those who call themselves 'the kirath.' But, according to her, their numbers are few, and they are disorganized. Alhana Starbreeze has forces on the border, but Mina does not fear them. She does not appear to fear anything," the Knight added with an admiration he could not conceal.

The One God! Ha! Targonne thought to himself, seeing far more in the messenger's mind than he was saying. Sorcery. This Mina is a witch. She has everyone ensorcelled—the elves, Dogah, and my Knights included. They are as smitten with this upstart chippy as the elves. What is she after?

The answer was obvious to Targonne.

She is after my position, of course. She is subverting the loyalty of my officers and winning the admiration of my troops. She plots against me. A dangerous game for such a little girl.

He mused, forgetting the weary messenger. Outside the room came the thud of booted feet and a loud voice demanding to see the Lord of the Night.

"My lord!" His aide hastened into the room, interrupting Targonne's dark thoughts. "Another messenger has arrived."

A second messenger entered the room, glanced askance at the first.

"Yes, what is *your* news?" Targonne demanded of the second.

"I have been contacted by Feur the Red, our agent in the service of the great green dragon overlord Beryl.

8

The red reports that she and a host of dragons bearing draconian soldiers have been ordered to undertake an assault on the Citadel of Light."

"The citadel?" Targonne struck his fist on the desk, causing a neatly stacked pile of steel coins to topple. "Is that green bitch of a dragon insane? What does she mean, attacking the citadel?"

"According to the red, Beryl has sent a messenger to tell you and her cousin Malystryx that this is a private quarrel and that there is no need for Malys to get involved. Beryl seeks a sorcerer who sneaked into her lands and stole a valuable magical artifact. She learned that the sorcerer fled for safety to the citadel, and she has gone to fetch him. Once she has him and the artifact, she will withdraw."

"Magic!" Targonne swore viciously. "Beryl is obsessed with magic. She thinks of nothing else. I have gray-robed wizards who spend all their time hunting for some blamed magical Tower just to placate that bloated lizard. Assaulting the citadel! What of the pact of the dragons? 'Cousin Malystryx' will most certainly see this as a threat from Beryl. This could mean all-out war, and that would wreck the economy."

Targonne rose to his feet. He was about to give an order to have messengers standing by, ready to carry this news to Malys, who must certainly hear of this from him, when he heard more shouting in the hallway.

"Urgent message for the Lord of the Night."

Targonne's aide, looking slightly frazzled, entered the room.

"What is it now?" Targonne growled.

"A messenger brings word from Marshal Medan in Qualinost that Beryl's forces have crossed the border into Qualinesti, pillaging and looting as they march. Medan urgently requests orders. He believes that Beryl intends to destroy Qualinesti, burn the forests to the ground, tear down the cities, and exterminate the elves."

"Dead elves pay me no tribute!" Targonne exclaimed, cursing Beryl with all his heart and soul. He began to pace behind his desk. "I cannot cut timber in a burned-out forest. Beryl attacks Qualinesti *and* the citadel. She is lying to me and to Malys. Beryl intends to break the pact. She plans war against Malys and against the Knighthood. I must find some way to stop her. Leave me! All of you," he ordered peremptorily. "I have work to do."

The first messenger bowed and left to eat and take what rest he could before the return flight. The second left to await orders. The aide departed to dispatch runners to wake other messengers and alert the blue dragons who would carry them.

After the aide and the messengers had gone, Targonne continued to pace the room. He was angry, infuriated, frustrated. Only a few moments before, he had been working on his accounts, content in the knowledge that the world was going as it should, that he had everything under control. True, the dragon overlords imagined that they were the ones in charge, but Targonne knew better. Bloated, enormous, they were—or had been—content to slumber in their lairs, allowing the Dark Knights of Neraka to rule in their names. The Dark Knights controlled Palanthas and Qualinost, two of the wealthiest cities on the continent. They would soon break the siege of Sanction and seize that seaport city, giving them access to New Sea. They had taken Haven, and he was even now drawing up plans to attack the prosperous crossroads town of Solace.

Now, he watched his plans topple in a heap like the stack of steel coins. Returning to his desk, Targonne laid out several sheets of foolscap. He dipped his pen into the ink and, after several more moments of profound thought, began to write.

General Dogah

Congratulations on your victory over the Silvanesti elves. These people have defied us for many years. However, I must warn you, do not trust them. I have no need to tell you that we do not have the manpower to hold Silvanesti if the elves decide to rise up in a body and rebel against us. I understand that they are sick and weakened, their population decimated, but they are tricky. Especially this king of theirs—Silvanoshei. He is the son of a cunning, treacherous mother and an outlawed father. He is undoubtedly in league with them. I want you to bring to me for interrogation any elves you believe might be able to provide me with information regarding any subversive plots of the elves. Be discreet in this, Dogah. I do not want to rouse the elves' suspicions.

Lord of the Night,
Targonne

He read over this letter, dusted the wet ink with sand to hasten the drying process, and set it aside. After a moment's thought, he set about composing the next.

To Dragon Overlord Malystryx, Your Most Exalted Majesty etc., etc.

It is with great pleasure that I make known to Your Most Illustrious Majesty that the elven people of Silvanesti, who have long defied us, have been utterly vanquished by the armies of the Dark Knights of Neraka. Tribute from these rich lands will soon be flowing into your coffers. The Knights of Neraka will, as usual, handle all the financial dealings to relieve you of such a mundane burden.

During the battle, the green dragon, Cyan Bloodbane, was discovered to have been hiding in Silvanesti. Fearing your wrath, he sided with the elves. Indeed, it was he who raised the magical shield that has so long kept us out of that land. He was slain during the battle. If possible, I will have his head found and delivered to Your Grace.

11

You may hear certain wild rumors that your cousin, Beryl-linthranox, has broken the pact of the dragons by attacking the Citadel of Light and marching her armies into Qualinesti. I hasten to assure Your Grace that such is not the case. Beryllin-thranox is acting under my orders. We have evidence that the Mystics of the Citadel of Light have been causing our own Mystics to fail in their magic. I deemed these Mystics a threat, and Beryllinthranox graciously offered to destroy them for me. As to Qualinesti, Beryllinthranox's armies are marching in order to join up with the forces of Marshal Medan. His orders are to destroy the rebels under the leadership of an elf known as the Lioness, who has harassed our troops and disrupted the flow of tribute.

As you see, I have everything under control. You need have no cause for alarm.

Lord of the Night,
Morham Targonne

He dusted sand on that letter and immediately launched into the next, which was easier to write due to the fact that there was some truth to this one.

To Khellendros the Blue Dragon, Most Esteemed, etc., etc.

You have undoubtedly heard that the great green dragon Beryllinthranox has launched an attack against the Citadel of Light. Fearing that you may misunderstand this incursion into lands so close to your territory, I hasten to reassure your lordship that Beryllinthranox is acting under my orders in this. The Mystics of the Citadel of Light have been discovered to be the cause of the failure of our Mystics in their magic. I would have made the request of you, Magnificent Khellendros, but I know that you must be keeping a close eye on the gathering of accursed Solamnic Knights in the city of Solanthus. Not wanting to call you away at this critical time, I requested that Beryllinthranox deal with the problem.

Lord of the Night,
Morham Targonne

Postscript: You are aware of the gathering of Solamnic Knights at Solanthus, are you not, Exalted One?

His last letter was easier still and took him very little thought.

Marshal Medan,

You are hereby ordered to hand over the capital city of Qualinost intact and undamaged to Her Grace, Beryllinthranox. You will arrest all members of the elven royal family, including King Gilthas and the Queen Mother, Laurana. They are to be given alive to Beryllinthranox, who may do with them what she pleases. In return for this, you will make clear to Beryllinthranox that her forces are to immediately cease their wanton destruction of forests, farms, buildings, etc. You will impress upon Beryllinthranox that although she, in her magnificence, does not need money, we poor unfortunate worms of mortals do. You have leave to make the following offer: Every human soldier in her army will be granted a gift of elven land, including all buildings and structures on the land. All high-ranking human officers in her armies will be given fine homes in Qualinost. This should curb the looting and destruction. Once matters have returned to normal, I will see to it that human settlers are moved in to take over the remainder of elven lands.
Lord of the Night,
Morham Targonne

Postscript 1: This offer of land does not apply to goblins, hobgoblins, minotaurs, or draconians. Promise them the equivalent value in steel, to be paid at a later date. I trust you will see to it *that these creatures are in the vanguard of the army and that they will take the heaviest casualties.*

Postscript 2: As to the elven residents of Qualinesti, it is probable that they will refuse to give up their ownership of their lands and property. Since by so doing they defy a direct order of the Knights of Neraka, they have broken the law and are hereby sentenced to death. Your soldiers are ordered to carry out the sentence on the spot.

Once the ink had dried, Targonne affixed his seal to each letter and, summoning his aide, dispatched them. As dawn broke, four blue dragonriders took to the skies.

This done, Targonne considered going to his bed. He knew, however, that he would not be able to rest with the specter of that accounting mistake haunting his otherwise pleasant dreams of neat charts and columns. He sat down doggedly to work, and as often happens when one has left a task upon which one has concentrated, he found the error almost immediately. The twenty-seven steel, fourteen silver, and five coppers were accounted for at last. Targonne made the correction with a precise pen stroke.

Pleased, he closed the book, tidied his desk, and left for a brief nap, confident that all was once more well with the world.

2

Attack on the Citadel of Light

eryl and her dragon minions flew over the Citadel of Light. The dragonfear they generated crashed down upon the inhabitants, a tidal wave that drowned courage in despair and terror. Four large red dragons flew overhead. The black shadows cast by their wings were darker than the deepest night, and every person the shadow touched felt his heart wither and his blood chill.

Beryllinthranox was an enormous green dragon who had appeared on Krynn shortly after the Chaos War; no one knew how or from where. Upon arrival, she and other dragons of her kind—most notably her cousin Malystryx—had attacked the dragons inhabiting Krynn, metallic and chromatic alike, waging war upon their own kind. Her body bloated from feeding off the dragons she had killed, Beryl circled high in the sky, far above the reds, who were her minions and her subjects, observing, watching. She was pleased with what she saw, pleased with the progress of the battle.

The citadel was defenseless against her. Had the great silver dragon, Mirror, been present, he might have dared defy her, but he was gone, mysteriously vanished. The Solamnic Knights, who had a fortress on Schallsea Isle, would make an heroic stand, but their numbers were few, and they could not hope to survive a concentrated attack from Beryl and her followers. The great green dragon would never have to fly within range of their arrows. She had only to breathe on them. A single poisonous blast from Beryl would kill every defender in the fort.

The Solamnic Knights were not going lie down and die. She could count on them to give her servants a lively battle. Their archers lined the battlements as their commanders strove to keep up their courage, even as the dragonfear unmanned many and left them weak and trembling. Knights rode with haste through island villages and towns, trying to quell the panic of the inhabitants and help them flee inland to the caves that were stocked and provisioned against just such an attack.

In the citadel itself, the Citadel Guards had always planned to use their mystical powers to defend themselves against a dragon attack. These powers had mysteriously waned over the past year, and thus the Mystics were forced to flee their beautiful crystal buildings and leave them to the ravages of the dragons. The first to be evacuated were the orphans. The children were frightened and cried for Goldmoon, for she was much loved by the children, but she did not come to them. Students and masters lifted the smallest children in their arms and soothed them, as they hastened to carry them to safety, telling them that Goldmoon would certainly come to them, but that she was now busy and that they must be brave and make her proud of them. As they spoke, the Mystics glanced at each other in sorrow and dismay.

Goldmoon had fled the citadel with the dawning. She had fled like one mad or possessed. None of the Mystics knew where she had gone.

The residents of Schallsea Isle left their homes and streamed inland, those debilitated by dragonfear urged and guided by those who had managed to overcome it. In the hills in the center of the island were large caves. The people had fondly believed that they would be safe from the ravages of the dragons inside these caves, but now that the attack had come, many were starting to realize how foolish such plans had been. The flames of the red dragons would destroy the forests and the buildings. As flames ravaged the surface, the noxious breath of the huge green would poison the air and the water. Nothing could survive. Schallsea would be an isle of corpses.

The people waited in terror for the attack to begin, waited for the flames to melt the crystal domes and the rock walls of the fortress, waited for the cloud of poison to choke the life from them. But the dragons did not attack. The reds circled overhead, watching the panic on the ground with gleeful satisfaction but making no move to kill. The people wondered what they were waiting for. Some of the foolish took hope, thinking that this might be nothing more than intimidation and that the dragons, having terrified everyone, would depart. The wise knew better.

In his room located high in the Lyceum, the main building of the crystal-domed Citadel of Light, Palin Majere watched through the enormous window—actually a wall of crystal—the coming of the dragons. He kept watch on the dragons while he desperately attempted to put back together the broken pieces of the magical artifact that was to have transported himself and Tasslehoff to the safety of Solace.

"Look at it this way," said Tas, with maddening kender cheerfulness, "at least the dragon won't get her claws on the artifact."

"No," said Palin shortly, "she'll get her claws on us."

"Maybe not," Tas argued, ferreting out a piece of the device that had rolled under the bed. "With the Device of Time Journeying being broken and its magic all gone—" He paused and sat up. "I guess its magic *is* all gone, isn't it, Palin?"

Palin didn't answer. He barely heard the kender's voice. He could see no way out of this. Fear shook him, despair gnawed at him until he was weak and limp. He was too exhausted to fight to stay alive, and why should he bother? It was the dead who were stealing the magic, siphoning it off for some unknown reason. He shivered, reminded of the feeling of those cold lips pressed against his flesh, of the voices crying, begging, pleading for the magic. They had taken it . . . and the Device of Time Journeying was now a hodgepodge of wheels, gears, rods, and sparkling jewels, lying scattered on the rug.

"As I was saying, with the magic gone"—Tas was still prattling—"Beryl won't be able to find us because she won't have the magic to guide her to us."

Palin lifted his head, looked at the kender.

"What did you say?"

"I said a lot of things. About the dragon not having the artifact and maybe not having us because if the magic is gone—"

"You may be right," Palin said.

"I am?" Tas was no end astonished.

"Hand me that," Palin instructed, pointing.

Appropriating one of the kender's pouches, Palin dumped out its contents and began to hastily gather up the bits and pieces of the artifact, stuffing them into the pouch.

"The guards will be evacuating people into the hills. We'll lose ourselves in the crowd. No, don't touch that!" he ordered sharply, slapping the kender's small hand that was reaching for the jeweled faceplate. "I must keep all the pieces together."

"I just wanted a memento," Tas explained, sucking on his red knuckles. "Something to remember Caramon by. Especially since I won't be using the artifact to go back in time now."

Palin grunted. His hands shook, and it was difficult for his twisted fingers to grasp some of the smaller pieces.

"I don't know why you want that old thing anyhow," Tas observed. "I doubt you can fix it. I doubt anyone can fix it. It looks to be *extremely* broken."

Palin shot the kender a baleful glance. "You said you had decided to use it to return to the past."

"That was then," said Tas. "Before things got really interesting here. What with Goldmoon sailing off in the gnome's submersible and now being attacked by dragons. Not to mention the dead people," he added, as an afterthought.

Palin didn't like the reminder. "Make yourself useful at least. Go out in the hallway and find out what's going on."

Tas did as he was told, heading for the door, although he continued to talk over his shoulder. "I told you about seeing the dead people. Right when the artifact busted. Didn't I? They were all over you, like leeches."

"Do you see any of them now?" Palin asked.

Tas glanced around. "No, not a one. But then," he pointed out helpfully, "the magic's gone, isn't it?"

"Yes." Palin snapped tight the strings on the bag that held the broken pieces. "The magic is gone."

Tas was reaching for the handle when a thundering knock nearly staved in the door.

19

"Master Majere!" a voice called. "Are you inside?"

"We're here!" Tasslehoff called.

"The citadel is under attack from Beryl and a host of red dragons," the voice said. "Master, you must make haste!"

Palin knew very well they were under attack. He expected death at any moment. He wanted nothing more than to run, and yet he remained on his knees, sweeping his broken hands over the rug, anxious to ascertain that he had not overlooked a single tiny jewel or small mechanism of the broken Device of Time Journeying.

Finding nothing, he rose to his feet as Lady Camilla, leader of the Solamnic Knights on Schallsea, strode into the room. She was a veteran with a veteran's calmness, thinking clearly and matter-of-factly. Her business was not to fight dragons. She could rely on her soldiers at the fortress to undertake that charge. Her business in the citadel was to safely evacuate as many people as possible. Like most Solamnics, Lady Camilla was highly suspicious of magic-users, and she regarded Palin with a grim look, as if she did not put it past him to be in league with the dragons.

"Master Majere, someone said they thought you were still here. Do you know what is happening outside?"

Palin looked out the window to see the dragons circling above them, the shadows of their wings floating over the surface of the flat, oily sea.

"I could not very well miss it," he answered coolly. He, for his part, did not much like Lady Camilla.

"What have you been doing?" Lady Camilla demanded angrily. "We need your help! I expected to find you working your magic to fight against these monsters, but one of the guards said he thought you were still in your room. I could not believe it, yet here you are, playing with a . . . a gewgaw!"

Palin wondered what Lady Camilla would say if she knew that the reason the dragons were attacking in the first place was to try to steal the "gewgaw."

"We were just leaving," Palin said, reaching out to grab the excited kender. "Come along, Tas."

"He's telling the truth, Lady Camilla," said Tasslehoff, noting the Knight's skepticism. "We *were* just leaving. We were heading for Solace but the magical device we were going to use for our escape broke—"

"That's enough, Tas." Palin shoved the kender out the door.

"Escape!" Lady Camilla repeated, her voice shaking in fury. "You planned to escape and leave the rest of us to die? I don't believe such cowardice. Not even of a wizard."

Palin kept firm hold of Tasslehoff's shoulder, pushed him roughly down the hallway toward the stairs.

"The kender is right, Lady Camilla," he said in caustic tones. "We *were* planning to escape. Something any *sensible* person would do in this situation, be he wizard or knight. As it turns out, we can't. We are stuck here with the rest of you. We will be heading for the hills with the rest of you. Or heading to our deaths, whichever the dragons decide. Move along, Tas! This is no time for your chatter!"

"But your magic—" Lady Camilla persisted.

Palin rounded on her. "I have no magic!" he said savagely. "I have no more power to fight these monsters than this kender! Less, perhaps, for his body is whole, whereas mine is broken."

He glared at her. She glared at him, her face pale and chill. They had reached the stairs that wound through the various levels of the Lyceum, stairs that had been crowded with people but were now empty. The residents of the Lyceum had joined the throngs fleeing the dragons, hoping to find shelter in the hills. Palin could see them streaming toward the island's interior. If the dragons attacked now and the reds breathed their flames upon these terrified masses, the slaughter would be horrific. Yet still the dragons circled above them, watching, waiting.

He knew very well why they were waiting. Beryl was trying to sense the artifact's magic. She was trying to determine which of these puny creatures fleeing from her carried the precious artifact. That is why she had not ordered her minions to kill. Not yet. He'd be damned if he was going to tell this to the Knight. She'd probably hand him over to the dragon.

"I assume you have duties elsewhere, Lady Camilla," Palin said, turning his back on her. "Do not concern yourself with us."

"Trust me," she retorted, "I will not!"

Shoving past him, she ran down the stairs, her sword clanking at her side, her armor rattling.

"Hurry up," Palin ordered Tas. "We'll lose ourselves in the crowd."

Kilting the skirts of his robes, Palin ran down the stairs. Tasslehoff followed, enjoying the excitement as only a kender can. The two exited the building, the last to do so. Just as Palin paused near the entryway to catch his breath and to determine which was the best way to go, one of the red dragons swooped low. People flung themselves screaming onto the ground. Palin shrank back against the crystal wall of the Lyceum, dragging Tas with him. The dragon flew by with a rush of wings, doing nothing except sending many running mad with terror.

Thinking the dragon might have seen him, Palin looked up into the sky, fearing the dragon might be planning to make another pass. What he saw perplexed and astonished him.

Large objects like enormous birds, filled the skies. At first Palin thought they were birds and then he saw glints of sunlight off metal.

"What in the Abyss is that?" he wondered.

Tasslehoff turned his face skyward, squinting against the sun. Another red dragon made a low swoop over the citadel.

"Draconian soldiers," said Tasslehoff calmly. "They're dropping off the backs of the dragons. I saw them do that in the War of the Lance." He gave an envious sigh. "I really do wish I'd been born a draconian sometimes."

"What did you say?" Palin gasped. "Draconians?"

"Oh, yes," said Tas. "Doesn't it look like fun? They ride on the backs of the dragons and then they jump off and—there, you can see them—see how they spread their wings to break their fall. Wouldn't it be wonderful, Palin? To be able to sail through the air like—"

"*That's* why Beryl hasn't let the dragons burn the place down!" Palin exclaimed in a rush of dismayed understanding. "She plans to use the draconians to find the magical artifact . . . to find us!"

Intelligent, strong, born to battle and bred to fight, draconians were the most feared of all the troops of the dragon overlords. Created during the War of the Lance by evil magicks from the eggs of metallic dragons, draconians are enormous lizardlike creatures who walk upright on two legs like humans. Draconians have wings, but these wings are short and will not lift their large and well-muscled bodies in sustained flight. The wings are suitable for allowing the creatures to float through the air, as they were doing now, enabling them to make a safe and gentle landing.

The moment the draconians hit the ground, they began to form into ranks in response to the shouted commands of their officers. The ranks of draconian soldiers spread out, seizing any person they could catch.

One group of draconians surrounded the Citadel Guards, ordered them to surrender. Outnumbered, the guards threw down their weapons. The draconians forced them to kneel on the ground, then cast magic spells on them, spells that entangled them in webs or sent them to sleep. Palin made a mental note to himself that the draconians were able to cast spells without apparent difficulty when every other mage on Ansalon could barely find enough magic to boil water. He found this fact ominous and would have liked to have had time to think about it further, but that didn't seem probable.

The draconians were not killing their prisoners. Not yet. Not until the prisoners had been questioned. They were left to lie where they had fallen, bound neatly in magic cobwebs. The draconian soldiers moved on, while other draconians began hauling the web-bound prisoners into the abandoned Lyceum.

Again, a red dragon flew overhead, slicing the air with its massive wings. Draconian troops leaped off the dragon's back. Their objective was now clear to Palin. The draconians were going to take and hold the Citadel of Light, use it as their base of operations. Once established, they would spread throughout the island, rounding up all civilians. Another force was probably attacking the Solamnic Knights, keeping them penned up in their fortress.

Do they have a description of Tas and me? Palin asked himself. Or have they been told to bring to Beryl any magic-user and kender they come across? Not that it matters, he realized bitterly. Either way, I'll soon be a prisoner again. Tormented and tortured. Chained up in the darkness, to rot in my own filth. I am helpless to save myself. I have no way to fight them. If I try to use my magic, the dead will siphon it off, take it for themselves, whatever good it does them.

He stood in the shadows of the crystal wall, his mind in turmoil, fear roiling inside him so that he was sick with it, thought he might die of it. He was not afraid of death. Dying was the easy part. Living as a prisoner . . . he could not face that. Not again.

"Palin," said Tas urgently. "I think they've seen us."

A draconian officer had indeed seen them. He pointed in their direction and issued orders. His troops started toward them. Palin wondered where Lady Camilla was and had a panicked notion to call for help. He discarded that immediately. Wherever she was, she had enough to do to help herself.

"Are we going to fight them?" Tas asked eagerly. "I have my special knife, Rabbit Slayer." He began to rummage inside his pouches, dumping out pieces of cutlery, bootlacings, an old sock. "Caramon named it that, because he said it would be good only for killing dangerous rabbits. I never met a dangerous rabbit, but it works pretty well against draconians. I just have to remember where I put it—"

I'll dash back inside the building, Palin thought, panic taking hold of him. I'll find a place to hide, any place to hide. He had an image of the draconians discovering him huddled, whimpering, in a closet. Dragging him forth . . .

Bitter gall filled Palin's mouth. If he ran away this time he would run away the next time and he would keep on running, leaving others to die for him. He was finished running. He would make his stand here.

I do not matter, Palin said to himself. I am expendable. Tasslehoff is the one who matters. The kender must not come to harm. Not in this time, not in this world. For if the kender dies, if he dies in a place and a time he is not meant to, the world and all of us on it—dragons, draconians, myself alike—will cease to exist.

"Tas," said Palin quietly, his voice steady, "I'm going to draw off these draconians, and while I'm doing that, you run into the hills. You'll be safe there. When the dragons leave—and I think they will, once they have captured me—I want you to go to Palanthas, find Jenna, and have her take you to Dalamar. When I say the word, you must run, Tas. Run as fast as ever you can."

The draconians were coming nearer. They were able to see him clearly now, and they had begun to talk loudly among themselves, pointing at him and jabbering. Judging by their excitement, one of his questions was answered. They had a description of him.

"I can't leave you, Palin!" Tas was protesting. "I admit that I was mad at you because you were trying to kill me by making me go back to be stepped on by a giant, but I'm mostly over that now and—"

"Run, Tas!" Palin ordered, angry with desperation. Opening the bag containing the pieces of the magical device, he took the faceplate of the device in his hand. "Run! My father was right. You must get to Dalamar! You must tell him—"

"I know!" Tas cried. He hadn't been listening. "We'll hide in the Hedge Maze. They'll never find us there. C'mon, Palin! Quickly!"

The draconians were shouting and calling out. Other draconians, hearing their yells, turned to look.

"Tas!" Palin rounded on him furiously. "Do as I tell you! Go!"

"Not without you," Tas said stubbornly. "What would Caramon say if he found out I left you here to die all by yourself? They're moving awfully fast, Palin," he added. "If we're going to try to make it to the Hedge Maze, I think we better go now."

Palin brought out the faceplate. With the Device of Time Journeying, his father had traveled back to the time of the First Cataclysm to try to save Lady Crysania and prevent his twin brother Raistlin from entering the Abyss. With this device, Tasslehoff had traveled here, bringing with him a mystery and a hope. With this device, Palin had gone back in time to find that time before the Second Cataclysm did not exist. The device was one of the most powerful and wondrous ever created by the wizards of Krynn. He was about to destroy it, and by destroying it, perhaps he was destroying them all. Yet, it was the only way.

He grasped the faceplate in his hand, gripped it so hard that the metal edges cut into his flesh. Crying out words of magic that he had not spoken since the gods had departed with the end of the Fourth Age, Palin hurled the faceplate at the advancing draconians. He had no idea what he hoped to accomplish. His was an act of despair.

Seeing the mage throwing something at them, the draconians skidded warily to a halt.

The faceplate struck the ground at their feet.

The draconians scrambled back, arms raised to protect their faces, expecting the device to explode.

The faceplate rolled on the ground, wobbled, and fell over. Some of the draconians started to laugh.

The faceplate began to glow. A jet of brilliant, blinding blue light streaked out, struck Palin in the chest.

The jolt shocked him, nearly stopping his heart. He feared for a horrible moment that the device was punishing him, exacting revenge upon him. Then he felt his body suffused with power. Magic, the old magic, burned inside him. The magic bubbled in his blood, intoxicating, exhilarating. The magic sang in his soul and thrilled his flesh. He cried out words to a spell, the first spell that came to mind, and marveled that he still remembered the words.

Not such a marvel, after all. Hadn't he recited them in a litany of grief, over and over to himself for all these many years?

Balls of fire flashed from his fingertips and struck the advancing draconians. The magic fire burned with such ferocity that the lizard-men burst into flame, became living torches. The blazing flames almost immediately consumed them, leaving them a mass of charred flesh, melted armor, piles of smoldering bones and teeth.

"You did it!" Tasslehoff shouted gleefully. "It worked."

Daunted by the horrific fate of their comrades, the other draconians were regarding Palin with hatred but also new and wary respect.

"Now will you run?" Palin shouted in exasperation.

"Are you coming?" Tas asked, balancing on his toes.

"Yes, damn it! Yes!" Palin assured him, and Tas dashed off.

Palin ran after him. He was a gray-headed, middle-aged man, who had once been in shape, but had not performed strenuous physical exertion like this in a long time. Casting the magic spell had drained him. He could already feel himself starting to weaken. He could not keep up this pace for long.

Behind him, an officer shouted furious orders. Palin glanced back to see the draconians once more in pursuit, their clawed feet tearing up the grassy lawns, sending divots of mud into the air. Draconians use their wings to help them run, and they were taking to the air, skimming over the ground at a rate that neither the middle-aged Palin nor the short-legged kender could ever hope to match.

The Hedge Maze was still some distance away. Palin's breath was coming in painful gasps. He had a sharp pain in his side, and his leg muscles burned. Tas ran gamely, but he was no longer a young kender. He stumbled and panted for air. The draconians were steadily gaining on them.

Halting, Palin turned to once again face his enemy. He sought the magic, felt it as a cold trickle in his blood, not a raging torrent. Reaching into the bag, he took hold of another piece of the Device of Time Journeying—the chain that was supposed to wind up inside the artifact. Shouting words that were more defiance than magic, Palin hurled the chain at the flapping-winged draconians.

The chain transformed, growing, lengthening, expanding until the links were as thick and strong as those of a chain attached to a ship's heavy anchor. The enormous chain struck the draconians in their midriffs. Writhing like an iron snake, it wrapped itself around and around the pursuing draconians. The links contracted, holding the monsters fast.

Palin could not take time to marvel. Catching hold of Tasslehoff's hand, he turned to run again, both of them racing frantically to reach the Hedge Maze ahead of their pursuers. For the moment the chase had ended. Wrapped in the chain, the draconians howled in pain and struggled desperately to escape its coils. No other draconians dared come after him.

Palin was exalted, thinking he had defeated his foes, then he caught movement out of the corner of his eyes. His elation evaporated. Now he knew why those draconians were not coming after him. They did not fear him. They were merely leaving the task of his capture to reinforcements, who were running to cut him off from the front.

An armed squadron of fifteen draconian soldiers took up positions between Palin, Tas, and the Hedge Maze.

"I hope . . . there's more of that device . . . left. . . ." Tas gasped with what breath he had available for talking.

Palin reached into the bag. His hand closed over a fistful of jewels that had once adorned the device. He saw the artifact again, saw its beauty and felt its power. His heart almost refused, but the hesitation lasted only a moment. He tossed the jewels at the draconians.

Sapphires, rubies, emeralds, and diamonds sparkled in the air as they rained down over the heads of the astonished draconians, falling around them like sand scattered by children playing at magic. The jewels shone in the sunlight. A few of the draconians, chortling in glee, bent to pick them up.

The jewels exploded, forming a thick cloud of glittering jewel dust that surrounded the draconians. Shouts of glee changed to curses and cries of pain as the gritty jewel dust clogged the eyes of those who had bent to grab them. Some had their mouths open, and the dust flew up their snouts, choking them. The fine dust penetrated beneath their scales, causing them to itch and scratch at themselves, yelping and howling.

While the draconians staggered around blindly bumping into each other, or rolled on the ground, or gasped for air, Palin and Tasslehoff circled around them. Another sprint and they both plunged into the green haven of the Hedge Maze.

The Hedge Maze had been constructed by Qualinesti Woodshapers, a gift from Laurana. The maze was designed to offer a place of beauty and solitude to all who entered, a place where people could walk, rest, meditate, study. A leafy embodiment of the maze that is man's heart, the Hedge Maze could never be mapped, as the gnome, Conundrum, had discovered to his immense frustration. Those who successfully walked the maze of their own hearts came at last to the Silver Stair located at the heart of the Hedge Maze, the culmination of the spiritual journey.

Palin did not have much hope that the draconians would lose him in the maze, but he did hope that the maze's own powerful magic would protect him and Tas, perhaps hide them from the eyes of the monsters. His hope was going to be put to the test. More draconians had joined in the pursuit, driven now by anger and the desire for revenge.

"Stop a moment," Palin said to Tas, who had no breath left to answer. He nodded and gulped air.

The two had reached the first bend in the Hedge Maze. No point in going farther unless Palin knew whether or not the draconians were going to be able to come after them. He turned to watch.

The first several draconians dashed inside the Hedge Maze and almost immediately came to a stop. Branches spread across the path, stems shot up from the ground. Foliage grew at an astonishing rate. Within moments, the path on which Palin and Tas had walked was overgrown with shrubbery so thick the mage could no longer see the draconians.

Palin breathed a sigh of relief. He had been right. The magic of the Hedge Maze would keep out those who entered with evil intent. He had a momentary fear that the draconians might use their wings to lift themselves over the maze, but, as he looked up, flowering vines twined overhead to form a canopy that would hide him from sight. For the moment, he and Tas were safe.

"Whew! That was close!" said Tasslehoff happily. "I thought we were goners there for a moment. You are a really good wizard, Palin. I saw Raistlin cast lots of spells, but I don't believe he ever caused draconians to sizzle up like bacon before, though I once saw him summon the Great Worm Catyrpelius. Did you ever hear about that one? Raistlin—"

A roar and a blast of flame interrupted Tasslehoff's tale. The bushes that had so recently grown to block the draconians burst into bright orange flame.

"The dragons!" Palin said with a bitter curse, coughing as the intense heat seared his lungs. "They're going to try to smoke us out."

In his elation at defeating the draconians, he had forgotten the dragons. The Hedge Maze could withstand almost all other attacks, but apparently it was not impervious to dragon fire. Another red breathed its fiery breath on the maze. Flames crackled, smoke filled the air. The way out was blocked off by a wall of flame. They had no choice but to run deeper into the maze.

Palin led the way down the aisle of green, made a right turn, and came to a halt when the hedgerow at the end of the path erupted up in a blaze of flame and smoke. Choking, Palin covered his mouth with his sleeve and searched for a way out. Another pathway opened in front of him, the bushes parting to let him and Tas through. They had only made it a short distance when, again, flames blocked their path. Still another path opened. Though the Hedge Maze itself was dying, it sought a way to save them. He had the impression that they were being led somewhere specific, but he had no idea where. The smoke made him dizzy and disoriented. His strength was starting to ebb. He staggered, more than ran. Tasslehoff, too, was falling prey to fatigue. His shoulders slumped, his breathing was ragged. His very topknot seemed to droop.

The red dragon that was attacking the maze did not want to kill them. The dragon could have done that long ago. The red was driving them like sheep, using fire to dog their footsteps, nip at their heels, try to force them out in the open. Still, the maze itself urged them on, revealing yet another path when their way was blocked.

Smoke swirled around them. Palin could barely see the kender right beside him. He coughed until his throat was raw, coughed until he retched. Whenever one of the hedge ways opened up, a flow of air would refresh him, but almost immediately the air became tainted with smoke and the smell of brimstone. They stumbled on.

A wall of flame burst in front of them. Palin fell back, looked frantically to the left to see another wall of flame. He turned to the right, and the maze crackled with fire. Heat seared his lungs. He could not breathe. Smoke swirled, stinging his eyes.

"Palin!" Tas pointed. "The stair!"

Palin wiped away the tears to see silver steps spiraling upward, vanishing in the smoke.

"Let's climb it!" Tas urged.

Palin shook his head. "It won't help. The stair doesn't lead anywhere, Tas," he croaked, his throat raw and bleeding, as a fit of coughing seized him.

"Yes, it does," Tas argued. "I'm not sure where, but I climbed it the last time I was here, when I decided that I should really go back and be stepped on by the giant. A decision I have since rethought," he added hastily. "Anyway I saw— Oh, look! There's Caramon! Hullo, Caramon!"

Palin raised his head, peered through the smoke. He was sick and faint, and when he saw his father, standing at the top of the Silver Stair, he did not wonder at the sight. Caramon had come to his son once before, in the Citadel of Light, come to him to urge him not to send Tasslehoff back to die. Caramon looked now as he had looked to his son before his death, old but still hearty and hale. His father's face was different, though. Caramon's face had always been quick to laughter, quick to smile. The eyes that had seen much sorrow and known much pain had always been light with hope. Caramon had changed. Now the eyes were different, lost, searching.

Tasslehoff was already clambering up the stairs, jabbering excitedly to Caramon, who said no word. There had been only a few stairs, when Tasslehoff began to climb. He was quite close to the top already. But when Palin placed his foot upon the first shining silver step, he looked up and saw the stairs appeared to be without number, never ending. He did not have the strength to climb all those stairs, and he feared he would be left behind. As his foot touched the stair, a breath of fresh air wafted over him. He gulped it eagerly. Lifting his face, he saw blue sky above him. He drew in another deep breath of fresh air and began to climb. The distance seemed short now.

Caramon stood at the top, waiting patiently. Lifting a ghostly hand, he beckoned to them.

Tasslehoff reached the top, only to find, as Palin had said, that the Silver Stair led nowhere. The staircase came to an abrupt end, his next step would carry him over the edge. Far below, the ugly black smoke of the dying hedge swirled like the waters of a maelstrom.

"What do I do now, Caramon?" Tas yelled.

Palin heard no reply, but apparently the kender did.

"How wonderful," Tas cried. "I'll fly just like the draconians!"

Palin shouted out in horror. He lunged, tried to grasp hold of the kender's shirttail, and missed.

With a cry of glee, Tasslehoff spread his arms like a bird and leaped straight off the final stair. He plunged downward and disappeared into the smoke.

Palin clung to the stair. In his desperate attempt to grab hold of Tas, he had almost toppled off. He waited, his heart in his throat, to hear the kender's death cry, but all he heard was the crackling of flame and the roaring of the dragons.

Palin looked into the swirling smoke and shuddered. He looked back at his father, but Caramon was not there. In his place flew the red dragon. Wings blotted out the patch of blue sky. The dragon reached out a talon, intending to pluck Palin from his stair and carry him back to his cell. He was tired, tired of being afraid. He wanted only to rest and to be rid of fear forever.

He knew now where the Silver Stair led.

Death.

Caramon was dead. His son would soon join him.

"At least," Palin said calmly, grimly, "I will nevermore be a prisoner."

He leaped off the stair—and fell heavily on his side on a hard stone floor.

The landing being completely unexpected, Palin made no attempt to break his fall. He rolled and tumbled, came up hard against a stone wall. Jolted by the impact, shocked and confused, he lay blinking at the ceiling and wondered that he was alive.

Tasslehoff bent over him.

"Are you all right?" he asked, but didn't wait for an answer. "Look, Palin! Isn't it wonderful? You told me to find Dalamar and I have! He's right here! But I can't find Caramon anymore. He's nowhere."

Palin eased himself carefully to a sitting position. He was bruised and battered, his throat hurt, and his lungs wheezed as though they were still filled with smoke, but he felt no stabbing pains, heard no bones crunch together. His astonishment and shock at the sight of the elf caused him to forget his minor injuries. Palin was shocked not only to see Dalamar—who had not been seen in this world for thirty years—he was shocked to see how Dalamar changed.

The long-lived elves do not appear to humans to age. Dalamar was an elf in the prime of manhood. He should have looked the same now as he had looked when Palin last saw him more than thirty years ago. He did not. So drastic was the change that Palin was not completely convinced that this apparition was Dalamar and not another ghost.

The elf's long hair that had once been as black as the wing of a raven was streaked with gray. His face, though still elegantly carved and beautifully proportioned, was wasted. The elf's pale skin was stretched tight over the bones of the skull, making it look as if his face were carved of ivory. The aquiline nose was beakish, the chin sharp. His robes hung loosely on an emaciated frame. His long-fingered, elegant hands were bony and chafed, the knuckles red and prominent. The veins on the backs of his hands traced a blue road map of illness and despair.

Palin had always liked and admired Dalamar, though he could not say why. Their philosophies were not remotely the same. Dalamar had been the servant of Nuitari, god of the Dark Moon and darker magicks. Palin had served Solinari, god of the Silver Moon, god of the magic of light. Both men had been devastated when the gods of magic had departed, taking the magic with them. Palin had gone into the world to seek out the magic they called "wild" magic. Dalamar had withdrawn from other magi, withdrawn from the world. He had gone seeking magic in dark places.

"Are you injured?" Dalamar asked. He sounded annoyed, not concerned for Palin's well-being, but only that Palin might require some sort of attention, an exertion of power on the part of the elf.

Palin struggled to stand. Speaking was painful. His throat hurt abominably.

"I am all right," he rasped, watching Dalamar as the elf watched him, wary, suspicious. "Thank you for helping us—"

Dalamar cut him off with a sharp, emphatic gesture of a pallid hand. The skin of the hand was so pale against the black robes that it seemed disembodied.

"I did what I had to do, considering the mess you had made of things." The pale hand snaked out, seized hold of Tas by the collar. "Come with me, kender."

"I'd be glad to come with you, Dalamar," Tas answered. "And, by the way, it really is me, Tasslehoff Burrfoot, so you needn't keep calling me 'kender' in that nasty tone. I'm very glad to see you again, except, you're pinching me. Actually you're hurting me quite a bit—"

"*In* silence," Dalamar said and gave the kender's collar an expert twist that effectively caused Tas to obey the order by half-choking him. Dragging the squirming kender with him, Dalamar crossed the small, narrow room to a heavy wooden door. He beckoned with a pale hand, and the door swung silently open.

Keeping a tight grasp on Tas, Dalamar paused in the doorway and turned to face Palin.

"You have much to answer for, Majere."

"Wait!" Palin croaked, wincing at the pain in his throat. "Where is my father? I saw him."

"Where?" Dalamar demanded, frowning.

"At the top of the Silver Stair," Tasslehoff volunteered. "We both saw him."

"I have no idea. I did not send him, if that is what you are thinking," said Dalamar. "Although, I appreciate his help."

He walked out, and the door slammed shut behind him. Alarmed, panicked, feeling himself start to suffocate, Palin hurled himself at the door.

"Dalamar!" he shouted, beating on the wood. "Don't leave me in here!"

Dalamar spoke, but it was only to chant words of magic.

Palin recognized the spell—a wizard lock.

His strength gone, he slid down the door and slumped to the cold, stone floor.

A prisoner.

3

Sun Arise

In the dark hour before the dawn, Gilthas, the king of the Qualinesti stood on the balcony of his palace. Rather, his body stood on the balcony. His soul walked the streets of the silent city. His soul walked every street, paused at every doorway, looked in every window. His soul saw a newlywed couple asleep, clasped in each other arms. His soul saw a mother sitting in a rocking chair, nursing her babe, the babe sleeping, the mother dozing, gently rocking. His soul saw young elf brothers sharing the same bed with a large hound. The two boys slept with their arms flung around the neck of the dog, all three dreaming of playing catch in sunlit meadows. His soul saw an elderly elf sleeping in the same house that his father had slept in and his father before him. Above his bed, a portrait of the wife who had passed on. In the next room, the son who would inherit the house, his wife by his side.

"Sleep long this night," Gilthas's soul said softly to each one he touched. "Do not wake too early in the morning, for

39

when you wake, it will not be the beginning of a new day but the end of all days. The sun you see in the sky is not the rising sun, but the setting sun. The daylight will be night and night the darkness of despair. Yet, for now, sleep in peace. Let me guard that peace while I can."

"Your Majesty," said a voice.

Gilthas was loath to pay heed. He knew that when he turned to listen, to answer, to respond, the spell would be shattered. His soul would return to his body. The people of Qualinesti would find their sleep disturbed by dreams of smoke and fire, blood and shining steel. He tried to pretend he had not heard, but even as he watched, he saw the bright silver of the stars start to fade, saw a faint, pale light in the sky.

"Your Majesty," said a voice, another voice.

Dawn. And with the dawn, death.

Gilthas turned around. "Marshal Medan," he said, a hint of coolness in his tone. He shifted his gaze from the leader of the Dark Knights of Neraka to the person standing next to him, his trusted servant. "Planchet. You both have news, by the looks of it. Marshal Medan, I'll hear yours first."

Alexius Medan was a human male in his fifties, and although he bowed deferentially to the king, the Marshal was the true ruler of Qualinesti and had been for more than thirty years, ever since the Dark Knights of Neraka seized Qualinesti during the Chaos War. Gilthas was known to all the world as the "Puppet King." The Dark Knights had left the young and apparently weak and sickly youth on the throne in order to placate the elven people and give them the illusion of elven control. In reality, it was Marshal Medan who held the strings that caused the arms of the puppet Gilthas to move, and Senator Palthainon, a powerful member of the Thalas-Enthia, who played the tune to which the puppet danced.

But as Marshal Medan had learned only yesterday, he had been deceived. Gilthas had not been a puppet but a most gifted actor. He had played the weak and vacillating king in order to mask his real persona, that of leader of the elven resistance movement. Gilthas had fooled Medan completely. The Puppet King had cut the strings, and the dances he performed were done to music of His Majesty's own choosing.

"You left us after dark and have been gone all night, Marshal," Gilthas stated, eyeing the man suspiciously. "Where have you been?"

"I have been at my headquarters, Your Majesty, as I told you before I left," Medan replied.

He was tall and well-built. Despite his fifty-five years—or perhaps because of them—he worked at keeping himself fighting fit. His gray eyes contrasted with his dark hair and dark brows and gave him an expression of perpetual gravity that did not lighten, even when he smiled. His face was deeply tan, weathered. He had been a dragonrider in his early days.

Gilthas cast a very slight glance at Planchet, who gave a discreet nod of his head. Both glance and nod were seen by the observant Medan, who looked more than usually grave.

"Your Majesty, I do not blame you for not trusting me. It has been said that kings cannot afford the luxury of trusting anyone—" the Marshal began.

"Especially the conqueror of our people, who has held us in his iron grasp for over thirty years," Gilthas interjected. Both elven and human blood ran in the young king's veins, though the elven dominated. "You release the grip on our throats to offer the same hand in friendship. You will understand me, sir, when I say that I still feel the bite of your fingers around my windpipe."

"Well put, Your Majesty," replied the Marshal with a

41

hint of smile. "As I said, I approve your caution. I wish I had a year to prove my loyalty—"

"To me?" Gilthas said with a slight sneer. "To the 'puppet'?"

"No, Your Majesty," Marshal Medan said. "My loyalty to the land I have come to consider my home. My loyalty to a people I have come to respect. My loyalty to your mother." He did not add the words, "whom I have come to love," though he might have said them in his heart.

The Marshal had been awake all night the night before, removing the Queen Mother to a place of safety, out of reach of the hands of Beryl's approaching assassins. He had been awake all day yesterday, having taken Laurana in secret to the palace where they had both met with Gilthas. It had been Medan's unhappy task to inform Gilthas that Beryl's armies were marching on Qualinesti with the intent of destroying the land and its people. Medan had not slept this night, either. The only outward signs of weariness were on the Marshal's haggard face, however, not in his clear, alert eyes.

Gilthas's tension relaxed, his suspicions eased. "You are wise, Marshal. Your answer is the only answer I would ever accept from you. Had you sought to flatter me, I would have known you lied. As it is, my mother has told me of your garden, that you have worked to make it beautiful, that you take pleasure not only in the flowers themselves but in planting them and caring for them. However, I must say that I find it difficult to believe that such a man could have once sworn loyalty to the likes of Lord Ariakan."

"I find it difficult to understand how a young man could have been tricked into running away from parents who doted on him to fly into a web spun by a certain senator," said Marshal Medan coolly, "a web that nearly led to the young man's destruction, as well as that of his people."

Gilthas flushed, hearing his own story repeated back to him. "What I did was wrong. I was young."

"As was I, Your Majesty," said the Marshal. "Young enough to believe the lies of Queen Takhisis. I do not flatter you when I say, Gilthas, that I have come to respect you. The role you played of the indolent dreamer, who cared more for his poetry than his people, fooled me completely. Although," the Marshal added dryly, "I must say that you and your rebels have caused me no end of trouble."

"And I have come to respect you, Marshal, and even to trust you somewhat," said Gilthas. "Though not completely. Is that good enough?"

Medan extended his hand. "Good enough, Your Majesty."

Gilthas accepted the Marshal's hand. Their handshake was firm and brief, on both sides.

"Now," said Medan, "perhaps your servant will tell his spies to cease following me about. We need everyone focused on the task ahead."

"What is your news, Marshal?" said Gilthas, neither agreeing nor disagreeing.

"It is relatively good news, Your Majesty," Medan stated. "All things considered. The reports we heard yesterday are true. Beryl's forces have crossed the border into Qualinesti."

"What good news can there be in this?" Gilthas demanded.

"Beryl is not with them, Your Majesty," said the Marshal. "Nor are any of her minions. Where they are and why they are not with the army, I cannot imagine. Perhaps she is holding them back for some reason."

"To be in on the final kill," said Gilthas bitterly. "The attack on Qualinost."

"Perhaps, Your Majesty. At any rate, they are not with the army, and that has bought us time. Her army is large, burdened with supply wagons and siege towers, and they are finding it difficult going through the forest. From the reports coming from our garrisons on the border, not only are they being harassed by bands of elves operating under the Lioness, but the very trees and plants and even the animals themselves are battling the enemy."

"Yes, they would," said Gilthas quietly, "but all these forces are mortal, as are we, and can only withstand so much."

"Indeed, Your Majesty. They could not withstand dragon fire, that is certain. Until the dragons arrive, however, we have a breathing space. Even if the dragons were to set the forests aflame, I calculate that it will take ten days for the army to reach Qualinost. That should give you time to institute the plan you outlined for us last night."

Gilthas sighed deeply and turned his gaze from the Marshal to the brightening sky. He made no response, but silently watched the sun rise.

"Preparations for evacuation should have begun last night," Medan stated in stern tones.

"Please, Marshal," said Planchet in a low voice. "You do not understand."

"He speaks truly. You do not understand, Marshal Medan," Gilthas said, turning around. "You could not possibly understand. You love this land, you say, but you cannot love it as we do. Our blood runs in every leaf and flower. The blood of every aspen tree flows through our veins. You hear the song of the sparrow, but we understand the words of that song. The axes and flames that fell the trees cut us and scorch us. The poison that kills the birds causes a part of us to die. This morning I must tell my people that they have to leave their homes, homes that trembled in the Cataclysm and yet stood firm. They must leave their bowers and their gardens and their waterfalls and grottos. They must flee, and where will they go?"

"Your Majesty," said Planchet, "on that score I, too, have good news for you. I received word in the night from the messenger of Alhana Starbreeze. The shield has fallen. The borders of Silvanesti are once more open."

Gilthas stared in disbelief, not daring to hope. "Can this be possible? Are you certain? How? What happened?"

"The messenger had no details, my lord. He started on his glad journey to bring us the good tidings the moment the elves knew it to be true. The shield is indeed fallen. Alhana Starbreeze walked across the border herself. I am expecting another messenger with more information soon."

"This is wonderful news," Gilthas exclaimed, ecstatic. "Our people will go to Silvanesti. Our cousins cannot deny us entry. Once there, we will combine our forces and launch an attack to retake our homeland."

Seeing Planchet regard him gravely, Gilthas sighed.

"I know, I know. You needn't remind me. I am leaping ahead of myself. But this joyful news gives me the first hope I have known in weeks. Come," Gilthas added, leaving the balcony and walking inside his chambers, "we must tell Mother—"

"She sleeps still, Your Majesty," said Planchet in a low voice.

"No, I do not," said Laurana. "Or, if I was, I will gladly wake to hear good news. What is this you say? The shield has fallen?"

Exhausted after the flight from her home in the night and a day of hearing nothing but dire news, Laurana had at last been persuaded to sleep. She had her own room in the royal palace, but Medan, fearful of Beryl's assassins, had given orders that the palace be cleared of all servants, ladies-in-waiting, elven nobility, clerks, and cooks. He had posted elven guards around the palace with orders to allow no one to enter except for himself and his aide. Medan might not have even trusted his aide, except that he knew him to be a Solamnic Knight and loyal to Laurana. Medan had then insisted that Laurana sleep on a couch in Gilthas's sitting room where her slumbers could be guarded. When Medan had departed for his headquarters, he had left behind the Solamnic, Gerard, as well as her son to watch over her during the night.

"The news is true, Mother," said Gilthas, coming to stand beside her. "The shield has fallen."

"It *sounds* wonderful," said Laurana cautiously. "Hand me my dressing gown, Planchet, so that I do not further disturb the Marshal's sensibilities. I don't trust the news, however. I find the timing disquieting."

Laurana's gown was a soft lilac color with lace at the throat. Her hair poured over her shoulders like warm honey. Her almond-shaped eyes were luminous, as blue as forget-me-nots. She was older than Medan by many, many years and looked far younger than he did, for the elven summer of youth and beauty diminishes into the winter of old age far more slowly than it does with humans.

Watching the Marshal, Gilthas saw in the man's face not the cool reserve of chivalry, but the pain of love, a hopeless love that could never be returned, could never even be spoken. Gilthas still did not like the Marshal, but this look softened his feelings for the man and even led him to pity him. The Marshal remained staring out the window until he could regain his stern composure.

"Say that the timing is fortuitous, Mother," urged

Gilthas. "The shield falls when we most need it to fall. If there were gods, I would suppose they watch over us."

"Yet there are no gods," Laurana replied, wrapping her dressing gown around her. "The gods have left us. So I do not know what to say to this news except be cautious and do not build your hopes upon it."

"I must tell the people something, Mother," Gilthas returned impatiently. "I have called a meeting of the Senate this very morning." He cast a glance at Medan. "You see, my lord, I have *not* been idle this night. We must begin the evacuation today if we are to have a hope of emptying the city of its thousands. What I must say to our people will be devastating, Mother. I need hope to offer them."

" 'Hope is the carrot they hang in front of the horse's nose to keep him plodding on,' " Laurana murmured.

"What did you say, Mother?" Gilthas asked. "You spoke so softly, I could not hear you."

"I was thinking of something someone said to me long ago. At the time I thought the person was embittered and cynical. Now I think perhaps he was wise." Laurana sighed, shook off her memories. "I am sorry, my son. I know this isn't helping."

A Knight, Medan's aide, entered the room. He stood respectfully silent, but it was clear from the tenseness of his posture that he was attempting to gain their attention. Medan was the first to notice him.

"Yes, Gerard, what is it?" Medan asked.

"A trivial matter. I do not want to disturb the Queen Mother," said Gerard with a bow. "Might we speak in private, my lord? If His Majesty will permit?"

"You have leave," said Gilthas, and turned back to try to persuade his mother.

Medan, with a bow, withdrew with Gerard, walking out on the balcony of the king's chamber, overlooking the garden.

Gerard wore the armor of a Dark Knight of Neraka, although he had removed the heavy breastplate for comfort's sake. He had washed away the blood and other traces of his recent battle with a draconian, but he still looked considerably the worse for wear. No one would have ever called the young Solamnic handsome. His hair was as yellow as corn, his face was scarred with pockmarks, and the addition of numerous fresh bruises, blue and green and purple, rising to the surface, did nothing to enhance his appearance. His eyes were his best feature, an intense, arresting blue. The blue eyes were serious, shadowed, and belied his words about the trivial nature of the interruption.

"One of the guards sent word that two people wait below, both demanding to enter the palace. One is a senator. . . ." He paused, frowning. "I can't recall the name—elven names are a muddle to me—but he is tall and had a way of looking down his nose at me as if I were an ant perched on the tip."

Medan's mouth twitched in amusement. "And has he the expression of someone who has just bitten into a bad fig?"

"Correct, my lord."

"Palthainon," said Medan. "The Puppet Master. I was wondering when he would turn up." Medan glanced through the glass-paned door at the king. "As the story goes in the old child's tale, Palthainon will find his puppet king has turned into a real one. Unlike the child's tale, I don't think this puppeteer will be pleased to lose his puppet."

"Should he be permitted to come up, my lord?"

"No," said Medan coolly. "The king is otherwise engaged. Let Palthainon await His Majesty's pleasure. Who else wants admittance?"

Gerard's expression darkened. He lowered his voice. "The elf Kalindas, my lord. He requests admittance. He has heard, he says, that the Queen Mother is here. He refuses to leave."

Medan frowned. "How did he find out the Queen Mother was in the palace?"

"I don't know, my lord," said Gerard. "He did not hear it from his brother. As you ordered, we did not permit Kelevandros to leave. When I was so weary I could not keep my eyes open anymore, Planchet kept watch to see that he did not try to slip out."

Medan cast a glance at Kelevandros. The elf, wrapped in his cloak, was still apparently sound asleep in a far corner of the room.

"My lord," said Gerard, "may I speak plainly?"

Medan gave a wry smile. "You've done nothing else since you entered my service, young man."

"I wouldn't exactly call it 'entering' your service, my lord," returned Gerard. "I am here because, as you must know or could have guessed, I deemed my remaining with you to be the best way to protect the Queen Mother. I know that one of those two elves is a traitor. I know that one of them has betrayed Laurana, the mistress who trusted them. That was how you knew to be waiting for Palin Majere that morning in the woods. One of those two told you. They were the only ones who knew. Am I right?" His voice was harsh, accusing.

Medan eyed him. "Yes, you are right. Believe me when I say, Sir Solamnic, that you do not look at me with more disgust than I look at myself. Yes, I used Kalindas. I had no choice. If the scum did not report to me, he would have reported directly to Beryl, and I would not have known what was going on. I did what I could to protect the Queen Mother. I knew well that she aided and abetted the rebels. Beryl would have killed Laurana long ago, if it hadn't been for me. So do not presume to judge me, young man."

"I am sorry, my lord," Gerard said, contrite. "I did not understand. What do we do? Should I send Kalindas away?"

"No, said Medan, rubbing his jaw that was gray and grizzled with a day's growth of stubble. "Better to have him here where I can keep an eye on him. There is no telling what mischief he might cause if he were wandering around loose."

"He could be . . . removed," Gerard suggested uncomfortably.

Medan shook his head. "Laurana might believe that one of her servants was a spy, but I doubt very much if her son would. Kelevandros would certainly not, and if we killed his brother he would raise such an outcry that we would have to kill him, as well. How will it look to the elven people, whose trust I must win, if they hear that I have started butchering elves on His Majesty's very doorstep? Besides, I need to ascertain if Kalindas has been in communication with Beryl's forces and what he told them."

"Very good, my lord," said Gerard. "I will keep close watch on him."

"*I* will keep watch on him, Gerard," the Marshal amended. "Kalindas knows you, or have you forgotten? He betrayed you, as well. If he finds you here with me, my trusted confidant, he will be immediately suspicious. He might do something desperate."

"You are right, my lord," Gerard said, frowning. "I had forgotten. Perhaps I could return to headquarters."

"You will return to headquarters, Sir Knight," Medan said. "Your own headquarters. I am sending you back to Solamnia."

"No, my lord," Gerard said stubbornly. "I refuse to go."

"Listen to me, Gerard," the Marshal said, resting his hand on the young man's shoulder, "I have not said this to His Majesty or the Queen Mother—although I think she already knows. The battle we are about to fight is the last desperate struggle of a drowning man going under for the third time. Qualinost cannot hope to stand against the might of Beryl's army. This fight is at best a delaying action to buy time for the refugees to flee."

"Then I will most certainly stay, my lord," Gerard said steadily, his tone defiant. "I could not in honor do otherwise."

"If I make this an order?" Medan asked.

"I would say you are not my commander and that I owe no allegiance to you," Gerard returned, his expression grim.

"And I would say you are a very selfish young man who has no concept of true honor," Medan replied.

"Selfish, my lord?" Gerard repeated, stung by the accusation. "How can it be selfish to offer my life for this cause?"

"You will be of more value to the cause alive than dead," Medan stated. "You did not hear me out. When I suggested that you return to Solamnia, I was not sending you to some safe haven. I had in mind that you will take word of our plight to the Knights' Council in Solanthus and ask for their aid."

Gerard regarded the Marshal skeptically. "You are asking for the aid of the Solamnics, my lord?"

"No," said Medan. "The Queen Mother is asking for the aid of the Solamnic Knights. You will be her representative."

Gerard was clearly still distrustful.

"I have calculated that we have ten days, Gerard," the Marshal continued. "Ten days until the army reaches Qualinost. If you leave immediately on dragonback, you could reach Solanthus the day after tomorrow at the latest. The Knights could not send an army, but mounted dragonriders could at least help guard the civilians." He smiled grimly. "Do not believe that I am sending you out of harm's way, sir. I expect you to come back with them, and then you and I will not fight each other, but side by side."

Gerard's face cleared. "I am sorry I questioned you, my lord. I will leave at once. I will need a swift mount."

"You will have one. My own Razor. You will ride him."

"I could not take your horse, sir," Gerard protested.

"Razor is not a horse," said Medan. "He is my dragon. A blue. He has been in my service since the Chaos War. What is the matter now?"

Gerard had gone extremely pale. "Sir," he said, clearing his throat, "I feel it only right that you know . . . I have never ridden a dragon. . . ." He swallowed, burning with shame. "I have never even seen one."

"It is high time you did," Medan said, clapping Gerard on the back. "A most exhilarating experience. I have always regretted that my duties as Marshal kept me from riding as much as I would have liked. Razor is stabled in a secret location outside Qualinost. I will give you directions and send written orders with my seal so that the stable master will know you come by my command. I will also send a message to Razor. Do not worry. He will bear you swiftly and in safety. You are not fearful of heights, are you?"

"No, my lord," Gerard said, gulping. What else could he say?

"Excellent. I will draw up the orders at once," Medan said.

Returning to the main chamber, motioning for Gerard to accompany him, Medan sat down at Planchet's desk and began to write.

"What of Kalindas, my lord?" Gerard asked in a low undertone.

Medan glanced at Laurana and Gilthas, who were together on the opposite side of the room, still conferring.

"It will not hurt him to cool his heels for awhile."

Gerard stood in silence, watching the Marshal's hand flow over the paper. Medan wrote swiftly and concisely. The orders did not take long, not nearly long enough as far as Gerard was concerned. He had no doubt that he was going to die, and he would much rather die with a sword in his hand than by toppling off the back of a dragon, falling with sickening terror to a bone-shattering end. Deeming himself a coward, he reminded himself of the importance and urgency of his mission, and thus he was able to take Medan's sealed orders with a hand that did not shake.

"Farewell, Sir Gerard," Medan said, clasping the young man by the hand.

"Only for a time, my lord," said Gerard. "I will not fail you. I will return and bring aid."

"You should leave immediately. Beryl and her followers would think twice about attacking a blue dragon, especially one belonging to the Dark Knights, but it would be best for you to take advantage of the fact that for the moment Beryl's dragons are not around. Planchet will show you the way out the back, through the garden, so that Kalindas does not catch sight of you."

"Yes, my lord."

Gerard lifted his hand in a salute, the salute a Solamnic Knight gives his enemy.

"Very well, my son, I agree," Laurana's voice reached them from across the chamber. She stood near a window. The first rays of the morning sunshine touched her hair like the hand of the alchemist, changed the honey to gold. "You convince me. You have your father's own way about you, Gilthas. How proud he would have been of you. I wish he could be here to see you."

"I wish he were here to offer his wise counsel," said Gilthas, leaning forward to kiss his mother gently on the cheek. "Now, if you will excuse me, Mother, I must write down the words that I will shortly be called upon to speak. This is so important, I do not want to make a mistake."

"Your Majesty," said Gerard, stepping forward. "If I might have a moment of your time. I want to pay my respects before I go."

"Are you leaving us, Sir Gerard?" Laurana asked.

"Yes, Madam," said Gerard. "The Marshal has orders for me. He dispatches me to Solamnia, there to plead your cause before the Council of Knights and ask for their aid. If I might have a letter from you, Your Majesty, in your hand with your seal, vouching for my credentials as your messenger and also stating the dire nature of the situation—"

"The Solamnics have never cared for Qualinesti before," Gilthas interrupted, frowning. "I see no reason why they should start now."

"They did care, once," said Laurana gently, looking searchingly at Gerard. "There was a Knight called Sturm Brightblade who cared very much." She held out her hand to Gerard, who bent low to touch her soft skin with his lips. "Go safely in the memory of that brave and gentle knight, Sir Gerard."

The story of Sturm Brightblade had never meant two coppers to Gerard before now. He had heard the tale of his death at the High Clerist's Tower so many times that it had grown stale in the telling. Indeed, he had even expressed his doubts that the episode had truly happened. Yet now he recalled that here was the comrade who had stood over the body of the dead Knight, the comrade who had wept for him even as she lifted the fabled dragonlance to defy his killer. Receiving her blessing in Sturm Brightblade's name, Gerard was humbled and chastened. He bent his knee before her, accepted the blessing with bowed head:

"I will, Madam," he said. "Thank you."

He rose to his feet, exalted. His fears over riding the dragon seemed paltry and ignoble now, and he was ashamed of them.

The young king looked chastened as well and gave Gerard his hand to shake. "Ignore my words, Sir Knight. I spoke without thought. If the Solamnics have been careless of Qualinesti, then it might be truly said that the Qualinesti have been careless of the Solamnics. For one to help the other would be the beginning of a new and better relationship for both. You shall have your letter."

The king dipped his pen in ink, wrote a few paragraphs on a sheet of fine vellum, and signed his name. Beneath his name, he affixed his seal, pressing into soft wax a ring he wore on his index finger. The ring left behind the image of an aspen leaf. He waited for the wax to harden, then folded the letter and handed it to Gerard.

"So I will convey to them, Your Majesty," said Gerard, accepting the letter. He looked once more at Laurana, to take with him in his mind her beautiful image for inspiration. He was disquieted to see sorrow darken her eyes as she gazed at her son, to hear her sigh softly.

Planchet told him how to find his way out of the garden. Gerard departed, scrambling awkwardly over the balcony, dropping heavily to the garden below. He looked up for one final wave, one final glimpse, but Planchet had closed the doors behind him.

Gerard recalled Laurana's look, her sadness, and he had a sudden terrible fear that this would be the last time he ever saw her, the last time he ever saw Qualinost. The fear was overwhelming, and his earlier resolve to stay and help them fight resurfaced. But he could not very well return now, not without looking foolish, or—

worse—a coward. Gripping the Marshal's orders in his hand, Gerard departed, running through the garden that was starting to come alive with the warm rays of the sun.

The sooner he reached the council, the sooner he would be back.

4

The Traitor

The room was quiet. Gilthas sat at his desk, writing his speech, the pen moving swiftly across the page. He had spent the night thinking of what to say. The words came rapidly, so that the ink seemed to flow from the heart and not his pen. Planchet was laying out a light breakfast of fruit, bread, and honey, although it seemed unlikely anyone would have much appetite. Marshal Medan stood at the window, watched Gerard depart through the garden. The Marshal saw the young Knight pause, perhaps he even guessed what Gerard was thinking. When Gerard turned and left, Medan smiled to himself and nodded.

"That was good of you, Marshal Medan," said Laurana, coming to stand at his side. She kept her voice low so as not to interrupt Gilthas in his work. "To send the young man safely away. For you do not truly believe the Solamnic Knights will come to our aid, do you?"

"No, I do not," said the Marshal, equally quiet. "Not because they will not, but because they cannot." He looked out the window, across the garden to the distant hills to the north. "They have their own problems. Beryl's attack means that the so-called Pact of the Dragons is broken. Oh, I am certain that Lord Targonne is doing his best to try to placate Malys and the others, but his efforts will be for naught. Many believe that Khellendros the Blue plays a game of cat and mouse. He pretends to be oblivious to all that is going on around him, but that is only to lull Malys and the others into complacency. In fact, it is my belief that he has long had his eye on Solanthus. He held off attacking only for fear that Beryl would consider such an attack a threat to her own territory to the south. But now he will feel that he can seize Solanthus with impunity. And so it will go from there. We may be the first, but we will not be the last.

"As to Gerard," Medan continued, "I returned to the Solamnic Knighthood a good soldier. I hope his commanders have sense enough to realize that."

He paused a moment, watching Gilthas. When the king had reached the end of a sentence, Medan spoke. "I am sorry to interrupt Your Majesty's work, but a matter has arisen that must be dealt with swiftly. A matter of some unpleasantness, I fear."

Medan shifted his gaze to Laurana. "Gerard reported to me that your servant, Kalindas, waits downstairs. It seems that he heard you were in the palace and was worried for you."

Medan watched Laurana carefully as he spoke. He saw her color wane, saw her troubled gaze flash across the room to Kelevandros, who was still sleeping.

She knows, Medan said to himself. If she does not know which of them is the traitor, yet she knows that one of them is. Good. That will make this easier.

"I will send Kelevandros to fetch him," Laurana said through pallid lips.

"I do not believe that would be wise," Medan replied. "I suggest that you ask Planchet to take Kalindas to my headquarters. My second-in-command, Dumat, will look after him. Kalindas will not be harmed, I assure you, Madam, but he must be kept safe, where he cannot communicate with anyone."

Laurana looked at the Marshal with sorrow. "My lord, I don't think . . . Is this necessary?"

"It is, Madam," he said firmly.

"I don't understand," Gilthas said, his voice tinged with anger. He rose to his feet. "My mother's servant is to be thrown in prison! Why? What is his crime?"

Medan was about to answer, but Laurana forestalled him.

"Kalindas is a spy, my son."

"A spy?" Gilthas was astonished. "For whom?"

"The Dark Knights," Laurana replied. "He reports directly to Marshal Medan, unless I am much mistaken."

Gilthas cast the Marshal a look of unutterable disgust.

"I make no apology, Your Majesty," Medan said calmly. "Nor, do I expect you to make any apology for the spies you have planted in my household."

Gilthas flushed. "A dirty business," he muttered.

"Indeed, Your Majesty. This makes an end of it. I, for one, will be glad to wash my hands. Planchet, you will find Kalindas waiting downstairs. Remove him to—"

"No, Planchet," said Gilthas peremptorily. "Bring him here to me. Kalindas has the right to answer his accuser."

"Do not do this, Your Majesty," Medan said earnestly. "Once Kalindas sees me here with you, he will know he has been unmasked. He is a dangerous man, cornered and desperate. He has no care for anyone. He will stop at nothing. I cannot guarantee Your Majesty's safety."

"Nevertheless," said Gilthas steadily, "elven law provides that Kalindas have the chance to defend himself against these charges. For too long, we have lived under your law, Marshal Medan. The law of the tyrant is no law at all. If I am to be king, then I make this my first act."

"Madam?" Medan turned to Laurana.

"His Majesty is right," said Laurana. "You have made your accusations, and we have listened. Kalindas must have his turn to tell his story."

"You will not find it a pretty one. Very well," Medan said, shrugging. "But we must be prepared. If I might suggest a plan of action . . ."

"Kelevandros," Laurana said, shaking the slumbering elf by the shoulder. "Your brother waits downstairs."

"Kalindas is here?" Kelevandros jumped to his feet.

"The guards refuse to allow him to enter," Laurana continued. "Go down and tell the guards they have my permission to bring him here."

"Yes, Madam."

Kelevandros hastened out the door. Laurana looked back at Medan. Her face was very pale, but she was calm, composed.

"Was that satisfactory?"

"Perfect, Madam," said Medan. "He was not the least suspicious. Take your seat at the table. Your Majesty, you should return to your work."

Laurana sighed deeply and sat down at the dining table. Planchet selected the very best fruit for her repast and poured her a glass of wine.

Marshal Medan had never admired Laurana's courage more than now, as he watched her take bites of fruit, chew and swallow, though the food must have tasted like ashes in her mouth. Opening one of the doors that led to the balcony, Medan moved outside, leaving the door ajar, so that he could hear and see what took place in the room without being seen himself.

Kalindas entered at his brother's heels.

"Madam, I have been frantic with concern for your safety. When that loathsome Marshal took you away, I feared he meant your death!"

"Did you, Kalindas?" Laurana said gently. "I am sorry to have caused you so much concern. As you see, I am safe here. Safe for the time being, at least. We have reports that Beryl's armies are marching on Qualinesti."

"Indeed, Madam, I heard that terrible rumor," said Kalindas, advancing until he stood close to the table at which she sat. "You are not safe here, Madam. You must take flight immediately."

"Yes, Madam," said Kelevandros. "My brother has told me that you are in danger. You and the king."

Gilthas had completed his writing. The parchment in his hand, the king rose from his desk, preparing to leave.

"Planchet," he said, "bring me my cloak."

"You are right to act swiftly, Your Majesty," said Kalindas, mistaking Gilthas's intent. "Madam, I will take the liberty of fetching your cloak, as well—"

"No, Kalindas," said Gilthas. "That is not what I meant."

Planchet returned with the king's cloak. Holding the garment over his right hand and arm, he moved to stand next to Gilthas.

"I have no intention of fleeing," Gilthas was saying. "I go now to make a speech to the people. We begin immediately to evacuate the population of Qualinost and make plans for the defense of the city."

Kalindas bowed to the king. "I understand. Your Majesty will make his speech, and then I will take you and your honored mother to a place of safety. I have friends waiting."

"I'll wager you do, Kalindas," said Marshal Medan, stepping through the door. "Friends of Beryl's waiting to assassinate both His Majesty and the Queen Mother. Where would these friends of yours happen to be?"

61

Kalindas's eyes darted warily from the Marshal to Gilthas and back to the Marshal. The elf licked dry lips. His gaze slid to Laurana. "I don't know what has been said about me, Madam—"

Gilthas intervened. "I will tell you what has been said, Kalindas. The Marshal has made the accusation that you are a spy in his employ. We have evidence that appears to indicate that this is true. By elven law, you are granted the right to speak in your defense."

"You don't believe him, do you, Madam?" Kelevandros cried. Shocked and outraged, he came to stand stolidly beside his brother. "Whatever this human has told you about Kalindas is a lie! The Marshal is a Dark Knight, and he is human!"

"Indeed, I am both those," said Medan. "I am also the one who paid your brother to spy upon the Queen Mother. I'll wager that if you search his person, you will find on him a stash of steel coins with the head of Lord Targonne stamped upon them."

"I knew someone in my household had betrayed me," Laurana said. Her voice ached with sorrow. "I received a letter from Palin Majere, warning me. That was how the dragon knew to wait for him and for Tasslehoff. The only person who could have warned the dragon was someone in my house. No one else knew."

"You are mistaken, Madam," Kelevandros insisted desperately. "The Dark Knights were spying on us. That is how they came to know. Kalindas would never betray you, Madam. Never! He loves you too well."

"Does he?" Medan asked quietly. "Look at his face."

Kalindas was livid, his skin whiter than the fine linen of the bed sheets. His lips curled back from his teeth in a sneer. His blue eyes were pale and glittering.

"Yes, I have a bag of steel coins," he said, spittle flecking his lips. "Coins paid to me by this human pig who thinks that by betraying me he may win the chance to crawl into your bed. Perhaps he already has. You are known to enjoy rutting with humans. Love you, Madam? This is how much I love you!"

Kalindas's hand darted inside his tunic. The blade of a dagger flashed in the sunlight.

Gilthas cried out. Medan drew his sword, but he had placed himself to guard the king. Medan was too far across the room to save Laurana.

She snatched up a wine glass and flung the contents into Kalindas's face. Half-blinded by the wine stinging his eyes, he stabbed wildly. The blow aimed for Laurana's heart struck her shoulder.

Cursing, Kalindas lifted the knife to strike again.

He gave a terrible cry. The knife fell from his hand. The blade of a sword protruded from his stomach. Blood soaked his shirt front.

Kelevandros, tears streaming down his cheeks, jerked his sword out of his brother's body. Dropping the weapon, Kelevandros caught hold of Kalindas, lowered him to the ground, cradled his dying brother in his arms.

"Forgive me, Kalindas!" Kelevandros said softly. He looked up, pleading. "Forgive him, Queen Mother—"

"Forgive!" Kalindas's lips, flecked with blood, twisted. "No!" He choked. His last words were squeezed out. "I curse them! I curse them both!"

He stiffened in his brother's arms. His face contorted. He tried again to speak, but blood gushed from his mouth, and with it went his life. Even in death, his eyes continued to stare at Laurana. The eyes were dark, and when the light of life faded in them, the shadows were lit with the cold glitter of his hate.

"Mother!" Gilthas sprang to her side. "Mother, you are hurt! Come, lie down."

"I am all right," Laurana said, though her voice shook. "Don't fuss. . . ."

"That was quick thinking on your part, Madam. Throwing the wine at him. He caught the rest of us flat-footed. Let me see." Medan peeled back the fabric of the sleeve that was soaked with blood. His touch was as gentle as he could make it. "The wound does not appear to be serious," he reported, after a cursory examination. "The dagger glanced off the bone. You will have a scar there, I am afraid, Madam, but the wound is clean and should heal well."

"It would not be the first scar I've borne," Laurana said with a wan smile. She clasped her hands together, to try to stop the trembling. Her gaze went involuntarily to the corpse.

"Throw something over that!" Medan commanded harshly. "Cover it up."

Planchet grabbed hold of the cloak he had been holding, spread it over Kalindas. Kelevandros knelt beside his brother, one hand holding the dead hand, the other holding the sword that had slain him.

"Planchet, summon a healer—" Gilthas began.

"No," Laurana countermanded his order. "No one must know of this. You heard the Marshal. The wound is not serious. It has already stopped bleeding."

"Your Majesty," said Planchet. "The meeting of the Thalas-Enthia . . . it is past time."

As if to emphasize this statement, a voice came from below, querulous and demanding. "I tell you I will wait no longer! A servant is permitted to see His Majesty, and I am kept waiting? You do not intimidate me. You dare not lay a hand on me, a member of the Thalas-Enthia. I will see His Majesty, do you hear? I will not be kept out!"

"Palthainon," said Medan. "After the last act of the tragedy, they send in the clowns." The Marshal started toward the door. "I will stall him as long as possible. Get this mess cleaned up!"

Laurana rose hurriedly to her feet. "He should not see me wounded like this. He must not know anything is wrong. I will wait in my own chambers, my son."

Gilthas was obviously reluctant to leave, but he knew as well as she did the importance of his talk before the Senate. "I will go to the Thalas-Enthia," he said. "First, Mother, I have a question to ask Kelevandros, and I want you to be here to hear it. Kelevandros, did you know of your brother's foul scheming? Were you part of it?"

Kelevandros was deathly pale and covered with his brother's blood, yet he faced the king with dignity. "I knew he was ambitious, yet I never thought . . . I never . . ." He paused, swallowed, and said quietly, "No, Your Majesty. I did not."

"Then I grieve for you, Kelevandros," said Gilthas, his harsh tone softening. "For what you had to do."

"I loved him," said Kelevandros in a low voice. "He was all the family I had left. Yet I could not let him harm our mistress."

Blood was starting to seep through the cloak. Kelevandros knelt over his brother's body, wrapped the cloak around it more tightly.

"With your permission, Your Majesty," he said with quiet dignity, "I will take my brother away."

Planchet made as if to help, but Kelevandros refused his assistance.

"No, he is my brother. My responsibility."

Kelevandros lifted Kalindas's body in his arms and, after a brief struggle, managed to stand upright. "Madam," he said, not raising his eyes to meet hers, "your home was the only home we ever knew, but I fear it would be unseemly—"

"I understand, Kelevandros," she said. "Take him there."

65

"Thank you, Madam."

"Planchet," Gilthas said, "go with Kelevandros. Give him what help he needs. Explain matters to the guard."

Planchet hesitated. "Your Honored Mother is wise. We should keep this secret, Your Majesty. If the people were to discover that his brother had made an attempt on the Queen Mother's life, I fear they might do Kelevandros some harm. And if they heard that Marshal Medan had been using elves to spy . . ."

"You are right, Planchet," Gilthas said. "See to it. Kelevandros, you should use the servant's—"

Realizing what he had been about to say, he stopped the words.

"The servant's entrance around back," said Kelevandros finished. "Yes, Your Majesty. I understand."

Turning, he bore his heavy burden out the door.

Laurana looked after them. "The curses of the dead always come true, they say."

"Who says?" Gilthas demanded. "Toothless old grannies? Kalindas had no high and noble goals. He did what he did out of greed alone. He cared only for the money."

Laurana shook her head. Her hair was gummed with her own blood, stuck to the wound. Gilthas started to add comforting words, but they were interrupted by a commotion outside the door. Marshal Medan could be heard tromping heavily up the stairs. He had raised his voice, to let them know he was coming and that he had company.

Laurana kissed her son with lips that were as pale as her cheeks. "You must leave now. My blessings go with you—and those of your father."

She left hurriedly, hastening down the hall.

"Planchet, the blood—" Gilthas began, but Planchet had already whisked a small ornamental table over the stain and planted himself in front of it.

Senator Palthainon entered the room with fuss and bustle. Fire smoldered in his eyes, and he began talking the instant his foot crossed the threshold.

"Your Majesty, I was told that you convened the Thalas-Enthia without first asking my approval—"

The senator halted in midword, the speech he had been rehearsing all the way up the stairs driven clean from his head. He had expected to find his puppet lying limp on the floor, tangled in his own strings. Instead, the puppet was walking out the door.

"I convened the Senate because I am king," said Gilthas, brushing past the senator. "I did not consult you, Senator, for the same reason. I am king."

Palthainon stared, began to burble and sputter. "What— What— Your Majesty! Where are you going? We must discuss this."

Gilthas paid no attention. He continued out the door, slammed it shut behind him. The speech he had written so carefully lay on the desk. After all, he would speak the words from his heart.

Palthainon stared after him, confounded. Needing someone to blame, he rounded on Marshal Medan. "This is your doing, Marshal. You put the fool boy up to this. What are you plotting, Medan? What is going on?"

The Marshal was amused. "This is none of my doing, Senator. Gilthas is king, as he says, and he has been king for many years. Longer than you realize apparently. As for what is going on"—Medan shrugged—"I suggest you ask His Majesty. He *may* deign to tell you."

"Ask His Majesty, indeed!" returned the senator with a blustering sneer. "I do not *ask* His Majesty anything. I tell His Majesty what to think and what to say, just as I always have. You are blathering, Marshal. I do not understand you."

"No, but you will," Medan advised the senator's

retreating back, as the elf picked up what shreds of dignity remained him and swept out of the chamber.

"Planchet," said Medan, after king and senator were gone and the palace was again quiet. "Bring water and bandages. I will attend to the Queen Mother. You should pull up the carpet. Take it out and burn it."

Armed with a wash basin and a roll of linen, Medan knocked at the door to Laurana's chambers. She bade him enter. He frowned to see her on her feet, looking out the window.

"You should lie down, Madam. Take this time to rest."

She turned to face him. "Palthainon will cause trouble in the Senate. You may be assured of that."

"Your son will skewer him, Madam," said the Marshal. "With words, not steel. He will let so much air out of that windbag I would not be surprised to see him come whizzing past the window. There," he added, "I made you smile."

Laurana did smile, but the next moment she swayed on her feet and reached to steady herself on the arm of a chair. Medan was at her side, helping her to sit down.

"Madam, you have lost a vast quantity of blood, and the wound continues to bleed. If I would not offend . . ." He paused, embarrassed. Coughing, he continued. "I could clean and dress the wound for you."

"We are both old soldiers, Marshal," said Laurana, sliding her arm out of the sleeve of her dressing gown. "I have lived and fought with men under circumstances where I could not afford to indulge in modesty. It is most kind of you to offer."

The Marshal reached to touch the warm skin and saw his hand—coarse, large, thick-fingered, and clumsy—in sharp contrast to the slender white shoulder of the elven woman, her own skin as smooth as the silken coverlet, the blood crimson and warm from the jagged cut. He snatched his hand back, the fingers clenched.

"I fear I hurt you, Madam," he said, feeling her flinch at his touch. "I am sorry. I am rough and clumsy. I know no other way."

Laurana clasped her hair with her hand, drew it over her shoulder, so that it was out of his way. "Marshal Medan, my son explained his plan for the defense of Qualinost to you. Do you think it will work?"

"The plan is a good one, Madam," said the Marshal, wrapping the bandage around her shoulder. "If the dwarves agree to it and do their part, it even has a chance of succeeding. I do not trust dwarves, however, as I warned His Majesty."

"A great many lives will be lost," said Laurana sadly.

"Yes, Madam. Those who remain to fight the rear-guard action may not be able to escape in time. The battle will be a glorious one," he added, tying off the bandage with a knot. "Like the old days. I, for one, would not miss it."

"You would give your life for us, Marshal?" Laurana asked, turning to look him full in the face. "You, a human and our enemy, will die defending elves?"

He pretended to be preoccupied with the wound, in order not to meet her penetrating gaze. He did not answer the question immediately but thought about it for a long time.

"I do not regret my past, Madam," he said at last. "I do not regret past decisions. I was born of common stock, a serf's son. I would have been a serf myself, illiterate, unschooled, but then Lord Ariakan found me. He gave me knowledge, he gave me training. Most important, he gave me faith in a power greater than myself. Perhaps you cannot understand this, Madam, but I worshipped Her Dark Majesty with all my soul. The Vision she gave me comes to me still in my dreams, although I cannot understand why, since she is gone."

"I understand, Marshal," said Laurana softly. "I stood in the presence of Takhisis, Queen of Darkness. I still feel the awe and reverence I experienced then. Although I knew her power to be evil, it was awful to behold. Perhaps that was because when I dared try to look into her eyes, I saw myself. I saw her darkness inside me."

"You, Madam?" Medan shook his head.

"I was the Golden General, Marshal," Laurana said earnestly. "A fine title. People cheered me in the streets. Children gave me bouquets of flowers. Yet I ordered those same people into battle. I orphaned many of those children. Because of me thousands died, when they might have lived to lead happy and productive lives. Their blood is on my hands."

"Do not regret your actions, Madam. To do so is selfish. Your regret robs the dead of the honor that is theirs. You fought for a cause you knew to be just and right. They followed you into battle—into death, if you will—because they saw that cause shining in you. That is why you were called the Golden General," he added. "Not for your hair."

"Still," she said, "I would like to give something back to them."

She fell silent, absorbed in her own thoughts. He started to leave, thinking that she would like to rest, but she detained him.

"We were speaking of you, Marshal," she said, resting her hand light upon his arm. "Why you are prepared to give your life for elves."

Looking into her eyes, he could have said he was prepared to lay down his life for one elf, but he did not. His love would not be welcome to her, whereas his friendship was. Counting himself blessed, he did not seek for more.

"I fight for my homeland, Madam," he replied simply.

"One's homeland is where one is born, Marshal."

"Precisely, Madam. My homeland is here."

His response gave her pleasure. Her blue eyes were soft with sympathy, glimmered with sudden tears. She was warmth and sweetness and perfume, and she was low in her spirits, shaken and hurt. He rose to his feet quickly, so quickly that he clumsily overturned the bowl of water he had used to wash the wound.

"I am sorry, Madam." He bent to wipe up the spill, glad to have the chance to hide his face. He rose again, did not look at her. "The bandage is not too tight, is it, Madam?" he asked gruffly.

"No, not too tight," said Laurana.

"Good. Then if you will excuse me, Madam, I must return to headquarters, to see if there have been any further reports of the army's progress."

With a bow, he turned on his heel and departed in haste, leaving her to her thoughts.

Laurana drew the sleeve of her gown over her shoulder. She flexed her fingers, rubbed her fingers over old calluses on her palm.

"I will give something back," she said.

5

Dragon Flight

The stables of the Dark Knights were located a considerable distance from Qualinesti. Not surprising, Gerard considered, since the stables housed a blue dragon. He had never been there, never had occasion to go, and had only a vague idea where the stables were. Medan's directions were easy to follow, however, and guided Gerard unerringly.

Mindful of the necessity for haste, he advanced at a jogging run. Gerard was soon winded, however. His wounds from his battle with the draconian throbbed. He'd had very little sleep, and he was weighted down with his armor. The thought that at the end of all this toil he would confront a blue dragon did not bring ease to his sore muscles or lighten the weight of his armor. Just the reverse.

He smelled the stables before he could see them. They were surrounded by a stockade with guards at the entrance. Alert and wary, they hailed him the moment they heard his footsteps. He replied with the proper code word and handed over Medan's orders. The guards peered at these intently, looked closely at Gerard, whom they did not recognize. There was no mistaking Medan's seal, however, and they let him pass.

The stables housed horses, griffons, and dragons, although not in the same location. Low, sprawling wooden buildings housed the horses. The griffons had their nests atop a cliff. Griffons prefer the heights, and they had to be kept far from the horses so that the horses were not made nervous by the smell of the beasts. The blue dragon, Gerard learned, was stabled in a cave beneath the cliff.

One of the stable hands offered to take Gerard to the dragon, and, his heart sinking so low that he seemed to walk on it with every reluctant step, Gerard agreed. They were forced to wait, however, due to the arrival of another blue dragon bearing a rider. The blue landed in a clearing near the horse stables, sending the horses into a panic. Gerard's guide left him, ran to calm the horses. Other stable hands shouted imprecations at the dragonrider, telling him he'd landed in the wrong spot and shaking their fists at him.

The dragonrider ignored them. Sliding from his saddle, he brushed away their jeers.

"I am from Lord Targonne," he said brusquely. "I have urgent orders for Marshal Medan. Fetch down one of the griffons to take me to headquarters and then see to my dragon. I want him properly housed and fed for the return flight. I leave tomorrow."

At the mention of the name Targonne, the stable hands shut their mouths and scattered to obey the Knight's commands. Several led the blue dragon to the caves beneath the mountains, while others began the long process of trying to whistle down one of the griffons. The proceeding took some time, for griffons are notoriously ill-tempered and will pretend to be deaf to a command in the hope that their master will eventually give up and go away.

Gerard was interested to hear what news the Dark Knight was taking with such speed to Medan. Seeing the Knight wipe his mouth, Gerard removed the flask from his belt.

"You appear to thirst, sir," he said, holding out the flask.

"I don't suppose you have any brandy in there?" asked the Knight, eyeing the flask eagerly.

"Water, I'm sorry to say," said Gerard.

The Knight shrugged, seized the flask and drank. His thirst slaked, he handed the flask back to Gerard. "I'll drink the Marshal's brandy when I meet with him." He eyed Gerard curiously. "Are you coming or going?"

"Going," said Gerard. "A mission for Marshal Medan. I heard you say you've come from Lord Targonne. How has his lordship reacted to the news that Beryl is attacking Qualinesti?"

The Knight shrugged, looked around with disdain. "Marshal Medan is the ruler of a backwater province. Hardly surprising that he was caught off-guard by the dragon's actions. I assure you, sir, Lord Targonne was not."

Gerard sighed deeply. "You have no idea how hard this duty is. Stuck here among these filthy elves who think that just because they live for centuries that makes them better than us. Can't get a mug of good ale to save your soul. As to the women, they're all so blasted snooty and proud.

"I'll tell you the truth, though." Gerard edged closer, lowered his voice. "They really want us, you know. Elf women like us human men. They just pretend they don't. They lead a fellow on and then scream when he tries to take what's been offered."

"I hear the Marshal sides with the vermin." The Knight's lip curled.

Gerard snorted. "The Marshal—he's more elf than human, if you ask me. Won't let us have any fun. My guess is that's about to change."

The Knight gave Gerard a knowing look. "Let's just say that wherever you're going, you'd best hurry back, or you're going to miss out."

Gerard regarded the Knight with admiration and envy. "I'd give anything to be posted at headquarters. Must be really exciting, being around his lordship. I'll bet you know everything that's happening in the whole world."

"I know my share," the Knight stated, rocking back on his heels and regarding the very stars in the sky with proprietory interest. "Actually I'm considering moving here. There'll be land for the asking soon. Elf land and fancy elf houses. And elf women, if that's what you like." He gave Gerard a disparaging glance. "Personally I wouldn't want to touch one of the cold, clammy hags. Turns my stomach to think of it. You had best have your fun with one of them fast, though, or she might not be around for the taking."

Gerard was able now to guess the import of Targonne's orders to Medan. He saw quite clearly the plan the Lord of the Night had in mind, and he was sickened by it. Seize elven property and elven homes, murder the owners, and hand the wealth out as gifts to loyal members of the Knighthood. Gerard's hand tightened around his sword. He would have liked to turn this Knight's proud stomach—turn it inside out. He would have to forego the pleasure. Leave that to Marshal Medan.

The Knight slapped his gloves against his thigh and glanced over at the stable hands, who were yelling at the griffons, who were continuing to ignore them.

75

"Louts!" he said impatiently. "I suppose I must do this myself. Well, a good journey to you, sir."

"And to you, sir," said Gerard. He watched the Knight stalk off to bully the stable hands, striking them with his fist when they did not give him the answers he thought he deserved. The stable hands slunk away, leaving the Knight to yell for the griffons himself.

"Bastard," said one of the men, nursing a bruised cheek. "Now we'll be up all night tending to his blasted dragon."

"I wouldn't work too hard at it," said Gerard. "I think the Knight's errand will take longer than he anticipates. Far longer."

The stable hand cast Gerard a sulky glance and, rubbing his cheek, led Gerard to the cave of the Marshal's blue dragon.

Gerard prepared nervously to meet the blue by recalling every bit of information he'd ever heard about dragons. Of primary importance would be controlling the dragonfear, which he had heard could be extremely debilitating. He took a firm grip on his courage and hoped he would do nothing to disgrace himself.

The stable hands brought the dragon forth from his lair. Razor was a magnificent sight. The sunlight gleamed on his blue scales. His head was elegantly shaped, eyes keen, nostrils flared. He moved with sinuous grace. Gerard had never been this close to a dragon, any dragon. The dragonfear touched Gerard, but the dragon was not exerting his power to panic the human, and Gerard felt the fear as awe and wonder.

The dragon, aware that he was being admired, shook his crest and flexed his wings, lashed his tail about.

An elderly man left the dragon's side, walked over to Gerard. The old man was short and bowlegged and scrawny. Squinty eyes were almost lost in a web of wrinkles, and he peered at Gerard with intense curiosity and suspicion.

"I am Razor's trainer, sir," said the old man. "I've never known the Marshal to allow another person on his dragon's back. What's going on?"

Gerard handed over Medan's orders. The old man stared at them with equal intensity, held the seal close to his nose to see it with what was probably his single good eye. Gerard thought for a moment that the old man was going to keep him from leaving, and he didn't know whether to be glad or disappointed.

"Well, there's a first time for everything," the old man muttered and handed back the orders. He looked at Gerard's armor, raised an eyebrow. "You're not thinking of taking to the air in that, are you, sir?"

"I . . . I suppose . . ." Gerard stammered.

The old man was scandalized. "You'd freeze your privates off!" He shook his head. "Now if you was going into battle on dragonback, yes, you'd want all that there metal, but you're not. You're flying far and you're flying fast. I have some old leathers of the Marshal's that'll fit you. Might be a trifle big, but they'll do. Is there any special way you would like us to place the saddle, sir? The Marshal prefers it set just back of the shoulder blades, but I've known other riders who want it between the wings. They claim the flight is smoother."

"I . . . I don't really know. . . ." Gerard looked at the dragon, and the knowledge struck home that he was really going to have go through with this.

"By Our Queen," stated the old man, amazed. "You've never sat a dragon afore, have you?"

Gerard confessed, red-faced, that he had not. "I hope it is not difficult," he added, remembering vividly learning to ride a horse. If he fell off the dragon as many times as he fell off the horse . . .

"Razor is a veteran, Sir Knight," stated the old man proudly. "He is a thorough soldier. Disciplined, obeys orders. Not temperamental like some of these blues can be. He and the general fought together as a team during the Chaos War and after. But when those freakish, bloated dragons came and began killing their own kind, the Marshal kept Razor hidden away. Razor wasn't happy about that, mind you. The rows they had."

The old man shook his head. He squinted up at Gerard. "I think I'm beginning to understand after all." He nodded his wizened head. "I've heard the rumors that the Green Bitch was heading this way."

He leaned close to Gerard, spoke in a loud whisper. "Don't let on to Razor, though, sir. If he thought he'd have a chance at that green beast what killed his mate, he'd stay and fight, Marshal or no Marshal. You just take him safe away from here, Sir Knight. Good luck to the both of you."

Gerard opened his mouth to say that he and Razor would be returning to fight just as soon as he had delivered his message, but he shut it again, fearing to say too much. Let the old man think what he wanted.

"Will . . . Razor mind that I am not Marshal Medan?" Gerard asked hesitantly. "I wouldn't want to upset the dragon. He might refuse to carry me."

"Razor is dedicated to the Marshal, sir, but once he understands that Medan has sent you, he will serve you well. This way, sir. I'll introduce you."

Razor listened attentively as a nearly tongue-tied Gerard haltingly explained his mission and exhibited Medan's orders.

"Where is our destination?" Razor demanded.

"I am not permitted to reveal that, yet," Gerard said apologetically. "I am to tell you once we are airborne. The fewer who know, the better."

The dragon gave a shake of his head to indicate his readiness to obey. He was not the talkative sort, apparently, and after that single question, he lapsed into disciplined silence.

Saddling the dragon took some time, not because Razor in any way hindered the operation, but the act of positioning the saddle and the harness with its innumerable buckles and straps was a complex and time-consuming procedure. Gerard put on the "leathers," consisting of a padded leather tunic with long sleeves that he pulled on over a pair of thick leather breeches. Leather gloves protected the hands. A leather cap that resembled an executioner's hood fit over his head, protected both head and neck. The leather tunic was overlarge, the leather pants were stiff, the leather helm stifling. Gerard found it almost impossible to see out of the eye-slits and wondered why they even bothered. The insignia of the Dark Knights— the death lily and the skull—had been incorporated into the stitching of the padding.

Other than that and his sword, nothing else marked Gerard as a Dark Knight. He placed the precious letter safely in a leather pack, tied the pack tightly to the dragon's saddle.

The sun was high in the sky by the time both dragon and rider were ready to leave. Gerard mounted the dragon awkwardly, requiring assistance from the stable hands and the dragon, who bore his incompetence with exemplary patience. Red-faced and embarrassed, Gerard had barely grasped the reins in his hand when Razor gave a galvanized leap straight into the air, powering himself upward with the strong muscles of his hind legs.

The jolt drove Gerard's stomach down somewhere around his boots, and he held on so tightly his fingers lost all feeling and went numb. But when the dragon spread his wings and soared into the morning, Gerard's spirit soared with him.

He had never before understood why anyone would want to be a part of a dragon-wing. He understood then. The experience of flight was exhilarating as well as terrifying. Memories came to him of childish dreams of flying like the eagles. He had even attempted to do so himself by jumping off the barn roof with arms extended, only to crash into a hayrick, nearly breaking his neck. A thrill of excitement warmed his blood and diluted the fear in his belly.

Watching the ground fall away beneath him, he marveled at the strange feeling that it was the world that was leaving him, not the other way around. He was entranced by the silence, a silence that was whole and complete, not what is termed silence by the land-bound. That silence is made up of various small sounds that are so constant we no longer hear them: the chirping of birds, the rustling of the wind in the leaves, the sound of distant voices, the murmur of brook and stream.

Gerard could hear nothing except the creak of the tendons of the dragon's wings, and when the dragon floated on the thermals, he could not hear even that. The silence filled him with a sensation of peace, euphoria. He was no longer a part of the world. He floated above its cares, its woes, its problems. He felt weightless, as if he had shed his bulky flesh and bone. The thought of going back down, of gaining back the weight, of resuming the burden, was suddenly abhorrent. He could have flown forever, flown to the place the sun went when it set, flown to places where the moon hid.

The dragon cleared the treetops.

"What direction?" Razor shouted, his voice booming, shaking Gerard out of his reverie.

"North," Gerard shouted. The wind rushing past his head whipped the words from his mouth. The dragon turned his head to hear better. "Solanthus."

Razor's eye regarded him askance, and Gerard was afraid the dragon might refuse. Solanthus was in nominally free territory. The Solamnic Knights had transformed Solanthus into a heavily fortified city, probably the most heavily fortified in all of Ansalon. Razor might very well wonder why he was being ordered to fly into an enemy stronghold, and if he didn't like the answer he might decide to dump Gerard from the saddle.

Gerard was ready with an explanation, but the dragon explained the situation to himself.

"Ah, a reconnaissance mission," he said and adjusted his course.

Razor maintained silence during the flight. This suited Gerard, who was preoccupied with his own thoughts, dark thoughts that cast a shadow over the beautiful panorama of the landscape sliding away far beneath him. He had spoken hopefully, positively of being able to persuade the Solamnic Knights to come to Qualinesti's aid, but now that he was on his way, he began to doubt that he would be able to persuade them.

"Sir," said Razor, "look below."

Gerard looked, and his heart seemed to plummet to the ground.

"Drop down," he ordered the dragon. He didn't know if he could be heard, and he accompanied his words with a gesture of his gloved hand. "I want a better view."

The dragon swooped out of the clouds, circled slowly in a descending spiral.

"That's close enough," said Gerard, indicating with a gesture that the dragon was to remain stationary.

Gerard bent over the saddle, grasping it with his gloved hands, and looked out over the dragon's left wing.

A vast army swarmed across the land, its numbers so large that it stretched like a great black snake for as far as he could see. A ribbon of blue that wound through the green forests was surely the White-rage River that formed the border of Qualinesti. The head of the black snake had already crawled over the border, was well inland.

Gerard leaned forward. "Would it be possible for you to increase your speed?" he shouted and illustrated his question with a jabbing finger, pointing north.

Razor grunted. "I can fly faster," he shouted, "but you will not find it comfortable."

Gerard looked down, estimating numbers, counting companies, supply wagons, gaining all the information he could. He gritted his teeth, bent in the saddle and gave the nod to proceed.

The dragon's enormous wings began to beat. Razor lifted his head to the clouds, soared up to reach them.

The sudden acceleration pressed Gerard into the saddle. He blessed the designer of the leather helm, understood the need for the eye-slits. Even then, the rushing wind half-blinded him, brought tears to his eyes. The motion of the dragon's wings caused the saddle to rock back and forth. Gerard's stomach heaved. Grimly he hung on and prayed that somewhere there were gods to pray to.

6

The March on Silvanost

No one quite knew how word came to spread throughout the capital city of Silvanost that the hands of the human girl named Mina were the hands of a healer. The elves might have heard news of her from the outside world, except that they had been long cut off from the outside world, covered by the shield that had been presumably protecting them but had been, in reality, slowly killing them. No elf could say where he had first heard this rumor, but he credited it to neighbor, cousin, or passerby.

The rumor started with the fall of darkness. It spread through the night, whispered on the flower-scented night breeze, sung by the nightingale, mentioned by the owl. The rumor spread with excitement and joy among the young, yet there were those among the older elves who frowned to hear it and who cautioned against it.

Strong among these were the kirath, the elves who had long patrolled and guarded the borders of Silvanesti. These elves had watched with grief as the shield killed every living thing along the border. They had fought the cruel dream cast by the dragon Cyan Bloodbane many years ago during the War of the Lance. The kirath knew from their bitter experience with the dream that evil can come in lovely forms, only to grow hideous and murderous when confronted. The kirath warned against this human girl. They tried to halt the rumors that were spreading through the city, as fast and bright and slippery as quicksilver. But every time the rumor came to a house where a young elven mother held to her breast her dying child, the rumor was believed. The warnings of the kirath went unheeded.

That night, when the moon lifted high in the heavens, the single moon, the moon that the elves had never grown accustomed to seeing in a sky where once the silver and the red moons had swung among the stars, the guards on the gates of Silvanost looked out along the highway leading into their city, a highway of moondust, to see a force of humans marching on Silvanost. The force was small, twenty Knights clad in the black armor of the Knights of Neraka and several hundred foot soldiers marching behind. The army was a shabby one. The foot soldiers stumbled, they limped, footsore and weary. Even the Knights were afoot, their horses having died in battle or been eaten by their starving riders. Only one Knight rode, and that was their leader, a slender figure mounted on a horse the color of blood.

A thousand elven archers, armed with the storied elven longbow, legendary for its accuracy, looked down upon this advancing army, and each picked out his or her target. There were so many archers that had the order been given to fire, each one of those advancing soldiers would have been stuck full with as many arrows as there are quills on the porcupine.

The elven archers looked uncertainly to their commanders. The archers had heard the rumors, as had their commanders. The archers had sick at home: wives, husbands, mothers, fathers, children, all dying of the wasting disease. Many of the archers themselves were in the first stages of the illness and remained at their posts only through sheer effort of will. So too with their commanders. The kirath, who were not members of the elven army, stood among the archers, wrapped in their cloaks that could blend in with the leaves and trees of the forests they loved, and watched grimly.

Mina rode unerringly straight toward the silver gates, rode into arrow range unflinching, her horse carrying its head proudly, neck arched, tail flicking. At her side walked a giant minotaur. Her Knights came behind her, the foot soldiers followed after. Now within sight of the elves, the soldiers took some pains to dress their lines, straighten their backs, march upright and tall with the appearance of being unafraid, although many must have quaked and shivered at the sight of the arrow tips shining in the moonlight.

Mina halted her horse before the gate. She raised her voice, and it carried as clear and ringing as the notes of a silver bell.

"I am called Mina. I come to Silvanost in the name of the One God. I come to Silvanost to teach my elven brothers and sisters of the One God and to accept them into the service of the One God. I call upon you, the people of Silvanost, to open the gates, that I may enter in peace."

"Do not trust her," urged the kirath. "Do not believe her!"

No one listened, and when one of the kirath, a man named Rolan, lifted his bow and would have fired a shaft at the human girl, those standing around him struck him down so that he fell bloody and dazed to the pavement. Finding that no one paid them any heed, the kirath picked up their fallen comrade and left the city of Silvanost, retreated back to their woodlands.

A herald advanced and read aloud a proclamation.

"His Majesty the king orders that the gates of Silvanost be opened to Mina, whom His Majesty names Dragonslayer, Savior of the Silvanesti."

The elven archers flung down their bows and gave a ragged cheer. The elven gatekeepers hastened to the gates that were made of steel and silver and magic. Though these gates looked as frail and fragile as spun cobweb, they were so bound by ancient magicks that no force on Krynn could break them, unless it was the breath of a dragon. But Mina, it seemed, had only to set her hand to the gates, and they opened.

Mina rode slowly into Silvanost. The minotaur walked at her stirrup, glowering distrustfully at the elves, his hand on his sword. Her soldiers came after, nervous, watchful, wary. The elves, after their initial cheer, fell silent. Crowds of elves lined the highway that was chalk-white in the moonlight. No one spoke, and all that could be heard was the jingle of chain mail and the rattle of armor and sword, the steady shuffling march of booted feet.

Mina had gone only a short distance, and some of the army still remained outside the gate, when she drew her horse to a halt. She heard a sound, and now she looked out into the crowd.

Dismounting, she left the highway and walked straight into the crowd of elves. The huge minotaur drew his sword and would have followed to guard her back, but she raised her hand in a wordless command, and he halted as though she had struck him. Mina came to a young elven woman trying vainly to stifle the whimperings of fretful child of about three years. It was the child's wail that had caught Mina's ears.

The elves drew aside to let Mina pass, flinching from her as though her touch pained them. Yet, after she had passed, some of the younger reached out hesitatingly to touch her again. She paid them no heed.

Approaching the elf woman, Mina said, speaking in Elvish, "Your baby cries. She burns with fever. What is wrong with her?"

The mother held the child protectively in her arms, bowed her head over the little girl. Her tears fell on the child's hot forehead.

"She has the wasting sickness. She has been ill for days now. She grows worse all the time. I fear that . . . she is dying."

"Give me the child," said Mina, holding out her hands.

"No!" The elven woman clasped the child to her. "No, do not harm her!"

"Give me the child," said Mina gently.

The mother lifted fearful eyes and looked into Mina's. The warm liquid amber flowed around the mother and the child. The mother handed the baby to Mina.

The little girl weighed almost nothing. She was as light as a will-o'-the-wisp in Mina's arms.

"I bless you in the name of the One God," said Mina, "and I call you back to this life."

The child's whimpering ceased. She went limp in Mina's arms, and the elder elves drew in hissing breaths.

"She is well now," Mina said, handing back the child to the mother. "The fever has broken. Take her home and keep her warm. She will live."

The mother looked fearfully into the face of her child and gave a cry of joy. The child's whimpering had ceased, and she had gone limp because she now slept peacefully. Her forehead was cool to the touch, her breathing easy.

"Mina!" the elf woman cried, falling to her knees. "Bless you, Mina!"

"Not me," said Mina. "The One God."

"The One God," the mother cried. "I thank the One God."

"Lies!" cried an elf, thrusting his way forward through the crowd. "Lies and blasphemy. The only true god is Paladine."

"Paladine forsook you," Mina said. "Paladine left you. The One God is with you. The One God cares for you."

The elf opened his mouth to make an angry rejoinder. Before he could speak, Mina said to him, "Your beloved wife is not with you here this night."

The elf shut his mouth. Muttering, he started to turn away.

"She is sick at home," Mina told him. "She has not been well for a long, long time. Every day, you watch her sink closer to death. She lies in bed, unable to walk. This morning, she could not lift her head from the pillow."

"She is dying!" the elf said harshly, keeping his head turned away. "Many have died. We bear our suffering and go on."

"When you return home," said Mina, "your wife will meet you at the door. She will take you by the hands, and you will dance in the garden as you once used to."

The elf turned to face her. His face was streaked with tears, his expression was wary, disbelieving. "This is some trick."

"No, it is not," Mina returned, smiling. "I speak the truth, and you know it. Go to her. Go and see."

The elf stared at Mina, then, with a hollow cry, pushed his way through those who surrounded him and vanished into the crowd.

Mina extended her hand toward an elven couple. Father and mother each held a young boy by the hand. The boys were twins, thin and listless, their young faces so pinched with pain they looked like wizened old men.

Mina beckoned to the boys. "Come to me."

The boys shrank away from her. "You are human," said one. "You hate us."

"You will kill us," said his brother. "My father says so."

"To be human, elf, or minotaur makes no difference to the One God. We are all children of the One God, but we must be obedient children. Come to me. Come to the One God."

The boys looked up at their parents. The elves stared at Mina, saying nothing, making no sign. The crowd around them was hushed and still, watching the drama. Finally, one boy let loose his mother's hand and came forward, walking weakly and unsteadily. He took hold of Mina's hand.

"The One God has the power to heal one of you," said Mina. "Which will it be? You or your brother."

"My brother," the child said immediately.

Mina rested her hand on the boy's head. "The One God admires sacrifice. The One God is pleased. The One God heals you both."

Healthful color flooded the pallid cheeks. The listless eyes blazed with life and vigor. The weak legs no longer trembled, the bent spines straightened. The other boy left his father and ran to join his twin, both flinging their arms around Mina.

"Bless you! Bless you, Mina!" some of the younger Silvanesti elves began to chant, and they gathered close to Mina, reaching out to seize hold of her, begging her to heal them, their wives, their husbands, their children. The crowd surged and heaved around her so that she was in danger of being adored to death.

The minotaur, Galdar, Mina's second-in-command and self-appointed guardian, waded into the mass. Catching hold of Mina, he bore her out of the press, thrusting aside the desperate elves with his strong arms.

Mounting her horse, Mina rose up in the stirrups and lifted her hand for silence. The elves hushed immediately, strained to hear her words.

"It has been given to me to tell you that all those who ask of the One God in humility and reverence will be healed of the sickness brought upon you by the dragon Cyan Bloodbane. The One God has freed you from this peril. Pray to the One God upon your knees, acknowledge the One God as the true god of the elves and you will be cured."

Some of the younger elves fell to their knees at once and began to pray. Others, the elder elves, refused. Never before had the elves prayed to any god except Paladine. Some began to mutter that the kirath had been right, but then those who had prayed lifted their heads to the moonlight and cried out in joy that the pain had left their bodies. At the sight of the miraculous healing, more elves dropped to their knees, raised their voices in praise. The elder elves, watching in dismay and disbelief, shook their heads. One in particular, who was dressed in the magical camouflaging cloak of the kirath, stared hard at Mina for long moments before vanishing among the shadows.

The blood-red horse proceeded forward at a walk. Mina's soldiers cleared her way through the press of bodies. The Tower of the Stars glimmered softly in the moonlight, pointing the way to heaven. Walking at her side, Galdar tried to breathe as little as possible. The stench of elf was overpowering, cloying, sickeningly sweet to the minotaur, like the scent of something long dead.

"Mina," said Galdar in a harsh growl, "these are *elves!*" He made no effort to conceal his disgust. "What does the One God want with elves?"

"The souls of all mortals are valuable to the One God, Galdar," Mina responded.

Galdar mulled this over but could not understand. Looking back at her, he saw, in the moonlight, the images of countless elves held prisoner in the warm golden amber of her eyes.

Mina continued through Silvanost as prayers to the One God, spoken in the Elvish language, rustled and whispered through the night.

Silvanoshei, son of Alhana Starbreeze and Porthios of the House of Solostaran, the heir to both kingdoms of the elves, the Qualinesti and the Silvanesti, stood with his face and hands pressed against the crystal windowpane, peering into the night.

"Where is she?" he demanded impatiently. "No, wait! I think I see her!" He stared long and then fell back with a sigh. "No, it is not her. I was mistaken. Why doesn't she come?" He turned around to demand in sudden fear, "You don't think anything has happened to her, Cousin?"

Kiryn opened his mouth to reply, but before he could say a word, Silvanoshei had spoken to a servant. "Find out what is happening at the gate. Return to me at once."

The servant bowed and departed, leaving the two alone in the room.

"Cousin," said Kiryn, keeping his voice carefully modulated, "that is the sixth servant you have sent this past half hour. He will return with the same message that they have all brought. The progress of the procession is slow, due to the fact that so many of our people want to see her."

Silvanoshei went back to the window, stared out again with an impatience he did not bother to hide. "It was a mistake. I should have been there to greet her." He cast a cold glance at his cousin. "I should not have listened to you."

91

"Your Majesty," said Kiryn with a sigh, "it would not have looked good. You, the king, welcoming in person the leader of our enemies. Bad enough that we have admitted her into the city in the first place," he added to himself, but Silvanoshei had sharp ears.

"Need I remind you, Cousin," said the king tersely, "that it was this same leader of our enemies who saved us from the machinations of the foul dragon Cyan Bloodbane? Because of her, I was brought back to life and given the chance to lower the shield he erected over us, the shield that was sucking out our very lives. Because of her, I was able to destroy the Shield Tree and save our people. If not for her, there would be no elves in the streets of Silvanost, only corpses."

"I am aware of that, Your Majesty," Kiryn said. "Yet I ask myself why? What are her motives?"

"I might ask the same of you, Cousin," Silvanoshei said coolly. "What are you motives?"

"I don't know what you mean," Kiryn said.

"Don't you? It has been brought to my attention that you are plotting behind my back. You have been seen meeting with members of the kirath."

"What of that, Cousin?" Kiryn asked mildly. "They are your loyal subjects."

"They are not my loyal subjects!" Silvanoshei said angrily. "They conspire against me!"

"They conspire against our enemies, the Dark Knights—"

"Mina, you mean. They conspire against Mina. That is the same as conspiring against me."

Kiryn sighed softly and said, "There is someone waiting to speak to Your Majesty."

"I will see no one," Silvanoshei said.

"I think you should see him," Kiryn continued. "He comes from your mother."

Silvanoshei turned away from the window and stared at Kiryn. "What are you saying? My mother is dead. She died the night the ogres raided our camp. The night I fell through the shield . . ."

"No, Cousin," said Kiryn. "Your mother, Alhana, lives. She and her forces have crossed the border. She has been in contact with the kirath. That is why . . . They tried to see you, Cousin, but were denied. They came to me."

Silvanoshei sank down into a chair. He lowered his head to his shaking hand to hide his sudden tears.

"Forgive me, Cousin," Kiryn said. "I should have found some better way to tell you—"

"No! You could have brought me no happier news!" Silvanoshei cried, lifting his face. "My mother's messenger is here?" He rose to his feet, walked impatiently toward the door. "Bring him in."

"He is not in the antechamber. He would be in danger here in the palace. I took the liberty—"

"Of course. I had forgotten. My mother is a dark elf," Silvanoshei said bitterly. "She is under penalty of death, as are those who follow her."

"Your Majesty now has the power to set that right," said Kiryn.

"By law, perhaps," said Silvanoshei. "But laws cannot erase years of hatred. Go and fetch him, then, wherever you have hidden him."

Kiryn left the room. Silvanoshei returned to the window, his thoughts a confused and joyous muddle. His mother alive. Mina returned to him. The two of them must meet. They would like each other. Well, perhaps not at first. . . .

He heard a scraping sound behind him, turned to see movement behind one of the heavy curtains. The curtain was drawn aside, revealing an opening in the wall, a secret passageway. Silvanoshei had heard stories from his mother about these passageways. As a lark, Silvanoshei had searched for the passages, but had found only this one. The passage led to the hidden garden, a garden now lifeless, its flowers having been killed by the blight of the shield.

Kiryn stepped out from behind the curtain. Another elf, cloaked and hooded, followed after him.

"Samar!" exclaimed Silvanoshei in a recognition that was both pleasurable and filled with pain.

His first impulse was to run forward, grasp Samar by the hand or perhaps even embrace him, so glad was he to see him and know he was alive and that his mother was alive. Kiryn was hoping for just such a reunion. He hoped that the news that his mother was near, that she and her forces had crossed the border would wrench Silvanoshei's mind away from Mina.

Kiryn's hopes were doomed to failure.

Samar did not see Silvanoshei the king. He saw Silvanoshei the spoiled child, dressed in fine clothes and glittering jewels, while his mother wore clothes she made of homespun and adorned herself in the cold metal of chain mail. He saw Silvanoshei residing in a grand palace with every comfort he could wish for, saw his mother shivering in a barren cave. Samar saw a vast bed with a thick down mattress and blankets of angora wool and sheets of silk, and he saw Alhana sleeping on the cold ground with her tattered cloak wrapped around her.

Anger pounded in Samar's veins, dimmed his vision, blurred his thinking. He blotted out Silvanoshei completely and saw only Alhana, who had been overcome with joy and emotion on hearing that Silvanoshei, whom she had believed to be dead, was alive. Not only alive but crowned king of Silvanesti—her dearest wish for him.

She had wanted to come immediately to see him, an act that would have placed in jeopardy not only her life but the lives of her people. Samar had pleaded long and hard to dissuade her from this course of action, and only the knowledge that she risked imperiling all for which she had labored so long had at last convinced her that he should go in her stead. He would take her love to her son, but he would not fawn or dote on the boy. Samar would remind Silvanoshei of a son's duty to a mother, be he king or commoner. Duty to his mother, duty to his people.

Samar's cold look halted Silvanoshei in midstep.

"Prince Silvanoshei," said Samar, with a very slight bow. "I trust I find you well. I certainly find you well-fed." He cast a scathing glance at the laden table. "That much food would feed your mother's army for a year!"

Silvanoshei's warm affection froze to solid ice in an instant. He forgot how much he owed Samar, remembered instead only that the man had never approved of him, perhaps never even liked him. Silvanoshei drew himself up to his full height.

"Undoubtedly you have not heard the news, Samar," Silvanoshei said with quiet dignity, "and so I forgive you. I am king of the Silvanesti, and you will address me as such."

"I will address you as what you are," Samar said, his voice shaking, "a spoiled brat!"

"How dare you—" Silvanoshei began hotly.

"Stop it! Both of you." Kiryn stared at them, aghast. "What are you two doing? Have you forgotten the terrible crisis that is at hand? Cousin Silvanoshei, you have known this man from childhood. You have told me many times that you admired and respected him as a second father. Samar risked his life to come to you. Is this how you repay him?"

Silvanoshei said nothing. He pressed his lips together, regarded Samar with an expression of injured dignity.

"And you, Samar," said Kiryn, turning to the elven warrior. "You are in the wrong. Silvanoshei is the crowned and anointed king of the Silvanesti people. You are Qualinesti. Perhaps the ways of your people are different. We Silvanesti revere our king. When you demean him, you demean us all."

Samar and the King were silent long moments, staring at each other—not as two friends who have been quick to quarrel and are glad to make up, but as two duelists who are sizing each other up even as they are forced to shake hands before the final contest. Kiryn was grieved to the heart.

"We have started out all wrong," he said. "Let us begin again."

"How is my mother, Samar?" Silvanoshei asked abruptly.

"Your mother is well . . . Your Majesty," Samar replied. He left a deliberate pause before the title, but he spoke it. "She sends her love."

Silvanoshei nodded. He was keeping a tight grip on himself. "The night of the storm. I thought . . . It seemed impossible that you could survive."

"As it turned out, the Legion of Steel had been keeping watch on the movements of the ogres, and so they came to our aid. It seems," Samar added, his voice gruff, "that you and your mother have been grieving together. When you did not return, we searched for you for days. We could only conclude that you had been captured by the ogres and dragged off to torment and death. When the shield fell and your mother crossed over into her homeland, we were met by the kirath. Her joy was boundless when she heard that not only were you alive, but that you were now king, Silvanoshei."

His tone hardened. "Then the reports of you and this human female—"

Silvanoshei flashed Kiryn an angry glance. "Now I understand the reason you brought him here, Cousin. To lecture me." He turned back to the window.

"Silvanoshei—" Kiryn began.

Samar strode forward, grabbed hold of Silvanoshei by the shoulder. "Yes, I am going to lecture you. You are behaving like a spoiled brat. Your honored mother did not believe the rumors. She told the kirath who spoke of this that they lied. What happens? I overhear you speaking of this human. I hear from your own lips that the rumors are true! You mope and whine for her, while a massive army of Dark Knights crosses the border. An army that was waiting at the border, prepared to cross when the shield came down.

"And, lo and behold, the shield fell! How did this army come to be there, Silvanoshei? Was it coincidence? Did the Dark Knights happen to arrive at the precise moment the shield happened to fall? No, Silvanoshei, the Dark Knights were there on the border because they *knew* the shield was going to fall. Now they march on Silvanost, five thousand strong, and you have opened the gates of the city to the female who brought them here."

"That is not true!" Silvanoshei returned heatedly, ignoring Kiryn's attempts to placate him. "Mina came to save us. She knew the truth about Cyan Bloodbane. She knew the dragon was the one responsible for raising the shield. She knew the shield was killing us. When I died at the hands of the dragon, she restored me to life. She—" Silvanoshei halted, his tongue cleaving to his palate.

"*She* told you to lower the shield," Samar said. "She told you *how* to lower the shield."

"Yes, I lowered the shield!" Silvanoshei returned defiantly. "I did what my mother has been striving to do for years! You know that to be true, Samar. My mother saw the shield for what it was. She knew it was not raised to protect us, and she was right. It was put in place to kill us. What would you have had me do, Samar? Leave the shield in place? Watch it suck the lives from my people?"

"You might have left it in place long enough to check to see if your enemy was massing on your border," Samar said caustically. "The kirath could have warned you, if you had taken time to listen to them, but no, you chose to listen to a human female, the leader of those who would see you and your people destroyed."

"The decision was mine alone to make," said Silvanoshei with dignity. "I acted on my own. I did what my mother would have done in my place. You know that, Samar. She herself told me of the time she flew on griffon-back straight into the shield in her efforts to shatter it. Time and again she tried and was flung back—"

"Enough!" Samar interrupted impatiently. "What's done is done." He had lost this round, and he knew it. He was quiet a moment, pondering. When he spoke again, there was a change in his voice, a note of apology in his tone. "You are young, Silvanoshei, and it is the province of youth to make mistakes, although this, I fear, may well prove fatal to our cause. However, we have not given up. We may yet be able to undo the damage you have—however well-meaning—caused."

Reaching beneath his cloak, Samar drew out another cloak and hood. "Dark Knights ride into our sacred city with impunity. I watched them enter. I saw this female. I saw our people, especially our young people, bewitched by her. They are blind to the truth. It will be our task to make them see again. Conceal yourself with this cloak, Silvanoshei. We will leave by the secret passage through which I entered, escape the city in the confusion."

"Leave?" Silvanoshei stared at Samar in astonishment. "Why should I leave?"

Samar would have spoken, but Kiryn interrupted, hoping to salvage his plan.

"Because you are in danger, Cousin," said Kiryn. "Do you think the Dark Knights will allow you to remain king? If they do, you will be no more than a puppet, like your cousin Gilthas. But, as king in exile, you will be a force to rally the people—"

Go? I cannot go, Silvanoshei said to himself. She is coming back to me. She draws closer every moment. This very night perhaps I will fold her in my arms. I would not leave though I knew death itself had come for me.

He looked at Kiryn and he looked at Samar and he saw not friends, but strangers, conspiring against him. He could not trust them. He could trust no one.

"You say that my people are in danger," said Silvanoshei. He turned his back, turned his gaze out the window, as if he were looking over the city below. In truth, he searched for her. "My people are in danger, and you would have me flee to safety and leave them to face the threat alone. What poor sort of king is that, Samar?"

"A live king, Your Majesty," Samar said dryly. "A king who thinks enough of his people to live for them instead of for himself. They will understand and honor you for your decision."

Silvanoshei glanced coolly over his shoulder. "You are wrong, Samar. My mother fled, and the people did not honor her for it. They despised her. I will not make the same mistake. I thank you for coming, Samar. You are dismissed."

Trembling, amazed at his own temerity, he turned back to the window, stared out unseeing.

"You ungrateful whelp!" Samar was half-choked with the gall of his rage, could barely speak. "You will come with me if I have to drag you!"

Kiryn stepped between Samar and the king.

"I think you had better leave, sir," Kiryn said, his voice calm, eyes level. He was angry with both of them, angry and disappointed. "Or I will be forced to summon the guards. His Majesty has made his decision."

Samar ignored Kiryn, glowered balefully at Silvanoshei. "I will leave. I will tell your mother that her son has made a noble, heroic sacrifice in the name of the people. I will *not* tell her the truth: that he stays for love of a human witch. I will not tell her, but others will. She will know, and her heart will break."

He tossed the cloak on the floor at Silvanoshei's feet. "You are a fool, young man. I would not mind if by your folly you brought ruin only on yourself, Silvanoshei, but you will bring ruin upon us all."

Samar left, stalking across the room to the secret passage. He flung the curtain aside with a violence that almost ripped it from its rings.

Silvanoshei cast a scathing glance at Kiryn. "Don't think I don't know what you were after. Remove me, and you ascend the throne!"

"You don't think that of me, Cousin," Kiryn said quietly, gently. "You can't think that."

Silvanoshei tried very hard to think it, but he failed. Of all the people he knew, Kiryn was the only one who seemed to have a true affection for him. For him alone. Not for the king. For Silvanoshei.

Leaving the window, he walked over, took Kiryn by the hand, pressed it warmly. "I'm sorry, Cousin. Forgive me. He makes me so angry, I don't know what I'm saying. I know you meant well." Silvanoshei looked after Samar. "I know that *he* means well, but he doesn't understand. No one understands."

Silvanoshei felt a great weariness come over him. He had not slept in a long time. He couldn't remember how long. Whenever he closed his eyes, he saw her face, heard her voice, felt the touch of her lips on his, and his heart leaped, his blood thrilled, and he lay awake, staring into the darkness, waiting for her to return to him.

"Go after Samar, Kiryn. Make certain he leaves the palace safely. I would not want any harm to come to him."

Kiryn gave his king a helpless glance, sighed, shook his head, and did as he was told.

Silvanoshei went back to the window.

7

Sailing the River of the Dead

t is a sad truism that the misfortunes of others, no matter how terrible, always pale in comparison to our own. At this moment in his life, if someone had told Conundrum that armies of goblins and hobgoblins, draconians, hired thugs, and murderers were marching on the elves, the gnome would have laughed in derision and rolled his eyes.

"They think *they* have trouble?" he would have said. "Hah! They should be down beneath the ocean in a leaky submersible with a crazed human woman who keeps insisting that I follow a bunch of dead people. Now *that* is trouble."

If Conundrum had been told that his friend the kender, who had provided him with the means to finally be able to achieve his life quest and map the Hedge Maze, was being held prisoner by the most powerful mage in all the world in the Tower of High Sorcery, Conundrum would have sneered.

"The kender thinks *he* has trouble! Hah! He should try

to operate the submersible all by himself when it requires a crew of twenty. There is trouble for you!"

In fact, the submersible worked far better with a crew of one, since the other nineteen simply added to the weight and got in the way and used up the air. The original voyage that left Mt. Nevermind and headed to the citadel had started with a crew of twenty, but the others had become lost, mislaid, or seriously burned along the way, leaving at last only Conundrum, who had been but a lowly passenger, in sole control. He knew nothing whatsoever about the complicated system of mechanics designed to power the MNS *Indestructible,* undoubtedly the reason the vessel had remained afloat as long as it had.

The vessel was designed in the shape of a large fish. It was made of wood, which made it light enough to float, and then covered with iron, which made it heavy enough to sink. Conundrum knew that there was a crank he had to crank in order to keep the vessel moving forward, another crank that made the vessel move up, and a third that made the vessel go down. He was somewhat vague on what the cranks actually did, although he recalled a gnome (perhaps the late captain) telling him that the rear crank caused the fins at the rear of the vessel to whirl about in a frenzied manner, stirring up the water and thus propelling the vessel forward. The crank at the bottom caused fins at the bottom to whirl, sending the vessel upward, while fins on the top reversed that process.

Conundrum knew that along with the cranking there were a good many gears that had to be constantly oiled. He knew this because all gnomes everywhere know that gears must be constantly oiled. He had been told that there were bellows that pumped air into the submersible, but he was unable to figure out how these worked and so concluded that it would be wisest, if less scientific, to bring the *Indestructible* up to the surface for air every few hours.

Since the bellows did not work and had never worked, this proved to be sound reasoning on his part.

At the start of his enforced journey, Conundrum asked Goldmoon why she had stolen his submersible, where she planned to go with it, and what she intended to do once they got there. It was then she made the startling pronouncement that she was following the dead, that the dead guided her and protected her, and the dead were leading her across New Sea to where she must go. When he asked, quite logically, why the dead had seen fit to tell her to steal his boat, she had said that diving underwater was the only means by which they could escape the dragon.

Conundrum tried to interest Goldmoon in the workings of the submersible and to elicit her help in the cranking—which was wearing on the arms—or at least the help of the dead, since they appeared to be the ones in charge of this trip. She paid no attention to him. Conundrum found his passenger exasperating, and he would have turned the *Indestructible* around on the spot and sailed back to his Hedge Maze, dragon or no dragon, but for the lamentable fact that he did not have the faintest idea how to make the boat go in any direction other than up, down, and forward.

Nor, as it turned out, did the gnome know how to make the boat stop, thus giving a new and unfortunate meaning to the term "landfall."

Due to either fate or the guidance of the dead, the *Indestructible* did not smash headlong into a cliff or run aground on a reef. Instead it plowed into a sandy beach, its fins still flapping, sending up great spumes of sand and seawater, mangling jellyfish, and terrorizing the sea birds.

The final mad plunge up onto the beach was jouncing and uncomfortable but not fatal to the passengers. Goldmoon and Conundrum escaped with only minor cuts and bruises. The same could not be said of the *Indestructible*.

Goldmoon stood on the deserted beach and breathed the fresh sea air deeply. She paid no attention to the cuts on her arms or the bruise on her forehead. This strange new body of hers had the capacity to heal itself. Within moments, the blood would dry, the flesh close together, the bruises fade away. She would continue to feel the pain of the injuries, but only on her true body, the body that was the weak and frail body of an elderly human.

She did not like this new body that had been miraculously bestowed on her—an unwilling recipient—the night of the terrible storm, but she had come to realize that its strength and health were essential in order to take her to wherever it was the dead wanted her to go. The old body would not have made it this far. It was near death. The spirit that resided in the old body neared death as well. Perhaps that was the reason Goldmoon could see the dead when others could not. She was closer now to the dead than to the living.

The pale river of spirits flowed over the windswept dunes, heading north. The long greenish-brown grass that grew on the dunes rippled with the wind of their passing. Gathering up the hem of her long white robes, the robes that marked her a Mystic of the Citadel of Light, Goldmoon made ready to follow.

"Wait!" cried Conundrum, who had been staring open-mouthed at the destruction of the *Indestructible*. "What are you doing? Where are you going?"

Goldmoon did not reply but continued on. Walking was difficult. She sank into the soft sand with every step. Her robes hampered her movements.

"You can't leave me," Conundrum stated. He waved an oil-covered hand. "I've lost an immense amount of time ferrying you across the sea, and now you have broken my boat. How am I going to return to my life quest—mapping the Hedge Maze?"

Goldmoon halted and turned to look back at the gnome. He was not a savory sight, with his scraggly hair and untidy beard, his face flushed with righteous indignation and smeared with oil and blood.

"I thank you for bringing me," she said, raising her voice to be heard above the freshening wind and the crashing waves. "I am sorry for your loss, but I can do nothing to help you." She shifted her head, gazed northward. "I have a journey I must make. I cannot linger here or anywhere." Looking back at the gnome, she added, kindly, "I would not leave you stranded. You may come with me, if you choose."

Conundrum looked at her, then back at the *Indestructible*, which had certainly not lived up to its name. Even he, a passenger, could see that repairs were going to be long and costly, to say nothing of the fact that since he'd never understood how the contraption worked in the first place, making it work again would present certain problems.

"Besides," he said to himself, more brightly, "I'm certain the owner has it insured, and he will no doubt be compensated for the loss."

This was taking an optimistic view of the matter. One might say an optimistic and completely unrealistic view, since it was a well known fact that the Guild of Insurers-EquityUnderandOverwritersCollisionAccidentalDismembermentFireFloodNotLiableforActsofGod had never paid out a single copper piece, although there were, following the Chaos War, innumerable lawsuits pending, contending that ActsofGod no longer counted, since there were no longer any gods. Due to the fact that the lawsuits had to go through the gnomish legal system, it was not expected that they would be settled during the litigants' lifetimes but would be handed down to the generations coming afterward, all of whom would be financially ruined by the accruing legal fees.

Conundrum had few belongings to retrieve from the wreckage. He had run off from the citadel so fast that he had left behind his most important belonging—the map of the Hedge Maze. The gnome was confident that the map would be found and, considering that it was a Marvel to end all Marvels, would naturally be placed in a most safe and secure part of the Citadel of Light.

The only thing salvaged from the wreckage was a knife that had belonged to the late captain. The knife was remarkable, for it had all sorts of tools attached to it and could do just about everything. It could open a bottle of wine, tell you which direction was north, and crack the shells of recalcitrant oysters. Its one drawback was that you couldn't cut anything with it, since it lacked a blade, the inventor having run out of room, but that was a minor inconvenience compared to the fact that you could use it to trim your nose hairs.

Thrusting the remarkable knife in the pocket of his ink-stained and oily robes, Conundrum floundered, sliding and stumbling along the beach. He paused once to turn and look back at the *Indestructible.* The submersible had the forlorn appearance of a beached whale and was already being covered over by drifting sand.

Conundrum set out after Goldmoon, who was following the river of the dead.

8

Balancing Accounts

Five days after Beryl's attack on the Citadel of Light, five days after the fall of the shield in Silvanesti and five days after the first ranks of Beryl's army crossed the border into the realm of Qualinesti, Lord Targonne sat at his desk going over the reports that had been flooding in from various parts of the continent of Ansalon.

Targonne found the report from Malys pleasing, at first. The enormous red dragon Malystryx, the dragon whom everyone acknowledged to be the true ruler of Ansalon, had taken the news of her cousin Beryl's aggression far better than Targonne had dared hope. Malys had ranted and raved, to be sure, but in the end she had stated that any move by Beryl to annex lands beyond Qualinesti would be viewed as a most serious affront to Malys and would be dealt with summarily.

The more Targonne thought about it, however, the more he began to have second thoughts. Malystryx had been too accommodating. She had received the news too calmly. He had the feeling that the giant red was plotting something and that whatever she was plotting would be catastrophic. For the moment, however, she was keeping to her laiȓ, apparently content to let him deal with the situation. That, he fully intended to do.

According to reports, Beryl had demolished the Citadel of Light, crushing the crystal domes in a fit of pique because, according to his agents, who had been on the scene and who had witnessed the destruction firsthand, she had not been able to locate the magical artifact that had been the reason for this misguided attack. The loss of life on the island might have been incalculable but for the fact that before she razed the buildings, Beryl had sent down squadrons of draconians to search for the artifact and the wizard who wielded it.

The delay provided time for the inhabitants to flee to safety inland. Targonne's agents, who had been attending the citadel in disguise, hoping to discover why their healing spells were going awry, had been among those who had fled to safety and were thus able to send back their reports. Beryl had departed early on in the battle, leaving her reds to finish the destruction for her. The draconians had gone after the refugees but had been fought off by the forces of the Solamnic Knights and some fierce tribal warriors who dwelt in the island's interior. The draconians had sustained heavy casualties.

Targonne, who did not like draconians, counted this as no great loss.

"Next report," he said to his aide.

The aide drew out a sheet of vellum. "A message from Marshal Medan, my lord. The Marshal apologizes for the delay in responding to your orders but says that your messenger met with a most unfortunate accident. He was flying to Qualinost when the griffon on which he was riding suddenly went berserk and attacked him. He was able to deliver his message, but he died of his injuries shortly thereafter. The Marshal states that he will comply fully with your orders and hand over the elven city of Qualinost to the dragon Beryl, along with the Queen Mother, both of whom he holds prisoner. The Marshal has disbanded the elven Senate, arrested the senators and the Heads of House. He was going to arrest the elven king, Gilthas, but the young man was smuggled out of the city and is now in hiding. The Marshal reports that Beryl's army is encountering attacks from elven forces and that these are slowing the army's march but otherwise doing little damage."

"That is good news, if it's true," Targonne said, frowning. "I have never quite trusted Medan. He was one of Ariakan's favorites, the main reason he was put in charge of Qualinesti. There were those stories Beryl put out that he had grown more elf than human, raising flowers and playing the lute."

"Thus far, he appears to have the situation under control, my lord," said the aide, glancing back over the neatly written page.

Targonne grunted. "We will see. Send a message to the great green bitch that she can have Qualinost and that I trust she will leave it intact and unspoiled. Include an account of the revenues we collected from Qualinost last year. That should convince her."

"Yes, my lord," said the aide, making a note.

"Anything new to report from Sanction?" Targonne asked in a resigned tone that indicated he would be shocked if there were.

The walled city of Sanction, located on the western shores of New Sea, controlled the only ports on New Sea for that part of Ansalon. During the War of the Lance, the city had been a stronghold of the dragon highlords, but it was now controlled by a mysterious and powerful wizard known as Hogan Bight. Thought to be acting independently, Bight had been wooed by the Dark Knights of Neraka, in hopes that he would ally with them and make the ports of Sanction available to them. Knowing that Bight was also being wooed by the Solamnics, the Dark Knights had laid siege to Sanction in order to hasten Bight's decision-making process. The siege had dragged on for long months now. The Solamnics had attempted to break it, but they had been routed by this very Mina who had now taken Silvanesti. Targonne supposed he should be grateful to Mina for having saved the day for him. He would have been a damn sight more grateful to her if he'd actually ordered her to do it.

"Sanction is still under siege, my lord," said the aide, after a moment's shuffle to the bottom of the pile. "The commanders complain they do not have enough men to take the city. They maintain that if General Dogah's forces had been allowed to march to Sanction instead of being diverted to Silvanesti, the city would now be in their hands."

"And I'm a gully dwarf," Targonne said with a snort. "Once Silvanesti is secure, we will deal with Sanction."

"Regarding Silvanesti, my lord." The aide returned to the top of the pile and extracted a sheet of paper. "I have here the report from the interrogation of the elven prisoners. The three—two males and a female—are members of what is known as the 'kirath,' a sort of border patrol, I believe."

He handed over the report. Immediately after hearing of the fall of Silvanesti, Targonne had ordered Dogah's troops to capture several elves alive and have them transported back to Jelek for interrogation. Targonne scanned the report briefly. His eyebrows lifted in astonishment, then came together in a frown. He could not believe what he was reading and started over at the beginning to see if he'd missed something.

Lifting his head, Targonne stared at his aide. "Have you read this?" he demanded.

"Yes, my lord," said the aide.

"The Mina girl is mad! Absolutely mad! Worse than that, I don't think she's even on our side! *Healing* the elves! She is *healing the bloody elves!*"

"So it would appear, my lord," said the aide.

Targonne picked up the paper to read aloud, " 'She has now a cult of young elven followers, who stand outside the palace where she has taken up residence, chanting her name.' And this. 'She has seduced the elven king Silvanoshei, who was publicly heard to say he is going to marry her. This news reportedly has greatly angered his mother, Alhana Starbreeze, who attempted to persuade her son to flee Silvanesti in advance of the arrival of the Dark Knights. Silvanoshei is said to be besotted with this Mina and refuses to leave her side.' "

Targonne threw down the report in anger. "This cannot go on. Mina is a threat, a danger. She must be stopped."

"That may prove difficult, my lord," said his aide. "You will see in Dogah's report that he approves and admires everything she does. He is infatuated by her. His men are loyal to her, as are her own. You will note that Dogah now signs his report, 'In the name of the One God.' "

"This Mina has bewitched them. Once she is gone and her spell is broken, they will return to their senses. But how to get rid of her? That is the problem. I don't want Dogah's forces turning on me. . . ."

Targonne picked up the report again, reread it. This time, he began to smile. He laid the report down, sat back, went over the plan in his mind. The numbers, he thought, added up nicely.

"Are the elven prisoners still alive?" he asked abruptly.

"Yes, my lord. It was thought you might have further need of them."

"You said there was a female among them?"

"One, my lord."

"Excellent. I have no further use for the males. Dispatch them in whatever way the executioner finds amusing. Have the female brought here to me. I will need a quill and ink—see to it that it's squeezed from berries or however the elves make it. And a scrollcase of elven design and manufacture."

"I believe there are some in the treasury room, my lord."

"Bring the least valuable. Finally, I want this." Targonne drew a diagram, handed it to the aide.

"Yes, my lord," the aide said, after a moment's perusal. "It will have to be specially made."

"Of course. Elven design. Emphasize that. And," Targonne added, "keep the cost to a minimum."

"Of course, my lord," said the aide.

"Once I have planted my instructions in the elf's mind, she is to be returned to Silvanesti and dropped off near the city of Silvanost. Have one of the messengers ready to depart this night."

"I understand, my lord," said the aide.

"One more thing," Targonne added, "I will be making a trip to Silvanesti myself sometime within the fortnight. I'm not sure when, so see to it that arrangements are made for me to leave whenever I have to."

"Why would you go there, my lord?" his aide asked, startled.

"Protocol will require my attendance at the funeral," Targonne replied.

9

The Ring of Tears

ilvanesti was an occupied land, Silvanost an occupied capital. The worst fears of the elves had been realized. It was to protect against this very disaster that they had authorized the creation of the magical shield. The embodiment of their fear and their distrust of the world, the shield had slowly drained them, drawing upon that fear to give itself unwholesome life. When the shield fell, the world, represented by the soldiers of the Dark Knights, marched into Silvanost, and sick and exhausted, the elves capitulated. They surrendered the city to their most feared foe.

The kirath predicted the worst. They spoke of slave camps, of looting and burning, of torment and torture. They urged the elves to fight until death had taken every one of them. Better to die free, said the kirath, than live as slaves.

A week passed and not a single elf male was dragged from his house and tortured. No elf babies were spitted on the ends of spears. No elf women were raped and left

114

to die on dung heaps. The Dark Knights did not even enter the city of Silvanost. They camped outside the city on the battlefield where Mina's troops had fought and lost and Mina herself had been made prisoner. The first order given to the soldiers of the Dark Knights was not to set fire to Silvanost but to burn the carcass of the green dragon, Cyan Bloodbane. A detachment even fought and defeated a band of ogres who had been elated to discover the shield had fallen and attempted an invasion of their own. Many among the younger elves were calling the Dark Knights saviors.

Babies were healed and played upon the grass that grew green in the fierce bright sunlight. Women strolled in their gardens, finding joy in the flowers that had withered beneath the shield, but which were now starting to bloom. Men walked the streets free and unfettered. The elf king, Silvanoshei, remained the ruler. The Heads of House were consulted on all matters. A confused observer might have said it was the Dark Knights who had capitulated to the Silvanesti.

To say that the kirath were disappointed would be unfair. They were loyal to their people, and they were glad—and most were thankful—that thus far the bloodbath they had expected had not occurred. Some of the older members of the kirath claimed that what was happening to the elves was far worse. They did not like this talk of a One God. They mistrusted the Dark Knights, who, they suspected, were not as peace-loving as they appeared. The kirath had heard rumors of comrades ambushed and spirited away on the backs of blue dragons. Those who disappeared were never heard of again.

Alhana Starbreeze and her forces had crossed the border when the shield fell. They now occupied territory to the north of the capital, about halfway between Silvanost and the border. They never remained in one location long but shifted from camp to camp, covering their movements, blending into the forests that many of them, including Alhana herself, had once known and loved. Alhana did not have much fear that she and her troops would be discovered. The five thousand troops of Dark Knights would have all they could do to hold Silvanost. The commander would be a fool to divide his forces and send them into unfamiliar territory, searching for elves who had been born and bred to the forests. Nonetheless Alhana had survived this long by never taking chances, and so the elves remained on the move.

Not a day passed, but that Alhana did not long to see her son. She lay awake nights making plans to sneak into the city, where her life was forfeit, not only from the Dark Knights, but from her very own people. She knew Silvanost, she knew the palace, for it had been her home. In the night the plans seemed sound, and she was determined to follow through with them. In the morning she would tell Samar, and he would bring up every difficulty, present her with every opportunity for disaster. He always won the argument, not so much because she feared what might happen to her if she were caught, but because she feared what might happen to Silvanoshei. She kept in touch with what was happening in Silvanost through the kirath. She watched and waited and agonized, and like all the other elves, she wondered what the Knights of Neraka were plotting.

It appeared to the kirath, to men and women such as Rolan, Alhana Starbreeze, and Samar and their meager resistance forces, that their people had once more fallen under the spell of a dream such as had been cast on the land during the War of the Lance. Except that this dream was a waking dream and none of them could battle it, for to do so would be to battle the dreamers. The kirath and Alhana made what plans they could for the day when the dream must end and the dreamer wake to a night-mare reality.

General Dogah's troops camped outside Silvanesti. Mina and her knights had moved into the Tower of the Stars. They had taken over one wing of the building, that which had previously belonged to the late Governor General Konnal. All the elves knew that their young king was enamored of Mina. The story of how she had brought Silvanoshei back from death had been made into a song sung by the young people throughout Silvanesti.

Never before would the elves have countenanced a marriage between one of their own and a human. Alhana Starbreeze had been declared a dark elf for having married "outside her kind" by marrying a Qua-linesti. Yet the young people—those who were near the same age as their king—had come to adore Mina. She could not walk the streets but that she was mobbed. The palace was surrounded, day and night, by young elves who sought to catch a glimpse of her. They were pleased and flattered to think that she loved their king, and they confidently expected to hear news of the mar-riage any day.

Silvanoshei expected it, too. He dreamed of her walk-ing into the palace, being led to his throne room, where he would be seated in regal state. In his dreams, she flung herself eagerly, adoringly into his arms. That had been five days ago. She had not yet asked to see him. On her arrival, she had gone straight to her quarters and remained there.

Five days had passed, and he had neither seen nor spoken to her. He made excuses for her. She feared to see him, feared her troops might not understand. She would come to him at night and declare her love for him, then swear him to secrecy. He lay awake nights in anticipation, but she did not come, and Silvanoshei's dream began to wither, as did the bouquet of roses and violets he had handpicked from the royal garden to present to her.

Outside the Tower of the Stars, the young elves chanted "Mina! Mina!" The words that had been so sweet to his ears only days before now stabbed him like knives. Standing at the window, hearing that name echo in the bitter emptiness of his heart, he made his decision.

"I am going to her," he said.

"Cousin—" Kiryn began.

"No!" Silvanoshei said, cutting off the reprimand he knew was coming. "I have listened to you and those fools of advisers long enough! 'She should come to you,' they say. 'It would be undignified for you to go to her, Your Majesty.' 'It is you who do her the honor.' 'You put yourself in a false position.' You are wrong. All of you. I have thought this over. I believe that I know the problem. Mina wants to come to me, but her officers will not let her. That great, hulking minotaur and the rest. Who knows but that they are holding her against her will?"

"Cousin," said Kiryn gently, "she walks the streets of Silvanost, she comes and goes freely from the palace. She meets with her officers and, from what I have heard, even the highest ranking defer to her in all things. You must face it, Cousin, if she wanted to see you, she would."

Silvanoshei was dressing himself in his very finest garments, and either he was pretending not to hear, or he had truly not heard. Kiryn's heart ached for his cousin. He had witnessed with alarm Silvanoshei's obsession with this girl. He had guessed from the beginning that she was using Silvanoshei to her own ends, though what those ends might be, Kiryn could not tell. Part of the reason he had hoped Silvanoshei would seek safety in the forest with the resistance movement was to take him away from Mina, break the hold she had over him. Kiryn's plans had failed, and he was at his wit's end.

Silvanoshei had no appetite. He had lost weight. He could not sleep but roamed around his room at night, leaping out of bed at every sound, thinking it was her coming to him. His long hair had lost its sheen and hung limp and ragged. His nails were bitten almost to the quick. Mina was healing the elven people. She was bringing them back to life. Yet she was killing their king.

Dressed in his royal robes that hung from his wasted frame, Silvanoshei enveloped himself in his cloth of gold and made ready to leave his chambers.

Kiryn, greatly daring, knowing that he risked rebuke, made one last attempt to stop him.

"Cousin," he said, his voice soft with the affection he truly felt, "do not do this. Do not demean yourself. Try to forget about her."

"Forget her," Silvanoshei said with a hollow laugh. "I might as well try to forget to breathe!"

Thrusting aside his cousin's hand, Silvanoshei swept out the door, the cloth of gold fluttering behind him.

Kiryn followed him, heartsick. Elven courtiers bowed as the king passed, many attempting to catch his eye. He paid them no heed. He wended his way through the palace until he reached the wing occupied by Mina and her Knights. In contrast to his chambers that were filled with people, the part of the tower where Mina had set up her command post was quiet and empty. Two of her Knights stood guard outside a closed door. At the sight of Silvanoshei, the Knights came to respectful attention, but they did not stand aside.

Silvanoshei gave them a baleful look. "Open the door," he commanded.

The Knights made no move to comply.

"I gave you an order," said Silvanoshei, flushing, the red staining the unhealthy pallor of his skin as if he were cut and bleeding.

"I am sorry, Your Majesty," said one of the Knights, "but our orders are to admit no one."

"I am not *no one!*" Silvanoshei's voice shook. "I am king. This is my palace. All doors open to me. Do as I tell you!"

"Cousin," Kiryn urged softly, "please come away!"

The door opened at that moment, not from without. It opened from within. The huge minotaur stood in the door, his head level with the top of the gilded frame. He had to stoop to pass through.

"What is this commotion?" the minotaur demanded in his rumbling voice. "You disturb the commander."

"His Majesty begs an audience with Mina, Galdar," said one of the Knights.

"I do not beg!" said Silvanoshei angrily. He glowered at the minotaur blocking the door. "Stand aside. I *will* speak to Mina. You cannot keep her locked away from me!"

Kiryn was watching the minotaur closely, saw the monster's lips twitch in what might have been the beginning of a derisive smile, but at the last moment, the minotaur rearranged his expression to one of somber gravity. Bowing his horned head, he stood aside.

"Mina," he said, turning on his heel, "His Majesty, the king of Silvanesti, is here to see you."

Silvanoshei swept into the room.

"Mina!" he cried, his heart in his voice, on his lips, in his outstretched hands, in his eyes. "Mina, why have you not come to me?"

The girl sat behind a desk covered with what looked to be map rolls. One map was spread out upon the desk, the curling edges held down with a sword at one corner, a morning star on the other. Kiryn had last seen Mina the day of the battle with Cyan Bloodbane. He had seen her dressed in the coarse robes of a prisoner, he had seen her being led to her execution.

She had changed since then. Her head had been shaved to only a fine down of red. The hair had grown back some, was thick and curly and flamed in the sunlight streaming through the crystal panes of the window behind her. She wore the black tunic of a Knight of Neraka over black chain mail. The amber eyes that gazed at Silvanoshei were cool, preoccupied, held the markings of the map, held roads and cities, hills and mountains, rivers and valleys. The eyes did not hold him.

"Silvanoshei," Mina said after a moment, during which the roads and cities caught in the golden amber were slowly overlaid by the image of the young elf. "Forgive me for not coming to pay my respects sooner, Your Majesty, but I have been extremely busy."

Caught in the amber, Silvanoshei struggled. "Mina! Respect! How can you use such a word to me? I love you, Mina. I thought . . . I thought you loved me."

"I do love you, Silvanoshei," said Mina gently, as one speaks to a fretful child. "The One God loves you."

Silvanoshei's struggles availed him nothing. The amber absorbed him, hardened, held him fast.

"Mina!" he cried in agony and lurched toward her.

The minotaur sprang in front of her, drew his sword.

"Silvan!" Kiryn shouted in alarm, catching hold of him.

Silvanoshei's strength gave way. The shock was too much. He crumpled and fell to the floor, clutching Kiryn's arm, nearly dragging his cousin down with him.

"His Majesty is unwell. Take him back to his room," said Mina, adding in a voice soft with pity, "Tell him I will pray for him."

Kiryn, with the help of the servants, managed to assist Silvanoshei to his chambers. They took secret hallways and stairs, for it would never do for the courtiers to see their king in such a pitiable condition. Once in his chambers, Silvanoshei flung himself on his bed and refused to speak to anyone. Kiryn stayed with him, worried until he was almost ill himself. He waited until, finally, he saw with relief that Silvanoshei slept, his exhaustion eventually overcoming his grief.

Thinking Silvanoshei was likely to sleep for hours, Kiryn went to his own rest. He gave orders to the servants that His Majesty was unwell and that he was not to be disturbed. The curtains over the windows were closed and drawn, the room darkened. The servants stole out, softly shutting the door behind them. Musicians sat outside the king's bedchamber, playing soft music to soothe his slumbers.

Silvanoshei slept heavily, as though drugged, and when he woke some hours later, he was stupefied and groggy. He lay staring into the shadows, hearing Mina's voice. *I was busy, too busy to come to you. . . . I will pray for you. . . .* Her words were sharp steel and inflicted a fresh wound every time he repeated them. He repeated them over and over. The sharp blade struck his heart and struck his pride. *He* knew she had once loved him, but now no one would believe that. All believed that she had used him, and they pitied him, just as she pitied him.

Angry, restless, he threw off the silken sheets and the embroidered down coverlet and left his bed. A thousand plans came to mind so that his brain was fevered with them. Plans to win her back, plans to humiliate her, noble plans to do grand things in spite of her, degrading plans to cast himself at her feet and plead with her to love him again. He found that none of the plans spread soothing salve over the terrible wounds. None of them eased this horrible pain.

He walked the length of his room and back many times, passing by his writing desk, but he was so preoccupied that he did not notice the strange scrollcase until the twentieth or twenty-first turn, when a shaft of dusty sunlight filtered through a chink in the velvet curtains, struck the scrollcase, and illuminated it, bringing it to his attention.

He paused, stared at the case, wondering. The scrollcase had not been there this morning. Of that, he was certain. It did not belong to him. It did not bear upon it the royal crest, nor was it as richly decorated as those that bore his messages. The case had a battered appearance, as if it had been often used.

The wild thought came to him that the scrollcase belonged to Mina. This notion was completely irrational, but when one is in love, all things are possible. He reached out his hand to snatch it up, then paused.

Silvanoshei was a young man who felt desperately in love, but he was not deranged enough to have forgotten the lessons in caution learned from spending most of his life running from those who sought to take his life. He had heard tales of scrollcases that harbored venomous snakes or were magically enchanted and spewed forth poisonous gas. He should summon a guard and have the case removed.

"Yet, after all, what does it matter?" he asked himself bitterly. "If I die, I die. That at least would end this torment. And . . . it might be from her!"

Recklessly, he caught up the scrollcase. He did take time to examine the seal, but the wax impression was smudged, and he couldn't make it out. Breaking the seal, he tugged impatiently at the lid with trembling fingers and finally pulled it off with such force that an object flew out and landed on the carpet, where it lay sparkling in the single shaft of sunlight.

He bent down to stare at it in wonder, then picked it up. He held between his thumb and forefinger a small ring, a circlet of rubies that had all been cut in a teardrop shape—or perhaps blood drop would better describe them. The ring was of exquisite workmanship. Only elves do such fine work.

His heart beat fast. The ring came from Mina. He knew it! Looking back inside the scrollcase, he saw a rolled missive. Dropping the ring on the desk, he drew out the letter. The first words quenched the flicker of hope that had so briefly warmed his heart. *My cherished son . . .* the letter began. But as he read, hope returned, a ravening flame, all-consuming.

My cherished son,

This letter will be brief as I have been very ill. I am recovered, but I am still very weak, too weak to write. One of my ladies acts as my scribe. The rumors that you are in love with a human girl have reached my ears. At first I was angry, but my illness carried me so close to death that it has taught me to think differently. I want only your happiness, Silvanoshei. This ring has magical properties. If you give it to one who loves you, it will ensure that her love for you will endure forever. If you give it to one who does not love you, the ring will cause her to love you with a passion equal to your own.

Take the ring with a mother's blessing, my beloved son, and give it to the woman you love with a kiss from me.

The letter was signed with his mother's name, though it was not her signature. The letter must have been written by one of the elven women who had once been Alhana's ladies-in-waiting but were now her friends, having chosen to share with her the harsh life of an outcast. He did not recognize the handwriting, but there was no reason he should. He felt a pang of worry over his mother's ill health, but was reassured to hear that she was better. His joy, as he looked at the ring and read once more of the ring's magical properties, was overwhelming. Joy overwhelmed reason, overwhelmed logic.

Cradling the precious ring in the palm of his hand, he brought it to his lips and kissed it. He began to make plans for a great banquet. Plans to show to all the world that Mina loved him and him alone.

10

The Betrothal Banquet

The Tower of the Stars was in a bustle of excitement and frantic preparation. His Majesty, the Speaker of the Stars, was giving a grand banquet in honor of Mina, the savior of the Silvanesti. Ordinarily, among the elves, such a banquet would have required months of preparation, days spent agonizing over guest lists, weeks of consultation with the cooks over the menu, more weeks spent arranging the table and deciding on the perfect choice for flowers. It was a mark of the king's youth, some said, and his impetuosity, that he had announced that the banquet would be held within twenty-four hours.

His minister of protocol wasted two of those twenty-four by attempting to remonstrate with His Majesty that such a feat was beyond the realm of possibility. His Majesty had been adamant, and so the minister had been forced to give way in despair and rush forth to marshal his forces.

The king's invitation was presented to Mina. She accepted in the name of herself and her officers. The minister was horrified. The elves had not intended to invite the officers of the Dark Knights of Neraka. So far as the longest lived among the elves could remember, no Silvanesti elf had ever shared a meal with a human on Silvanesti soil. Mina was different. The elves had begun to consider Mina as one of themselves. Rumors were circulating among her followers that she had elven blood in her; the fact that she was a commander in the army of the Dark Knights of Neraka having conveniently slipped their minds. Mina helped foster this belief, never appearing in public in her black armor, but always dressing in silvery white.

At this point, an argument arose. The aide to the minister of protocol maintained that during the War of the Lance, when the *daughter of Lorac* (who was Alhana Starbreeze, but since she was a dark elf and her name could not be mentioned, she was referred to in this manner) had returned to Silvanost, she had brought with her several human companions. There was no record of whether or not they had dined while on Silvanesti soil, but it was to be presumed they had. Thus a precedent had been set. The minister of protocol observed that they might have dined, but, if so, the dining was informal, due to the unfortunate circumstances of the time. Thus, such a dinner did not count.

As for the notion of the minotaur dining with elves, that was simply out of the question.

Flustered, the minister hinted to Mina that her officers would be bored with the proceedings, which they would find long and tedious, particularly since none of them spoke Elvish. They would not like the food, they would not like the wine. The minister was certain that her officers would be much happier dining as they were accustomed to dine in their camp outside of the walls of Silvanost. His Majesty would send food, wine, and so forth.

127

"My officers will attend me," Mina said to him, "or I will not come."

At the thought of delivering this message to His Majesty, the minister decided that eating dinner with humans would be less traumatic. General Dogah, Captain Samuval, the minotaur Galdar, and Mina's Knights would all attend. The minister could only hope fervently that the minotaur would not slurp his soup.

His Majesty was in a festive mood, and his gaiety affected the palace staff. Silvanoshei was a favorite among the servants and staff members, and all had noted his wan appearance and were anxious about him. The staff was pleased at the change in him and did not question it. If a banquet would lift him from the doldrums, they would throw the most lavish banquet that had ever been seen in Silvanesti.

Kiryn was less pleased at the change, viewed it with unease. He alone noted that Silvanoshei's gaiety had a frantic quality to it, that the color in his cheeks was not the rosy color of health but seemed to have been burned into the pale flesh. He could not question the king, for Silvanoshei was immersed in preparations for the grand event, overseeing everything to make certain all was perfect, down to personally selecting the flowers that were to grace the table. He claimed he had no time to talk.

"You will see, Cousin," Silvanoshei said, pausing a moment in his headlong rush to grasp Kiryn's hand and squeeze it. "She does love me. You will see."

Kiryn could only conclude that Silvanoshei and Mina had been in contact and that she had somehow reassured him. This was the only explanation for Silvanoshei's erratic behavior, although Kiryn, thinking over again all that Mina had said the day before, found it difficult to believe that those cruel words of hers had been an act.

But she was human, and the ways of humans were never to be understood.

Elven royal banquets are always held outdoors, at midnight, beneath the stars. In the old days, before the War of the Lance, before the coming of Cyan Bloodbane and the casting of the dream, rows and rows of tables would have been set up in the tower's garden to accommodate all the elves of House Royal. Many nobles had died fighting the dream. Many more had died of the wasting sickness brought on them by the shield. Of those who had survived, most refused the invitation—a terrible affront to the young king. Rather it would have been an affront, if Silvanoshei had paid any heed to it. He said only, with a laugh, that the old fools would not be missed. As it was, only two long tables were required now, and the elder elves of House Servitor, who remembered the past glory of Silvanesti, let fall tears as they polished the delicate silver and set the fragile, eggshell-thin porcelain dishes upon the cobweb-fine lace table coverings.

Silvanoshei was dressed and ready long before midnight. The hours until the banquet appeared to him to have been mounted on the backs of snails, they crawled so slowly. He worried that all might not be right, although he had been to check the laying of the tables eight times already and was with difficulty dissuaded from going down a ninth. The discordant sound of the musicians tuning their instruments was sweetest music to him, for it meant that there was only a single hour remaining. He threatened to backhand the minister of protocol, who said that the king could not possibly make his regal appearance until all the guests had entered. Silvanoshei was the first to arrive and charmed and bewildered all his guests by greeting them personally.

He carried the ruby ring in a jeweled box in a velvet pouch inside his blue velvet doublet and beneath his silken shirt. He checked continuously to make certain the box was still there, pressing his hand over his breast so often that some of the guests took note and wondered uneasily if their young king suffered from some heart complaint. They had not seen His Majesty so joyful since his coronation, however, and they were soon caught up in his merriment and forgot their fears.

Mina came with the midnight, and Silvanoshei's joy was complete. She wore a gown of white silk, simple, with no ornamentation. Her only jewelry was the pendant that she always wore, a pendant round and plain with no decoration or design. She herself was in high spirits. Those elves she knew, she greeted by name, graciously accepting their blessings and their thanks for the miracles she had performed. She was as slender as any elf maid and almost as beautiful said the young elves, which was, for them, a high compliment, one rarely paid to any human.

"I thank you for the honor you do me this night, Your Majesty," said Mina when she came to make her bow to Silvanoshei.

He would not let her bow but took her hand and raised her up. "I wish I had time to do more," he said. "Someday you will see a true elven celebration." *Our wedding*, his heart sang to him.

"I do not mean this honor," she said, dismissing with a glance the beautifully decorated tables, the fragrant flowers and the myriad candles that illuminated the night. "I thank you for the honor you do me this night. The gift you intend to give me is one I have long wanted, one for which I have long prepared. I hope I may be worthy of it," she added quietly, almost reverently.

Silvanoshei was astonished and for a moment felt the pleasure in his gift—that was to have been a marvelous surprise—diminished. Then the import of her words struck him. *The honor he would do her. The gift she had long wanted. She hoped she may be worthy.* What could that mean except that she spoke of the gift of his love?

Ecstatic, he kissed fervently the hand she offered him. He promised himself that within hours he would kiss her lips.

The musicians ceased playing. Silver chimes rang out, announcing dinner. Silvanoshei took his place at the head table, leading Mina by the hand and seating her on his right. The other elves and the human officers took their places, or at least so Silvanoshei presumed. He could not have sworn to that, or the fact that there was anyone else present or that the stars were in the sky, or that the grass was beneath his feet.

He was aware of nothing except Mina. Kiryn, seated opposite Silvanoshei, tried to speak to his cousin, but Silvanoshei never heard a word. He did not drink wine. He drank Mina. He did not eat fruit or cake. He devoured Mina. The pale moon did not light the night. Mina lit the night. The music was harsh compared to Mina's voice. The amber of her eyes surrounded him. He existed in a golden stupor of happiness, and as if drunk on honey wine, he did not question anything. As for Mina, she spoke to her neighbors, enchanting them with her fluent Elvish and her talk of the One God and the miracles this god performed. She rarely spoke to Silvanoshei, but her amber gaze was often on him, and that gaze was not warm and loving but cool, expectant.

Silvanoshei might have been uneasy at this, but he touched the box over his heart for reassurance, brought to mind Mina's words to him, and his unease vanished.

Maidenly confusion, he told himself, and gazed at her as she talked of this One God, proud to watch her hold her own among the elven wise and scholars such as his cousin, Kiryn.

"You will forgive me if I ask a question about this One God, Mina," said Kiryn deferentially.

"I not only forgive you," Mina answered with a slight smile. "I encourage you. I do not fear questions, though some might fear the answers."

"You are an officer in the Dark Knights of Takhisis—"

"Neraka," Mina corrected. "We are the Dark Knights of Neraka."

"Yes, I heard your organization had made that change, Takhisis having departed—"

"As did the god of the elves, Paladine."

"True." Kiryn was grave. "Although the circumstances of their departures are known to be different. Still, that is not relevant to my question. In their brief history, the Dark Knights of whatever allegiance have held that the elves are their sworn and bitter enemies. They have never made secret their manifesto that they plan to purge the world of elves and seize their lands for their own."

"Kiryn," Silvanoshei intervened angrily, "this is hardly suitable—"

Mina rested her hand on his. Her touch was like fire licking his flesh. The flames both seared and cauterized.

"Let your cousin speak, Your Majesty," said Mina. "Please continue, sir."

"I do not understand, therefore, why now you conquer our lands and . . ." He paused, looked stern.

"And let you live," Mina finished for him.

"Not only that," said Kiryn, "but you heal our sick in the name of this One God. What care can this One God—a god of our enemies—have for elves?"

Mina sat back. Lifting a wineglass, she revolved the fragile crystal goblet in her hand, watching as the candles seemed to burn in the wine. "Let us say that I am the ruler of a large city. Inside the city's walls are thousands of people who look to me for protection. Now, within this city are two strong and powerful families. They hate and detest each other. They have sworn each other's destruction. They fight among themselves whenever they meet, creating strife and enmity in my city. Now, let us say that my city is suddenly threatened. It is under attack from powerful forces from the outside. What happens? If these two families continue to quarrel, the city will surely fall. But if the families agree to unite and battle this foe together, we have a chance to defeat our common enemy."

"That common enemy would be what—the ogres?" asked Kiryn. "They were once your allies, but I have heard since that they have turned on you—"

Mina was shaking her head. "The ogres will come to know the One God. They will come to join the battle. Be blunt, sir," she said, smiling with encouragement. "You elves are always so polite. You need not be fearful of hurting my feelings. You will not anger me. Ask the question that is in your heart."

"Very well," said Kiryn. "You are responsible for revealing the dragon to us. You are responsible for the dragon's death. You led us to know the truth about the shield. You have given us our lives when you could have taken them. Nothing for nothing, they say. Tit for tat. What do you expect us to give you in return? What is the price we must pay for all this?"

"Serve the One God," Mina said. "That is all that is required of you."

"And if we do not choose to serve this One God?" Kiryn said, frowning and grave. "What then?"

"The One God chooses us, Kiryn," said Mina, gazing at the wavering drop of flame flickering in the wine. "We do not choose the One. The living serve the One God. So do the dead. Especially the dead," she added in a voice so low and soft and wistful that only Silvanoshei heard her.

Her tone and her strange look frightened him.

"Come, Cousin," Silvanoshei said, flashing Kiryn a warning, irate glance. "Let us make an end to these philosophical discussions. They give me a headache." He gestured to the servants. "Pour more wine. Bring on the fruit and cake. Tell the musicians to resume playing. That we may drown him out," he said with a laugh to Mina.

Kiryn said no more, but sat regarding Silvanoshei with a troubled and worried expression.

Mina did not hear Silvanoshei. Her gaze was sifting through the crowd. Jealous of anyone who stole her attention from himself, Silvanoshei was quick to notice that she was searching for someone. He marked where her gaze roamed and saw that she was locating every one of her officers. One by one, her gaze touched each of them and one by one, each of them responded, either by a conscious look of understanding or, with the minotaur, a slight nod of the horned head.

"You need not worry, Mina," Silvanoshei said, an edge to his voice, to show he was displeased, "your men are behaving themselves well. Much better than I had hoped. The minotaur has only broken his wineglass, shattered a plate, torn a hole in the tablecloth, and belched loudly enough to be heard in Thorbardin. All in all, a most highly successful evening."

"Trivialities," she murmured. "So trivial. So meaningless."

Mina clasped Silvanoshei's hand suddenly, her grip tightening around his heart. She looked at him with the amber eyes. "I prepare them for what is to come, Your Majesty. You imagine that the danger has passed, but you are mistaken. Danger surrounds us. There are those who fear us. Those who seek our destruction. We must not be lulled into complacency by gentle music and fine wine. So I remind my officers of their duty."

"What danger?" asked Silvanoshei, now thoroughly alarmed. "Where?"

"Close," said Mina, drawing him into the amber. "Very close."

"Mina," said Silvanoshei, "I was going to wait to give this to you. I had a speech all prepared. . . ." He shook his head. "I've forgotten every word of it. Not that it matters. The words I truly want to say to you are in my heart, and you know them. You've heard them in my voice. You've seen them every time you see me."

Thrusting his trembling hand into the breast of his doublet, he drew forth the velvet bag. He reached inside, brought out the silver box and placed it on the table in front of Mina.

"Open it," he urged her. "It's for you."

Mina regarded the box for long moments. Her face was very pale. He heard her give a small, soft sigh.

"Don't worry," he said wretchedly. "I'm not going to ask anything of you in return. Not now. I hope that someday you might come to love me or at least think fondly of me. I think you might someday, if you will wear this ring."

Seeing that she made no move to touch the box, Silvanoshei seized hold of it and opened it.

The rubies in the ring glittered in the candlelight, each shining like a drop of blood—Silvanoshei's heart's blood.

"Will you take it, Mina?" he asked eagerly, desperately. "Will you take this ring and wear it for my sake?"

Mina reached out her hand, a hand that was cold and steady. "I will take the ring and I will wear it," she said. "For the sake of the One God."

She slipped the ring onto the index finger of her left hand.

Silvanoshei's joy was boundless. He was annoyed at first that she had dragged this god of hers into the matter, but perhaps she was merely asking the One God's blessing. Silvanoshei would be willing to ask that, too. He would be willing to fall onto his knees before this One God, if that would gain him Mina.

He watched her expectantly, waiting for the ring's magic to work on her, waiting for her to look at him with adoration.

She looked at the ring, twisted it on her finger to see the rubies sparkle. For Silvanoshei, no one else was present. No one except the two of them. The other people at the table, the other people at the banquet, the other people in the world were a blur of candlelight and music and the fragrance of gardenia and rose, and all of it was Mina.

"Now, Mina," he said, ecstatic. "You must kiss me."

She leaned near him. The magic of the ring was working. He could feel her love. His arms encircled her. But before their lips could touch, her lips parted in a gasp. Her body stiffened in his arms. Her eyes widened in shock.

"Mina!" he cried, terrified, "what is wrong?"

She screamed in agony. Her lips formed a word. She tried to speak it, but her throat closed, and she gagged. Frantic, she clutched at the ring and tried to drag it off her finger, but her body convulsed, painful spasms wracking her slender frame. She pitched forward onto the table, her arms thrust out, knocking over glasses, scattering the plates. She made an inarticulate, animal sound, terrible to hear. Her life rattled in her throat. Then she was still. Horribly still. Her eyes fixed in her head. Their amber gaze stared accusingly at Silvanoshei.

Kiryn rose to his feet. His action was involuntary. He had no immediate plan. His thoughts were a confusion. His first thought was for Silvanoshei, that he should try to somehow engineer his escape, but he immediately abandoned that idea. Impossible with all the Dark Knights around. At that moment, although he did not consciously know it, Kiryn abandoned Silvanoshei. The Silvanesti people were now Kiryn's, his care and his responsibility. He could do nothing to save his cousin. Kiryn had tried, and he had failed. But he might be able to save his people. The kirath must hear of this. They must be warned so they could be prepared to take whatever actions might be necessary.

The other elves who sat around them were rigid with shock, too stunned to move, unable to comprehend what had just occurred. Time slowed and stopped altogether. No one drew breath, no eye blinked, no heart beat—all were frozen in disbelief.

"Mina!" Silvanoshei cried in desperation and reached out to hold her.

Suddenly, all was turmoil. Mina's officers, crying out in rage, surged through the crowd, smashing chairs, overturning tables, knocking down anyone who impeded their progress. Elves cried out, screamed. Some of the more astute grabbed husband or wife and fled in haste. Among these was Kiryn. As the Dark Knights surrounded the table where Mina lay still and unmoving, Kiryn cast one last, aching glance at his unfortunate cousin and, with a heavy heart and deep foreboding, slipped away into the night.

An enormous hand, a hand covered in brown fur, seized the king's shoulder in a bone-crushing grasp. The minotaur, his hideous face monstrous with fury and with grief, lifted Silvanoshei from his chair and, snarling a curse, flung the young elf aside, as he might have flung away a piece of refuse.

Silvanoshei smashed through an ornamental trellis and tumbled backward into the hole where the Shield Tree had once stood. He lay dazed, breathless, then faces, grim, human faces, contorted in murderous rage, surrounded him. Rough hands seized him and hauled him from the pit. Pain shot through his body, and he moaned. The pain might have come from broken bones. Perhaps every bone in his body was broken. The true pain came from his shattered heart.

The knights hauled Silvanoshei to the banquet table. The minotaur had his hand on Mina's neck.

"The lifebeat is gone. She is dead," he said, his lips flecked with foam. Turning, he jabbed a shaking finger at Silvanoshei. "There is her murderer!"

"No!" Silvanoshei cried. "I loved her! I gave her my ring—"

The minotaur seized hold of Mina's lifeless hand. He gave the circlet of rubies a vicious tug, dragged it off her finger. Thrusting the ring under Silvanoshei's nose, the minotaur shook it.

"Yes, you gave her a ring. A poisoned ring! You gave her the ring that killed her!"

Jutting from one of the rubies was a tiny needle. On that needle glistened a drop of blood.

"The needle is operated by a spring," the minotaur announced, now holding the ring high for all to see. "When the victim touches the ring or turns it upon her finger, the needle activates and pierces the flesh, sending its deadly poison into the bloodstream. I'll wager," he added grimly, "that we discover the poison is a kind whose use is well known to elves."

"I didn't . . . " Silvanoshei cried from the agony of his grief. "It wasn't the ring. . . . It couldn't . . . "

His tongue cleaved to the roof of his mouth. He saw again Samar standing in his chambers. Samar, who knew all the secret passages in the palace. Samar, who had tried to force Silvanoshei to flee, who had made no secret of his hatred and distrust of Mina. Yet, the note had been written in a woman's hand. His mother . . .

A blow sent Silvanoshei reeling. The blow came from the minotaur's fist, but, in truth, Silvanoshei did not feel it, though it broke his jaw. The true blow was the knowledge of his guilt. He loved Mina, and he had slain her.

The minotaur's next blow brought darkness.

II

The Wake

he stars faded slowly with the coming of dawn, each bright, glittering pinprick of flame quenched by the brighter fire of Krynn's sun. Dawn brought no hope to the people of Silvanost. A day and a night had passed since the death of Mina. By orders of General Dogah, the city had been sealed off, the gates shut. The inhabitants were told to remain in their houses for their own safety, and the elves had no thought of doing otherwise. Patrols marched the streets. The only sounds that could be heard were the rhythmic tramp of booted feet and the occasional sharp command of an officer.

Outside Silvanost, in the encampment of the Dark Knights of Neraka, the three top officers came together in front of what had once been Mina's command tent. They had arranged a meeting for sunrise, and it was almost time. They arrived simultaneously and stood staring at one another uneasily, irresolutely. None wanted to enter that empty tent. Her spirit lingered there. She was present in every object, and that presence only made her absence more acutely felt. At last, Dogah, his face grim, thrust aside the tent flap and marched in. Samuval followed, and Galdar came, last of all.

Inside the tent, Captain Samuval lit an oil lamp, for night's shadows still held residence. The three looked bleakly about. Although Mina had taken quarters in the palace, she preferred to live and work among her troops. The original command tent and a few pieces of furniture had been lost to the ogres. This tent was elven in make, gaily colored. The humans considered that it looked more like a tent for harlequins than for military men, but they were grudgingly impressed by the fact that it was lightweight, easy to pack and to assemble, and kept out the elements far better than the tents supplied by the Dark Knights.

The tent was furnished with a table, borrowed from the palace, several chairs, and a cot, for Mina sometimes slept here if she worked late into the night. No one had been inside this tent since the banquet. Her belongings had not been touched. A map, marked in her hand-writing, remained spread out upon the table. Small blocks and arrows indicated troop movements. Galdar glanced at it without interest, thinking it was a map of Silvanesti. When he saw that it wasn't, he sighed and shook his horned head. A battered tin cup, half-filled with cold tarbean tea, held down the eastern corner of the world. A guttered candle stood on the northwest. She had worked up until the time of departure for the banquet. A flow of melted wax had run down the side of the candle, streamed into the New Sea. A rumble sounded deep in Galdar's chest. He rubbed the side of his snout, looked away.

"What's that?" Samuval asked, moving closer to stare at the map. "I'll be damned," he said, after a moment. "Solamnia. Looks like we have a long march ahead of us."

The minotaur scowled. "March! Bah! Mina is dead. I felt for her lifebeat. It is not there. I think something went wrong!"

"Hush, the guards," Samuval warned, with a glance at the tent flap. He had closed and tied shut the opening, but two soldiers stood outside.

"Dismiss them," said Dogah.

Samuval stalked over to the tent flap, poked his head out. "Report to the mess tent. Return in an hour."

He paused briefly to look at a tent that stood beside the command tent. That tent had been the tent where Mina slept, and it was now where her body lay in state. They had placed her upon her cot. Dressed in her white robes, she lay with her hands at her sides. Her armor and weapons had been piled at her feet. The tent flaps had been rolled up, so that all could see her and come to pay her homage. The soldiers and Knights had not only come, they had stayed. Those who were not on duty had kept vigil throughout the day after her death and into the long night. When they had to go on duty, others took their places. The soldiers were silent. No one spoke.

The silence was not only the silence of grief but of anger. Elves had killed their Mina, and they wanted the elves to pay. They would have destroyed Silvanost the night when they first heard, but their officers had not permitted it. Dogah, Samuval, and Galdar had endured many bad hours following Mina's death trying to keep the troops in line. Only by repeating over and over the words, "By Mina's command," had they at last brought the enraged soldiers under control.

Dogah had put them to work, ordering them to cut down trees to make a funeral pyre. The soldiers, many with tears streaming down their faces, had performed their grim task with a fierce will, cutting down the trees of the Silvanesti forest with as much delight as if they were cutting down elves. The elves in Silvanost heard the death cries of their trees—the woods of Silvanesti had never before felt the blade of an axe—and they grieved deeply, even as they shuddered in fear. The soldiers had worked all day yesterday and all through the night. The pyre was now almost ready. But ready for what? Her three officers were not quite certain.

They took their seats around the table. Outside the tent, the camp was noisy with the thud of the axes and the crews hauling the giant logs to the growing pyre that stood in the center of the field where the elven army had defeated Mina's troops and had yet, in the end, fallen to her might. The noise had a strangely quiet quality to it. There was no laughing or bantering, no singing of work songs. The men carried out their duties in grim silence.

Dogah rolled up the map, stowed it away. General Dogah was a grim-faced, heavily bearded human of around forty. A short man, he appeared to be as wide as he was tall. He was not corpulent but stocky, with massive shoulders and a bull neck. His black beard was as thick and curly as a dwarf's, and this and his short stature gave him the nickname among his troops of Dwarf Dogah. He was not related to dwarves in any way, shape or form, as he was quick to emphasize with his fists if anyone dared suggest such a thing. He was most decidedly human, and he had been a member of the Dark Knights of Neraka for twenty of his forty years.

He was technically the highest-ranking officer among them, but, being the newest member of Mina's command group, he was at somewhat of a disadvantage in that her officers and troops did not know him and had been immediately distrustful of him. Dogah had been suspicious of them and, in particular, of this upstart wench who had, he discovered to his immense shock and outrage, sent him forged orders, had brought him to Silvanesti on what had appeared at first to be a kender's errand.

He had arrived at the border with several thousand troops, only to find that shield was up and they could not enter. Scouts reported that a huge ogre army was massing, ready to deal a death blow to the Dark Knights who had stolen their land. Dogah and his forces were trapped. They could not retreat, for to do so would have meant a march back through ogre lands. They could not advance. Dogah had cursed Mina's name loudly and viciously, and then the shield had fallen.

Dogah had received the report with astonishment. He had gone himself to look in disbelief. He had been loath to cross, fearing that elven warriors would suddenly spring up, as thick as the dust of the dead vegetation that coated the ground. But there on the other side, waving to him from horseback, was one of Mina's Knights.

"Mina bids you cross in safety, General Dogah!" the Knight had called. "The elven army is in Silvanost, and they have been considerably weakened both by their battle with the dragon, Cyan Bloodbane, and by the wasting effects of the shield. They do not pose a threat to you. You may proceed in safety."

Dogah had been dubious, but he had crossed the border, his hand on his sword, expecting at any moment to be ambushed by a thousand pointy-ears. His army had met with no resistance, none at all. Those elves they had encountered had been easily captured and were at first killed, but then they had been sent to Lord Targonne, as his lordship ordered.

Dogah had remained wary, however, his troops nervous and on alert. There was still the city of Silvanost. Then came the astonishing report that the city had fallen to a handful of soldiers. Mina had entered in triumph and was now ensconced in the Tower of the Stars. She awaited Dogah's arrival with impatience, and she bade him make haste.

It was not until Dogah had entered the city and strode its streets with impunity did he come finally to believe that the Dark Knights of Neraka had captured the elven nation of Silvanesti. The enormity of this feat overwhelmed him. The Dark Knights had accomplished what no other force in history had been able to do, not even the grand armies of Queen Takhisis during the War of the Lance. He had looked forward with intense curiosity to meeting this Mina. He had, in truth, not really believed that she could be the person responsible. He had guessed that perhaps it was some older, wiser officer who was truly in command, using the girl as a front to keep the troops happy.

Dogah had discovered his mistake immediately on first meeting her. Watching carefully, he had seen how every single officer deferred to her. Not only that, they regarded her with a respect that was close to worship. Her lightest word was a command. Her commands were obeyed instantly and without question. Dogah had been prepared to respect her, but after a few moments in her presence, he was both charmed and awed. He had joined wholeheartedly the ranks of those who adored her. When he had looked into Mina's amber eyes, he had been proud and pleased to see a tiny image of himself.

Those eyes were closed now, the warm fire that lit the amber quenched.

Galdar leaned across the table to hiss, "I say again, something has gone wrong." He sat back, scowling. The fur that covered his face was streaked with two dark furrows. "She looks dead. She feels dead. Her skin is cold. She does not breathe."

"She told us the potion would have that effect," said Samuval irritably. The fact that he was irritable was a certain sign of his nervousness.

"Keep your voices down," Dogah ordered.

"No one can hear us over that infernal racket," Samuval returned, referring to the erratic staccato of the axes.

"Still, it is best not to take chances. We are the only three who know Mina's secret, and we must guard the secret as we promised. If word got out, the news would spread like a grass fire in the dry season and that would ruin everything. The soldiers' grief must appear to be real."

"Perhaps they are wiser than we are," Galdar muttered. "Perhaps they know the truth, and *we* are the ones who have been deluded."

"What would you have us do, minotaur?" Dogah demanded, his black brows forming a solid bar across his thick nose. "Would you disobey her?"

"Even if she is . . ." Samuval paused, not wanting to speak aloud the ill-omened word. "Even if something did go wrong," he amended, "those commands she gave us would be her last commands. I, for one, will obey them."

"I also," said Dogah.

"I will not disobey her," said Galdar, choosing his words carefully, "but let us face it, her commands are contingent upon one thing happening, and thus far her prediction has not yet come to pass."

"She foretold an attempt on her life," argued Captain Samuval. "She foretold that the foolish elf would be the cat's paw. Both came true."

"Yet, she did *not* foretell the use of the poison ring," Galdar said, his voice harsh. "You saw the needle. You saw that it punctured her skin."

He drummed his fingers on the table, glanced at his comrades from beneath narrowed eyes. He had something on his mind, something unpleasant to judge by the frown, but he seemed uncertain whether to speak his thought or not.

"Come, Galdar," said Samuval finally. "Out with it."

"Very well." Galdar looked from one to the other. "You have both heard her say that even the dead serve the One God."

Dogah shifted his bulk in the chair that creaked beneath his weight. Samuval picked at the wax from the guttered candle. Neither made any response.

"She promised the One God would confound her enemies," Galdar continued, his tone heavy. "She never promised we should see her again alive—"

"Hail the command tent," a voice shouted. "I have a message from Lord Targonne. Permission to enter?"

The three officers exchanged glances. Dogah rose hastily to his feet and hurriedly untied the flaps. The messenger entered. He wore the armor of a dragonrider, and he was wind-blown and dust-covered. Saluting, he handed Dogah a scrollcase.

"No reply is expected, my lord," the messenger said.

"Very well. You are dismissed." Dogah eyed the seal on the scrollcase and again exchanged glances with his comrades.

When the messenger had gone, Dogah cracked the seal with a sharp rap on the table. The other two looked on expectantly as he opened the case and withdrew the scroll. He unfurled it, cast his gaze over it, and lifted his eyes, glittering black with triumph.

"He is coming," he said. "Mina was right."

"Praise the One God," said Captain Samuval, sighing with relief. He nudged Galdar. "What do you say now, friend?"

Galdar shrugged, nodded, said nothing aloud. When the others had gone, shouting for their aides, giving orders to make ready for his lordship's arrival, Galdar remained alone in the tent where Mina's spirit lingered.

"When I touch your hand and feel your flesh warm again, then I will praise the One God," he whispered to her. "Not before."

Lord Targonne arrived about an hour after sunrise, accompanied by six outriders. His lordship rode a blue dragon, as did the others. Unlike many high-ranking Knights of Neraka, Targonne did not keep a personal dragon but preferred to use one from the stables. This cut down on his own out-of-pocket expenditures, or so he always claimed. In truth, if he had wanted to keep his own dragon, he would have done so and charged the care and feeding to the Knighthood. As it was, Targonne did not keep a dragon because he neither liked nor trusted dragons. Perhaps this was because as a mentalist, Targonne knew perfectly well that dragons neither liked nor trusted him.

He took no pleasure in dragon flight and avoided it when possible, preferring to make his journeys on horseback. In this instance, however, the sooner this annoying girl went up in flames the better, as far as Targonne was concerned, and he was willing to sacrifice his own personal comfort to see this accomplished. He brought other dragonriders with him not so much because he wished to make a show or that he feared attack, but that he was convinced his dragon was going to do something to imperil him—either take it into its head to plummet from the skies or be struck by lightning or dump him off deliberately. He wanted additional riders around him so that they could rescue him.

His officers knew all this about Targonne. In fact, Dogah was laughing about this to Galdar and Captain Samuval as they watched the blue dragons fly in tight circles to a landing. Mina's army was drawn up in formation on the battlefield, with the exception of the few who were still at work on the pyre. Mina's funeral would be held at noon, the hour she herself had chosen.

"Do you think any of them would really risk their necks to save the mercenary old buzzard?" Samuval asked, watching the circling blues. "From what I've heard, most of his staff would just as soon see him bounce several times off sharp rocks while falling into a bottomless chasm."

Dogah grunted. "Targonne makes certain he will be saved. He takes along as escort only those officers to whom he owes large sums of money."

The blue dragons settled to the ground, their wings stirring up great clouds of dust. The dragonriders emerged from the cloud. Sighting the waiting honor guard, they headed in that direction. Mina's cadre of officers approached to greet his lordship.

"Which one is he?" asked Captain Samuval, who had never met the leader of the Knights of Neraka. The captain's curious gaze ranged over the tall, well-built, grim-faced Knights who were moving with rapid stride toward him.

"The little runt in the middle," said Galdar.

Thinking the minotaur was making sport of him, Captain Samuval chuckled in disbelief and looked to Dogah for the truth. Captain Samuval saw Dogah's gaze focus tensely on the short man who was almost bent double from coughing in the dust, waving his hand to clear the air. Galdar was also keeping close watch on the little man. The minotaur's hands clenched and unclenched.

Targonne did not cut a very prepossessing figure. He was short, squat and somewhat bowlegged. He did not like wearing full armor, for he found it chafed him, and he made concession to his rank by wearing only a breast-plate. Expensive, hand-tooled, it was made of the finest steel, embossed in gold, and suited his exalted station. Due to the fact that Lord Targonne was stoop-shouldered, with a caved-in chest and slightly curved back, the breast-plate did not fit well, but hung forward, giving the unfortunate impression of a bib tied around the neck of a child, rather than the armor of a valiant Knight.

Samuval was not impressed with Targonne's appearance, but nonetheless, he had heard stories about Targonne's ruthless and cold-blooded nature and thus did not find it at all strange that these two officers were so apprehensive of this meeting. All knew that Targonne had been responsible for the untimely death of the former leader of the Knights, Mirielle Abrena, and a great many of her followers, though no one ever mentioned such a thing aloud.

"Targonne is sly, cunning, and subtle, with an amazing ability to probe deeply into the minds of those he encounters," warned Dogah. "Some even claim that he uses this ability to infiltrate the minds of enemies and bend them to his will."

Small wonder, thought Samuval, that the mighty Galdar, who could have lifted Targonne and tossed him around like a child, was panting with nervousness. The rank bovine odor was so strong that Samuval edged upwind to keep from gagging.

"Be prepared," Galdar warned in a low rumble.

"Let him look into our minds. He will be surprised by what he finds there," Dogah said dryly, moving forward, saluting his superior.

"So, Galdar, it is good to see you again," Targonne said, speaking pleasantly. The last time Targonne had seen the minotaur, he had lost his right arm in battle. Unable to fight,

Galdar had hung around Neraka, hoping for employment. Targonne might have rid himself of the useless creature, but he considered the minotaur a curiosity.

"You have come by a new arm. That bit of healing must have cost you a pretty steel piece or two. I wasn't aware that our officers were so highly paid. Or perhaps you found your own private stash. I suppose you are aware, Galdar, of the rule that states all treasure discovered by those in the service of the Knighthood is to be turned over to the Knighthood?"

"The arm was a gift, my lord," said Galdar, staring straight over Targonne's head. "A gift of the One God."

"The One God." Targonne marveled. "I see. Look at me, Galdar. I like eyes at a level."

Reluctantly, Galdar lowered his gaze to meet Targonne's. Immediately Targonne entered the minotaur's mind. He had a glimpse of roiling storm clouds, fierce winds, driving rain. A figure emerged from the storm and began to walk toward him. The figure was a girl with a shaved head and amber eyes. The eyes looked into Targonne's, and a bolt of lightning struck the ground in front of him. Dazzling, shattering white light flared. He could see nothing for long seconds and stood blinking his eyes to clear them. When he was able to see once more, Targonne saw the empty valley of Neraka, the rain-slick black monoliths, and the storm clouds vanishing over the mountains. Probe and pierce as he might, Targonne could not get past these mountains. He could not take himself out of the accursed valley. He withdrew his thought from Galdar's mind.

"How did you do that?" Targonne demanded, eyeing the minotaur and frowning.

"Do what, my lord?" Galdar protested, clearly astonished. The astonishment was real, he wasn't feigning. "I didn't do anything, sir. I've just been standing here."

Targonne grunted. The minotaur had always been a freak. He would gain more from a human. He turned to Captain Samuval. Targonne was not pleased to find this man among the officers greeting him. Samuval had once been a Knight, but he had either quit or been drummed out; Targonne couldn't remember the details. Most likely drummed out. Samuval was nothing but a draggle-tail mercenary leading his own company of archers.

"*Captain* Samuval," said Lord Targonne, laying nasty emphasis on the low rank. He sent his gaze into Samuval's brain.

Flight after flight of arrows arched through the air with the vicious whir of a thousand wasps. The arrows found their marks, piercing black armor and black chain mail. Black-fletched arrows struck through men's throats and brought down their horses. The dying screamed, horrible to hear, and still the arrows flew and the bodies began to mount, blocking the pass so that those behind were forced to turn and fight the enemy who had almost made it through the pass, almost ridden to glory.

An arrow was fired at him, at Targonne. It flew straight and true, aiming for his eye. He tried to duck, to flee, to escape, but he was held fast. The arrow pierced his eye, glanced through to the brain. Pain exploded so that he clutched at his head, fearing his skull might split apart. Blood poured down over his vision. He could see nothing except blood, no matter where he looked.

The pain ended swiftly, so swiftly that Targonne wondered if he had imagined it. Finding himself clutching at his head, he made as if to brush back his hair from his face and made another attempt to look into the mind of Captain Samuval. He saw only blood.

He tried to stanch the flow, to clear his vision, but the blood continued to pour down around him, and eventually he gave it up. Blinking, having the strange feeling that his eyelids were gummed together, he glared frowningly at this annoying captain, searching for some signs that the man was not what he appeared to be—not a bluff and ordinary soldier, but a wizard of high intelligence and cunning, a rogue Gray Robe or mystic in disguise. The captain's eyes were eyes that followed the arrow's flight until it hit its target. Nothing more.

Targonne was vastly puzzled and starting to grow frustrated and angry. Some force was at work here, thwarting him, and he was determined to ferret it out. He left the captain. Who cared about a blasted sell-sword anyway? Next to him stood Dogah, and Targonne relaxed. Dogah was Targonne's man. Dogah was to be trusted. Targonne had walked the length and breadth of Dogah's mind on previous occasions. Targonne knew all the dark secrets tucked away in shadowed corners, knew that he could count on Dogah's loyalty. Targonne had deliberately saved Dogah for last, knowing that if he had questions, Dogah would answer them.

"My lord," said General Dogah before Targonne could open his mouth, "let me first state for the record that I believed the orders I received telling me to march to Silvanesti came from you. I had no idea they had been forged by Mina."

Since the orders commanding Dogah to march to Silvanesti had provided the Dark Knights of Neraka with one of the greatest victories ever in the history of the Knighthood, Targonne did not like to be reminded of the fact that he was not the one who had given them.

"Well, well," he said, highly displeased, "perhaps I had more to do with those than you imagine, Dogah. The Knight Officer who issued those orders may have indicated that she was acting on her own, but the truth was that she was obeying my commands."

The girl was dead. Targonne could afford to play fast and loose with the truth. She was certainly not going to contradict him.

He continued blandly, "She and I agreed between us to keep this secret. The mission was so risky, so hazardous, so fraught with possibilities of failure, that I feared to mention it to anyone, lest word leak out to the elves and put them on their guard. And then, there is the dragon Malys to be considered. I did not want to raise her hopes, to give her expectations that might not come to pass. As it is, Malystryx is astonished at our great triumph and holds us in even higher regard than before."

All the while he was speaking, Targonne was attempting to probe Dogah's brain. Targonne could not manage it, however. A shield rose before his eyes, a shield that shimmered eerily in the light of a blazing sun. He could see beyond the shield, see dying trees and a land covered with gray ash, but he could not enter the shield nor cause it to be lifted.

Targonne grew increasingly angry, and thus he became more bland, more friendly. Those who knew him well were most terrified of him whenever he linked arms with them and spoke to them as chums.

Targonne linked arms with General Dogah.

"Our Mina was a gallant officer," he said in mournful tones. "Now the accursed elves have assassinated her. I am not surprised. That is like them. Skulking, sneaking, belly-crawling worms. They are too cowardly to attack face to face, and so they resort to this."

"Indeed, my lord," said Dogah, his voice grating, "it is a coward's act."

"They will pay for it, though," Targonne continued. "By my head, they will pay! So that's her funeral pyre, is it?"

He and Dogah had walked slowly, arm in arm, across

the field of battle. The minotaur and the captain of archers followed slowly after.

"It's massive," said Targonne. "A bit too massive, don't you think? She was a gallant officer but only a junior officer. This pyre"—he indicated the immense stack of trees with a wave of his hand—"could well be the pyre of a leader of the Knighthood. A leader such as myself."

"Indeed it could, my lord," agreed Dogah quietly.

The base of the pyre was formed of six enormous trees. The work crews had wrapped chains around the logs, then dragged them into position in the center of the battlefield. The logs were soaked with any sort of inflammable liquid the men had been able find. The place reeked of oils, resins and spirits, and the fresh green blood of the trees. Atop this pile of logs, the men had thrown more logs, huge amounts of brush, and dead wood they had scavenged from the forest. The stack was now almost eight feet in height and ten feet in length. Climbing on ladders, they laid willow branches across the top, weaving them into a latticework of leaves. On this platform they would lay Mina's body.

"Where is the body? I would like to pay my last respects," said Targonne in dirgelike tones.

He was led to the tent where Mina lay in state, guarded by a group of silent soldiers, who parted to allow him to pass. Targonne stuck a mental needle in several as he walked among them, and their thoughts were only too clear, only too easy to read: loss, grief, sorrow, white-hot anger, vengeance. He was pleased. He could turn such thoughts as these to his own purposes.

He looked down at the corpse and was not in the least moved or touched beyond an annoyed wonder that this hoyden should have managed to garner such a loyal— one might say fanatical—following. He played to his audience, however, and saluted her and spoke the proper words. Perhaps the men noted some lack of sincerity in his voice, for they did not cheer him, as he considered he had the right to expect. They seemed to pay very little attention to him at all. They were Mina's men, and if they could have followed her into death to bring her back, they would have done so.

"Now, Dogah," said Targonne, when they were alone inside the command tent, "relate to me the circumstances of this tragic business. It was the elf king who murdered her, or so I understand. What have you done with him?"

Dogah related laconically the events of the previous night. "We questioned the young elf—his name is Silvanoshei. He is a sly one. He pretends to be almost mad with grief. A cunning actor, my lord. The ring came from his mother, the witch Starbreeze. We know from spies in the king's household that one of her agents, an elf named Samar, paid a secret visit to the king not long ago. We have no doubt that, between them, they plotted this murder. The elf made a show of being in love with Mina. She took pity on him and accepted the ring from his hand. The ring was poisoned, my lord. She died almost instantly.

"As to the elf king, we have him in chains. Galdar broke his jaw, and so it has been difficult to get much out of him, but we managed." Dogah smiled grimly. "Would your lordship like to see him?"

"Hanged, perhaps," said Targonne and gave a small, dry chuckle at his little pleasantry. "Drawn and quartered. No, no, I have no interest in the wretch. Do what you please with him. Give him to the men, if you like. His screams will help assuage their grief."

"Yes, my lord." General Dogah rose to his feet. "Now, I must attend to preparations for the funeral. Permission to withdraw?"

Targonne waved his hand. "Certainly. Let me know when all is made ready. I will make a speech. The men will like that, I know."

Dogah saluted and withdrew, leaving Targonne alone in the command tent. He rifled through Mina's papers, read her personal correspondence, and kept those that appeared to implicate various officers in plots against him. He perused the map of Solamnia and shook his head derisively. What he found only proved that she had been a traitor, a dangerous traitor and a fool. Priding himself on the brilliance of his plan and its success, he settled back in his chair to take a short nap and recover from the rigors of the journey.

Outside the tent, the three officers conferred.

"What's he doing in there, do you suppose?" Samuval asked.

"Rummaging through Mina's things," Galdar said with a baleful glare back at the command tent.

"Much good may it do him," said Dogah.

The three eyed each other, ill at ease.

"This is not going as planned. What do we do now?" Galdar demanded.

"We do what we promised her we would do," Dogah replied gruffly. "We prepare for the funeral."

"But it wasn't supposed to happen like this!" Galdar growled, insistent. "It is time she ended it."

"I know, I know," Dogah muttered with a dark, side-long glance at the tent where Mina lay, pale and still. "But she hasn't, and we have no choice to but to carry on."

"We could stall," suggested Captain Samuval, gnawing on his lower lip. "We could make some excuse—"

"Gentlemen." Lord Targonne appeared at the entrance to the tent. "I thought I heard you out here. I believe you have duties to attend to in regard to this funeral. This is no time to be standing around talking. I fly only in daylight, never at night. I must depart this afternoon. I cannot stay lollygagging around here. I expect the funeral to be held at noon as planned. Oh, by the way," he added, having ducked into the tent and then popped his head back out again, "if you think you might have trouble lighting the pyre, I would remind you that I have seven blue dragons at my command who will be most pleased to offer their assistance."

He withdrew, leaving the three to stare uneasily at one another.

"Go fetch her, Galdar," said Dogah.

"You don't mean to put her on that pyre?" Galdar hissed through clenched teeth. "No! I refuse!"

"You heard Targonne, Galdar," Samuval said grimly. "That was a threat, in case you misunderstood him. If we don't obey him, her funeral pyre won't be the only thing those blasted dragons set ablaze!"

"Listen to me, Galdar," Dogah added, "if we don't go through with this, Targonne will order his own officers to do so. I don't know what's gone wrong, but we have to play this out. Mina would want us to. You are second in command. It is your place to bring her to the pyre. Do you want one of us to take over?"

"No!" Galdar said with a vicious snap of his teeth. "I will carry her. No one else! I will do this!" He blinked, his eyes were red-rimmed. "But I do so only because she commanded it. Otherwise, I would let his dragons set fire to all the world and myself with it. If she *is* dead, I see no reason to go on living."

Inside the command tent, Targonne overheard this statement. He made a mental note to get rid of the minotaur at the first opportunity.

12

The Funeral

Pacing slowly and solemnly, Galdar carried Mina's body in his arms to the funeral bier. Tears ran in rivulets down the minotaur's grief-ravaged face. He could not speak, his throat was choked with his sorrow. He held her cradled in his arms, her head resting on the right arm she had given to him. Her body was cold, her skin a ghastly white. Her lips were blue, her eyelids closed, the eyes behind them fixed and unmoving.

When he had arrived at the tent where her body lay, he had attempted, surreptitiously, to find some sign of life in her. He had held his steel bracer up to her lips, hoping to see the slight moistness of breath on the metal. He had hoped, when he picked her up in his arms, to be able to feel the faint beating of her heart.

No breath stirred. Her heart was still.

I will seem to be as one dead, she had told him. *Yet I live. The One God performs this deception that I may strike out at our enemies.*

She had said that, but she had also said that she would wake to accuse her murderer and call him to justice, and here she lay, in Galdar's arms, as cold and pale as a cut lily frozen in the snow. He was about to place that fragile lily on the top of a pile of wood that would blaze into a raging inferno with a single spark.

Mina's Knights formed a guard of honor, marching behind Galdar in the funeral procession. They wore their armor, polished to a black sheen, and kept their visors lowered, each hiding his own grief behind a mask of steel. Unbidden by their commanders, the troops formed a double line leading from the tent to the bier. Soldiers who had followed her for weeks stood side by side with those who had just newly arrived but who had already come to adore her. Galdar walked slowly between the rows of soldiers, never pausing as their hands reached out to touch her chill flesh for one last blessing. Young soldiers wept unashamedly. Scarred and grizzled veterans looked grim and stern and brushed hastily at their eyes.

Walking behind Galdar, Captain Samuval led Mina's horse, Foxfire. As was customary, her boots were reversed in the stirrups. Foxfire was edgy and restless, perhaps due to the proximity of the minotaur—the two had formed a grudging alliance, but neither truly liked the other—or perhaps the raw emotions of the soldiers affected the animal, or perhaps the horse, too, felt Mina's loss. Captain Samuval had his hands full controlling the beast, who snorted and shivered, bared his teeth, rolled his eyes until the whites showed, and made dangerous and unexpected lunges into the crowd.

The sun was near its zenith. The sky was a strange, cobalt blue, a winter sky in summer, with a winter sun that burned bright but gave no warmth, a sun that seemed lost in the empty blue vastness. The line of men came to an end. Galdar stood before the huge pyre. A litter wound round with ropes rested on the ground at the minotaur's feet. Men with tear-grimed faces stood atop the pyre, waiting to receive their Mina.

Galdar looked to his right. Lord Targonne stood at attention. He wore his grief mask, probably the same one he'd worn at the funeral of Mirielle Abrena. He was impatient for the end of the ceremony, however, and he permitted his gaze to shift often to watch the progress of the sun—a not-so-subtle reminder to Galdar to speed matters along.

General Dogah stood at Galdar's left. The minotaur shot the commander a speaking glance.

We have to stall! Galdar pleaded.

Dogah lifted his gaze to the sun that was almost directly overhead. Galdar looked up to see seven blue dragons circling, taking an unusual interest in the proceedings. As a rule, dragons find such ceremonies boring in the extreme. Humans are like bugs. They lead short and frantic lives, and like bugs, humans are constantly dying. Unless the human and the dragon have formed a particular bond, dragons little care what becomes of them. Yet, now Galdar watched them fly above Mina's funeral pyre. The shadows of their wings slid repeatedly over her still face.

If Targonne meant the dragons to intimidate, he was succeeding. Dogah felt the cringe of dragonfear twist his heart, already wrung by grief. He lowered his gaze in defeat. There was nothing to be done.

"Carry on, Galdar," Dogah said quietly.

Galdar knelt from his great height and with uncommon gentleness placed Mina's body on the litter. Somewhere someone had found a fine woven silk cloth of gold and of purple. Probably stolen from the elves. Galdar arranged Mina's body on the litter, her hands folded over her breast. He drew the cloth over her, as a father might lovingly cover a slumbering child.

"Good-bye, Mina," Galdar whispered.

Half-blinded by his tears that were rolling unchecked down his snout, he rose to his feet and made a fierce gesture. The soldiers atop the pyre pulled on the ropes. The ropes tightened, went taut, and the litter bearing Mina's body rose slowly to the top of the pyre. The soldiers settled the litter, rearranged the cloth over her. Each one stooped to kiss her cold forehead or kiss her chill hands. Then they climbed down from the top of the pyre.

Mina remained there, alone.

Captain Samuval brought Foxfire to a halt at the foot of the pyre. The horse, now seemingly aware that he was on show, stood quiet with dignity and pride.

Mina's Knights gathered around the pyre. Each held in his hand a lighted torch. The flames did not waver or flicker, but burned steadily. The smoke rose straight into the air.

"Let us get on with it," said Lord Targonne in annoyed tones. "What do you wait for?"

"A moment longer, my lord," said Dogah. Raising his voice, he shouted, "Bring the prisoner."

Targonne cast Dogah a baleful glance. "What do we need him for?"

Because it was Mina's command, Dogah might have said. He offered the first explanation that came into his mind.

"We plan to throw him onto the pyre, my lord," said Dogah.

"Ah," said Targonne, "a burnt offering." He chuckled at his little jest and was annoyed when no one else did.

Two guards led forth the elf king who had been responsible for Mina's death. The young man was festooned in chains—fetters on his wrists and ankles were attached to an iron belt around his waist, an iron collar had been locked around his neck. He could scarcely walk for the weight and had to be assisted by his captors. His face was bruised practically beyond recognition, one eye swollen shut. His fine clothes were covered with blood.

His guards brought him to a halt at the foot of the pyre. The young man lifted his head. He saw Mina's body resting atop the pyre. The elf went so white that he was paler than the corpse. He let out a low, wretched cry and lurched suddenly forward. His guards, thinking he was trying to escape, seized hold of him roughly.

Silvanoshei had no thought of escape, however. He heard them cursing him and talking of throwing him onto the fire. He didn't care. He hoped they would, that he might die and be with her. He stood with his head bowed, his long hair falling over his battered face.

"Now that we are finished with the histrionics," said Lord Targonne snappishly, "may we proceed?"

Galdar's lips curled back from his teeth. His huge fist clenched.

"By my beard, here come the elves," Dogah exclaimed in disbelief.

It had been Mina's command that all elves who wanted to attend the ceremony were to be permitted to do so, and they were not to be harassed or threatened or harmed, but welcomed in the name of the One God. Mina's officers had not expected any elves would come. Fearing retribution, most elves had locked themselves in their houses, preparing to defend their homes and families or, in some cases, making plans to flee into the wilderness.

Yet now out of the city gates came pouring a vast gathering of Silvanesti elves, mostly the young, who had been Mina's followers. They bore flowers in their hands—those flowers that had survived the ravaging touch of the shield—and they walked with slow and

measured tread to the tune of the mournful music of
muted harp and somber flute. The human soldiers had
good reason to resent this appearance of their enemy,
those they held responsible for their beloved commander's death. A muttering arose among the troops, hardening into a growl of anger and a warning to the elves to
keep their distance.

Galdar took heart. Here was the perfect way to stall! If
the men would decide to ignore their orders and take out
their fury on these elves, Galdar and the other officers
could not be expected to stop them. He glanced skyward.
Blue dragons would not interfere with the slaughter of
elves. After such an unseemly disruption, the funeral
would certainly have to be postponed.

The elves proceeded toward the pyre. The shadows
of the dragons' wings flowed over them. Many blanched
and shuddered. The dragonfear that touched even
Galdar must be horrible for these elves. For all they
knew, they would be brutally attacked by the human
soldiers who had good reason to hate them. Yet still
they came to pay homage to the girl who had touched
them and healed them.

Galdar could not help but pay grudging homage to
their courage. So, too, did the men. Perhaps because Mina
had touched them all, human and elf felt a bond that day.
The growls of anger and muttered threats died away. The
elves took their places a respectful distance from the pyre,
as if they were aware they had no right to come closer.
They lifted their hands. A soft breeze sprang up from the
east, caught the flowers they bore, and carried them in a
cloud of fragrance to the pyre, where the white petals
floated down around Mina's body.

The chill sunlight illuminated the pyre, illuminated
Mina's face, shimmered in the golden cloth so that it
seemed to burn with its own fire.

"Are we expecting anyone else?" Targonne demanded sarcastically. "Dwarves, perhaps? A contingent of kender? If not, then get this over with, Dogah!"

"Certainly, my lord. First, you said you intended to speak her eulogy. As you said, my lord, the troops would appreciate hearing from you."

Targonne glowered. He was growing increasingly nervous, and he could not explain why. Perhaps it was the strange way these three officers stared at him, with hatred in their eyes. Not that this was particularly unusual. There were many people on Ansalon who had good reason to hate and fear the Lord of the Night. What made Targonne uneasy was the fact that he could not enter their minds to discover what they were thinking, what they were plotting.

Targonne felt suddenly threatened, and he could not understand why that should make him nervous. He was surrounded by his own bodyguard, Knights who had good reason to make certain that he remained alive. He had seven dragons at his command, dragons who would make short work of humans and elves alike, if the Lord of the Night ordered. Still he could not argue away the feeling of imminent peril.

The feeling made him irritated, annoyed, and sorry he had ever come. This hadn't turned out as he had planned. He had come to flaunt this victory as his own, to bask in the renewed adulation of the troops and their officers. Instead, he found himself overshadowed by a dead girl.

Clearing his throat, Targonne straightened. In a voice that was cold and flat, he said, "She did her duty."

The officers and men regarded him expectantly, waited for him to go on.

"That is her eulogy," Targonne said coldly. "A fitting eulogy for any soldier. Dogah, give the command to light the pyre."

Dogah said no word, but cast a helpless look at the other two officers. Captain Samuval was bleak, defeated. Galdar gazed with his soul in his eyes to the top of the pyre, where Mina lay still, unmoving.

Or did she move? Galdar saw a quiver in the cloth of gold that covered her. He saw color return to her wan cheek, and his heart leaped with hope. He stared enthralled, waiting for her to rise. She did not, and he came to the bitter realization that the stirring of the cloth was caused by the gentle breeze and the mockery of warmth was the pale light of the sun.

Lifting his voice in a ragged howl of grief and rage, Galdar snatched a torch from the hand of one of Mina's Knights and hurled it with all the might of his strong right arm onto the top of Mina's funeral pyre.

The flaming torch landed at Mina's feet, set the cloth that covered her ablaze.

Raising their own voices in hollow cries, the Knights under Mina's command flung their own torches onto the pyre. The oil-soaked wood burst into flame. The fires spread rapidly, flames reaching out like eager hands to join together and encircle the pyre. Galdar kept watch. He stared at the top to keep sight of her, blinking painfully as smoke stung his eyes and cinders landed in his fur. At last the heat was so intense that he was forced to retreat, but he did not do so until he lost sight of Mina's dear body in the thick smoke coiling around her.

Lord Targonne, coughing and flapping his hands at the smoke, backed away immediately. He waited long enough to make certain that the fire was blazing merrily, then turned to Dogah.

"Well," said his lordship, "I'll be off—"

A shadow blotted out the sun. Bright day darkened to night in the pause between one heartbeat and the next. Thinking it might be an eclipse—albeit a strange and sudden one—Galdar lifted amazed eyes, still stinging from the smoke, to the heavens.

A shadow blotted out the sun, but it was not the round shadow of the single moon. Silhouetted against tendrils of fire was a sinuous body, a curved tail, a dragon's head. Seen against the sun, the dragon appeared as black as time's ending. When it spread its massive wings, the sun vanished completely, only to reappear as a burst of flame in the dragon's eye.

Darkness deep and impenetrable fell upon Silvanost and, in that instant, the flames that consumed the pyre were doused by a breath that was neither heard nor felt.

Galdar gave a roar of triumph. Samuval dropped to his knees, his hands covering his face. Dogah gazed at the dragon with wonder. Mina's Knights stared upward in awe.

The darkness grew deeper, until Targonne could barely see those standing next to him.

"Get me out of here! Quick!" he ordered tersely.

No one obeyed his commands. His Knight escorts stared at the strange, immense dragon that had blotted out the sun, and they seemed, one and all, to have been changed to stone by the sight.

Now thoroughly frightened, feeling the darkness closing in around him, Targonne kicked at his Knights and swore at them. Fear shook him and shredded him and turned his bowels to water. One moment he threatened his officers he would see them flayed alive, the next he was promising them a fortune in steel to save him.

The darkness grew yet deeper. White lightning flared, splitting the unnatural night. Thunder crashed, shaking the ground. Targonne started to yell for his dragons to come rescue him.

The yell died in this throat.

The white lightning illuminated a figure standing atop the pyre, a figure wearing shining black armor and shrouded in a cloth of gold that was charred and burnt. The blue dragons flew above her, the lightning crackled around her. Swooping low over the ash-laden pyre, each blue dragon bowed its head to her.

"Mina!" The blue dragons sounded the paean. "Mina!"

"Mina!" Galdar sobbed and fell to his knees.

"Mina!" whispered General Dogah in relief.

"Mina!" Captain Samuval shouted in vindication.

Behind them, in the darkness, the elves took the word and made of it a song. "Mina . . . Mina . . ." The soldiers joined in, chanting, "Mina . . . Mina!"

The darkness lifted. The sun shone, and it was warm and dazzling to the eye. The strange dragon descended through the ethers. Such was the terror and the awe of its coming that few in the crowd could lift their shuddering gazes to look at it. Those who managed, and Galdar was one of them, saw a dragon such as they had never before beheld on Krynn. They were not able to look on it long, for the sight made their eyes water and burn, as if they stared into the sun.

The dragon was white, but not the white of those dragons who live in the lands of perpetual snow and frost. This dragon was the white of the flame of the forger's hottest fire. The white that is in direct opposition to black. The white that is not the absence of color but the blending together of all colors of the spectrum.

As the strange looking dragon drifted lower to the ground, its wings did not stir the air, nor did the ground shake from the impact when it landed. The blue dragons, all seven of them, lowered their heads and spread their wings in homage.

"Death!" they cried together in a single voice, fell and terrible. "The dead return!"

Now they could see that the dragon was not a living dragon. It was a ghostly dragon, a dragon formed of the souls of the chromatic dragons who had died during the Age of Mortals, killed by their own kind.

The death dragon lifted its front clawed foot and, turning it upward, placed that foot upon the top of the pyre. Mina stepped upon the upturned claw. The death dragon lowered her reverently to the charred, blackened, and ash-covered ground.

"Mina! Mina!" The soldiers were stamping their feet, clashing sword on shield, yelling until they were hoarse, and still the chant rang out. The elven voices had made of her name a madrigal whose beauty enchanted even the most obdurate and hardened human heart.

Mina gazed at them all in pleasure that warmed the amber eyes so that they shone purest gold. Overwhelmed by the love and the adoration, she seemed at a loss as to how to respond. At length, she acknowledged the tribute with an almost shy wave of her hand and a grateful smile.

She reached out and clasped the hands of Dogah and Captain Samuval, who could not speak for their joy. Then Mina walked over to stand in front of Galdar.

The minotaur fell on his knees, his head bent so low that the horns brushed the ground.

"Galdar," said Mina gently.

He lifted his head.

Mina held out her hand. "Take it, Galdar," she said.

He took hold of her hand, felt the flesh warm to the touch.

"Praise the One God, Galdar," Mina told him. "As you promised."

"Praise the One God!" Galdar whispered, choking.

"Will you always doubt, Galdar?" Mina asked him.

He looked at her fearfully, afraid of her anger, but he saw that her smile was fond and caring.

"Forgive me, Mina," he faltered. "I won't doubt anymore. I promise."

"Yes, you will, Galdar," Mina said, "but I am not angry. Without doubters, there would be no miracles."

He pressed her hand to his lips.

"Now arise, Galdar," said Mina, her voice hardening as the amber in her eyes hardened. "Arise and lay hands on the one who sought to kill me."

Mina pointed to the assassin.

She did not point at the wretched Silvanoshei, who was staring at her with dumb amazement and disbelief.

She pointed at Targonne.

13

Avenging the Dead

orham Targonne had no use for miracles. He had seen them all in his time, seen the smoke and seen the mirrors. Like everything else in this world, miracles could be bought and sold on the open market like fish and yesterday's fish at that, for most of them stunk to the heavens. He had to admit that the show he'd just witnessed was good, better than most. He couldn't explain it, but he was convinced that the explanation was there. He had to find it. He would find it in this girl's mind.

He sent a mental probe into Mina's red-crowned head, launched it as swift and straight as a steel-tipped arrow. When he found out the truth, he would denounce her to her addlepated believers. He would reveal to them how truly dangerous she was. They would thank him. . . .

In her mind, he saw eternity, that which no mortal is ever meant to see.

No mortal mind can encompass the smallness that holds the vastness.

No mortal eye can see that blinding light for the illuminating darkness.

Mortal flesh withers in the cooling fire of the burning ice.

Mortal ears cannot bear to hear the roaring silence of the thundering quiet.

Mortal spirits cannot comprehend the life that begins in death and the death that lives in life.

Certainly not a mortal mind like Targonne's. A mind that divides honor by ambition and multiplies gain by greed. The numbers that were the sum of his life were halved and halved again and halved again after that, and he was, in the end, a fraction.

The great are humbled by even a glimpse of eternity. The mean tremble in fear. Targonne was horrified. He was a rat in that immense vastness, a cornered rat who could not find a corner.

Yet, even at the end, the cornered rat is a cunning rat. Cunning was all Targonne had left to him. Looking about, he saw that he had no friends, no allies. All he had were those who served him out of fear or ambition or need, and every one of these petty concerns were so much dust swept away by an immortal hand. His guilt was plain for even the stupidest to see. He could deny it or embrace it.

Awkwardly, the bib of his ill-fitting breastplate thumping and banging against his bony knees, Targonne knelt before Mina in an attitude of the most abject humility.

"Yes, it is true," he blubbered, squeezing out a meager tear or two. "I sought to have you killed. I had no choice. I was ordered to do it." He kept his head humbly lowered, but managed to steal a glance to see how his speech was being received. "Malystryx ordered your death. She fears you, and with good reason!"

Now he thought it was time he could lift his head, and he arranged his face to match his words. "I was wrong. I admit it. I feared Malystryx. Now I see my fear is unfounded. This god of yours, this One God—a most wonderful and magnificent and powerful god." He clasped his hands. "Forgive me. Let me serve you, Mina. Let me serve your god!"

He looked into the amber eyes and saw himself, a tiny vermin, scurrying frantically until the amber flowed over him and held him immobile.

"I foretold that someday you would kneel before me," said Mina, and her tone was not smug, but gentle. "I forgive you. More important, the One God forgives you and accepts your service."

Targonne, grinning inside, started to rise.

"Galdar," Mina continued, "your sword."

Galdar drew a huge, curved-bladed sword, lifted it. He held it poised a moment over Targonne's head, long enough to allow the coward a moment to fully comprehend what was going to happen. Targonne's shriek of terror, the squeal of the dying rat, was cut off by the sweep of the blade that severed the man's head from his neck. Blood spattered on Mina. The head rolled to Mina's feet and lay there in a gruesome pool, facedown in the mud and the ash.

"Hail, Mina! Lord of the Night!" General Dogah shouted.

"Hail, Mina! Lord of the Night!" The soldiers picked up the cheer, and their voices carried it to heaven.

Amazed by what they had seen and heard, the elves were horrified by the brutal murder, even of one who had so richly deserved punishment. Their hymns of praise faded out discordantly. They stared to see that Mina did not even bother to wipe away the blood.

"What are your orders, Mina?" Dogah asked, saluting.

"You and the men under your command will remain here to hold the land of Silvanesti in the name of the Dark Knights of Neraka," Mina said. "You will send rich tribute to Dragon Overlord Malystryx in my name. That should placate her and keep her eye turned inward."

Dogah stroked his beard. "Where are we to find this rich tribute, Mina?"

She motioned Captain Samuval to release Foxfire. The horse danced up to her, nuzzled her. Mina stroked the horse's neck affectionately and began to remove the saddlebags.

"Where do you suppose you will find it, Dogah?" she asked. "In the Royal Treasury in the Tower of the Stars. In the homes of the members of House Royal and in the storerooms of the elven merchants. Even the poorest of these elves," she continued, tossing the saddlebags onto the ground, "have family heirlooms hidden away."

Dogah chuckled. "What of the elves themselves?"

Mina cast a glance at the headless corpse that was being rolled unceremoniously onto the base of the funeral pyre.

"They promised to serve the One God, and the One God needs them now," Mina said. "Let those who have pledged themselves to the One God fulfill that pledge by working with us to maintain control over the land."

"They won't do that, Mina," Dogah said grimly. "Their service won't extend that far."

"You will be surprised, Galdar," said Mina. "Like all of us, the elves have sought something beyond themselves, something in which to believe. The One God has given that to them, and many will come to the service of the One God. The Silvanesti who are faithful to the One will erect a Temple to the One in the heart of Silvanost. Elven priests of the One will be granted the power of healing and given the means to perform other miracles.

"First, though, Dogah, the One will expect them to prove that loyalty. They should be the first to hand over their riches, and they should be the ones who take the riches from those who prove recalcitrant. The elves who claim to be loyal to the One God will be expected to reveal to us all those who are enemies of the One God, even if those enemies are their own lovers, wives, fathers, or children. All this you will ask of them, and those who are truly faithful will make the sacrifice. If they do not, they may serve the One God dead as well as alive."

"I understand," said Dogah.

Mina knelt to unbuckle the straps of the saddle that encircled Foxfire's belly. Her Knights would have leaped to do this for her, but the moment one made a move toward the horse, Foxfire curled back his lip and halted the man with a jealous eye.

"I leave you in charge, Dogah. I ride this day with those under my command for Solamnia. We must be there in two days."

"Two days!" Galdar protested. "Mina, Solamnia is at the other end of the continent! A thousand miles away, across the New Sea. Such a feat is impossible—"

Mina straightened, looked the minotaur full in the eye.

Galdar gulped, swallowed. "Such a feat would be impossible," he amended contritely, "for anyone but you."

"The One God, Galdar," Mina corrected him. "The One God."

Removing the saddle from Foxfire, she placed it on the ground. Last, she took off the bridle and tossed it down next to the saddle. "Pack that with the rest of my things," she commanded.

Putting her arms around the horse's neck, Mina spoke softly to the animal. Foxfire listened attentively, head bowed, ears forward to catch the slightest whisper. At length Foxfire nodded his head. Mina kissed the horse and stroked him lovingly. "You are in the hands of the One God," she said. "The One God bring you safe to me at my need."

Foxfire lifted his head, shook his mane proudly, then wheeled and galloped off, heading for the forest. Those in his path were forced to jump and scramble to get out of his way, for he cared not whom he trampled.

Mina watched him depart, then, as if by accident, she noticed Silvanoshei.

The elf had witnessed all that had passed with the dazed look of one who walks in a dream and cannot wake. He watched the fire blaze in grief that approached madness. He witnessed Mina's triumphant return to life with disbelief that flared into joy. So convinced was Silvanoshei of his own guilt, that when he heard her accuse her assassin, he waited to die. Even now he could not comprehend what had happened. Silvanoshei knew only that his love was alive. He gazed at her in wonder and in despair, in hope and in dejection, seeing all, understanding nothing.

She walked over to him. He tried to rise, but the chains weighed him down and hobbled him so he found it difficult to move.

"Mina . . ." He tried to speak, but he could only mumble through the swelling and the pain of his broken jaw.

Mina touched his forehead, and the pain vanished, the jaw healed. The bruises disappeared, the swelling subsided. Seizing her hands, he pressed them passionately to his lips.

"I love you, Mina!"

"I am not worthy of your love," she said.

"You are, Mina! You are!" he gabbled. "I may be a king, but you are queen—"

"You misunderstand me, Silvanoshei,' Mina said softly. "Your love should not be for me but for the One God who guides and directs me."

She withdrew her hands from his grasp.

"Mina!" he cried in despair.

"Let your love for me lead you to the One God, Silvanoshei," Mina said to him. "The hand of the One God brought us together. The hand of the One God forces us to separate now, but if you allow the One God to guide you, we will be together again. You are the Chosen of the One God, Silvanoshei. Take this and keep it in faith."

She took from her finger the ruby ring, the poison ring. Dropping the ring in his trembling palm, she turned and walked away without a glance.

"Mina!" Silvanoshei cried, but she did not heed him.

His manacled hands hung listlessly before him. He paid no attention to anything going on around him. He continued to kneel on the bloody ground, clutching the ring, staring at Mina, his heart and his soul in his eyes.

"Why did you tell him that, Mina?" Galdar asked in a low voice as he hurried to accompany her. "You care nothing for the elf, that is obvious. Why lead him on? Why bother?"

"Because he could be a danger to us, Galdar," Mina replied. "I leave behind a small force of men to rule over a large nation. If the elves ever find a strong leader, they could unite and overthrow us. He has it within him to be such a leader."

Galdar glanced back, saw the elf groveling on the ground. "That sniveling wretch? Let me slay him." Galdar placed his hand on the hilt of his sword that was stained with Targonne's blood.

"And make of him a martyr?" Mina shook her head. "No, far better for us if he is seen to worship the One God, seen to ignore the cries of his people. For those cries will change to curses.

"Have no fear, Galdar," she added, drawing on a pair of soft leather riding gloves. "The One God has seen to it that Silvanoshei is no longer a threat."

"Do you mean the One God did this to him?" Galdar asked.

Mina flashed him a glance of amber. "Of course, Galdar. The One God guides all our destinies. His destiny. Yours. Mine."

She looked at him long, then said softly, almost to herself, "I know what you are feeling. I had difficulty accepting the will of the One as opposed to my own. I fought and struggled against it for a long time. Let me tell you a story, and perhaps you will understand.

"Once, when I was a little girl, a bird flew inside the place where I lived. The walls were made of crystal, and the bird could see outside, see the sun and the blue sky and freedom. The bird hurled itself at the crystal, trying frantically to escape back into the sunshine. We tried to catch it, but it would not let us near. At last, wounded and exhausted, the bird fell to the floor and lay there quivering. Goldmoon picked up the bird, smoothed its feathers with her hand, and healed its wounds. She carried it out into the sunlight and set it free.

"I was like that bird, Galdar. I flung myself against the crystal walls of my creation, and when I was battered and bruised, the One God lifted me and healed me and now guides me and carries me, as the One God guides and carries us all. Do you understand, Galdar?"

He was not sure he did. He was not sure he wanted to, but he said, "Yes, Mina," because he wanted to please her, to smooth the frown from her forehead and bring the light back to her amber eyes.

She looked at him long, then she turned away, saying briskly, "Summon the men. Have them collect their gear and make ready to depart for Solamnia."

"Yes, Mina," said Galdar.

She paused, looked back at him. A corner of her mouth twitched. "You do not ask how we will get there, Galdar," she said.

"No, Mina," he said. "If you tell me to fly, I trust that I will sprout wings."

Mina laughed gaily. She was in excellent spirits, sparkling and ebullient. She pointed to the horizon.

"There, Galdar," she said. "There is how a minotaur will fly."

The sun was falling toward night, sinking into a pool of blood and fire. Galdar saw a spectacle thrilling in its terrible beauty. Dragons filled the sky. The sun gleamed on red wings and blue, shining through them like fire glowing through stained glass. The scales of the black dragons shimmered with dark iridescence, the scales of the green dragons were emeralds scattered against cobalt.

Red dragons—powerful and enormous, blue dragons—small and swift, black dragons—vicious and cruel, white dragons—cold and beautiful, green dragons—noxious and deadly. Dragons of all colors, male and female, old and young, they came at Mina's call. Many of these dragons had been hiding deep in their lairs, terrified of Malys and of Beryl, of Khellendros, one of their own who had turned on them. They had hidden away, afraid they would find their skulls upon one of the totems of the dragon overlords.

Then had come the great storm. Above the fearsome winds, blasting lightning, and booming thunder, these dragons had heard a voice telling them to prepare, to make ready, to come when summoned.

Tired of living in fear, longing for revenge for the deaths of their mates, their children, their comrades, they answered the call, and now they flew to Silvanesti, their many-colored scales forming a terrible rainbow over the ancient homeland of the elves.

The dragons' scales glittered in the sunshine so that each might have been encrusted with a wealth of jewels. The shadows of their passing rippled along the ground beneath them, flowing over hillock and farmhouse, lake and forest.

The swift-flying blues took the lead, wing tip to wing tip, keeping time with matching strokes, taking pride in their precision. The ponderous reds brought up the rear, their enormous wings moving a single sweeping flap to every four of the faster blues. Blacks and greens were scattered throughout.

The elves felt the terror of their coming. Many collapsed, senseless, and others fled in the madness of their fear. Dogah sent his men after them, bidding them to make certain no elf escaped into the wilderness.

Mina's men ran to collect their gear and any supplies that could be carried on dragonback. They brought Mina's maps to her, she said she needed nothing else. They were ready and waiting to mount by the time the first of the dragons began to circle down and land upon the battlefield. Galdar mounted a gigantic red. Captain Samuval chose a blue. Mina rode the strange dragon, the dragon she termed the "death dragon."

"We travel by darkness," said Mina. "The light of neither moon nor star will shine this night so our journey may remain secret."

"What is our destination?" Galdar asked.

"A place where the dead gather," she said. "A place called Nightlund."

Her dragon spread its ghastly wings and soared into the air effortlessly, as if it weighed no more than the ashes that drifted up from the pyre, where they were burning Targonne's body. The other dragons, bearing the soldiers of Mina's army upon their backs, took to the skies. Clouds foamed up from the west, blotting out the sun, gathering thick around the multitude of dragons.

Dogah returned to the command tent. He had work to do: comandeering storehouses to hold the loot, establishing slave-labor camps, interrogation centers and prisons, brothels to keep the men entertained. He had noted, when in Silvanost, a temple dedicated to an old god, Mishakal. He would establish the worship of the One God there, he decided. An appropriate place.

As he made his plans, he could hear the screams of elves who were probably, even now, being dispatched into the One God's service.

Out on the battlefield, Silvanoshei remained where Mina had left him. He had been unable to take his eyes from her. In despair, he had watched her depart, clinging to the rag of hope she had left him as a child clings to the tattered blanket he clutches to keep away the terrors of the night. He did not hear the cries of his people. He heard only Mina's voice.

The One God. Embrace the One God, and we will be together again.

14

The Chosen of the One God

en members of the kirath and ten elves of Alhana's army were hiding in the forests outside Silvanost to watch the funeral. They were hiding there when the dragons came. Wearing the magical cloaks of the kirath that made them invisible to any who might be watching for them, the elves were able to creep within close proximity of the funeral pyre. They saw everything that happened but were helpless to intervene. They could do nothing to save their people. Their numbers were too small. Help would come later. These elves were here with one mission, one purpose, and that was to rescue their young king.

The elves heard death all around them. The stumps of dying trees cried out in agony. The ghost of Cyan Bloodbane hissed and howled in the wind. These elves had fought the dream with courage. They had fought ogres without blanching. Forced to listen to the song of death, they felt their palms sweat and their stomachs clench.

The elves hiding in the forest were reminded of the dream, yet this was worse, for the dream had been a dream of death, and this was real. They watched their brethren mourn the death of the strange human girl child, Mina. As the Knights cast their torches onto the pyre, the elves did not cheer, even in their hearts. They watched in wary silence.

Crouched among the boughs severed from a living aspen that had been left to wither and die, Alhana Starbreeze saw flames crackle on the pyre and smoke begin to rise to the heavens. She kept her gaze on her son, Silvanoshei, who had been dragged in chains and now appeared on the verge of collapse. Beside her, Samar muttered something. He had not wanted her to come, he had argued against it, but this time she insisted on having her way.

"What did you say, Commander?" Kiryn whispered.

"Nothing," Samar returned, with a glance at Alhana.

He would not speak ill of Alhana's son to anyone but himself, especially not to Kiryn, who never ceased to defend Silvanoshei, to maintain that the king was in the grip of some strange power.

Samar liked Kiryn. He admired the young man for having had the wit, resourcefulness, and foresight to escape the calamitous banquet, to seek out the kirath, and alert them to what had happened. But Kiryn was a Silvanesti, and although he claimed he had remained loyal all these years to Alhana, Samar did not trust him.

A hand touched his arm, and in spite of himself, Samar started, unable to repress a shudder. He looked around, half-angry, though if he had heard the sounds of the elven scout approaching, he would have severely reprimanded such carelessness.

"Well," he growled, "what did you find out?"

"It is true, what we heard," the woman said, her voice softer than the ghostly whispers. "Silvanoshei was responsible for the human girl's death. He gave her a ring, a ring he told people came from his mother. The ring was poisoned. The human died almost instantly."

"I sent no such ring!" Alhana said, seeing the cold stares of the kirath. For years, they had been told Alhana Starbreeze was a dark elf. Perhaps some had even believed it. "I fight my enemies face to face. I do not poison them, especially when I know that it is my people who will suffer the consequences!"

"This smacks of treachery," Samar said. "Human treachery. This Lord Targonne is known to have made his way to the top by climbing a ladder of the corpses of his enemies. This girl was just one more rung—"

"Commander! Look!" The scout pointed.

The elves hiding amid the shadows of the death-singing forest watched in amazement to see the human girl rise whole and alive from the blazing pyre. The humans were proclaiming it a miracle. The elves were skeptical.

"Ah, I thought there would be some trick in this," Samar said.

Then came the strange death dragon, and the elves turned dark and shadowed eyes to each other.

"What is this?" Alhana wondered aloud. "What does it portend?"

Samar had no answer. In his hundreds of years, he had roamed almost every portion of Ansalon and had encountered nothing like this horrible creature.

The elves heard the girl accuse Targonne, and although many could not understand her language, they were able to guess the import of her words by the expression on the doomed human's face. They watched his headless corpse topple to the ground without comment or surprise. Such barbarous behavior was only to be expected of humans.

As the flight of many colored dragons formed a hideous rainbow in the skies above Silvanesti, the song of death rose to a shrieking paean. The elves shrank among the shadows and shivered as the dragonfear swept over them. They flattened themselves among the dead trees. They were able to do nothing but think of death, to see nothing but the image of their own dying.

The dragons departed, bearing the strange girl away with them. The Dark Knights of Neraka swept down upon the Silvanesti people, carrying salvation in one hand, death in the other.

Alhana's heart hurt almost to breaking at the sound of the screams of those first to fall victim to the wrath of the Dark Knights. Smoke was already starting to rise from the beautiful city. Yet she reached out a hand to detain Rolan of the kirath, who was on his feet, sword in hand.

"Where do you think you are going?" Alhana demanded.

"To save them," Rolan said grimly. "To save them or die with them."

"A witless act. Would you throw away your life for nothing?"

"We must do something!" Rolan cried, his face livid. "We must help them!"

"We are thirty," Alhana answered. "The humans outnumber us dozens to one." She looked back grimly, pointed to the fleeing Silvanesti. "If our people would stand and fight, we might be able to help them, but—look at that! Look at them! Some flee in confusion and panic. Others stand and sing praises to this false god!"

"The human is clever," Samar said quietly. "With her trickery and her promises, she seduced your people as surely as she seduced that poor besotted boy out there. We can do nothing to help them. Not now—not until reason prevails. But we might be able to help him."

Tears streamed down Rolan's cheeks. Every elven death cry seemed to strike him, for his body shuddered at each. He stood irresolute, blinking his eyes and watching the gray tendrils of smoke rising from Silvanost. Alhana did not weep. She had no more tears left.

"Samar, look!" Kiryn pointed. "Silvanoshei. They are taking him away. If we're going to do something, we'd better do it fast, before they reach the city and lock him up in some dungeon."

The young man stood on the battlefield in the shadow of Mina's pyre and appeared stunned to the point of insensibility. He did not look to see what was happening to his people. He did not make any move at all. He stared as if transfixed at where she had stood. Four humans—soldiers, not Knights—had been left to guard him. Seizing hold of him, two began to drag him off. The other two followed along, swords drawn, keeping careful watch.

Only four of them. The rest of the Knights and soldiers had raced off to effect the subjugation and looting of Silvanost, about a mile distant. Their camp was empty, abandoned except for these four and the prince.

"We do what we came to do," Alhana said. "We rescue the prince. Now is our chance."

Samar rose up from his hiding place. He gave a piercing cry, that of a hawk, and the woods were alive with elven warriors, emerging from the shadows.

Samar motioned his warriors forward. Alhana rose too, but she remained behind a moment, placed her hand upon Rolan's shoulder.

"Forgive me, Rolan of the Kirath," Alhana said. "I know your pain, and I share it. I spoke in haste. There *is* something we can do."

Rolan looked at her, the tears still glimmering in his eyes.

"We can vow to return and avenge the dead," she said.

Rolan gave a fierce nod.

Gripping her weapon, Alhana caught up with Samar, and they soon joined the main body of the elven warriors, who ran silently, unseen, from out the whispering shadows.

Silvanoshei's captors hauled him back toward Silvanost. The four men were put out, grumbling that they were missing the fun of looting and burning the elven city.

Silvanoshei stumbled over the uneven ground, blind, deaf, oblivious to everything. He could not hear the cries, he could not smell the smoke of destruction nor see it rising from his city. He saw only Mina. He smelled only the smoke of her pyre. He heard only her voice chanting the litany of the One God. The god she worshiped. The god who had brought them together. *You are the Chosen.*

He remembered the night of the storm, the night the ogres had attacked their camp. He remembered how the storm had made his blood burn. He had likened it to a lover. He remembered the desperate run to try to save his people, and the lightning bolt that had sent him tumbling down the ravine and into the shield.

The Chosen.

How had he been able to pass through the shield, when no others could do so?

That same lightning bolt blazed through his mind.

Mina had passed through the shield.

The Chosen. The hand of the One God. An immortal hand that had touched him with a lover's caress. The same hand had thrown the bolt to block his path and raised the shield to let him enter. The immortal hand had pointed his way to Mina on the battlefield, had guided the arrows that felled Cyan Bloodbane. The hand had rested against his own hand and given him the strength to uproot the lethal Shield Tree.

The immortal hand cupped around him, held him, healed him, and he was comforted as he had been in his mother's arms the night the assassins had tried to slay him. He was the Chosen. Mina had told him so. He would give himself to the One God. He would allow that comforting hand to guide him along the chosen path. Mina would be there waiting for him at the end.

What did the One God want of him now? What was the plan for him? He was a prisoner, chained and manacled.

Silvanoshei had never prayed to any god. After the Chaos War, there had been no gods to answer prayers. His parents had told him that mortals were on their own. They had to make do in this world, rely on themselves. It seemed to him, looking back, that mortals had made a hash of things.

Perhaps Mina had been right when she told him that he did not love her, he loved the god in her. She was so confident, so certain, so self-possessed. She never doubted. She was never afraid. In a world of darkness where everyone else was stumbling blindly, she alone was granted the gift of sight.

Silvanoshei did not even know how to pray to a god. His parents had never spoken of the old religion. The subject was a painful one for them. They were hurt, but they were also angry. The gods, with their departure, had betrayed those who had put their faith in them.

But how did he know for certain that the One God cared for him? How did he know that he was truly the Chosen?

He determined to test the One God, a test to reassure himself, as a child assures himself by small tests that his parents really do love him.

Silvanoshei prayed, humbly, "If there is something you want me to do, I cannot do it if I am prisoner. Set me free, and I will obey your will."

"Sir!" shouted one of the soldiers who had been guarding the rear. "Behind—" Whatever he had been about to say ended in a shriek. The tip of a sword protruded from his gut. He had been stabbed in the back, the blow so fierce that it had pierced the chain mail shirt he wore. He fell forward and was trampled under a rush of elven warriors.

The guards holding Silvanoshei let loose as they turned to fight. One managed actually to draw his sword, but he could make no use of it, for Rolan sliced off his arm. Rolan's next cut was to the throat. The guard fell in a pool of his own gore. The other guard was dead before he could reach his weapon. Samar's blade swept the head from the man's neck. The fourth man was dispatched handily by Alhana Starbreeze, who thrust her sword in his throat.

So lost was he in religious fervor that Silvanoshei was barely aware of what was happening, of grunts of pain and stifled cries, the thud of bodies falling to the ground. First he was being hauled away by soldiers, then, looking up, he saw the face of his mother.

"My son!" Alhana cried softly. Dropping her bloody sword, she gathered Silvanoshei into her embrace and held him close.

"Mother?" Silvanoshei said dazedly. He could not understand, for at first, when the arms wrapped around him in maternal love, he had seen another face. "Mother . . ." he repeated, bewildered. "Where— How—"

"My Queen," said Samar warningly.

"Yes, I know," said Alhana. She reluctantly released her son. Wiping away her tears, she said, "I will tell you everything, my son. We will have a long talk, but now is not the time. Samar, can you remove his chains?"

"Keep watch," Samar ordered an elf. "Let me know if anyone has spotted us."

"Not likely, Commander," was the grim return. "They are too busy with their butchery."

Samar examined the manacles and the chains and shook his head. "There is no time to remove these, Silvanoshei, not until we are far from Silvanost and pursuit. We will do what we can to help you along the way, but you must be strong, Your Highness, and bear this burden awhile longer."

Samar looked and spoke doubtfully. He had seen Silvanoshei a sodden mess on the battlefield. He was prepared to find the young elf shattered, demoralized, uncaring whether he lived or died, unwilling to make an effort to do either.

Silvanoshei stood upright. He had been confused at first. His rescue had come too quickly. The sight of his mother had shaken him, but now that he had time to think, he saw with elation that the One God had been responsible. The One God had answered his prayer. He *was* the Chosen. The manacles cut his flesh so that it bled, but he bore the pain gladly as a testament to his love for Mina and his newfound faith in the One God.

"I do not need you or anyone to help me, Samar," Silvanoshei said with quiet calm. "I can bear this burden for as long and as far as necessary. Now, as you say, we must make haste. My mother is in danger."

Enjoying Samar's look of astonishment, Silvanoshei shoved past the startled warrior and began to hobble clumsily toward the forest.

"Help him, Samar," Alhana ordered, retrieving her sword. She watched her son with fondness and pride— and faint unease. He had changed, and although she told herself that his ordeal would have changed anyone, she found this change disturbing. It wasn't so much that he had grown from a boy to a man. It was that he had grown from her boy into a man she did not know.

Silvanoshei felt imbued with strength. The chains weighed nothing, were gossamer and silk. He began to run, awkwardly, occasionally tripping and stumbling, but he was doing as well for himself as he might have done with assistance. The elven warriors surrounded him, guarding him, but no one was there to stop them. The Knights of Neraka were acting swiftly to seize Silvanost and wrap the city in its own chains, forged of iron and fire and blood.

The elves and their freed captive traveled north for a short distance, far enough that they could not smell the smoke of destruction. They turned east and, under Rolan's guidance, came to the river, where the kirath had boats ready to carry the prince upstream, north to the camp of Alhana's forces. Here they would rest for a short time. They lit no fires, set careful watch.

Silvanoshei had managed to keep up with the rest, although by the end of the journey his breath was coming in painful gasps, his muscles burned, and his hands were covered with the blood that ran from his chafed wrists. He fell more than once, and at last, because his mother pleaded with him, he permitted the other elves to assist him. No word of complaint passed his lips. He held on with a grim determination that won even Samar's approval.

Once they reached the riverbank and relative safety, the elves hacked at his fetters with axes. Silvanoshei sat still, unflinching, though the axe blades sometimes came perilously close to cutting off a foot or slicing into his leg. Sparks flew, but the chains would not break, and eventually, after all the axe blades were notched, the elves were forced to give up. Without a key they could not remove the iron manacles round Silvanoshei's ankles and his wrists.

Alhana assured her son that once they arrived at his mother's camp, the blacksmith would be able to make a key that would fit the locks and so remove them.

"Until then, we travel by boat the rest of the way. The journey will not be nearly so difficult for you, my son."

Silvanoshei shrugged, unconcerned. He bore the pain and discomfort with quiet fortitude. Chains clanking, he wrapped himself in a blanket and lay down on the ground, again without complaint.

Alhana sat beside her son. The night was hushed, as if all living things held their breath in fear. Only the river continued to speak, the swift-flowing water rushing past them, talking to itself in a deep, sorrowful murmur, knowing what terrible sights it would see downstream, loath to continue on its journey, yet unable to halt the flow.

"You must be exhausted, my son," Alhana said, her own voice low, "and I will not keep you from your sleep long, but I want to tell you that I understand. You have lived through a difficult time. You have experienced events that might have overwhelmed the best and wisest of men, and you are only a youth. I must confess that I feared to find you crushed by what happened this day. I was afraid that you were so entangled in the snares of the human witch that you would never be free of her. Her tricks are impressive, but you must not be fooled by them. She is a witch and a charlatan and makes people see what they want to see. The power of the gods is gone in this world. I see no evidence that it has returned."

Alhana paused to allow Silvanoshei to comment. The young man was silent. His eyes, glittering with starlight, were wide open and gazing into the darkness.

"I know that you must grieve over what is now happening in Silvanost," Alhana continued, disappointed that he did not respond. "I promise you as I promised Rolan of the kirath that we will come back in strength to free the people and drive the legions of darkness from that fair city. You will be restored as king. That is my dearest wish.

You have proven by the courage and strength I see in you this night that you are worthy to hold that holy trust, assume that great responsibility."

A pale smile flickered over Silvanoshei's lips. "So I have proven myself to you, have I, Mother? You think that at last I am worthy of my heritage?"

"You did not need to prove yourself to me, Silvanoshei," said Alhana, regretting her words the moment she had spoken them. She faltered, tried to explain. "If I gave you that impression, I never meant to. I love you, my son. I am proud of you. I think that the strange and terrible events of which you have been a part have forced you to grow up rapidly. You have grown, when you might have been crushed by them."

"I am glad to have earned your good opinion, Mother," Silvanoshei said.

Alhana was bewildered and hurt by his cool and detached demeanor. She did not understand but, after some thought, put it down to the fact that he had endured much and must be worn out. Silvanoshei's face was smooth and placid. His eyes were fixed on the night sky with such intensity that he might have been counting every single pinpoint of bright, white light.

"My father used to tell a story, Mother," said Silvanoshei, just as she was about to rise. The prince rolled over on his side, his chains clanking and rattling, a discordant sound in the still night. "A story of a human woman—I can't recall her name. She came to the Qualinesti elves during another time of turmoil and danger, bearing a blue crystal staff, saying that she was sent to them by the gods. Do you recall this story, Mother?"

"Her name was Goldmoon," said Alhana. "The story is a true one."

"Did the elves believe her when she said that she came bearing a gift of the gods?"

"No, they did not," Alhana said, troubled.

"She was termed a witch and a charlatan by many elves, among them my own father. Yet she did bring a gift from the gods, didn't she?"

"My son," Alhana began, "there is a difference—"

"I am very tired, Mother." Silvanoshei drew his blanket up over his shoulders and rolled over, so that his back was to her. "May your rest be blessed," he added.

"Peaceful rest, my son," said Alhana, bending down to kiss his cheek. "We will speak of this more in the morning, but I would remind you that the Dark Knights are killing elves in the name of this so-called One God."

There came no sound from the prince except the bitter music of the chains. Either he stirred in discomfort, or he was settling himself for sleep. Alhana had no way of telling, for Silvanoshei's face was hidden from her.

Alhana made the rounds of the camp, checking to see that those who stood guard duty were at their posts. Assured that all were watchful and alert, she sat down at the river's edge and thought with despair and anger of the terror that reigned in Silvanost this night.

The river mourned and lamented with her until she imagined that she began to hear words in its murmurings.

> Sleep, love; forever sleep
> Your soul the night will keep
> Embrace the darkness deep
> Sleep, love; forever sleep.

The river left its banks. Dark water overflowed, rose up, and drowned her.

Alhana woke with a start to find it was morning. The sun had lifted above the treetops. Drifting clouds raced past, hiding the sun from sight, then restoring it to view, so that it seemed as if the orb were winking at some shared joke.

Angry that she had been so undisciplined as to let herself slumber when danger was all around them, she jumped to her feet. To her dismay, she found that she was not the only one who had slept at her post. Those on guard duty slumbered standing up, their chins on their chests, their eyes closed, their weapons lying on the ground at their feet.

Samar lay beside her. His hand was outstretched, as if he had been about to speak to her. Sleep had felled him before he could say a word.

"Samar!" she said, shaking him. "Samar! Something strange has happened to us."

Samar woke immediately, flushed in shame to find that he had failed in his duty. He gave an angry roar that roused every elf.

"I am at fault," he said, bitterly chagrined. It is a wonder to me that our enemies did not take advantage of our weakness to slit our throats! I had intended to leave with the dawn. We have a long journey, and we have lost at least two hours of travel. We must make—"

"Samar!" Alhana cried, her voice piercing his heart. "Come quickly! My son!"

Alhana pointed to an empty blanket and four broken manacles—manacles no axe had been able to cut. In the dirt near the blanket were deep prints of two booted feet and prints of a horse's hooves.

"They have taken him," she said, frightened. "They have taken him away in the night!"

Samar tracked the hoof prints to the water's edge, and there they vanished. He recalled, with startling clarity, the red horse that had galloped riderless into the forest.

"No one took him, My Queen," Samar said. "One came to fetch him. He went eagerly, I fear."

Alhana stared across the sun-dappled river, saw it bright and sparkling on the surface, dark and wild and dangerous beneath. She recalled with a shudder the words she had heard the river sing last night.

Sleep, love. Forever sleep.

15

Prisoners, Ghosts, the Dead, and the Living

alin Majere was no longer a prisoner in the Tower of High Sorcery. That is to say, he was and he was not. He was not a prisoner in that he was, not confined to a single room in the Tower. He was not chained or bound or physically restrained in any way. He could roam freely about the Tower but no farther. He could not leave the Tower. A single door at the lower level of the Tower permitted entry and egress, and that was enchanted, sealed shut by a wizard lock.

Palin had his own room with a bed but no chair and no desk. The room had a door but no window. The room had a fire grate, but no fire, and was chill and dank. For food, there were loaves of bread, stacked up in what had once been the Tower's pantry, along with crockery bowls—most of which were cracked and chipped—filled with dried fruit. Palin recognized bread that had been created by magic and not the baker, because it was tasteless and pale and had a spongy texture. For drink, there was water in pitchers that continually refilled themselves. The water was brackish and had an unpleasant odor.

Palin had been reluctant to drink it, but he could find nothing else, and after casting a spell on it to make certain it did not contain some sort of potion, he used it to wash down the knots of bread that stuck in his throat. He cast a spell and summoned a fire into existence, but it didn't help lift the atmosphere of gloom.

Ghosts haunted the Tower of High Sorcery. Not the ghosts of the dead who had stolen his magic. Some sort of warding spell kept them at bay. These ghosts were ghosts of his past. At this turning, he encountered the ghost of himself inside this Tower, arriving to take the dread Test of magic. At that turning, he imagined the ghost of his uncle, who had predicted a future of greatness for the young mage. Here he found the ghost of Usha when he had first met her: beautiful, mysterious, fond, and loving. The ghosts were sorrowful, shades of promise and hope, both dead. Ghosts of love, either dead or dying.

Most terrible was the ghost of the magic. It whispered to him from the cracks in the stone stairs, from the torn threads in the carpet, from the dust on the velvet curtains, from the lichen that had died years ago but had never been scraped off the wall.

Perhaps because of the presence of the ghosts, Palin was strangely at home in the Tower. He was more at home here than he was at his own light, airy, and comfortable home in Solace. He didn't enjoy admitting that to himself. He felt guilty because of it.

After days of wandering alone through the Tower, locked up with himself and the ghosts, he understood why this chill, dread place was home. Here in the Tower he had been a child, a child of the magic. Here the magic had watched over him, guided him, loved him, cared for him. Even now he could sometimes smell the scent of faded rose petals and would recall that time, that happy time. Here in the Tower all was quiet. Here no one had any claim on him. No one expected anything of him. No one looked at him with pity. He disappointed no one.

It was then he realized he had to leave. He had to escape from this place, or he would become just another ghost among many.

Having spent the greater portion of his four days as a prisoner roaming the Tower, much as a ghost might roam the place it was doomed to frequent, he was familiar with the physical layout of the Tower. It was similar to what he remembered, but with differences. Every Master of the Tower altered the building to suit his or her needs. Raistlin had made the Tower of High Sorcery his own when he was Master. He had shared it with no one except a single apprentice, Dalamar, the undead who served them, and the Live Ones, poor, twisted creatures who lived out their miserable, misbegotten lives below the surface of the ground in the Chamber of Seeing.

Upon Raistlin's death, Dalamar was made Master of the Tower of High Sorcery. The Tower had been located in the lord city of Palanthas, which considered itself the center of the known world. Previously the Tower of High Sorcery had been a sinister object, one of foreboding and terror. Dalamar was a forward-thinking mage, despite being an elf and a Black Robe (or perhaps because he was an elf and a Black Robe). He wanted to flaunt the power of mages, not hide it, and so he had opened the Tower to students, adding rooms in which his apprentices could live and study.

Fond of comfort and luxury as any elf, he had brought into the Tower many objects that he collected over his travels: the wondrous and the hideous, the beautiful and the awful, the plain and the curious. The objects were all gone, at least so far as Palin could discover. Dalamar might have stashed them in his chamber, which was also wizard-locked, but Palin doubted it. He had the impression that if he entered Dalamar's living quarters he would find them as bare and empty as the rest of the dark and silent rooms in the Tower. These things were part of the past. Either they had been broken in the cataclysmic upheaval of the Tower's move from Palanthas, or their owner had cast them off in pain and in anger. Palin guessed the latter.

He recalled very well when he had heard the news that Dalamar had destroyed the Tower, rather than permit the great blue dragon Khellendros to seize control of it. The citizens of Palanthas woke to a thundering blast that shook houses, cracked streets, broke windows. At first, the people thought they were under attack by dragons, but after that initial shock, nothing further happened.

The next morning, they were awestruck and astonished and generally pleased to find that the Tower of High Sorcery—long considered an eyesore and a haven of evil— had disappeared. In its place was a reflecting pool where, if one looked, it was said one could see the Tower in the dark waters. Thus many began to circulate rumors that the Tower had imploded and sunk into the ground. Palin had never believed those rumors, nor, as he had discussed with his longtime friend and fellow mage Jenna, did he believe Dalamar was dead or the Tower destroyed.

Jenna had agreed with him, and if anyone would know it would be she, for she had been Dalamar's lover for many years and was the last to see him prior to his departure more than thirty years ago.

"Perhaps not so long ago as that," Palin muttered to himself, staring in frustration and simmering anger out the window. "Dalamar knew exactly where to find us. Knew where to lay his hands on us. Only one person could have told him. Only one person knew: Jenna."

He probably should be glad the powerful wizard had rescued them. Otherwise he and Tasslehoff would be sitting in the dragon Beryl's prison cell under far less propitious circumstances. Palin's feelings of gratitude toward Dalamar had effectively evaporated by now. Once he might have shaken Dalamar's hand. Now, he wanted only to wring the elf's neck.

The Tower's relocation from Palanthas to wherever it was now—Palin hadn't the vaguest idea, he could see nothing but trees around it—had brought about other changes. Palin saw several large cracks in the walls, cracks that might have alarmed him for his own safety had he not been fairly certain (or at least hoped) that Dalamar had shored up the walls with magic. The spiral staircase had always been treacherous to walk, but now was doubly so, due to the fact that some of the stairs had not survived the move. Tasslehoff climbed nimbly up and down the stairs like a squirrel, but Palin held his breath every time.

Tasslehoff—who had explored every inch of the Tower during the first hour of his arrival—reported that the entrance to one of the minarets was completely blocked off by a caved-in wall and that the other minaret was missing half the roof. The fearful Shoikan Grove that had once so effectively guarded the Tower had been left behind in Palanthas, where it stood now as a sad curiosity. The Tower was surrounded by a new grove—a grove of immense cypress trees.

Having lived among the vallenwoods all his life, Palin was accustomed to gigantic trees, but he was impressed by the cypresses. Most of the trees stood far taller than the Tower, which was dwarfed by comparison. The cypresses held their enormous green-clothed arms protectively over the Tower, shielding it from the view of roaming dragons, particularly Beryl, who would have given her fangs and her claws and her green scaly tail thrown into the bargain for knowledge of the whereabouts of the Tower that had once reigned so proudly in Palanthas.

Peering out of one of the few upper-story windows still in existence in the Tower—many others that he had remembered had been sealed up—Palin looked out upon a thick forest of cypress that rolled in undulating waves of green to the horizon. No matter what direction he looked, he saw only those spreading green boughs, an ocean of limbs and branches, leaves and shadow. No path cut through these boughs, not even an animal path, for the forest was eerily quiet. No bird sang, no squirrel scolded, no owl hooted, no dove mourned. Nothing living roamed the forest. The Tower was not a ship bobbing upon this ocean. It was submerged in the depths, lost to the sight and knowledge of those who lived in the world beyond.

The forest was the province of the dead.

One of the remaining windows was located at the very bottom of the Tower, a few feet from the massive oaken door. The window looked out upon the forest floor, a floor that was thick with shadow, for sunlight very rarely managed to penetrate through the leaves that formed a canopy above.

Amid the shadows, the souls roamed. The aspect was not a pleasant one. Yet Palin found himself fascinated, and often he would stand here, shivering in the cold, his arms folded for warmth in the sleeves of his robes, gazing out upon the restless, ever-moving, ever-shifting congregation of the dead.

He would watch until he could stand it no more, then he would turn away, his own soul riven with pity and horror, only to be drawn back again.

The dead could not enter the Tower seemingly. Palin did not sense them near him as he had felt them in the citadel. He did not feel that strange tickling sensation when he used his magic to cast spells, a sensation he had set down as gnats or bits of cobweb or a straggling strand of hair or any of a hundred other ordinary occurrences. Now he knew that what he had felt had been the hands of the dead, stealing the magic from him.

Locked up in the Tower alone with Tasslehoff, Palin guessed that it was Dalamar who had been giving the dead their orders. Dalamar had been usurping the magic. Why? What was he doing with it? Certainly, Palin thought sardonically, Dalamar was not using the magic to redecorate.

Palin might have asked him, but he could not find Dalamar. Nor could Tasslehoff, who had been recruited to help in the search. Admittedly, there were many doors in the Tower that were magically locked to both Palin and the kender—especially the kender.

Tasslehoff put his ear to these doors, but not even the kender with his sharp hearing had been able to detect any sounds coming from behind any of them, including one that led to what Palin remembered were Dalamar's private chambers.

Palin had knocked at this door, knocked and shouted, but he had received no answer. Either Dalamar was deliberately ignoring him, or he was not there. Palin had first thought the former and was angry. Now he was starting to think the latter, and he was uneasy. The notion came to his mind that he and Tas had been brought here, then abandoned, to live out their days as prisoners in this Tower, surrounded and guarded by the dead.

"No," Palin amended, talking softly to himself as he stared out the window on the lower floor, "the dead are not guards. They, too, are prisoners."

The souls clogged the shadows beneath the trees, unable to find rest, unable to find peace, wandering in aimless, constant motion. Palin could not comprehend the numbers—thousands, thousands of thousands, and thousands more beyond that. He saw no one he recognized. At first, he had hoped to find his father again, hoped that Caramon could give him some answers to the myriad questions teeming in his son's fevered mind. Palin soon came to realize that his search for one soul among the countless many was as hopeless as searching for a single grain of sand on a beach. If Caramon had been free to come to Palin, his father would surely have done so.

Palin recalled vividly now the vision he had seen of his father in the Citadel of Light. In that vision, Caramon had fought his way to his son through a mass of dead pressing around Palin. Caramon had been trying to tell his son something, but before he could make himself understood, he had been seized by some unseen force and dragged away.

"I think it's awfully sad," said Tasslehoff. He stood with his forehead pressed against the window, peering out the glass. "Look, there's a kender. And another. And another. Hullo!" Tasslehoff tapped with his hands on the window. "Hullo, there! What have you got in your pouches?"

The spirits of the dead kender ignored this customary kender greeting—a question no living kender could have resisted—and were soon lost in the crowd, disappearing among the other souls: elves, dwarves, humans, minotaurs, centaurs, goblins, hobgoblins, draconians, gully dwarves, gnomes, and other races—races Palin had never before seen but had only read about. He saw what he thought were the souls of the Theiwar, the dark dwarves, a cursed race. He saw the souls of the Dimernesti, elves who live beneath the sea and whose very existence had long been disputed. He saw souls of the Thanoi, the strange and fearsome creatures of Ice Wall.

Friend and foe were here. Goblin souls passed shoulder to shoulder with human souls. Draconian souls drifted near elven souls. Minotaur and dwarf roamed side by side. No one soul paid attention to another. One was not aware of the other or seemed to know the other existed. Each ghostly soul went on his or her way, intent upon some quest—some hopeless quest by the looks of it, for on the face of every spirit Palin saw searching and longing, dejection and despair.

"I wonder what it is they're all looking for," Tasslehoff said.

"A way out," replied Palin.

He slung over his shoulder a pack containing several loaves of the magicked bread and a waterskin. Making up his mind, not taking time to think for fear he would argue himself out of his decision, he walked to the Tower's main door.

"Where are you going?" asked Tas.

"Out," said Palin.

"Are you taking me with you?"

"Of course."

Tas looked longingly at the door, but he held back, hovering near the stairs. "We're not going back to the citadel to look for the Device of Time Journeying, are we?"

"What's left of it?" Palin returned bitterly. "If any of it remained undamaged, which I doubt, the bits and pieces were probably picked up by Beryl's draconians and are now in her possession."

"That's good," Tas said, heaving a relieved sigh. Absorbed in arranging his pouches for the journey, he missed Palin's withering glare. "Very well, I'll go along. The Tower was an extremely interesting place to visit, and I'm glad we came here, but it does get boring after awhile. Where do you suppose Dalamar is? Why did he bring us here and then disappear?"

"To flaunt his power over me," said Palin, coming to stand in front of the door. "He imagines that I am finished. He wants to break my spirit, force me to grovel to him, beg him to release me. He will find that he has caught a shark in his net, not a minnow. I had once thought he might be of some help to us, but no more. I will not be a pawn in his khas game."

Palin looked very hard at the kender. "You don't have any magical objects on you? Nothing you've discovered here in the Tower?"

"No, Palin," said Tas with round-eyed innocence. "I haven't discovered anything. Like I said, it's been pretty boring."

Palin persisted. "Nothing you've found that you are intending to return to Dalamar, for example? Nothing that fell into your pouches when you weren't looking? Nothing that you picked up so that someone wouldn't trip over it?"

"Well . . ." Tas scratched his head. "Maybe . . ."

"This is very important, Tas," Palin said, his tone serious. He cast a glance out the window. "You see the dead out there? If we have anything magic, they will try to take it from us. Look, I have removed all my rings and my earring that Jenna gave me. I have left behind my pouches of spell components. Just to be safe, why don't you leave your pouches here, as well? Dalamar will take good care of them," he added in reassuring tones, for Tas was clutching his pouches next to his body and staring at him in horror.

"Leave my pouches?" Tas protested in agony. Palin might as well have asked the kender to leave his head or his topknot. "Will we come back for them?"

"Yes," said Palin. Lies told to a kender are not really lies, more akin to self-defense.

"I guess . . . in that case . . . since it is important . . . " Tas removed his pouches, gave each of them a fond, parting pat, then stowed them safely in a dark corner beneath the stair. "I hope no one steals them."

"I don't think that's likely. Stand over there by the stairs, Tas, where you will be out of the way, and do not interrupt me. I'm going to cast a spell. Alert me if you see anyone coming."

"I'm the rear guard? You're posting me as rear guard?" Tas was captivated and immediately forgot about the pouches. "No one ever posted me as rear guard before! Not even Tanis."

"Yes, you're the . . . er . . . rear guard. You must keep careful watch, and not bother me, no matter what you hear or see me doing."

"Yes, Palin. I will," Tasslehoff promised solemnly, and took up his position. He came bouncing back again. "Excuse me, Palin, but since we're alone here, who is it I'm supposed to be rear-guarding against?"

Palin counseled patience to himself, then said, "If, for example, the wizard-lock includes magical guards, casting a counterspell on the lock might cause these guardians to appear."

Tas sucked in a breath. "Do you mean like skeletons and wraiths and liches? Oh, I hope so—that is, no I don't," he amended quickly, catching sight of Palin's baleful expression. "I'll keep watch. I promise."

Tas retreated back to his post, but just as Palin was calling the words to the spell to his mind, he felt a tug on his sleeve.

"Yes, Tas?" Palin fought the temptation to toss the kender out the window. "What is it now?"

"Is it because you're afraid of the wraiths and liches that you haven't tried to escape before this?"

"No, Tas," said Palin quietly. "It was because I was afraid of myself."

Tas considered this. "I don't think I can rear guard you against yourself, Palin."

"You can't, Tas," Palin said. "Now return to your post."

Palin figured that he had about fifteen seconds of peace before the novelty of being rear guard wore off and Tasslehoff would again be pestering him. Approaching the door, he closed his eyes and extended his hands.

He did not touch the door. He touched the magic that enchanted the door. His broken fingers . . . He remembered a time they had been long and delicate and supple. He felt for the magic, groped for it like a blind man. Sensing a tingling in his fingertips, his soul thrilled. He had found a thread of magic. He smoothed the thread and found another thread and another until the spell rippled beneath his touch. The fabric of the magic was smooth and sheer, a piece of cloth cut from a bolt and hung over the door.

The spell was not simple, but it was certainly not that complex. One of his better students could have undone this spell. Palin's anger increased. Now his pride was hurt.

"You always did underestimate me," Palin muttered to the absent Dalamar. He plucked a thread, and the fabric of magic came apart in his hands.

The door swung open.

Cool air, crisp with the sharp smell of the cypress, breathed into the Tower, as one might try to breathe life through the lips of a drowned man. The souls in the shadows of the trees ceased their aimless roaming, and hundreds turned as one to stare with their shadowed eyes at the Tower. None moved toward it. None made any attempt to approach it. They hung, wavering, in the whispering air.

"I will use no magic," Palin told them. "I have only food in my pack, food and water. You will leave me alone." He motioned to Tas, an unnecessary gesture, since the kender was now dancing at his side. "Keep near me, Tas. This is no time to go off exploring. We must not get separated."

"I know," said Tas excitedly. "I'm still the rear guard. Where is it we're going, exactly?"

Palin looked out the door. Years ago, there had been stone stairs, a courtyard. Now his first step out of the Tower of High Sorcery would fall onto a bed of brown, dead cypress needles that surrounded the Tower like a dry moat. The cypress trees formed a wall around the brown moat, their branches serving as a canopy under which they would walk. Standing in the shadows of the trees, watching, were the souls of the dead.

"We're going to find a path, a trail. Anything to lead us out of this forest," Palin said.

Thrusting his hands in the sleeves of his robes, to emphasize the fact that he was not going to use them, he strode out the door and headed straight for the tree line. Tas followed after, discharging his role as rear guard by attempting to look backward while walking forward, a feat of agility that apparently took some practice, for Tas was having a difficult time of it.

"Stop that!" said Palin through clenched teeth the second time Tasslehoff bumbled into him. They were nearing the tree line. Palin removed his hand from his sleeve long enough to grasp Tas by the shoulder and forcibly turn him around. "Face forward."

"But I'm the rear—" Tas protested. He interrupted himself. "Oh, I see. It's what's in front of us you're worried about."

The dead had no bodies. These they had left behind, abandoning the shells of cold flesh as butterflies leave the cocoon. Once, like butterflies, these spirits might have flown free to whatever new destination awaited them. Now they were trapped as in an enormous jar, constrained to wander aimlessly, searching for the way out.

So many souls. A river of souls, swirling about the boles of the cypress trees, each one a drop of water in a mighty torrent. Palin could barely distinguish one from another. Faces flitted past, hands or arms or hair trailing like diaphanous silken scarves. The faces were the most terrible, for they all looked at him with a hunger that caused him to hesitate, his steps to slow. Whispered breath that he had mistaken for the wind touched his cheek. He heard words in the whispers and shivered.

The magic, they said. *Give us the magic.* They looked at him. They paid no attention to the kender. Tasslehoff was saying something. Palin could see his mouth moving and almost hear the words, but he couldn't hear. It was as if his ears were stuffed with the whispers of the dead.

"I have nothing to give you," he told the souls. His own voice sounded muffled and faraway. "I have no magical artifacts. Let us pass."

He came to the tree line. The whispering souls were a white, frothing pool among the shadows of the trees. He had hoped that the souls would part before him, like the early morning fog lifting from the valleys, but they remained, blocking his way. He could see dimly through them, see more trees with the eerie white mist of souls wavering beneath. He was reminded of the hordes of mendicants that crowded the streets of Palanthas, grimy hands outstretched, shrill voices begging.

He halted, cast a glance back at the Tower of High Sorcery, saw a broken, crumbling ruin. He faced forward.

They did not harm you in the past, he reminded himself. You know their touch. It is unpleasant but no worse than walking into a cobweb. If you go back there, you will never leave. Not until you are one of them.

He walked into the river of souls.

Chill, pale hands touched his hands, his arms. Chill, pale eyes stared at him. Chill, pale lips pressed against his lips, sucked the breath from him. He could not move for the swirling souls that had hold of him and were dragging him under. He could hear nothing except the whispered roar of their terrible voices. He turned, trying to find the way back, but all he saw were eyes, mouths, and hands. He turned and turned again, and now he was disoriented and confused, and there were more of them and still more.

He couldn't breathe, he couldn't speak, he couldn't cry out. He fell to the ground, gasping for air. They rose and ebbed around him, touching, pulling, yanking. He was shredded, torn asunder. They searched through the fibers of his being.

Magic . . . magic . . . give us the magic. . . .

He slipped beneath the awful surface and ceased to struggle.

Tasslehoff saw Palin walk into the shadows of the trees, but the kender did not immediately follow after him. Instead he attempted to gain the attention of several dead kender, who were standing beneath the trees, watching Palin.

"I say," said Tas very loudly, over the sound of buzzing in his ears, a sound that was starting to be annoying, "have you seen my friend, Caramon? He's one of you."

Tas had been about to tell them that Caramon was dead, like them, but he refrained, thinking that it might make them sad to be reminded of the fact.

"He's a really big human, and the last time I saw him alive he was very old, but now that he's dead—no offense—he looks young again. He has curly hair and a very friendly smile."

No use. The kender refused to pay the least bit of attention to him.

"I hate to tell you this, but you are extremely rude," Tas told the kender as he walked past. He might as well follow Palin, since no one was going to talk to him. "One would think you'd been raised by humans. You must not be from Kendermore. No Kendermore kender would act that— Now that's odd. Where did he go?"

Tas searched the forest ahead of him as well as he could, considering the poor ghosts, who were whirling about in a frenetic manner, enough to make a fellow dizzy.

"Palin! Where are you? I'm supposed to be the rear guard, and I can't be the rear guard if you're not in front."

He waited a bit to see if Palin answered his call, but if the sorcerer did, Tas probably wouldn't be able to hear it over the buzzing that was starting to give him a pain in the head. Putting his fingers in his ears to try to shut out the sound, Tas turned to look behind him, thinking that perhaps Palin had forgotten something and gone back to the Tower to fetch it. Tas could see the Tower, looking small beneath the cypress trees, but no sign of Palin.

"Drat it!" Tas took his fingers out of his ears to wave his hands, trying to disperse the dead who were really making a most frightful nuisance of themselves. "Get out of here. I can't see a thing. Palin!"

It was like walking through a thick fog, only worse, because fog didn't look at you with pleading eyes or try to grab hold of you with wispy hands. Tasslehoff groped his way forward. Tripping over something, probably a tree root, he fell headlong on the forest floor. Whatever he had fallen over jerked beneath his legs. It's not a tree root, he thought, or if it is, the root belongs to one of the more lively varieties of tree.

Tas recognized Palin's robes, and after a moment more, he recognized Palin. He hovered over his friend in consternation.

Palin's face was exceedingly white, more white than the spirits surrounding him. His eyes were closed. He gasped for air. One hand clutched at this throat, the other clawed at the dirt.

"Get away, you! Go! Leave him alone," Tas cried, endeavoring to drive away the dead souls, who seemed to be wrapping themselves around Palin like some evil web. "Stop it!" the kender shouted, jumping up and stamping his foot. He was starting to grow desperate. "You're killing him!"

The buzzing sound grew louder, as if hornets were flying into his ears and using his head for a hive. The sound was so awful that Tasslehoff couldn't think, but he realized he didn't have to think. He only had to rescue Palin before the dead turned him into one of themselves.

Tas glanced behind him again to get his bearings. He could see the Tower or catch glimpses of it, at any rate, through the ever-shifting mist of the souls. Running around to Palin's head, Tas took hold of the man by the shoulders. The kender dug his heels into the ground and gave a grunt and a heave. Palin was not large as humans went—Tas envisioned himself trying to drag Caramon—but he was a full-grown man and deadweight, at this point more dead than alive. Tas was a kender and an older kender at that. He dragged Palin over the rough, needle-strewn ground and managed to move him a couple of feet before he had to drop him and stop to catch his breath.

The dead did not try to stop Tas, but the buzzing noise grew so loud that he had to grit his teeth against it. He picked up Palin again, glanced behind once more to reassure himself that the Tower was still where he thought it was, and gave another tug. He pulled and panted and floundered, but he never lost his grip on Palin. With a final great heave that caused his feet to slip out from under him, he dragged Palin out of the forest onto the bed of brown needles that surrounded the Tower.

213

Keeping a wary eye on the dead, who hovered in the dark shadows beneath the trees, watching, waiting, Tas crawled around on all fours to look anxiously at his friend.

Palin no longer gasped for air. He gulped it down thankfully. His eyes blinked a few times, then opened wide with a look that was wild and terrified. He sat up suddenly with a cry, thrusting out his arms.

"It's all right, Palin!" Tas grabbed hold of one of Palin's flailing hands and clutching it tightly. "You're safe. At least I think you're safe. There seems to be some sort of barrier they can't cross."

Palin glanced over at the souls writhing in the darkness. Shuddering, he averted his gaze, looked back at the door to the Tower. His expression grew grim, he stood up, brushing brown needles from his robes.

"I saved your life, Palin," Tas said. "You might have died out there."

"Yes, Tas, I might have," Palin said. "Thank you." Stopping, he looked down at the kender, and his grim expression softened. He put a hand on Tas's shoulder. "Thank you very much."

He glanced again at the Tower, and the grimness returned. A frown caused the lines on his face to turn dark and jagged. He continued to stare fixedly at the Tower and, after drawing in a few more deep breaths, he walked toward it. He was very pale, almost paler than when he had been dying, and he looked extremely determined. As determined as Tas had ever seen anyone.

"Where are you going now?" Tas asked, game for another adventure, although he wouldn't have minded a brief rest.

"To find Dalamar."

"But we've looked and looked—"

"No, we haven't," Palin said. He was angry now, and he intended to act before his anger cooled. "Dalamar has no right to do this! He has no right to imprison these wretched souls."

Sweeping through the Tower door, Palin began to climb the spiral staircase that led into the upper levels of the building. He kept close to the wall that was on his right, for the stairs had no railing on his left. A misstep would send him plummeting down into darkness.

"Are we going to free them?" Tas asked, clambering up the staircase behind Palin. "Even after they tried to kill you?"

"They didn't mean to," Palin said. "They can't help themselves. They are being driven to seek out the magic. I know now who is behind it, and I intend to stop him."

"How will we do that?" Tas asked eagerly. Palin hadn't exactly included him in this adventure, but that was probably an oversight. "Stop him, I mean? We don't even know where he is."

"I'll stop him if I have to tear this Tower down stone by stone," was all Palin would say.

A long and perilous climb up the spiral staircase through the near darkness brought them to a door.

"I already tried this," Tas announced. Examining it, he gave it an experimental shove. "It won't budge."

"Oh, yes, it will," said Palin.

He raised his hands and spoke a word. Blue light began to glow, flames crackled from his fingers. He drew a breath and reached out toward the door. The flames burned brighter.

Suddenly, silently, the door swung open.

"Stop, Tas!" Palin ordered, as the kender was about to bound inside.

"But you opened it," Tas protested.

"No," said Palin, and his voice was harsh. The blue flames had died away. "No, I didn't."

He took a step forward, staring intently into the room. The few rays of sunlight that managed to struggle through the heavy, overhanging boughs of the cypress trees had to work to penetrate the years of silt and mud that covered the windows outside and the layer of dust that caked the inside. No sound came from within.

"You stay out in the hall, Tas."

"Do you want me to be rear guard again?" Tas asked.

"Yes, Tas," said Palin quietly. He took another step forward. His head cocked, he was listening for the slightest sound. He moved slowly into the room. "You be the rear guard. Let me know if you see anything coming."

"Like a wraith or a ghoul? Sure, Palin."

Tas stood in the hall, hopping from one foot to the other, trying to see what was happening in the room.

"Rear guard is a really important assignment," Tasslehoff reminded himself, fidgeting, unable to hear or see anything. "Sturm was always rear guard. Or Caramon. I never got to be rear guard because Tanis said kender don't make good rear guards, mainly because they never stay in the rear—

"Don't worry! I'm coming, Palin!" Tas called, giving up. He dashed into the room. "Nothing's sneaking up behind us. Our rears are safe. Oh!"

Tas came to a halt. He didn't have much choice in the matter. Palin's hand had a good, strong hold on his shoulder.

The room's interior was gray and chill, and even on the warmest, brightest summer day would always be gray and chill. The wintry light illuminated shelves containing innumerable books. Next to these were the scroll repositories, like honeycombs, a few filled, but most empty. Wooden chests stood on the floor, their ornate carvings almost obliterated by dust. The heavy curtains that covered the windows, the once-beautiful rugs on the floors, were dust-covered, the fabric rotting and frayed.

At the far end of the room was a desk. Someone was sitting behind the desk. Tas squinted, tried to see in the dim, gray light. The someone was an elf, with long, lank hair that had once been black but now had a gray, jagged streak that ran from the forehead back.

"Who's that?" he asked in a loud whisper.

The elf sat perfectly still. Tas, thinking he was asleep, didn't want to wake him.

"Dalamar," said Palin.

"Dalamar!" Tas repeated, stunned. He twisted his head to look up at Palin, thinking this might be a joke. If it was, Palin wasn't laughing. "But that can't be right! He's not here. I know because I banged on the door and shouted 'Dalamar' real loud, like that, and no one answered."

"Dalamar!" Tas raised his voice. "Hullo! Where have you been?"

"He can't hear, Tas," Palin said. "He can't see you or hear you."

Dalamar sat behind his desk, his thin hands folded before him, his eyes staring straight ahead. He had not moved as they entered. His eyes did not shift, as they surely must have, at the sound of the kender's shrill voice. His hands did not stir, his fingers did not twitch.

"Maybe he's dead," Tas said, a funny feeling squirming in his stomach. "He certainly looks dead, doesn't he, Palin?"

The elf sat unmoving in the chair.

"No," said Palin. "He is not dead."

"It's a funny way to take a nap, then," Tas remarked. "Sitting straight up. Maybe if I pinched him—"

"Don't touch him!" Palin warned sharply. "He is in stasis."

"I know where that is," Tas stated. "It's north of Flotsam, about fifty miles. But he's not in Stasis, Palin. He's right here."

217

The elf's eyes, which had been open and unseeing, suddenly closed. They remained closed for a long, long time. He was coming back from the stasis, back from the enchantment that had taken his spirit out into the world, leaving his body behind. He drew air in through his nose, keeping his lips pressed tightly shut. His fingers curled, and he winced, as if in pain. He curled them and uncurled them and began to rub them.

"The circulation stops," Dalamar said, opening his eyes and looking at Palin. "It is quite painful."

"My heart bleeds for you," said Palin.

Dalamar's gaze went to Palin's own broken, twisted fingers. He said nothing, continued to rub his hands.

"Hullo, Dalamar!" Tas said cheerfully, glad for a chance to be included in the conversation. "It's nice to see you again. Did I tell you how much you have changed from the time I saw you at Caramon's first funeral? Do you want to hear about it? I made a really good speech, and then it began to rain and everyone was already sad, and that made it sadder, but then you cast a magic spell, a wonderful spell that made the raindrops sparkle and the sky was filled with rainbows—"

"No!" Dalamar said, making a sharp, cutting motion with his hand.

Tas was about to go on to the other parts of the funeral, since Dalamar didn't want to talk about the rainbows, but the elf gave him a peculiar look, raised his hand, and pointed.

Perhaps I'm going to Stasis, Tas thought, and that was the last conscious thought he had for a good, long while.

16

A Bored Kender

alin placed the comatose kender in one of the
shabby, dust-covered and mildewed chairs
that stood at the far end of the library, a portion
that was in shadow. Affecting to be settling Tas, Palin took
the opportunity to look closely at Dalamar, who remained
seated behind the desk, his head bowed into his hands.

Palin had seen the elf only briefly on first arriving. He
had been shocked then at the ruinous alteration in the features of the once handsome and vain elven wizard: the
gray-streaked black hair, the wasted features, the thin
hands with their branching blue veins like rivers drawn
on a map, rivers of blood, rivers of souls. And this, their
master . . . Master of the Tower.

Struck by a new thought, Palin walked over to the
window and looked down into the forest below, where
the dead flowed still and silent among the boles of the
cypress trees.

"The wizard-lock on the door below," Palin said
abruptly. "It was not meant to keep us in, was it?"

No answer came from Dalamar. Palin was left to answer himself. "It was meant to keep them out. If that is true, you might want to replace it."

Dalamar, a grim look on his face, left the room. He returned long moments later. Palin had not moved. Dalamar came to stand beside him, looked into the mist of swirling souls.

"They gather around you," Dalamar said softly. "Their grave-cold hands clasp you. Their ice lips press against your flesh. Their chill arms embrace you, dead fingers clutch at you. You know!"

"Yes," said Palin. "I know." He shook off the remembered horror. "You can't leave, either."

"My body cannot leave," Dalamar corrected. "My spirit is free to roam. When I depart, I must always come back." He shrugged. "What is it the *Shalafi* used to say? 'Even wizards must suffer.' There is always a price." Dalamar lowered his gaze to Palin's broken fingers. "Isn't there?"

Palin thrust his hands into the sleeves of his robes. "Where has your spirit been?"

"Traveling Ansalon, investigating this fantastical time-traveling story of yours," Dalamar replied.

"Story? *I* told you no story," Palin returned crisply. "I haven't spoken one word to you. You've been to see Jenna. *She* was the one who told you. And she said that she hadn't seen you in years."

"She did not lie, Majere, if that's what you're insinuating, although I admit she did not tell you all the truth. She has not *seen* me, at least not my physical form. She has heard my voice, and that only recently. I arranged a meeting with her after the strange storm that swept over all Ansalon in a single night."

"I asked her if she knew where to find you."

"Again, she told you the truth. She does *not* know where to find me. I did not tell her. She has never been here. No one has been here. You are the first, and believe me"—Dalamar's brows constricted—"if you had not been in such dire straits, you would not be here now. I do not pine for company," he added with a dark glance.

Palin was silent, uncertain whether to believe him or not.

"For mercy's sake, don't sulk, Majere," Dalamar said, willfully misinterpreting Palin's silence. "It's undignified for a man of your age. How old are you anyway? Sixty, seventy, a hundred? I can never tell with humans. You look ancient enough to me. As for Jenna 'betraying' your confidence, it is well for you and the kender that she did, else I would have not taken an interest in you, and you would now be in Beryl's tender care."

"Do not try to taunt me by remarking on the fact that I am old," Palin said calmly. "I know I have aged. The process is natural in humans. In elves, it is not. Look in a mirror, Dalamar. If the years have taken a toll on me, they have taken a far more terrible toll on you. As for pride"—Palin shrugged in his turn—"I lost that a long time ago. It is hard to remain proud when you can no longer summon magic enough to heat my morning tea. I think you have reason to know that."

"Perhaps I do," Dalamar replied. "I know that I have changed. The battle I fought with Chaos stole hundreds of years from me, yet I could live with that. I was victorious, after all. Victor and loser, all at the same time. I won the war and was defeated by what came after. The loss of the magic.

"I risked my life for the sake of the magic," Dalamar continued, his voice low and hollow. "I would have given my life for the sake of the magic. What happened? The magic departed. The gods left. They left me bereft, powerless, helpless. They left me—ordinary!"

Dalamar breathed shallowly. "All that I gave up for the magic—my homeland, my nation, my people . . . I

used to consider I had made a fair trade. My sacrifice—
and it was a wrenching sacrifice, though only another elf
would understand—had been rewarded. But the reward
was gone, and I was left with nothing. Nothing. And
everyone knew it.

"It was then I began to hear rumors—rumors that Khellendros the Blue was going to seize my Tower, rumors that
the Dark Knights were going to attack it. My Tower!" Dalamar gave a vicious snarl. His thin fist clenched. Then, his
hand relaxed, and he gave a grating laugh.

"I tell you, Majere, gully dwarves could have taken
over my Tower, and I could have done nothing to stop
them. I had once been the most powerful wizard in
Ansalon, and now, as you said, I could not so much as
boil water."

"You were not alone." Palin was unsympathetic. "All
of us were affected the same way."

"No, you weren't," Dalamar retorted passionately.
"You could not be. You had not sacrificed as I had sacrificed. You had your father and mother. You had a wife
and children."

"Jenna loved you—" Palin began.

"Did she?" Dalamar grimaced. "Sometimes I think
we only used each other. She could not understand me
either. She was like you, with her damnable human hope
and optimism. Why are you humans like that? Why do
you go on hoping when it is obvious that all hope is lost?
I could not stomach her platitudes. We quarreled. She
left, and I was glad to see her leave. I had no need of her.
I had no need of anyone. It was up to me to protect my
Tower from those great, bloated wyrms, and I did what I
had to do. The only way to save the Tower was to appear
to destroy it. And I did so. My plan worked. No one
knows the Tower is here. No one will, unless I want it to
be found."

"Moving the Tower must have taken an immense amount of magical power—a bit more than would be required to boil water," Palin observed. "You must have had some of the old magic left to you."

"No, I assure you, I did not," Dalamar said, his passion cooling. "I was as barren as you."

He gave Palin a sharp and meaningful glance. "Like you, I understood magic was in the world, if one knew where to look for it."

Palin avoided Dalamar's intense gaze. "I do not know what you're implying. I discovered the wild magic—"

"Not alone. You had help. I know, because I had the same help. A strange personage known as the Shadow Sorcerer."

"Yes!" Palin was astonished. "Hooded and cloaked in gray. A voice that was as soft as shadow, might have belonged to either man or woman."

"You never saw a face—"

"But I did," Palin protested. "In that last terrible battle, I saw she was a woman. She was an agent of the dragon Malystryx—"

"Indeed?" Dalamar lifted an eyebrow. "In my last 'terrible' battle, I saw that the Shadow Sorcerer was a man, an agent for the dragon Khellendros who, according to my sources, had supposedly left this world in search of the soul of his late master, that demon-witch Kitiara."

"The Shadow Sorcerer taught you wild magic?"

"No," Dalamar replied. "The Shadow Sorcerer taught me death magic. Necromancy."

Palin looked back out the window to the roaming spirits. He looked around the shabby room with its books of magic that were so many ghosts, lined up on the shelves. He looked at the elf, who was thin and wasted, like a gnawed bone. "What went wrong?" he asked at last.

"I was duped," Dalamar returned. "I was given to believe I was master of the dead. Too late, I discovered I was not the master. I was the prisoner. A prisoner of my own ambition, my own lust for power.

"It is not easy for me to say these things about myself, Majere," Dalamar added. "It is especially hard for me to say them to you, the darling child of magic. Oh, yes. I knew. You were the gifted one, beloved of Solinari, beloved of your Uncle Raistlin. You would have been one of the great archmages of all time. I saw that. Was I jealous? A little. More than a little. Especially of Raistlin's care for you. You wouldn't think I would want that, would you? That I would hunger for his approval, his notice. But I did."

"All this time," said Palin, his gaze returning to the trapped souls, "I have been jealous of you."

"The silence of the empty Tower twined around them.

"I wanted to talk to you," Palin said at last, almost loathe to break that binding silence. "To ask you about the Device of Time Journeying—"

"Rather late for that now," Dalamar interrupted, his tone caustic. "Since you destroyed it."

"I did what I had to do," Palin returned, stating it as fact, not apology. "I had to save Tasslehoff. If he dies in a time that is not his own, our time and all in it will end."

"Good riddance." Dalamar gave a wave of his hand, walked back to his desk. He walked slowly, his shoulders stooped and rounded. "Oblivion would be welcome."

"If you truly thought that you would be dead by now," Palin returned.

"No," said Dalamar, stopping to glance out another window. "No, I said oblivion. Not death." He returned to his desk, sank down into the chair. "*You* could leave. You have the magical earring that would carry you through the portals of magic back to your home. The earring will work here. The dead cannot interfere."

"The magic wouldn't carry Tasslehoff," Palin pointed out, "and I won't leave without him."

Dalamar regarded the slumbering kender with a speculative, thoughtful gaze. "He is not the key," he said musingly, "but perhaps he is the picklock."

Tasslehoff was bored.

Everyone on Krynn either knows, or should know, how dangerous a bored kender can be. Palin and Dalamar both knew, but unfortunately they both forgot. Their combined memory lapse is perhaps understandable, given their preoccupation with trying to find the answers to their innumerable questions. What was worse, not only did they forget that a bored kender is a dangerous kender, they forgot the kender completely. And that is well nigh inexcusable.

The reunion of these old friends had gotten off to a pretty good start, at least as far as Tas was concerned. He had been awakened from his unexpected nap in order to explain his role in the important events that had transpired of late. Perching on the edge of Dalamar's desk and kicking his heels against the wood—until Dalamar curtly told him to stop—Tasslehoff gleefully joined in the conversation.

He found this entertaining for a time. Palin described their visit to Laurana in Qualinesti, his discovery that Tasslehoff was really Tasslehoff and the revelation about the Device of Time Journeying, and his subsequent decision to travel back in time to try to find the other time Tasslehoff had told him about. Since Tasslehoff had been intimately involved in all this, he was called upon to provide certain details, which he was happy to do.

He would have been more happy had he been allowed to tell his complete tale without interruption, but Dalamar said he didn't have time to hear it. Having always been told when he was a small kender that one can't have everything (he had always wondered why one couldn't have everything but had at last arrived at the conclusion that his pouches weren't big enough to hold it all), Tas had to be content with telling the abbreviated version.

After he had described how he had come to Caramon's first funeral and found Dalamar head of the Black Robes, Palin head of the White Robes, and Silvanoshei king of the united elven nations, and the world mostly at peace and there were no—repeat—*no* humungous dragons running about killing kender in Kendermore, Tasslehoff was told that his observations were no longer required. In other words, he was supposed to go sit in a chair, keep still, and answer questions only when he was asked.

Going back to the chair that stood in a shadowy corner, Tasslehoff listened to Palin telling about how he had used the Device of Time Journeying to go back into the past, only to find that there wasn't a past. That was interesting, because Tasslehoff had been there to see that happen, and he could have provided eyewitness testimony if anyone had asked him, which no one did. When he volunteered, he was told to be quiet.

Then came the part where Palin said how the one thing he knew for a fact was that Tasslehoff should have died by being squished by Chaos and that Tasslehoff had not died, thus implying that everything from humungous dragons to the lost gods was all Tasslehoff's fault.

Palin described how he—Palin—had told him—Tasslehoff—that he had to use the Device of Time Journeying to return to die and that Tasslehoff had most strongly and—logically, Tas felt compelled to point out—refused to do this. Palin related how Tasslehoff had fled to the citadel to seek Goldmoon's protection by telling Goldmoon that Palin was trying to murder him. How Palin had arrived to say that, no, he was not and found Gold-moon growing younger, not older. That caused the conversation to take a bit of a detour, but they soon—too soon, as far as Tas was concerned—returned to the main highway.

Palin told Dalamar that Tasslehoff had finally come to the conclusion that going back in time was the only honorable thing to do—and here Palin most generously praised the kender for his courage. Then Palin explained that before Tas could go back, the dead had broken the Device of Time Journeying and they had been attacked by draconians. Palin had been forced to use the pieces of the device to fend off the draconians, and now pieces of the device were scattered over most of the Hedge Maze, and how were they going to send the kender back to die?

Tasslehoff rose to present the novel idea that perhaps the kender should *not* be sent back to die, but at this juncture Dalamar fixed Tas with a cold eye and said that in his opinion the most important thing they could do to help save the world, short of slaying the humungous dragons, was to send Tasslehoff back to die and that they would have to figure out some way to do it without the Device of Time Journeying.

Dalamar and Palin began snatching books from the shelves, paging through them, muttering and mumbling about rivers of time and Graygems and kender jumping in and mucking things up and a lot of other mind-numbing stuff. Dalamar magicked up a fire in the large fireplace, and the room that had been cold and dank, grew warm and stuffy, smelling of vellum, mildew, lamp oil, and dead roses. Since there was no longer anything of interest to see or hear, Tasslehoff's eyes decided to close. His ears agreed with his eyes, and his mind agreed with his ears, and all of them took another brief nap, this one of his own choosing.

Tas woke to something poking him uncomfortably in the posterior. His nap had apparently not been as brief as he thought, for it was dark outside the window—so dark that the darkness had overflowed from outside and was now inside. Tasslehoff could not see a thing. Not himself, not Dalamar, and not Palin.

Tasslehoff squirmed about in the chair in order to stop whatever was sticking him in a tender region from sticking him. It was then, after he woke up a bit, that he realized the reason he couldn't see either Palin or Dalamar was that they were no longer in the room. Or, if they were, they were playing at hide and seek, and while that was a charming and amusing game, the two of them didn't seem the type to go in for it.

Leaving his chair, Tasslehoff fumbled his way to Dalamar's desk, where he found the oil lamp. A few embers remained in the fireplace. Tas felt about on the desk until he discovered some paper. Hoping that the paper didn't have a magic spell written on it or if did, it was a spell that Dalamar didn't want anymore, Tas stuck the end of the paper in the fireplace, lit it, and lit the oil lamp.

Now that he could see, he reached into his back pocket to find out what had been poking him. Taking out the offending object, he held it to the oil lamp.

"Uh, oh!" Tas exclaimed.

"Oh, no!" he cried.

"How did *you* get here?" he wailed.

The thing that had been poking him was the chain from the Device of Time Journeying. Tas threw it onto the desk and reached back into his pocket. He pulled out another piece of the device, then another and another. He pulled out all the jewels, one by one. Spreading the pieces on the desk, he gazed at them sadly. He might have actually shaken his fist at them, but such a gesture would not have been worthy of a Hero of the Lance, and so we will say here that he did not.

As a Hero of the Lance, Tas knew what he should do. He should gather up all the pieces of the device in his handkerchief (make that Palin's handkerchief) take them straightway to wherever Palin and Dalamar were, and hand them over and say, quite bravely, that he was prepared to go back and die for the world. That would be a Noble Deed, and Tasslehoff had been ready once before to do a Noble Deed. But one had to be in the proper mood for being Noble, and Tas discovered he wasn't in that mood at all. He supposed that one also had to be in the proper mood to be stepped on by a giant, and he wasn't in that particular mood either. After seeing the dead people roaming about aimlessly outside—especially the dead kender, who didn't even care what they had in their pouches—Tasslehoff was in the mood to live and go on living.

He knew this was not likely to happen if Dalamar and Palin discovered that he had the magical device in his pocket, even if it was broken. Fearing that any moment Palin and Dalamar might remember they'd left him here and come back to check on him or offer him dinner, Tasslehoff hurriedly gathered up the pieces of the magical device, wrapped them in the handkerchief, and stuffed them in one of his pouches.

That was the easy part. Now came the hard part.

Far from being Noble, he was going to be Ignoble. He thought that was the right word. He was going to Escape.

Leaving by the front door was out. He had tried the windows already, and they were no help. You couldn't even break them by heaving a rock through the glass like you could an ordinary, respectable window. Tas had heaved, and the rock had bounced off and landed on his foot, smashing his toes.

"I have to consider this logically," Tas said to himself. It may be noted as a historical fact that this was the only time a kender ever said such a thing and only goes to show how truly dire was the situation in which he found himself. "Palin got out, but he's a wizard, and he had to use magic to do it. However, using logic, I say to myself— if nothing but a wizard can get out can anything other than a wizard get in? If so, what and how?"

Tas thought this over. While he thought, he watched the embers glow in the fireplace. Suddenly he let out a cry and immediately clapped his hand over his mouth, afraid that Palin and Dalamar would hear and remember him.

"I've got it!" he whispered. "Something does get in! Air gets in! And it goes out, too. And where it goes, I can go."

Tasslehoff kicked and stomped on the embers until they went out. Picking up the oil lamp, he walked into the fireplace and took a look around. It was a large fire-place, and he didn't have to stoop all that much to get inside. Holding the lamp high, he peered up into the darkness. He was almost immediately forced to lower his head and blink quite frantically until he dislodged the soot that had fallen into his eyes. Once he could see again, he was rewarded by a lovely sight—the wall of the chimney was not smooth. Instead it was nubbly, wonderfully nubbly, with the ends and fronts and sides of large stones sticking out every which way.

"Why, I could climb up that wall with one leg tied behind my back," Tasslehoff exclaimed.

This not being something he did on a regular basis, he decided that it would be far more efficient to use two legs. He couldn't very well climb and hang onto the oil lamp, so he left that on the desk, thoughtfully blowing out the flame first so that he wouldn't set anything on fire. Entering the chimney, he found a good foot- and handhold right off and began his climb.

He had gone only a short distance—moving slowly because he had to feel his way in the darkness and pausing occasionally to wipe gunk out of his eyes—when he heard voices coming from below. Tasslehoff froze, clinging like a spider to the wall of the chimney, afraid to move lest he send a shower of soot raining down into the fireplace. He did think, rather resentfully, that Dalamar might at least have spent some magic on a chimney sweep.

The voices were raised and heated.

"I tell you, Majere, your story makes no sense! From all we have read, you should have seen the past flow by you like a great river. In my opinion, you simply miscast the spell."

"And I tell you, Dalamar, that while I may not have your vaunted power in magic, I did *not* miscast the spell. The past was not there, and it all goes wrong at the very moment Tasslehoff was supposed to die."

"From what we have read in Raistlin's journal, the death of the kender should be a drop in time's vast river and should not affect time one way or the other."

"For the fourteenth time the fact that Chaos was involved alters matters completely. The kender's death becomes vitally important. What of this future he says he visited? A future in which everything is different?"

"Bah! You are gullible, Majere! The kender is a liar. He made it all up. Where is that blasted scroll? That should explain everything. I know it is here somewhere. Look over there in that cabinet."

Tasslehoff was understandably annoyed to hear himself referred to as a liar. He considered dropping down and giving Dalamar and Palin both a piece of his mind but reflected that, if he did so, it would be difficult to explain why exactly he'd gone up the chimney in the first place. He kept quiet.

"It would help if I knew what I was looking for."

"A scroll! I suppose you know a scroll when you see one."

"Just find the damn thing!" Tasslehoff muttered. He was growing quite weary of hanging onto the wall. His hands were starting to ache, and his legs to quiver, and he feared he wasn't going to be able to hold on much longer.

"I know what a scroll looks like, but—" A pause. "Speaking of Tasslehoff, where is he? Do you know?"

"I neither know nor care."

"When we left, he was asleep in the chair."

"Then he's probably gone to bed, or he's attempting to pick the lock of the door to the laboratory again."

"Still, don't you think we should—"

"Found it! This is it!" The sound of paper being unrolled. "*A Treatise on Time Journeying Dealing Specifically with the Unacceptability of Permitting Any Member of the Graygem Races to Journey Back in Time Due to the Unpredictability of Their Actions and How This Might Affect Not Only the Past but the Future.*"

"Who's the author?"

"Marwort."

"Marwort! Who termed himself Marwort the Illustrious? The Kingpriest's pet wizard? Everyone knows that when he wrote about the magic, the Kingpriest guided his hand. Of what use is this? You can't believe a word that traitor says."

"So the history of our Order has recorded, and therefore no one studies him. But I have often found what he has to say interesting—if one reads between the lines. For example, notice this paragraph. The third one down."

Tasslehoff's stiff fingers began to slip. He gulped and readjusted his hold on the stones and wished Palin and Dalamar and Marwort gone with all his heart and soul.

"I can't read by this light," Palin said. "My eyes are not what they used to be. And the fire has gone out."

"I could light the fire again," Dalamar offered.

Tasslehoff nearly lost his grip on the stones.

"No," said Palin. "I find this room depressing. Let us take it back where we can be comfortable."

They doused the light, leaving Tas in darkness. He heaved a sigh of relief. When he heard the door close, he began his climb once again.

He was not a young, agile kender anymore, and he soon found that climbing chimneys in the dark was wearing work. Fortunately, he had reached a point in the chimney where the walls started to narrow, so that at least he could lean his back against one wall while keeping himself from slipping by planting his feet firmly against the wall opposite.

He was hot and tired. He had grime in his eyes and soot up his nose and his mouth. His legs were scraped, his fingers rubbed raw, his clothes ripped and torn. He was bored of being in the dark, bored of the stones, bored of the whole business—and he didn't appear to be any closer to the way out than when he'd started.

"I really don't see why it is necessary to have this much chimney," Tasslehoff muttered, cursing the Tower's builder with every grimy foothold.

Just when he thought that his hands were going to refuse to clamp down on another stone and that his legs were going to drop off and fall to the bottom, something filled his nose, and for a change it wasn't soot.

"Fresh air!" Tasslehoff breathed deeply, and his spirits revived.

The whiff of fresh air wafting down from above lent strength to Tasslehoff's legs and banished the aches from his fingers. Peering upward in hope of seeing stars or maybe the sun—for he had the notion that he'd been climbing for the past six months or so—he was disappointed to see only more darkness. He'd had darkness enough to last a lifetime, maybe even two lifetimes. However, the air was fresh, and that meant outside air, so he clambered upward with renewed vigor.

At length, as all things must do, good or otherwise, the chimney came to an end.

The opening was covered with an iron grate to keep birds and squirrels and other undesirables from nesting in the chimney shaft. After what Tasslehoff had already been through, an iron grate was nothing more than a minor inconvenience. He gave it an experimental shove, not expecting anything to come of it. Luck was with him, however. The bolts holding the grate in place had long since rusted away—probably sometime prior to the First Cataclysm—and at the kender's enthusiastic push the gate popped off.

Tasslehoff was unprepared for its sudden departure. He made a desperate grab but missed, and the grate went sailing into the air. The kender froze again, squinched shut his eyes, hunched his shoulders, and waited for the grate to strike the ground at the bottom with what would undoubtedly be a clang loud enough to wake any of the dead who happened to be snoozing at the moment.

He waited and waited and kept on waiting. Considering the amount of chimney he'd had to climb, he supposed it must be a couple of hundred miles to the bottom of the Tower, but, after awhile, even he was forced to admit that if the grate had been going to clang it would have done so by now. He poked his head up out of the hole and was immediately struck in the face by the end of a tree branch, while the sharp pungent smell of cypress cleaned the soot from his nostrils.

He shoved aside the tree branch and looked around to get his bearings. The strange and unfamiliar moon of this strange and unfamiliar Krynn was very bright this night, and Tasslehoff was at last able to see something, although that something was only more tree branches. Tree branches to the left of him, tree branches to the right. Tree branches up, and tree branches down. Tree branches as far as the eye could see. He looked over the edge of the chimney and found the grate, perched in a branch about six feet below him.

Tasslehoff tried to determine how far he was from the ground, but the branches were in the way. He looked to the side and located the top of one of the Tower's two broken minarets. The top was about level with him. That gave him some idea of how far he had climbed and, more importantly, how far the ground was below.

That was not a problem, however, for here were all these handy trees.

Tasslehoff pulled himself out of the chimney. Finding a sturdy limb, he crawled carefully out on it, testing his weight as he went. The limb was strong and didn't so much as creak. After chimney climbing, tree climbing was simple. Tasslehoff shinnied down the trunk, lowered himself from limb to friendly and supportive limb, and finally, as he gave a sigh of exultation and relief, his feet touched firm and solid ground.

Down here, the moonlight was not very bright, hardly filtering through the thick leaves at all. Tas could make out the Tower but only because it was a black, hulking blot amongst the trees. He could see, very far up, a patch of light and figured that must be the window in Dalamar's private chamber.

"I've made it this far, but I'm not out of the woods yet," he said to himself. "Dalamar told Palin we were near Solanthus. I recall someone saying something about the Solamnic Knights having a headquarters at Solanthus, so that seems like a good place to go to find out what's become of Gerard. He may be dull, and he certainly is ugly, and he doesn't like kender, but he is a Solamnic Knight, and one thing you can say about Solamnic Knights is that they aren't the type to send a fellow back in time to be stepped on. I'll find Gerard and explain everything to him, and I'm sure he'll be on my side."

Tasslehoff remembered suddenly that the last time he'd seen Gerard, the Knight had been surrounded by Dark Knights firing arrows at him. Tas was rather downhearted at this thought, but then it occurred to him that Solamnic Knights were plentiful and if one was dead, you could always find another.

The question now was, how to find his way out of the forest.

All this time he'd been on the ground, the dead were flowing around him like fog with eyes and mouths and hands and feet, moving past him and over him, but he hadn't really taken any notice, he'd been too busy thinking. He noticed now. Although being surrounded by dead people with their sad faces and their hands that plucked at one of his pouches wasn't the most comfortable experience in the world, he thought perhaps they might make up for being so extremely cold and creepy by providing him with directions.

"I say, excuse me, sir— Madam, excuse me— Hobgoblin, old chum, could you tell me— I beg your pardon, but that's my pouch. Hey, kid, if I give you a copper would you show— Kender! Fellow kender! I need to find a way to reach— Drat," Tasslehoff said after several moments spent in a futile attempt to converse with the dead. "They don't seem to see me. They look right through me. I'd ask Caramon, but just when he might be useful, he isn't around. I don't mean to be insulting," he added in irritable tones, trying without success to find a path through the cypress trees that pressed thick around him, "but there really are a lot of you dead people! Far more than is necessary."

He continued searching for a path—any sort of a path— but without much luck. Walking in the dark was difficult, although the dead were lit with a soft white light that Tas thought was interesting at first but after awhile, seeing that the dead looked very lost, sorrowful, and terrified, he decided that darkness—any darkness— would be preferable.

At least, he could put some distance between himself and Palin and Dalamar. If he, a kender who was never lost, was lost in these trees, he had no doubt that a mere human and a dark elf—wizards though they might be— would be just as lost and that by losing himself he was also losing them.

He kept going, bashing into trees and knocking his head against low branches, until he took a nasty tumble over a tree root and fell down onto a bed of dead cypress needles. The needles were sweet-smelling, at least, and they were decently dead—all brown and crispy—not like some other dead he could mention.

His legs were pleased that he wasn't using them anymore. The brown needles were comfortable, after you got used to them sticking you in various places, and, all in all, Tasslehoff decided that since he was down here he might as well take this opportunity to rest.

He crawled to the base of the tree trunk, settled himself as comfortably as possible, pillowing his head on a bed of soft green moss. It was not surprising, therefore, that the last thing he thought of, as he was drifting off to sleep, was his father.

Not that his father was moss-covered.

It was his father telling him, "Moss always grows on the side of a tree facing—"

Facing . . .

Tas closed his eyes.

Now, if he could just remember what direction . . .

237

"North," he said and woke himself up.

Realizing that he now could tell what direction he was traveling, he was about to roll over and go back to sleep when he looked up and saw one of the ghosts standing over him, staring down at him.

The ghost was that of a kender, a kender who appeared vaguely familiar to Tas, but then most kender appear familiar to their fellow kender since the odds are quite likely that in all their ambulations, they must have run into each other sometime.

"Now, look," said Tasslehoff, sitting up. "I don't mean to be rude, but I have spent most of the day escaping from the Tower of High Sorcery, and—as I am certain you know—escaping from sorcerous towers makes a fellow extremely tired. So if you don't mind, I'm just going to go to sleep."

Tas shut his eyes, but he had the feeling the ghost of the kender was still there, still looking down at him. Not only that, but Tas continued to see the ghost of the kender on the backs of his eyelids, and the more he thought about it the more he was quite certain he had definitely met that kender somewhere before.

The kender was quite a handsome fellow with a taste in clothes that others might have considered garish and outlandish but that Tasslehoff considered charming. The kender was festooned with pouches, but that wasn't unusual. What was unusual was the expression on the kender's face—sad, lost, alone, seeking.

A cold chill shivered through Tasslehoff. Not a thrilling, excited chill, like you feel when you're about to pull the glittering ring off the bony finger of a skeleton and the finger twitches! This was a nasty, sickening kind of chill that scrunches up the stomach and squeezes the lungs, making it hard to breathe. Tas thought he would open his eyes, then he thought he wouldn't. He squinched them shut very hard so they wouldn't open by themselves and curled into an even tighter ball. He knew where he had seen that kender before.

"Go away," he said softly. "Please."

He knew quite well, though he couldn't see, that the ghost hadn't gone away.

"Go away, go away, go away!" Tas cried frantically, and when that didn't work, he opened his eyes and jumped to his feet and yelled angrily at the ghost, "Go away!"

The ghost stood staring at Tasslehoff.

Tasslehoff stood staring at himself.

"Tell me," Tas said, his voice quivering, "why are you here? What do you want? Are you . . . are you mad because I'm not dead yet?"

The ghost of himself said nothing. It stared at Tas a little longer, then turned and walked away, not as if it wanted to but because it couldn't help itself. Tas watched his own ghost join a milling throng of other restless spirits. He watched until he could no longer distinguish his ghost from any other.

Tears stung his eyes. Panic seized him. He turned and ran as he had never run before. He ran and ran, not looking where he was going, smashing into bushes, caroming off tree trunks, falling down, getting up, running some more, running and running until he fell down and couldn't get up because his legs wouldn't work anymore.

Exhausted, frightened, horrified, Tasslehoff did something he had never done.

He wept for himself.

17
Mistaken Identity

hile Tasslehoff was recalling with fond nostalgia his travels with Gerard, it may be truthfully stated that at this time Gerard was not thinking fond thoughts about the kender. He wasn't thinking any sort of thoughts about the kender at all. Gerard assumed, quite confidently, that he would never have anything more to do with kender and put Tasslehoff out of his mind. The Knight had far more important and worrisome matters to consider.

Gerard wanted desperately to be back in Qualinesti, assisting Marshal Medan and Gilthas to prepare the city for the battle with Beryl's forces. In his heart, he was there with the elves. In reality, he was on the back of the blue dragon, Razor, flying north—the exact opposite direction from Qualinesti, heading for Solanthus.

They were passing over the northern portion of Abanasinia—Gerard was able to see the vast shining expanse of New Sea from the air—when Razor started to descend. The dragon informed Gerard that he needed to rest and eat. The flight over New Sea was long, and once they started out over the water there would be nowhere to stop until they reached land on the other side.

Although he grudged the time, Gerard was in whole-hearted agreement that the dragon should be well-rested before the flight. The blue extended his wings to slow his descent and began to circle around and around, dropping lower with every rotation, his destination a large expanse of sandy beach. The sea was entrancing seen from above. Sunlight striking the water made it blaze like molten fire. The dragon's flight seemed leisurely to Gerard until Razor drew closer to the ground, or rather, when the ground came rushing up to meet them.

Gerard had never been so terrified in his life. He had to clamp his teeth tightly shut to keep from shrieking at the dragon to slow down. The last few yards, the ground leaped up, the dragon plummeted down, and Gerard knew he was finished. He considered himself as brave as the next man, but he couldn't help but shut his eyes until he felt a gentle bump that rocked him slightly forward in the saddle. The dragon settled his muscular body comfortably, folded his wings to his sides and tossed his head with pleasure.

Gerard opened his eyes and spent a moment recovering from the ordeal, then climbed stiffly from the saddle. He'd been afraid to move during much of the flight for fear he'd fall, and now his muscles were cramped and sore. He hobbled around for a bit, groaning and stretching out the kinks. Razor watched him with condescending, if respectful, amusement.

Razor lumbered off to find something to eat. The dragon looked clumsy on land, compared to the air. Trusting that the dragon would keep watch, Gerard wrapped himself in a blanket and lay down on the sun-warmed sand. He meant only to rest his eyes. . . .

Gerard woke from the sleep he had never meant to take to find the dragon basking in sunlight, gazing out across the water. At first, Gerard thought he had been napping only a few hours, then he noted that the sun was in a much different portion of the sky.

"How long have I been asleep?" he demanded, clambering to his feet and shaking the sand out of his leathers.

"All the night and much of the morning," the dragon replied.

Cursing the fact that he had wasted time sleeping, noting that he had left the dragon burdened with the saddle, which was now knocked askew, Gerard began to apologize, but Razor passed it off.

At that, the dragon appeared uneasy, as if something were preying on his mind. Razor looked often at Gerard as if about to speak and then seemingly decided against it. He snapped his mouth shut and twitched his tail moodily. Gerard would have liked to have encouraged the dragon's confidences, but he did not feel they knew each other that well, so he said nothing.

He had a bad several minutes tugging and pulling the saddle back into position and redoing some of the harness, all the while conscious of more precious time slipping by. At last he had the saddle positioned correctly, or at least so he hoped. He had visions of his grand plans ending in failure as the saddle slid off the dragon in midflight, dumping Gerard to an ignominious death.

Razor was reassuring, however, stating that the saddle felt secure to him, and Gerard trusted to the dragon's expertise, having none of his own. They flew off just as dusk was settling over the sea. Gerard was concerned about flying at night, but as Razor sensibly pointed out, night flying was much safer these days than flying by daylight.

The dusk had a strange smoky quality to it that caused the sun to blaze red as it sank below the smudged horizon line. The smell of burning in the air made Gerard's nose twitch. The smoke increased, and he wondered if there was a forest fire somewhere. He looked down below to see if he could spot it but could find nothing. The gloom deepened and blotted out the stars and the moon, so that they flew in a smoke-tinged fog.

"Can you find your way in this, Razor?" Gerard shouted.

"Strangely enough, I can, sir," Razor returned. He fell into one of the uncomfortable silences again, then said abruptly, "I feel obliged to tell you something, sir. I must confess to a dereliction of duty."

"Eh? What?" Gerard cried, hearing only about one word in three. "Duty? What about duty?"

"I was waiting for your return at about noon time yesterday when I heard a call, sir. The call was as a trumpet, summoning me to war. I had never heard the like, sir, not even in the old days. I . . . I almost followed it, sir. I came close to forgetting my duty and departing, leaving you stranded. I will turn myself in for disciplinary action upon our return."

If this had been another human talking, Gerard would have said comfortingly that the man must have been dreaming. He couldn't very well say that to a creature hundreds of years older and more experienced than himself, so all he ended up saying was that the dragon had remained and that was what counted. At least Gerard knew now why Razor had appeared so uneasy.

Talk ended between them. Gerard could see nothing and only hoped that they would not fly headlong into a mountain in the darkness. He had to trust Razor, however, who appeared to be able to see where he was going, for he flew confidently and swiftly. At length Gerard relaxed enough to be able to pry loose his fingers from the saddle horn.

Gerard had no notion of the passing of time. It seemed they had been flying for hours, and he even dozed off again, only to wake with a horrific start in a cold sweat from a dream that he was falling to find that the sun was rising.

"Sir," said Razor. "Solanthus is in sight."

He could see the towers of a large city just appearing over the horizon. Gerard ordered Razor to land some distance from Solanthus, find a place where the blue could rest, and remain safely in hiding, not only from the Solamnic Knights, but from Skie, otherwise known as Khellendros, the great blue dragon, who had held his own against Beryl and Malystryx.

Razor found what he considered a suitable location. Under the cover of a cloud bank, he made an easy landing, spiraling downward in wide sweeping circles onto a vast expanse of grasslands near a heavily wooded forest.

The dragon smashed and trampled the grass when he landed, digging gouges into the dirt with his clawed feet and thrashing the grass with his tail. Anyone who came upon the site would be able to guess at once that some mighty creature had walked here, but this area was remote. A few farms could be seen, carved out of the forest. A single road wound snakelike through the tall grass, but it was several miles distant.

Gerard had sighted a stream from the air, and he was looking forward to nothing so much as a swim in the cool water. His own stench was so bad that he came near making himself sick, and he was itchy from sand and dried sweat. He would bathe and change clothes—rid himself of the leather tunic, at least, that marked him a Dark Knight. He'd have to enter Solanthus dressed like a farm hand—shirtless, clad only in his breeches. He had no way to prove he was a Solamnic Knight, but Gerard was not worried. His father had friends in the Knighthood, and almost certainly Gerard would find someone who knew him.

As for Razor, if the dragon asked why they were here,

Gerard was prepared to explain that he was under Medan's orders to spy upon the Solamnic Knighthood.

The dragon did not ask questions. Razor was far more interested in discovering a place to hide and rest. He was in the territory of the mighty Skie now. The enormous blue dragon had discovered that he could gain strength and power by preying on his own kind, and he was hated and feared by his brethren.

Gerard was anxious that Razor find a hiding place. The dragon was graceful in the air, his wings barely moving as he soared silently on the thermals. On the ground, the blue was a lumbering monster, his feet trampling and smashing, his tail knocking over small trees, sending animals fleeing in terror. He brought down a stag with a snap of his jaws, and, hauling the carcass by the broken neck in his teeth, brought it along with him to enjoy at his leisure.

This made conversation difficult, but he answered Gerard's questions concerning Skie with grunts and nods. Strange rumors had circulated about the mighty blue dragon, who was the nominal ruler of Palanthas and environs. Rumors had it that the dragon had vanished, that he'd handed over control to an underling. Razor had heard these rumors, but he discounted them.

Investigating a depression in a rocky cliff to see if it would make a suitable resting place, Razor dropped the deer carcass by the bank of the stream.

"I believe that Skie is involved in some deep plot that will result in his downfall," Razor told Gerard. "If so, it will be a punishment for slaying his own kind. If we even are his own kind," he added, as an afterthought.

"He's a blue dragon, isn't he?" Gerard asked, looking longingly at the creek and hoping the dragon settled himself soon.

"Yes, sir," said Razor. "But he has grown so that he is far larger than any blue ever seen on Krynn before.

He is larger than the reds—except Malystryx—a great bloated monster. My brethren and I have often commented on it."

"Yet he fought in the War of the Lance," said Gerard. "Is this satisfactory? There don't appear to be any caves."

"True, sir. He was a loyal servant to our departed queen. But one has to wonder, sir."

Unable to find a cave large enough to hold him, Razor pronounced the depression a good start, declared his intention to widen it by blasting chunks of rock out of the side of the cliff. Gerard watched from a safe distance as the blue dragon spat bolts of lightning that blew huge holes in the solid rock, sending boulders splashing into the water and causing the ground to shake beneath his feet.

Certain that the noise of the splitting rock, the blasting explosions, and the concussive thunder must be heard in Solanthus, he feared a patrol would be sent out to investigate.

"If the Solanthians hear anything at all, sir," Razor said during a rest break, "they will think it is merely a coming storm."

Once he had created his cave and the dust had settled and the numerous small avalanches had stopped, Razor retired inside to rest and enjoy his meal.

Gerard removed the saddle from the dragon's back—a proceeding that took some time since he was not familiar with the complicated harness. Razor offered his assistance, and once this was done and Gerard had dragged the heavy saddle into a corner of the cave, out of the way, he left the dragon to his meal and his slumber.

Gerard traveled downstream a good distance until he found a place shallow enough for bathing. He stripped off his leathers and undergarments and waded, naked, into the rippling stream.

The water was deep and cold. He gasped, shivered, and, gritting his teeth, plunged in headfirst. He was not a particularly good swimmer, so he stayed clear of the deeper part of the stream where the current ran swift. The sun was warm, the cold tingled his skin, felt invigorating. He began to splash and leap about, at first to keep the blood flowing and then because he was enjoying himself.

For a few moments, at least, he was free. Free of all his worries and anxieties, free of responsibility, free of anyone telling him what to do. For a few moments, he let himself be a child again.

He tried to catch fish with his bare hands. He dog-paddled beneath the overhanging willow trees. He floated on his back, enjoying the warmth of the sun on his skin and the refreshing contrasting cold of the water. He scrubbed off the caked-on dirt and blood with a handful of grass, all the while wishing he had some of his mother's tallow soap.

Once he was clean, he could examine his wounds. They were inflamed but only slightly infected. He had treated them with a salve given to him by the Queen Mother, and they were healing well. Peering at his reflection in the water, he grimaced, ran his hand over his jaw. He had a stubbly growth of beard, dark brown, not yellow, like his hair. His face was ugly enough without the beard, which was patchy and splotchy and looked like some sort of malignant plant life crawling up his jaw.

He thought back to the time in his youth when he'd tried in vain to grow the silky flowing mustache that was the pride of the Solamnic Knighthood. His mustache proved to be rough and bristly, stuck out every which way like his recalcitrant hair. His father, whose own mustache was full and thick, had taken his son's failure

247

as a personal affront, irrationally blaming whatever was rebellious inside Gerard for manifesting itself through his hair.

Gerard turned to wade back to where he had left his leathers and his pack, intending to retrieve his knife and shave off the stubble. A flash of sunlight off metal half-blinded him. Looking up on the bank, he saw a Solamnic Knight.

The Knight was clad in a leather vest, padded for protection, worn over a knee-length tunic that was belted at the waist. The flash of metal came from a half-helm that covered the head but had no visor. A red ribbon fluttered from the top of the half-helm, the padded vest was decorated with a red rose. A long bow slung over the shoulders indicated that the Knight had been out hunting, as evidenced by the carcass of a stag hanging over the back of a pack mule. The Knight's horse was nearby, head down, grazing.

Gerard cursed himself for not having kept closer watch. Had he been paying attention, instead of larking about like a schoolboy, he would have heard horse and rider approaching.

The Knight's booted foot was planted firmly atop Gerard's sword belt and sword. The Knight held a long sword in one gloved hand. In the other, a coil of rope.

Gerard could not see the Knight's face, due to the shadows of the trees, but he had no doubt that the expression would be grim and stern and undoubtedly triumphant.

He stood in the middle of the stream that was growing colder by the second and pondered on the odd quirk in human nature that makes us feel we are far more vulnerable naked than when wearing clothes. Shirt and breeches will not stop arrow, knife, or sword, yet had he been dressed, Gerard would have been able to face this Knight with confidence. As it was, he stood in the stream and gaped at the Knight with about as much intelligence as the fish that were making darts at his bare legs.

"You are my prisoner," said the Solamnic, speaking Common. "Come forth slowly and keep your hands raised so that I may see them."

Gerard's discomfiture was complete. The Knight's voice was rich and mellow and unquestioningly feminine. At that moment, she turned her head to glance warily about her, and he saw two long thick braids of glossy blue-black hair streaming out from beneath the back of the half-helm.

Gerard felt his skin burn so hot that it was a wonder the water around him didn't steam.

"Lady Knight," he said when he could find his voice, "I concede readily that I am your prisoner, at least for the moment, until I can explain the unusual circumstances, and I would do as you command, but I am . . . as you can see . . . not dressed."

"Since your clothes are here on the bank, I did not think that you would be," the Knight returned. "Come out of the water now."

Gerard thought briefly of making a dash for it to the opposite bank, but the stream ran deep and swift, and he was not that good a swimmer. He doubted if he could manage it. He pictured himself floundering in the water, drowning, calling for help, destroying what shreds of dignity he might have left.

"I don't suppose you would turn your head, Lady, and allow me to dress myself?" he asked.

"And let you stab me in the back?" Laughing she leaned forward. "Do you know, Knight of Neraka, I find it amusing that you, a champion of evil, who has undoubtedly slaughtered any number of innocents, burned villages, robbed the dead, looted, and raped, are such a shrinking lily."

She was pleased with her joke. The emblem of the Dark Knights on which her foot rested, was the skull and the lily.

"If it makes you feel better," the Lady Knight continued, "I have served in the Knighthood for twelve years, I have held my own in battle and tourney. I have seen the male body not only unclothed but ripped open. Which is how I will view yours if you do not obey me." She raised her sword. "Either you come out or I will come in after you."

Gerard began to splash through the water toward the bank. He was angry now, angry at the mocking tone of the woman, and his anger in part alleviated his embarrassment. He looked forward to fetching his pack and exhibiting his letter from Gilthas, proving to this female jokester that he was a true Knight of Solamnia here on an urgent mission and that he probably outranked her.

She watched him carefully every step of the way, her face evincing further amusement at the sight of his nakedness—not surprising, since his skin was shriveled like a prune, and he was blue and shaking with the cold. Arriving at the bank, he cast one furious glance at her and reached for his clothes. She continued to stand with her foot on his sword, her own sword raised and at the ready.

He dressed himself in the leather trousers he'd brought with him. He was going to ignore the tunic, that lay crumpled on the bank, hoping that she might not notice the emblem stitched on the front. She lifted it with the tip of her sword, however, and tossed it at him.

"Wouldn't want you to get sunburned," she said. "Put it on. Did you have a nice flight?"

Gerard's heart sank, but he made a game try. "I don't know what you mean. I walked—"

"Give it up, Neraka," she said to him. "I saw the blue dragon. I saw the beast land. I marked its trail and followed it and found you." She regarded him with interest, all the while keeping the sword pointed at him and dangling the length of rope in her hands. "So what were you intending to do, Neraka? Spy on us, maybe? Pretend to be some loutish farm lad coming to the city for a good time? You appear to have the lout part down well."

"I am not a spy," he said through teeth clenched to keep them from chattering. "I know that you're not going to believe this, but I am not a Dark Knight of Neraka. I am a Solamnic, like yourself—"

"Oh, that is rich! A blue Solamnic riding a blue dragon." The Lady Knight laughed heartily, then flicked her hand and, with alacrity tossed the loop of rope over his head. "Don't worry. I won't hang you here, Neraka. I mean to take you back to Solanthus. You can tell your tale to an admiring audience. The inquisitor has been in low spirits these days. You'll cheer him right up, I'm sure."

She jerked the rope, grinned to see Gerard grab it to keep from choking. "Whether you arrive there alive, half-alive, or barely breathing is up to you."

"I'll prove it," Gerard stated. "Let me open my pack—"

He looked down on the ground. The pack was not there.

Gerard searched frantically along the riverbank. No pack. And then he remembered. He had left the pack with the letter hooked to the dragon's saddle. The saddle and the pack were back in the cave with the blue dragon.

He bowed his head that was dripping wet, too overwhelmed to swear. The hot words were in his heart but they couldn't make it past the lump in his throat to reach his tongue. Raising his head, he looked at the Lady

Knight, looked her full in the eyes that, he noted, were tree-leaf green.

"I swear to you, Lady, on my honor as a true Knight that I am a Solamnic. My name is Gerard uth Mondar. I am stationed in Solace, where I am one of the honor guard for the Tomb of the Last Heroes. I can offer no proof of what I say, I admit that, but my father is well known among the Knighthood. I am certain there are Lord Knights in Solanthus who will recognize me. I have been sent to bring urgent news to the Council of Knights in Solanthus. In my pack, I have a letter from Gilthas, king of the elves—"

"Ah, yes," she said, "and in my pack I have a letter from Mulberry Miklebush, queen of the kender. Where is this pack with this wonderful letter?"

Gerard muttered something.

"I didn't catch that, Neraka?" She bent nearer.

"It's attached to the saddle of the . . . blue dragon," he said glumly. "I could go fetch it. I give you my word of honor that I would return and surrender myself."

She frowned slightly. "I don't, by any chance, have hay stuck in my hair, do I?"

Gerard glared at her.

"I thought I might," she said. "Because you obviously think I have just fallen out of the hay wagon. Yes, Sweet Neraka, I'll accept the word of honor of a blue dragonrider, and I'll let you run off and fetch your pack *and* your blue dragon. Then I'll wave my hankie to you as you both fly away."

She prodded him in the belly with her sword.

"Get on the horse."

"Listen, Lady," Gerard said, his anger and frustration growing. "I know that this looks bad, but if you'll use that steel-covered head of yours for thinking, you'll realize that I'm telling the truth! If I were a real dragonrider of

Neraka, do you think you'd be standing here poking me with that sword of yours? You'd be food for my dragon about now. I am on an urgent mission. Thousands of lives are at stake— Stop that, damn you!"

She had been prodding him with her sword at every third word, steadily forcing him to fall back until he bumped into her horse. Furious, he thrust aside the sword with his bare hand, slicing open his palm.

"I do love to hear you talk, Neraka," she said. "I could listen to you all day, but, unfortunately, I go on duty in a few hours. So mount up, and let's be off."

Gerard was now so angry that he was seriously tempted to summon the dragon. Razor would make short work of this infuriating female, who had apparently been born with solid steel in her head instead of on top of it. He controlled his rage, however, and mounted the horse. Knowing full well what she intended to do with him, he put his hands behind his back, wrists together.

Sheathing her sword, keeping a firm grip on the rope that was around his neck, she tied his wrists together with the same length of rope, adjusting it so that if he moved his arms or any part of his body, he'd end up strangling himself. All the while, she kept up her jocular banter, calling him Neraka, Sweet Neraka, and Neraka of Her Heart and other mocking endearments that were galling in the extreme.

When all was ready, she took her horse's reins and led the horse through the forest at a brisk walk.

"Aren't you going to gag me?" Gerard demanded.

She glanced over her shoulder. "Your words are music to my ears, Neraka. Speak on. Tell me more about the king of the elves. Does he dress in green gossamer and sprout wings from his back?"

"I could yet summon the dragon," Gerard stated. "I do not because I do not want to hurt you, Lady Knight.

This proves what I have been telling you, if you'd only think about it."

"It might," she conceded. "You may well be telling the truth. But you may well not be telling the truth. You might not be summoning the dragon because the beasts are notoriously untrustworthy and unpredictable and would just as soon kill you as me. Right, Neraka?"

Gerard was beginning to understand why she had not gagged him. He could think of nothing to say that would not incriminate himself or make matters worse. Her argument about the evil nature of blue dragons was one he might have made himself before he had come to know Razor. Gerard had no doubt that if he summoned Razor to deal with this Knight, the dragon would make short work of her and leave Gerard untouched. But while Gerard would have preferred Razor to this annoying female as a traveling companion any day, he could not very well countenance the horrible death of a fellow Solamnic, no matter how obnoxious she might be.

"When I reach Solanthus, I will send a company to slay the dragon," she continued. "He cannot be far from here. Judging from the explosions I heard, we will have no trouble finding evidence of his hiding place."

Gerard was reasonably certain that Razor could take care of himself, and that left him concerned for the welfare of his fellow Knights. He decided that the best course of action he could take now was to wait until he came before the council. Once there, he could explain himself and his mission. He was confident the council would believe him, despite his lack of credentials. Undoubtedly there would be someone on the council who knew him or knew his father. If all went well, he would return to Razor and both he, the dragon, and a force of Knights would fly to Qualinesti. After this Knight had made her most abject and humble apologies.

They left the wooded stream bank behind, entered the grasslands not far from where the dragon had alighted. Gerard could see in the distance the road leading to Solanthus. The tops of the city's towers were just visible over the tips of the tall grass.

"There is Solanthus, Neraka," she said, pointing. "That tall building there on your left is—"

"My name is *not* Neraka. My name is Gerard uth Mondar. What are you called," he asked, adding in a muttered undertone, "besides godawful?"

"I heard that!" she sang out. She glanced at him over her shoulder. "My name is Odila Windlass."

"Windlass. Isn't that some sort of mechanical device on board a ship?"

"It is," she replied. "My people are seafaring."

"Pirates, no doubt," he remarked caustically.

"Your wit is as small and shriveled as certain other parts of you, Neraka," she returned, grinning at his embarrassment.

They had reached the road by now, and their pace increased. Gerard had ample opportunity to study her as she walked alongside him, leading the horse and the pack mule. She was tall, considerably taller than he was, with a shapely, muscular build. She did not have the dark skin of the seafaring Ergothians. Her skin was the color of polished mahogany, indicating a blending of races somewhere in her past.

Her hair was long, falling in two braids to her waist. He had never seen such black hair, blue-black, like a crow's wing. Her brows were thick, her face square-jawed. Her lips were her best feature, being full, heart-shaped, crimson, and prone to laughter, as she had already proven.

Gerard would not concede that she had any good features. He had little use for women, considering them conniving, sneaking, and mercenary. Of the women he

255

distrusted and disliked most, he decided that dark-haired, dark-complexioned female Knights who laughed at him ranked at the top of his list.

Odila continued to talk, pointing out the sights of Solanthus on the theory that he would get to see little of the city from his cell in the dungeons. Gerard ignored her. He went over in his mind what he was going to say to the Knights' Council, how best to portray the admittedly sinister-looking circumstances of his arrival. He rehearsed the eloquent words he would use to present the plight of the beleaguered elves. He hoped against hope that someone would know him. He was forced to concede that in the irritating female's place, he would not have believed him either. He had been a dolt for forgetting that pack.

Recalling the desperate situation of the elves, he wondered what they were doing, how they were faring. He thought back to Marshal Medan, Laurana, and Gilthas, and he forgot himself and his own troubles in his earnest concern for those who had come to be his friends. So lost in thought was he that he rode along without paying attention to his surroundings and was astonished to look up and realize that night had fallen while they were on the road and that they had reached the outer walls of Solanthus.

Gerard had heard that Solanthus was the best fortified city in all of Ansalon, even surpassing the lord city of Palanthas. Now, gazing up at the immense walls, black against the stars, walls that were only the outer ring of defenses, he could well believe it.

An outer curtain wall surrounded the city. The wall consisted of several layers of stone packed with sand, slathered over with mud and then covered with more stone. On the other side of the curtain wall was a moat. Gates in several locations pierced the curtain wall. Large drawbridges led over the moat. Beyond the moat was yet another wall, this one lined with murder holes and slits for archers. Large kettles that could be filled with boiling oil were positioned at intervals. On the other side of this wall, trees and bushes had been planted so that any enemy succeeding in taking this wall would not be able to leap down into the city unimpeded. Beyond that lay the streets of the city and its buildings, the vast majority of which were also constructed of stone.

Even at this late hour, people stood at the gatehouse waiting to enter the city. Each person was stopped and questioned by the gatehouse guards. Lady Odila was well known to the guards and did not have to stand in line, but was passed through with merry jests about her fine "catch" and the success of her hunting.

Gerard bore the jokes and crude comments in dignified silence. Odila kept up the mirth until one guard, at the last post, shouted, "I see you had to hog-tie this man to keep him, Lady Odila."

Odila's smile slipped. The green leaf eyes glittered emerald. She turned and gave the guard a look that caused him to flush red, sent him hastening back into the guardhouse.

"Dolt," she muttered. She tossed her black braids, affected to laugh, but Gerard could see that the verbal arrow had struck something vital in her, drawn blood.

Odila led the horse among the crowds in the city streets. People stared at Gerard curiously. When they saw the emblem on his chest, they jeered and spoke loudly of the executioner's blood-tipped axe.

A slight flutter of doubt caused Gerard a moment's unease, almost a moment's panic. What if he could not convince them of the truth? What if they did not believe him? He pictured himself being led to the block, protesting his innocence. The black bag being drawn over his head, the heavy hand pressing his head down on the bloodstained block. The final moments of terror waiting for the axe to fall.

Gerard shuddered. The images he conjured up were so vivid that he broke out into a cold sweat. Berating himself for giving way to his imagination, he forced himself to concentrate on the here and now.

He had presumed, for some reason, that Lady Odila would take him immediately before the Knights' Council. Instead, she led the horse down a dark and narrow alley. At the end stood an enormous stone building.

"Where are we?" he asked.

"The prison house," said Lady Odila.

Gerard was amazed. He had been so focused on speaking to the Knights' Council that the idea that she should take him anywhere else had never occurred to him.

"Why are you bringing me here?" he demanded.

"You have two guesses, Neraka. The first—we're attending a cotillion. You are going to be my dancing partner, and we're going to drink wine and make love to each other all night. Either that"— she smiled sweetly— "or you're going to lock you up in a cell."

She ordered the horse to halt. Torches burned on the walls. Firelight glowed yellow from a square, barred window. Guards, hearing her approach, came running to relieve her of her prisoner. The warden emerged, wiping the back of his hand across his mouth. They'd obviously interrupted his dinner.

"Given a choice," said Gerard acidly, "I'll take the cell."

"I'm glad," Odila said, with a fond pat on his leg. "I would so hate to see you disappointed. Now, alas, I must leave you, Sweet Neraka. I am on duty. Don't pine away, missing me."

"Please, Lady Odila," said Gerard, "if you can be serious for once, there must be someone here who knows the name uth Mondar. Ask around for me. Will you do that much?"

Lady Odila regarded him for a moment with quiet intensity. "It might prove amusing, at that." She turned away to speak to the warden. Gerard had the feeling he had made an impression on her, but whether good or bad, whether she would do what he had asked or not, he could not tell.

Before she left, Lady Odila gave a concise account of all of Gerard's crimes—how she'd seen him fly in on a blue dragon, how he had landed far outside the city, and how the dragon had taken pains to hide himself in a cave. The warden regarded Gerard with a baleful eye and said that he had an especially strong cell located in the basement that was tailor-made for blue dragonriders.

With a parting gibe and a wave of her hand, Lady Odila mounted her horse, grabbed the reins of the pack mule, and cantered out of the yard, leaving Gerard to the mercies of the warden and his guards.

In vain Gerard protested and argued and demanded to see the Knight Commander or some other officer. No one paid the least attention to him. Two guards hauled him inside with ruthless efficiency, while two other guards stood ready with huge spiked-tipped clubs should he make an attempt to escape. They cut loose his bonds, only to replace the rope with iron manacles.

The guards hustled him through the outer rooms where the warden had his office and the jailer his stool and table. The iron keys to the cells hung on hooks ranged in neat rows along the wall. Gerard caught only a glimpse of this, before he was shoved and dragged, stumbling, down a stair that ran straight and true to a narrow corridor below ground level. They led him to his cell with torches—he was the only prisoner down on this level, apparently—and tossed him inside. They gave him to know that there was a bucket for his waste and a straw mattress for sleeping. He would receive two meals a day, morning and night. The door, made of heavy oak with a small iron grate in the top, began to close. All this happened so fast that Gerard was left dazed, disbelieving.

The warden stood in the corridor outside his cell, watching to make certain to the last that his prisoner was safe.

Gerard flung himself forward, wedging his body between the wall and the door.

"Sir!"—he pleaded—"I must speak before the Knights' Council! Let them know Gerard uth Mondar is here! I have urgent news! Information—"

"Tell it to the inquisitor," said the warden coldly.

The guards gave Gerard a brutal shove that sent him staggering, manacles clanking, back into his cell. The cell door shut. He heard the sounds of their feet clomping up the stairs. The torch light diminished and was gone. Another door slammed at the top of the stairs.

Gerard was left alone in darkness so complete and silence so profound that he might have been cast off this world and left to float in the empty nothingness that was said to have existed long before the coming of the gods.

18

BERYL'S MESSENGER

 arshal Medan sat stolidly at his desk in his office that was located in the massive and ugly building the Knights of Neraka had constructed in Qualinost. The Marshal considered the building every bit as ugly as did the elves, who averted their eyes if they were forced to walk anywhere near its hulking, gray walls, and he rarely entered his own headquarters. He detested the barren, cold rooms. Due to the humid air, the stone walls accumulated moisture and always seemed to be sweating. He felt stifled whenever he had to remain here extended periods of time and the feeling was not in his imagination. For the greater protection of those inside, the building had no windows, and the smell of mold was all-pervasive.

Today was worse than ever. The smell clogged his nose and gave him a swelling pain behind his eyes. Due to the pain and the pressure, he was listless and lethargic, found it difficult to think.

"This will never do," he said to himself and was just about to leave the room to take a refreshing walk outside when his second-in-command, a Knight named Dumat, knocked at the wooden door.

The Marshal glowered, returned to seat himself behind the desk, and gave a horrific snort in an effort to clear his nose.

Taking the snort for permission to enter, Dumat came in, carefully shutting the door behind him.

"He's here," he said, with a jerk of his thumb over his shoulder.

"Who is it, Dumat?" Medan asked. "Another draco?"

"Yes, my lord. A bozak. A captain. He's got two baaz with him. Bodyguards, I'd say."

Medan gave another snort and rubbed his aching eyes.

"We can handle three dracos, my lord," said Dumat complacently.

Dumat was a strange man. Medan had given up trying to figure him out. Small, compact, dark-haired, Dumat was in his thirties, or so Medan supposed. He really knew very little about him. Dumat was quiet, reserved, rarely smiled, kept to himself. He had nothing to say of his past life, never joined the other soldiers in boasting of exploits either on the battlefield or between the sheets. He had come to the Knighthood only a few years earlier. He told his commander only what was necessary for the records and that, Medan had always guessed, was probably all lies. Medan had never been able to figure out why Dumat had joined the Knights of Neraka.

Dumat was not a soldier. He had no love for battle. He was not prone to quarreling. He was not sadistic. He was not particularly skilled at arms, although he had proven in a barracks brawl that he could handle himself in a fight. He was even-tempered, though there were smoldering embers in the dark eyes that told of fires burning somewhere deep inside. Medan had never been more astonished in his life than the day almost a year ago when Dumat had come to him and said that he had fallen in love with an elven woman and wanted to make her his wife.

Medan had done all he could to discourage relations between elves and humans. He was in a difficult situation, dealing with explosive racial tensions, trying to retain control of a populace that actively hated its human conquerors. He had to maintain discipline over his troops, as well. He laid down strict rules against rape and those who, in the early days of the elven occupation, broke the rules were given swift, harsh punishment.

But Medan was experienced enough in the strange ways of people to know that sometimes captive fell in love with captor and that not all elf women found human males repulsive.

He had interviewed the elf woman Dumat wanted to marry, to make certain she was not being coerced or threatened. He found that she was not some giddy maiden, but a grown woman, a seamstress by trade. She loved Dumat and wanted to be his wife. Medan represented to her that she would be ostracized from the elven community, cut off from family and friends. She had no family, she told him, and if her friends did not like her choice of husband, they were no true friends. He could not very well argue this point, and the two were married in a human ceremony, since the elves would not officially recognize such a heinous alliance.

The two lived happily, quietly, absorbed in each other. Dumat continued to serve as he had always done, obeying orders with strict discipline. Thus, when Medan had to decide which of his Knights and soldiers he could trust, he had chosen Dumat as among those few to remain with him to assist in the last defense of Qualinost. The rest were sent away south to assist the Gray Robes in their continuing fruitless and ludicrous search for the magical

Tower of Wayreth. Medan had told Dumat plainly what he faced, for the Marshal would not lie to any man, and had given him a choice. He could stay or take his wife and depart. Dumat had agreed to stay. His wife, he said, would remain with him.

"My lord," said Dumat, "is something wrong?"

Medan came to himself with a start. He had been woolgathering, staring at Dumat all the while so that the man must be wondering if his nose was on crooked.

"Three draconians, you said." Medan forced himself to concentrate. The danger was very great, and he could not afford any more mental lapses.

"Yes, my lord. We can deal with them." Dumat was not boastful. He was merely stating a fact.

Medan shook his head and was sorry he'd done so. The pain behind his eyes increased markedly. He gave another ineffectual snort. "No, we can't keep killing off Beryl's pet lizard men. She will eventually get suspicious. Besides, I need this messenger to report back to the great green bitch, assure her that all is proceeding according to plan."

"Yes, my lord."

Medan rose to his feet. He eyed Dumat. "If something goes wrong, be prepared to act on my command. Not before."

Dumat gave a nod and stepped aside to allow his commander to precede him, falling into step behind.

"Captain Nogga, my lord," said the draconian, saluting.

"Captain," said the Marshal, advancing to meet the draconian.

The bozak was enormous, topping Medan by a lizard head, massive shoulders and wing tips. The baaz bodyguards—shorter, but just as muscular—were attentive, alert, and armed to the teeth, of which they had a good many.

"Her Majesty Beryl has sent me," Captain Nogga announced. "I am to apprise you of the current military situation, answer any questions you might have, and take stock of the situation in Qualinost. Then I am to report back to Her Majesty."

Medan bowed his acknowledgment. "You must have had a perilous journey, Captain. Traveling through elven territory with only a small guard. It is a wonder you were not attacked."

"Yes, we heard that you were having difficulty maintaining order in this realm, Marshal Medan," Nogga returned. "That is one of the reasons Beryl is sending in her army. As to how we came, we flew here on dragonback. Not that I fear the pointy-ears," he added disparagingly, "but I wanted to take a look around."

"I hope you find everything to your satisfaction, Captain," Medan said, not bothering to hide his ire. He had been insulted, and the draconian would have thought it strange if he did not respond.

"Indeed, I was pleasantly surprised. I had been prepared to find the city in an uproar, with rioting in the streets. Instead I find the streets almost empty. I must ask you, Marshal Medan, where are the elves? Have they escaped? Her Majesty would be most unhappy to hear that."

"You flew over the roads," Medan said shortly. "Did you see hordes of refugees fleeing southward?"

"No, I did not," Nogga admitted. "However—"

"Did you see refugees heading east, perhaps?"

"No, Marshal, I saw nothing. Therefore I—"

"Did you notice, as you flew over Qualinost, on the outskirts of the city, a large plot of cleared land, freshly dug-up ground?"

"Yes, I saw it," Nogga replied impatiently. "What of it?"

"That is where you will find the elves, Captain," said Marshal Medan.

"I don't understand," Captain Nogga said.

"We had to do something with the bodies," Medan continued offhandedly. "We couldn't leave them to rot in the streets. The elderly, the sickly, the children, and any who put up resistance were dispatched. The rest are being retained for the slave markets of Neraka."

The draconian scowled, his lips curled back. "Beryl gave no orders concerning slaves going to Neraka, Marshal."

"I respectfully remind you and Her Majesty that I receive my orders from Lord of the Night Targonne, not from Her Majesty. If Beryl wishes to take up the matter with Lord Targonne, she may do so. Until then, I follow my lord's commands."

Medan straightened his shoulders, a movement that brought his hand near his sword hilt. Dumat had his hand on his sword hilt, and he moved quietly, with seeming nonchalance, to stand near the two baaz. Nogga had no idea that his next words might be his last. If he demanded to see the mass grave or the slave pens, the only thing he would end up seeing would be Medan's sword sticking out of his scaly gut.

As it was, the draconian shrugged. "I am acting on orders myself, Marshal. I am an old soldier, as are you. Neither of us has any interest in politics. I will report back to my mistress and, as you so wisely suggest, urge her to talk it over with your Lord Targonne."

Medan eyed the draconian intently, but, of course, there was no way to read the expression on the lizard's face. He nodded and, removing his hand from his sword hilt, strode past the draconian to stand in the doorway, where he could take a breath of fresh, sweet-scented air.

"I have a complaint to register, Captain." Medan glanced over his shoulder at Nogga. "A complaint against a draconian. One called Groul."

"Groul?" Nogga was forced to clump over to where Medan stood. The draconian's eyes narrowed. "I intended to ask about Groul. He was sent here almost a fortnight ago, and he has not reported back."

"Nor will he," said Medan brusquely. He drew in another welcome breath of fresh air. "Groul is dead."

"Dead!" Nogga was grim. "How did he die? What is this about a complaint?"

"Not only was he foolish enough to get himself killed," Medan stated, "he killed one of my best agents, a spy I had planted in the house of the Queen Mother." He cast a scathing glance at Nogga. "In future, if you must send draconian messengers, make certain that they arrive sober."

Now it was Nogga's turn to bristle. "What happened?"

"We are not certain," Medan said, shrugging. "When we found the two of them—Groul and the spy—they were both dead. At least we have to assume that the pile of dust next to the elf's corpse was Groul. What we do know is that Groul came here and delivered to me the message sent by Beryl. He had already imbibed a fair quantity of dwarf spirits. He reeked of them. Presumably after he left me, he fell in with the agent, an elf named Kalindas. The elf had long complained over the amount of money he was being paid for his information. My guess is that Kalindas confronted Groul and demanded more money. Groul refused. The two fought and killed each other. Now I am short one spy, and you are short one draconian soldier."

Nogga's long, lizard tongue flicked from between his teeth. He fiddled with his sword hilt.

"Strange," said Nogga at last, his red-eyed gaze intent upon the Marshal, "that they should end up slaying each other."

"Not so strange," Medan returned dryly. "When you consider that one was soused and the other was slime."

Nogga's teeth clicked together. His tail twitched, scraping across the floor. He muttered something that Medan chose to ignore.

"If that is all, Captain," the Marshal said, turning his back yet again upon the draconian and walking toward his office, "I have a great deal of work to do. . . ."

"Just a moment!" Nogga rumbled. "The orders Groul carried stated that the Queen Mother was to be executed and her head given over to Beryl. I assume these orders have been carried out, Marshal. I will take the elf's head now. Or did yet another strange circumstance befall the Queen Mother?"

Pausing, Medan rounded on his heel. "Surely the dragon was not serious when she gave those orders?"

"Not serious!" Nogga scowled.

"Beryl's sense of humor is well known," said the Marshal. "I thought Her Majesty was having a jest with me."

"It was no jest, I assure you, my lord. Where is the Queen Mother?" Nogga demanded, teeth grating.

"In prison," Medan said coolly. "Alive. Waiting to be handed over to Beryl as my gift when the dragon enters Qualinost in triumph. Orders of Lord Targonne."

Nogga had opened his mouth, prepared to accuse Medan of treachery. The draconian snapped it shut again.

Medan knew what Nogga must be thinking. Beryl might consider herself the ruler of Qualinesti. She might consider the Knights to be acting under her auspices, and in many ways they were. But Lord Targonne was still in command of the Dark Knights. More importantly, he was known to be in high favor with Beryl's cousin, the great red dragon Malystryx. Medan had been wondering how Malys was reacting to Beryl's sudden decision to move troops into Qualinesti. In that snap of Nogga's jaws, Medan had his answer. Beryl had no desire to antagonize Targonne, who would most certainly run tattling to Malys that he was being mistreated.

"I will see the elf bitch," Nogga said sullenly. "To make certain there are no tricks."

The Marshal gestured toward the stairs that led to the dungeons located below the main building. "The corridor is narrow," the Marshal said, when the baaz would have followed after their commander. "We will all be a tight fit."

"Wait here," Nogga growled to the baaz.

"Keep them company," said Medan to Dumat, who nodded and almost, but not quite, smiled.

The draconian stumped down the spiral stairs. Cut out of the bedrock, the stairs were rough and uneven. The dungeons were located far underground, and they soon lost the sunlight. Medan apologized for not having thought to bring a torch with him and hinted that perhaps they should go back.

Nogga brushed that aside. Draconians can see well in the darkness, and he was having no difficulty. Medan followed several paces after the captain, groping his way in the darkness. Once, quite by accident, he stepped hard on Nogga's tail. The draconian grunted in irritation. Medan apologized politely. They wound their way downward, finally arrived at the bottom of the stairs.

Here torches burned on the walls, but by some strange fluke they gave little light and created a great deal of smoke. Reaching the bottom of the stairs, Nogga blinked and grumbled, peering this way and that in the thick atmosphere. Medan shouted for the gaoler, who came to meet them. He wore a black hood over his head, in the manner of an executioner, and was a grim and ghostly figure in the smoke.

"The Queen Mother," Medan said.

The gaoler nodded and led them to a cell that was nothing more than an iron-barred cage set into a rock wall. He pointed silently inside.

An elf woman crouched on the floor of the cell. Her long golden hair was lank and filthy. Her clothes were rich, but torn and disheveled, stained with dark splotches that might have been blood. Hearing the Marshal's voice, she rose to meet them, stood facing them defiantly. Although there were six cells in the dungeon, the rest were empty. She was the only prisoner.

The draconian approached the cell. "So this is the famous Golden General. I saw the elf witch once long ago in Neraka at the time of the fall."

He looked her up, and he looked her down, slowly, insultingly.

Laurana stood at ease, calm and dignified. She regarded the draconian steadfastly, without flinching. Marshal Medan's hand clasped spasmodically over the hilt of his sword.

I need this lizard alive, he reminded himself.

"A pretty wench," said Nogga with a leer. "I remember thinking so at the time. A fine wench to bed, if one can stomach the stench of elf."

"A wench who proved something of a disaster to you and your kind," Medan could not refrain from observing, though he realized almost the moment the words were said that the remark had been made a mistake.

Nogga's eyes flared in anger. His lips curled back from his teeth, the tip of his long tongue flicked out. Staring at Laurana, he sucked his tongue in with a seething breath. "By the lost gods, elf, you will not look at me so smugly when I am through with you!"

The draconian seized hold of the iron-barred door. Muscles on his gigantic arms bunched. With a jerk and a pull, he wrenched the door free of its moorings and flung the door to one side, nearly crushing the gaoler, who had to make a nimble jump to save himself. Nogga bounded inside the cell.

Caught off guard by the draconian's sudden violent outburst, Medan cursed himself for a fool and leaped to stop him. The gaoler, Planchet, was closer to the draconian, but his way was impeded by the iron door that Nogga had tossed aside and that was now leaning at a crazy angle against one of the other cells.

"What are you doing, Captain?" Medan shouted. "Have you lost your senses? Leave her alone! Beryl will not want her prisoner damaged."

"Bah, I'm only having a little fun," Nogga growled, reaching out his hand.

Steel flashed. From the folds of her dress, Laurana snatched a dagger.

Nogga skidded to a halt, his clawed feet scraping against the stone floor. He stared down in astonishment to find the dagger pressed against his throat.

"Don't move," Laurana warned, speaking the draconian's own language.

Nogga chuckled. He had recovered from his initial amazement. Defiance added spice to his lust, and he knocked aside the dagger with his clawed hand. The blade slit his scaled skin, spattering blood, but he ignored the wound. He seized hold of Laurana. Still holding the dagger, she stabbed at him, while she struggled in his strong grasp.

"I said let her go, Lizard!"

Locking his fists together, Medan struck Nogga a solid thwack on the back of the head. The blow would have felled a human, but Nogga was barely distracted by it. His clawed hands tore at Laurana's dress.

Planchet finally managed to kick aside the cell door. Grabbing hold of a flaring torch, he brought it down on the draconian's head. Cinders flew, the torch broke in half.

"I'll be back to you in a moment," Nogga promised with a snarl and flung Laurana against the wall. Teeth bared, the draconian turned to face his assailants.

"Don't kill him!" Medan ordered in Elvish, and punched the draconian in the gut, a blow that doubled him over.

"Do you think there's a chance we might?" Planchet gasped, driving his knee into the draconian's chin, snapping his head back.

Nogga sank to his knees, but he was still trying to regain his feet. Laurana grabbed hold of a wooden stool and brought it down on the draconian's head. The stool smashed into splinters, and Nogga slumped to the floor. The draconian lay on his belly, legs spraddled, the fight gone out of him at last.

The three of them stood breathing heavily, eyeing the draconian.

"I am deeply sorry, Madam," said Medan, turning to Laurana.

Her dress was torn. Her face and hands were spattered with the draconian's blood. His claws had raked across the white skin of her breasts. Drops of blood oozed from the scratches, sparkled in the torchlight. She smiled, exultant, grimly triumphant.

Medan was enchanted. He had never seen her so beautiful, so strong and courageous, and at the same time so vulnerable. Before he quite knew what he was doing, he put his arms around her, drew her close.

"I should have known the creature would try something like this," Medan continued remorsefully. "I should never have put you at such risk, Laurana. Forgive me."

She lifted her gaze to meet his. She said a soft word of reassurance and then, ever so gently, she slipped out of his grasp, her hand drawing the tatters of her dress modestly over her breasts.

"No need to apologize, Marshal," she said, her eyes alight with mischief. "To be truthful, I found it quite exhilarating."

She looked down at the draconian. Her voice hardened, her hand clenched. "Many of my people have already given their lives in this battle. Many more will die in the last fight for Qualinost. At last I feel I am doing my share, small though that may be."

When she looked back up at him, the mischief sparkled. "But I fear we have damaged your messenger, Marshal."

Medan grunted something in response. He dared not look at Laurana, dared not remember her warmth as she had rested, just a moment, in his arms. All these years, he had been proof against love, or so he had convinced himself. In reality, he had fallen in love with her long ago, pierced through by love for her, for the elven nation. What bitter irony that only now, at the end, had he come to fully understand.

"What do we do with him, sir?" Planchet asked. The elf was limping, favoring a sore knee.

"I'll be damned if I'm going to haul that heavy carcass of his up the stairs," Medan said harshly. "Planchet, escort your mistress to my office. Bolt the door behind you and remain there until you receive word that it is safe to leave. On your way there, tell Dumat to come down here and bring those baaz with him."

Planchet removed his cloak and wrapped it around Laurana's shoulders. She held the cloak fast over her torn dress with one hand and placed her other hand on Medan's arm. She looked up into his eyes.

"Are you certain you will be all right, Marshal?" she asked softly.

She was not talking about leaving him alone with the draconian. She was talking about leaving him alone with his pain.

"Yes, Madam," Medan said, and he smiled in his turn. "Like you, I found it exhilarating."

She sighed, lowered her gaze, and for a moment it seemed as if she would say something else. He didn't want to hear it. He didn't want to hear her say that her heart was buried with her husband Tanis. He didn't want to hear that he was jealous of a ghost. It was enough for him to know that she respected him and trusted him. He took hold of her hand, as it lay on his arm. Lifting her fingers, he pressed them to his lips. She smiled tremulously, reassured, and allowed Planchet to lead her away.

Medan remained in the dungeons alone, glad of the quiet, glad of the smoke-tinged darkness. He massaged his aching hand and, when he was once more master of himself, he picked up the bucket of water that they used to douse the torches and flung the filthy liquid in Captain Nogga's face.

Nogga snuffled and spluttered. Shaking his head muzzily, he heaved himself up off the floor.

"You!" he snarled and swung round, waving his meaty fist. "I'll have you—"

Medan drew his sword. "I would like nothing better than to drive this steel into your vitals, Captain Nogga. So don't tempt me. You will go back to Beryl, and you will tell Her Majesty that in accord with the orders of my commander, Lord Targonne, I will turn over the elven capital of Qualinost to her. I will, at the same time, hand over the Queen Mother, alive and undamaged. Understood, Captain?"

Nogga glanced around, saw that Laurana was gone. His red eyes glinted in the darkness. He wiped a dribble of blood and saliva from his mouth, regarded Medan with a look of inveterate hatred.

"At that time, I will return," said the draconian, "and we will settle the score that lies between us."

"I look forward to it," said Medan politely. "You have no idea how much."

Dumat came running down the stairs. The baaz were right behind him, weapons in hand.

"Everything is under control," Medan stated, returning

his sword to its sheath. "Captain Nogga forgot himself for a moment, but he has remembered again."

Nogga gave an incoherent snarl and slouched out of the cell, wiping away blood and spitting out a broken tooth. Motioning to the baaz, he made his way back up the stairs.

"Provide an honor guard for the captain," Medan ordered Dumat. "He is to be escorted safely to the dragon that brought him here."

Dumat saluted and accompanied the draconians up the stairs. Medan lingered a moment longer in the darkness. He saw a splotch of white on the floor, a tattered bit of Laurana's dress, torn off by the draconian. Medan reached down, picked it up. The fabric was as soft as gossamer. Smoothing it gently with his hand, he tucked it into the cuff of his shirt sleeve, and then went upstairs to see the Queen Mother safely home.

19

Desperate Game

The great green dragon, Beryl, flew in wide circles over the forests of Qualinesti and tried to do away with her doubts by reassuring herself that all was proceeding as planned. As *she* planned. Events were moving forward at a rapid pace. Too rapid, to her mind. She had ordered these events. She. Beryl. No other. Therefore why the strange and nagging feeling that she was not in control, that she was being pushed, rushed? That someone at the gaming table had jostled her elbow, causing her to toss the dice before the other players had laid down their bets.

It had all started so innocently. She had wanted nothing more than what was rightfully hers—a magical artifact. A wondrous magical artifact that had no business being in the hands of the crippled, washed-up human mage who had acquired it—mistakenly at that, from some runt of a mewling kender. The artifact belonged to her. The artifact was in her territory, and everything in her territory belonged to her. All knew that. No one could dispute the point. In her quite rightful effort to acquire this artifact, she had somehow ended up sending her armies to war.

Beryl blamed her cousin Malystryx.

Two months ago, the green dragon had been happily wallowing in her leafy bower with never a thought of going to war against the elves. Well, perhaps that was not quite true. She had been building up her armies, using the vast wealth amassed from the elves and humans under her subjugation to buy the loyalties of legions of mercenaries, hordes of goblins and hobgoblins, and as many draconians as she could lure to her with promises of loot, rapine, and murder. She held these slavering dogs on a tight leash, tossing them bits of elf now and again to whet their appetites. Now she had unleashed them. She had no doubt that she would win.

Yet, she sensed that there was another player in the game, a player she could not see, a player watching from the shadows, one who was betting on another game: a bigger game with higher stakes. A player who was betting that she, Beryl, would lose.

Malystryx, of course.

Beryl did not watch the north for Solamnic Knights with their silver dragons or the mighty blue dragon Skie. The silvers had purportedly vanished, according to her spies, and it was common knowledge—again among her spies—that Skie had gone mad. Obsessed with a human master, he had disappeared for a time, only to return with some story of having been in a place he called the Gray.

Beryl did not watch the east where lived the black dragon Sable. The slimy creature was content with her foul miasma. Let her rot there. As to the white, Frost, the white dragon did not live who could challenge a green of Beryl's power and cunning. No, Beryl watched the northeast, watched for red eyes that remained constantly on the horizon of her fear.

Now it seemed Malystryx had made her move at last, a move that was both unexpected and cunning. The Green had discovered only days earlier that almost all her minion dragons—dragons native to Krynn, who had sworn allegiance to Beryl—had deserted her. Only two red dragons remained and she did not trust them. Had never trusted reds. No one could tell her for certain where the others had gone, but Beryl knew. These lesser dragons had switched sides. They had gone over to Malystryx. Her cousin was undoubtedly laughing at Beryl right now. Beryl gnashed her teeth and belched a cloud of noxious gas, spewed it forth as if she had her treacherous cousin in her claws.

Beryl saw Malys's game. The Red had tricked her. Malys had forced Beryl to enter into this war against the elves, forced her to commit her troops to the south, all the while building up her strength as Beryl expended hers. Malys had tricked Beryl into destroying the Citadel of Light— those Mystics had long been stinging parasites beneath Malys's scales. Beryl suspected now that Malys had been the one to plant the magical device where Beryl would hear of it.

Beryl had considered calling back her armies, but she immediately abandoned that plan. Once unleashed, the dogs would never return to her hand. They had the smell, the taste of elven blood, and they would not heed her call. Now she was glad that she had not.

From her vast height, Beryl looked down in pride to see the enormous snake that was her military might winding its way through the thick forests of Qualinesti. Its forward movement was slow. An army marches on its stomach, so the saying goes. The troops could move only as fast as the heavily laden supply wagons. Her forces dared not forage, dared not live off the land, as they might have done. The animals and even the vegetation of Qualinesti had entered the fray.

Apples poisoned those who ate them. Bread made from elven wheat sickened an entire division. Soldiers reported comrades strangled by vines or killed by trees that let fall huge limbs with crushing force. This was a foe easily defeated, however. This foe could be fought with fire. Clouds of smoke from the burning forests of Qualinesti turned day into night over much of Abanasinia. Beryl watched the smoke billowing into the air, watched the prevailing winds carry it westward. She breathed in the smoke of the dying trees in delight. As her armies moved slowly but inexorably forward, Beryl grew stronger daily.

As for Malys, she would smell the smoke of war, and she would sniff in it the stench of her own doom.

"For though you may have tricked me into acting, Cousin," Beryl told those wrathful red eyes glowering at her from the west, "you have done me a favor. Soon I will rule over a vast territory. Thousands of slaves will do my bidding. All of Ansalon will hear of my victory over the elves. Your armies will desert you and flock to my standard. The Tower of High Sorcery at Wayreth will be mine. No longer will the wizards be able to hide it and its powerful magicks from me. The longer you skulk in the shadows, waiting, the stronger I grow. Soon your great ugly skull will crown my totem, and I will be the ruler of Ansalon."

Thus Beryl began already to calculate her winnings. Still she could not rid herself of the disquieting feeling that from somewhere in the shadows, outside the circle, another player waited, another player watched.

Far, far below, eyes did watch Beryl, but they were not the eyes of a player in this game, or at least, he could not flatter himself that he was a player. His were the bones that rattled in the cup and were flung upon the table, to bounce about aimlessly until they came to rest ignominiously in a corner and the winner was declared.

Gilthas stood at the hidden entrance to one of the underground tunnels, keeping watch on Beryl. The dragon was enormous, huge, monstrous. Her scaled body, bloated, misshapen, was so ponderous that it seemed impossible her wings could lift the loathsome mass of flesh off the ground. Impossible until one noticed the thick and heavy musculature of the shoulders and the sheer width and breadth of the wingspan. Her shadow spread across the land, blotting out the haze-dimmed sun, turning bright day to horrid night.

Gilthas shivered as the shadow of the dragon's wings swept over him, chilling him. Although the wings were soon gone, he felt as if he remained in the black shadow of death.

"Is it safe, Your Majesty?" a quivering voice asked.

No, you foolish child! Gilthas wanted to rage. No it is not safe! Nowhere in this wide world is safe for us. The dragon keeps watch on us from the sky day and night. Her army, thousands strong, marches on the land, killing, burning. They have blotted out the very sun with the smoke of death. We may delay them, at the cost of precious lives, but we cannot stop them. Not this time. We run, but where do we run to? Where is the safe haven we seek? Death. Death is the only refuge. . . .

"Your Majesty," called the voice again.

Gilthas roused himself with an effort. "It is not safe," he cautioned in low tones, "but for the moment the dragon is gone. Come now quickly! Quickly."

This tunnel was one of many tunnels built by the dwarves who were helping hundreds of elven refugees escape the city of Qualinost and smaller settlements to the north, areas that had already fallen to Beryl's army. The tunnel's entrance was only a couple of miles south of the city proper—the dwarves had extended their tunnels to reach the city itself, and even now, as Gilthas spoke to these refugees, who had been caught above ground, other elves walked through the tunnel behind him.

The elves had begun to evacuate Qualinost six days ago, the day Gilthas had informed the people that their land was under attack by the forces of the dragon Beryl. He had told the elves the truth, the brutal truth. The only hope they had of surviving this war was to leave behind that which they loved most, their homeland. Even then, though they might survive as a people, Gilthas had not been able to give them any assurance that they would survive as a nation.

He had given the Qualinesti their orders. The children must leave. They were the hope of the race, and they should be protected. Caretakers for the children should go with them, be it mothers, fathers, grandparents, aunts, uncles, cousins. Those elves who were able to fight, those who were trained warriors, were asked to stay behind to fight the battle to defend Qualinost.

He had not promised the elves that they would escape to a safe haven for he could not promise that they would find such a haven. He would not tell his people comforting lies. Too long, the Qualinesti people had slept snugly beneath the blanket of comforting lies. He had told them the truth and, with quiet fortitude, they had accepted it.

He had been proud of his people in that moment and in the sorrowful moments that came after. Mates parted, one to go with the children, the other staying behind. Those remaining kissed their children lovingly, held them close, bade them be good and be obedient. As Gilthas told his people no lies, the elven parents told their children none. Those staying behind did not promise that they would see their loved ones again. They bade them do only one thing: Remember. Always remember.

At Gilthas's gesture, the elves who had been in hiding slipped out from the shadows of the trees, whose leafy boughs had provided them protection from Beryl's searching eyes. The forest had been quiet with the coming of the dragon, animal noises hushed, bird song silenced. All living things crouched, trembling, until Beryl had passed. Now that the dragon was gone, the forest came alive. The elves took their children by their hands, assisting the elderly and the infirm, and slid and slipped down the sides of a narrow ravine. The tunnel's entrance was at the bottom, concealed by a lean-to made of tree branches.

"Hurry!" Gilthas motioned, keeping watch for the dragon's return. "Hurry!"

The elves hastened past him and into the darkness of the tunnel beyond, where they were met by dwarves, who pointed out the way to go. One of those dwarves who was gesturing and saying in Elvish, "Left, left, keep to the left, mind that puddle there," was Tarn Bellowsgranite, King of the Dwarves. He was dressed as any dwarven laborer, his beard caked with dirt, and his boots covered in mud and crushed rock. The elves never guessed his royal stature.

The elves looked relieved at first when they reached the safety of the dark tunnel and they were glad to duck inside. As they confronted the line of dwarves, pointing and gesturing for them to move deeper below ground, relief changed to unease. Elves are not happy below ground. They do not like confined places. They like to see the sky above their heads and the branching trees and breathe the fresh air. Below ground, they feel stifled and closed in. The tunnels smelled of darkness, of black loam and the gigantic worms, the Urkhan, that burrowed through the rock. Some elves hesitated, glanced back outside, where the sun shone brightly. One older elf, whom Gilthas recognized as belonging to the Thon-Thalas, the elven Senate, turned around and started to go back.

"I can't do this, Your Majesty," the senator said to Gilthas in apology. He was gasping for breath, his face was pale. "I'm suffocating! I'll die down there!"

Gilthas started to reply, but Tarn Bellowsgranite stepped forward, blocked the senator's path.

"Good sir," said the dwarf, cocking one eye at the elf senator, "yes, it's dark down here and, yes, it smells bad, and, yes, the air is not the freshest. But, consider this, good sir." Tarn raised one grubby finger. "How dark will it be inside the dragon's belly? How bad will *that* smell?"

The senator looked down at the dwarf and managed a wan smile. "You are right, sir. I had not considered that particular argument. It is a cogent one, I admit."

The senator looked back down the corridor. He looked outside, drew a deep breath of fresh air. Reaching out, he touched Gilthas on the hand, a mark of respect. Bowing to the dwarf, the elf ducked his head, and plunged into the tunnel, holding his breath, as if he would hold it for the miles he would have to travel below ground.

Gilthas smiled. "You've said those words before, Thane, I'll wager."

"Many times," said the dwarf, stroking his beard and grinning. "Many times. If not me, then the others." He gestured to the dwarven helpers. "We use the same argument. It never fails." He shook his head. "Elves living below ground. Who would have thought it, eh, Your Majesty?"

"Someday," said Gilthas in reply, "we'll have to teach dwarves to climb trees."

Bellowsgranite snorted, laughed at the thought. Shaking his head, he went stomping down the tunnel, shouting encouragement to the dwarves who were working to keep the passageway clear of falling rock and to make certain the braces they used to shore up the tunnel were strong and secure.

The last elves to enter the tunnel were a group of twelve, members of a single family. The eldest daughter, who had almost come into her majority, had volunteered to take the children. Father and mother—both trained warriors—would remain to fight to save their city.

Gilthas recognized the girl, remembered her from the masquerade he had held not so long ago. He remembered her dancing, dressed in her finest silken gown, her hair adorned with flowers, her eyes shining with happiness and excitement. Now her hair was uncombed and unwashed, adorned with the dead leaves in which she had been hiding. Her dress was torn and travel-stained. She was frightened and pale, but resolute and firm, not giving way to her fear, for the younger children looked to her for courage.

The journey from Qualinost had been slow. Since the day Beryl had caught a group of elves on the road and killed them all with a blast of her poisonous breath, the elves had dared not travel in the open. The elves had kept to the forests for protection, holding as still as the rabbit in the presence of the fox when the green dragon swept overhead. Thus their progress was slow, heartbreakingly slow.

As Gilthas watched, the girl picked up a toddler from a nest of leaves and pine needles. Summoning the other children to her side, she ran toward the tunnel. The children followed her, the elder children carrying the younger on their backs.

Where was she going? Silvanesti. A land that was to this girl nothing more than a dream. A sad dream, for she had heard all her life that the Silvanesti disliked and distrusted their Qualinesti cousins. Yet now she was on her way to beg them for sanctuary. Before they could even reach Silvanesti, she and her siblings would have to travel miles below ground, then emerge to cross the arid, empty Plains of Dust.

"Quickly, quickly!" Gilthas urged, thinking he caught a glimpse of the dragon above the treetops.

When the last child was inside, he reached out, grabbed the tree-branch lean-to, and dragged it across the opening, concealing it from sight.

The girl paused inside the tunnel to take a quick head count. Satisfied all her brood were with her, she managed a smile for Gilthas and, lifting her head and adjusting the toddler to more comfortable position on her back, started to enter the tunnel proper.

One of the younger boys held back. "I don't want to go, 'Trina," he said, his voice quavering. "It's dark in here."

"No, no, it's not," said Gilthas. He pointed to a globe, hanging from the ceiling. A soft warm glow shone from inside the globe, illuminating the darkness. "You see that lantern?" Gilthas asked the child. "You'll find those lanterns all through the tunnel. Do you know what makes that light?"

"Fire?" asked the boy doubtfully.

"A baby worm," said Gilthas. "The adult worms dig the tunnels for us, and their young light our way. You're not afraid now, are you?"

"No," said the young elf. His sister cast him a scandalized look, and he flushed. "I mean, no, Your Majesty."

"Good," said Gilthas. "Then off you go."

A deep voice sang out in Dwarvish, repeating it in Elvish, "Make way! Worm a'coming! Make way!"

The dwarf spoke in Elvish but as if he had a mouthful of rocks. The children did not understand. Gilthas made a jump for the girl. "Get back!" he shouted to the other children. "Get back against the wall! Quickly!"

The floor of the tunnel began to shake.

Catching hold of the startled girl, he dragged her out of the center of the tunnel. She was terrified, and the child she carried began to wail in fear. Gilthas took the toddler in his arms, soothed her as best he could. The other children crowded around him, wide-eyed, staring. Some began to whimper.

"Watch this," he said, smiling at them. "No need to be afraid. These are our saviors."

The head of one of the gigantic worms the dwarves used for burrowing came into sight at the far end of the tunnel. The worm had no eyes, for it was accustomed to living in darkness below ground. Two horns protruded from the top of its head. A dwarf, seated in a large basket on the worm's back, held the reins of a leather harness in his hands. The harness wrapped around the two horns and allowed the wormrider to guide the Urkhan as an elf rider guided his horse.

The worm paid little attention to the dwarf on its back. The Urkhan was interested only in its dinner. The worm spewed liquid onto the solid rock at the side of the tunnel. The worm-spit hissed on the rock, began to bubble. Large chunks of rock split apart and fell to the tunnel floor. The Urkhan's maw opened, seized a chunk, and swallowed it.

The worm crawled nearer, a fearsome sight. Its enormous, undulating, slime-covered body was reddish brown in color and filled half the tunnel. The floor of the tunnel shook beneath the worm's weight. Urkhan wranglers, as they were called, helped the rider guide the worm by reins attached to straps wrapped around its body.

As the worm came closer to Gilthas and the children, it suddenly swung its blind head around, started to veer toward their side of the tunnel. For one moment, Gilthas feared they would be crushed. The girl clutched at him. He pressed her back against the wall, shielding her and as many of the children as he could with his body.

The wranglers knew their business and were quick to react. Bawling loud curses, the dwarves began to drag on the reins and beat on the Urkhan with their fists and sticks. The creature gave a great, snuffling snort and, shaking its huge head, turned back to its meal.

"There now, you see. That wasn't so bad," Gilthas said cheerfully.

The children did not look particularly reassured, but at a sharp word from their sister they fell back into line and began to straggle down the tunnel, keeping wary eyes on the worm as they crept past it.

Glithas remained behind, waiting. He had promised his wife that he would meet her at the entrance to the tunnel. He was starting to return to the entryway when felt her hand upon his shoulder.

"My love," she said.

Her touch was gentle, her voice soft and soothing. She must have entered the tunnel when he was helping the children. He smiled to see her, and the darkness of despair the dragon had brought down on him departed in the glow of the larva light that glistened in her mane of golden hair. A kiss or two was all they had time to share, for both had news to impart and urgent matters to discuss.

Both began speaking simultaneously.

"My husband, the news we heard is true. The shield has fallen!"

"My wife, the dwarves have agreed!"

They both stopped, looked at each other, and laughed.

Gilthas could not remember the last time he had laughed or heard his wife laugh. Thinking this a good omen, he said, "You first."

She was about to continue, then she glanced around, frowned. "Where is Planchet? Where are your guards?"

"Planchet remained behind to help the Marshal foil some draconians. As to my guards, I ordered them to return to Qualinost. Don't scold, my dear." Gilthas smiled. "They are needed there to help ready the defenses. Where are your guards, Madam Lioness?" he asked in mock severity.

"Around," she said, smiling. Her elf soldiers could be quite close at hand, and he would never see them or hear them, not unless they wanted him to. Her smile faded from her lips and eyes. "We came upon the young elf girl and the children. I offered to send one of my people with her, but she refused. She said she would not think of taking a warrior from the battle."

"A few weeks ago she danced at her first ball. Now, she cowers in a tunnel and runs for her life." He could not go on for a moment for the emotion choking him. "What courage our people have!" he said huskily.

The two stood in the tunnel. The floor shook beneath them. The dwarven wranglers bellowed and shouted. Dwarves crouched by the entrance, waiting to assist more refugees. Other elves, coming from farther down the tunnel, walked past them. Seeing their king, they nodded and smiled and acted as if this, escaping through a dark and shaking tunnel, guided by dwarves, were an every-day occurrence.

Clearing his throat, Gilthas said, more briskly, "You have verified the first reports we heard?"

The Lioness brushed a tangle of her shining hair from her face. "Yes, but what the fall of the shield means, whether this is good or bad, cannot be told."

"What happened? How did this come about? Did the Silvanesti lower it themselves?"

She shook her head, and the golden, curling, rampant mass of hair that gave her the nickname of the Lioness covered her face once more. Fondly, her husband smoothed the locks back with his hand. He loved to look upon her face. Some noble Qualinesti elven women, with their cream and rose-petal complexions, looked with disdain on the Kagonesti, whose skin was tanned a deep brown from days spent in the sunshine.

Unlike his face, wherein one could see traces of his human heritage in his square jaw and slightly more rounded eyes, her face was all elven: heart-shaped, with almond eyes. Her features were strong, not delicate, her gaze bold and decisive. Seeing him look at her with love and admiration, the Lioness captured his hand, kissed his palm.

"I have missed you," she said softly.

"And I, you." He sighed deeply, drew her close. "Will we ever be at peace, do you think, Beloved? Will there ever be a time when we can sleep until long, long after sunrise, then wake and spend the rest of the day doing nothing except loving each other?"

She did not answer him. He kissed the mane of hair and held her close.

"What of the shield?" he said at last.

"I talked to a runner who saw it was down, but when he tried to find Alhana and her people, they had moved on. That is not unexpected. Alhana would have immediately crossed the border into Silvanesti. We may not hear anything more from her for some time."

"I had not let myself hope that this news was true," Gilthas said, "but you ease my care and lift my fear. By lowering the shield, the Silvanesti show they are willing to enter the world again. I will send emissaries immediately to tell them of our plight and ask for their aid. Our people will travel there and find food and rest and shelter. If our plans fail and Qualinost falls, with our cousins' help, we will build a large army. We will return to drive the dragon from our homeland."

The Lioness put her hand over his mouth. "Hush, Husband. You are spinning steel out of moonbeams. We have no idea what is happening in Silvanesti, why the shield was lowered, what this may portend. The runner reported that all living things that grew near the shield were either dead or dying. Perhaps this shield was not a blessing to the Silvanesti but a curse.

"There is also the fact," she added relentlessly, "that our cousins the Silvanesti have not acted very cousinly in the past. They named your Uncle Porthios a dark elf. They have no love for your father. They deem you a half-breed, your mother something worse."

"They cannot deny us entry," Gilthas said firmly. "They will not. You will not deprive me of my moonbeams, my dear. I believe the lowering of the shield is a sign of a change of heart among the Silvanesti. I have hope to offer our people. They will cross the Plains of Dust. They will reach Silvanesti, and once there our cousins will welcome them. The journey will not be easy, but you know better than anyone the courage that lives in the hearts of our people. Courage such as we saw in that young girl."

"Yes, the journey will be hard," the Lioness said, regarding her husband earnestly. "Our people will succeed, but they will need a leader: one who will urge us to keep going when we are tired and hungry and thirsty and there is no rest, no food, no water. If our king travels with us, we will follow him. When we arrive in Silvanesti, our king must be our emissary. Our king must speak for us, so that we do not seem a mob of beggars."

"The senators, the Heads of House—"

"—will squabble among themselves, Gilthas, you know that. One third will want to march west instead of east. Another third will want to march north instead of south. And the other third will not want to march at all. They will fight over this for months. If they ever did manage to reach Silvanesti, the first thing they would do is drag up all the quarrels for the past three centuries, and that will be an end to everything. You, Gilthas. You are the only one who has a hope of making this work. You are the only one who can unify the various factions and lead the people across the desert. You are the only one who can smooth the way with the Silvanesti."

"And yet," Gilthas argued, "I cannot be in two places at once. I cannot fight to defend Qualinost and lead our people into the Plains of Dust."

"No, you cannot," the Lioness agreed. "You must put someone else in charge of the defense of Qualinost."

"What sort of king flees to safety and leaves his people to die in his stead?" Gilthas demanded frowning.

"The sort of king who makes certain that the last sacrifice of those who stay behind will not be made in vain," said his wife. "Do not think that because you do not remain to fight the dragon that you will have the easier task. You are asking a people born to the woods, born to lush gardens and bountiful water, to venture into the Plains of Dust, an arid land of shifting sand dunes and blazing sun. Place me in charge of Qualinost—"

"No," he said shortly. "I will not hear of it."

"My love—"

"We will not discuss it. I have said no, and I mean it. How can I do what you tell me I must do, without you at my side?" Gilthas demanded, his voice rising in his passion.

She gazed at him in silence, and he grew calmer.

"We will not speak of this anymore," he told her.

"Yet we must speak of it sometime."

Gilthas shook his head. His lips compressed into a tight, grim line. "What other news?" he asked abruptly.

The Lioness, who knew her husband's moods, understood that continuing to argue would be fruitless. "Our forces harass Beryl's armies. Yet, their numbers are so great that we are as gnats attacking a pack of ravening wolves."

"Withdraw your people. Order them south. They will be needed to guard the survivors if Qualinost falls."

"I thought that would be your command," she said. "I have already done so. From now on, Beryl's troops will move unimpeded, looting and burning and killing."

Gilthas felt the hope that had warmed his blood seep away, leaving him once again despairing, chilled.

"Yet we will have our revenge upon her. You said that the dwarves have agreed to your plan." The Lioness, sorry she had spoken so harshly, tried to lift him from the dark mood she saw settling on him.

"Yes," he said. "I spoke to Tarn Bellowsgranite. Our meeting was fortuitous. I had not expected to find him in the tunnels. I had thought I would have to ride to Thorbardin to speak with him, but he has taken charge of the work himself, and thus we were able to settle the matter at once."

"He knows that perhaps some of his own people may die defending elves?"

"He knows better than I can tell him what the cost will be to the dwarves. Yet they are willing to make the sacrifice. 'If once the great green dragon swallows Qualinesti, she will next have an appetite for Thorbardin,' he told me."

"Where is the dwarven army?" the Lioness demanded. "Skulking underground, prepared to defend Thorbardin. An army of hundreds of thousands, doughty warriors. With them, we could withstand Beryl's assault—"

"My dear," said Gilthas, gently, "the dwarves have a right to defend their homeland. Would we elves rush to their aid if they were the ones attacked? They have done much for us. They have saved the lives of countless people, and they are prepared to sacrifice their lives for a cause that is not their own. They should be honored, not castigated."

The Lioness glared at him, defiant for a moment, then she said with a shrug and a rueful smile. "You are right, of course. You see both sides, whereas I see only one. This is why I say again, you must be the one to lead our people."

"I said we would speak of this later," Gilthas returned, his voice cool.

"I wonder," he said, changing the subject, "does that young girl cry when she is alone and wakeful in the night, her charges slumbering around her, trusting in her even when the darkness is deep?"

"No," the Lioness answered. "She does not cry, for one of them might wake and see her tears and lose faith."

Gilthas sighed deeply, held his wife close. "Beryl has crossed the border into our land. How many days before the army reaches Qualinost?"

"Four," the Lioness replied.

20

The March into Nightlund

ina's small army, only a few hundred in number, made up of the group of Knights who had followed her from the ghastly valley of Neraka to Sanction to Silvanesti, and now to this strange land.

The dragons flew through darkness so deep that Galdar could not see Captain Samuval flying on the dragon next to him. Galdar could not even see his own dragon's long tail or wings for the darkness that shrouded them. He saw one dragon only and that was the strange dragon Mina rode, the death dragon, for it shimmered with a ghostly iridescence that was both terrible and beautiful. Red, blue, green, white, red-blue, as two of the souls of the dead dragons combined, then white-green, constantly changing until he grew dizzy and was forced to look away.

But his gaze was drawn back to the death dragon, marveling, awed. He wondered how Mina found courage to ride a beast that seemed as insubstantial as the morning mist, for he could see through the dragon, see the darkness beyond it. Mina had no qualms apparently, and her faith was justified, for the dragon bore her safely through the skies of Ansalon and deposited her gently and reverently on the ground.

The other dragons landed on a vast plain, allowed their riders to dismount, then took to the air again.

"Listen for my call," Mina told the dragons. "I will have need of you."

The dragons—giant reds and fleet blues, sly blacks, aloof whites and cunning greens—bowed low their heads, spread their wings, and bent their proud necks before her. The death dragon circled once above her head and then vanished as if it had been absorbed into the darkness. The other dragons lifted their wings and flew away, heading different directions. Their departure created a great wind that nearly blew the men over. The dragons were gone, and they were left on foot, with no mounts, in a strange land, with no idea where they were.

It was then Mina told them.

"Nightlund," she said.

Once this land had been ruled by a Solamnic Knight named Soth. Given the chance by the gods to halt the Cataclysm, Lord Soth had failed and brought down a curse upon himself and the land. Since the time of the Cataclysm, other doomed souls, both living and dead, had found in Nightlund a place of refuge and they had come to dwell within its deep shadows. Hearing that the land had become a hideout for those fleeing the law, the Solamnic Knights, who ruled this land, had made several attempts to clean them out. These proved futile, and soon the Knights quit entering the forest, leaving it to Soth, the accursed knight, to rule. Nightlund was a no-man's-land, where none of the living came, if they could help it,

This land had an evil reputation, even among the Dark Knights of Neraka, for the dead had no allegiances to any government of the living. Mina's Knights and soldiers formed ranks and marched after her without a murmur of complaint. They were so confident of her now, they believed in her—and in the One God—so strongly, that they did not question her judgment.

Mina's soldiers entered Nightlund with impunity. They encountered no enemy—living or dead. They marched beneath huge cypress trees that had been old at the time of the forging of the Graygem. They saw no living creature, no squirrel or bird, mouse or chipmunk, no deer or bear. They saw no dead, either, for none of them possessed magic, and thus the dead took no interest in them. But the soldiers and knights sensed the dead around them, sensed it as one senses he is being watched by unseen eyes. After several days of marching through the eerie forest, the men who had followed Mina into Nightlund without hesitation were starting to have second thoughts.

The fur on the back of Galdar's neck prickled and twitched, and he was continually whipping his head around to see if something was creeping up on him. Captain Samuval complained—in low tones and only when Mina could not hear him—that he had "the horrors." When asked what malady this might be, he could not explain, except to say that it made his feet and hands cold so that no fire could warm them and gave him an ache in his belly. The sharp crack of a falling branch sent men diving to the ground, to lie quivering in terror until someone told them what it was. Shamefaced, they would rise and carry on.

The men doubled the watch at night, though Mina told them that they had no need to set a watch at all. She did not explain why, but Galdar guessed that they were being guarded by those who had no more need of sleep. He did not find this particularly reassuring, and he often woke from a dream of hundreds of people standing around him, staring down at him with eyes that were empty of all except pain.

Mina was strangely silent during this march. She walked in the front of the line, refused all company, said no word to any man, yet Galdar could sometimes see her lips moving, as though she were speaking. When he once ventured to ask to whom she spoke, she replied, "To them," and made a sweeping gesture with her hand that encompassed nothing.

"The dead, Mina?" Galdar asked hesitantly.

"The souls of the dead. They have no more need of the shells that once housed them."

"You can see them?"

"The One God gives me that power."

"But I can't."

"I could cause you to see them, Galdar," Mina said to him, "but you would find it most unpleasant and disconcerting."

"No, Mina, no, I don't want to see them," Galdar said hastily. "How . . . how many of them are there?"

"Thousands," she replied. "Thousands upon thousands and thousands more after that. The souls of all who have died in this world since the Chaos War, Galdar. That is how many. And more join their ranks daily. Elves dying in Silvanesti and Qualinesti, soldiers dying defending Sanction, mothers dying in childbirth, children dying of sickness, the elderly dying in their beds—all these souls are flowing into Nightlund in a vast river. Brought here by the One God, prepared to do the bidding of the One God."

"You said since the end of the Chaos War. Where did the souls go before that?"

"The blessed souls went to other realms beyond. Cursed souls were doomed to remain here, until they learned the lessons they were meant to learn in life. Then they, too, left for the next stage. The old gods encouraged the souls to leave. The old gods gave the souls no choice. The old gods ignored the fact that the souls did not want to depart. They longed to remain within the world and do what they could to assist the living. The One God saw this and granted the souls the gift that they could remain in the world and serve the One God. So they do, Galdar. And so they will."

Mina looked at him with her amber eyes. "You would not want to leave, would you, Galdar?"

"I would not want to leave you, Mina," he replied. "That is what I fear most about dying. That I would have to leave you."

"You never will, Galdar," Mina said to him, her voice gentle. The amber warmed. Her hand touched his arm, and her touch was as warm as the amber. "I promise you that. You never will."

Galdar was uneasy. He hesitated to say the next, for fear she would be displeased, but he was her second-in-command, and he was responsible not only to her but to those under his command.

"How long are we going to stay here, Mina? The men don't like it in this forest. I can't say that I blame them. The living have no place here. We're not wanted."

"Not long," she said. "I must pay a visit to someone who lives within this forest. Yes, he *lives*," she emphasized the word. "A wizard by the name of Dalamar. Perhaps you've heard of him?"

Galdar shook his head. He had as little to do with wizards as possible and took no interest in them or their business.

"After that," Mina continued, "I must leave for a brief time—"

"Leave?" Galdar repeated, involuntarily raising his voice.

"Leave?" Captain Samuval came hurrying over. "What is this? Who is leaving?"

"Mina," said Galdar, his throat constricting.

"Mina the only reason the troops stay is because of you," said Samuval. "If you go—"

"I will not be gone long," said Mina, frowning.

"Long or short, Mina, I'm not sure we can control the men," said Captain Samuval. He kept jerking his head about, constantly looking over his shoulder. "And I don't blame them. This land is cursed. Ghosts crawl all over it. I can feel them crawling all over me!"

He shivered and rubbed his arms and glanced fearfully about. "You can't see them except out of the corner of your eye. And when you look at them, they're gone. It's enough to drive a man stark, staring mad."

"I will speak to the men, Captain Samuval," Mina replied. "You and Galdar must speak to them, as well, and you must show them by example that you are not afraid."

"Even though we are," the minotaur growled.

"The dead will not harm you. They have been ordered to congregate here for one purpose and one purpose alone. The One God commands them. They serve the One God, and through the intercession of the One God, they serve me."

"What is this purpose, Mina? You keep saying that, but you tell us nothing."

"All will be revealed. You must be patient and have faith," Mina said. The amber eyes cooled and hardened.

Galdar and Samuval exchanged glances. Samuval held still, no longer jerked his head about or rubbed his arms, afraid of offending Mina.

"How long will you be gone?" Galdar asked.

"You will come with me to the wizard's Tower. Then I travel north, to speak to the dragon who rules Palanthas, the dragon known as Khellendros or, as I prefer to call him, Skie."

"Skie? He's not even around anymore. All know that he departed on some strange quest."

"The dragon is there," Mina said. "He waits for me, though he does not know it."

"Waits to attack you, maybe," said Samuval with a snort. "He's not like one of our blue dragons, Mina. This Skie is a butcher. He devours his own kind to gain power, just like Malystryx."

"You should not go alone, Mina," Galdar urged tersely. "Take some of us with you."

"The Hand of the One God brought down Cyan Blood-bane," Mina said sternly. "The Hand of the One God will bring down Skie, if he thwarts the God's commands. Skie will obey. He has no choice. He cannot help himself.

"You will obey me, too, Galdar, Captain Samuval," Mina added. "As will the men." Her tone and her look softened. "You have no need to fear. The One God rewards obedience. You will be safe in the forest of the dead. They guard you. They have no thought of harming you. Resume the march, Galdar. We must make haste. Events in the world move swiftly, and we are called."

"We are called," muttered Galdar, after Mina had departed, traveling deeper into the forest. "We are always called, it seems."

"Called to victory," observed Captain Samuval. "Called to glory. I don't mind that. Do you?"

"No, not that part," Galdar admitted.

"Then what's wrong—besides this place frightens the pudding out of us." Samuval glanced around the shadowed forest with a shudder.

"I guess I'd like to think I had some say in the matter," Galdar muttered. "Some choice."

"In the military?" Samuval chortled. "Your mama must have dropped you on your head when you were a calf if you think that!"

He looked down the path. Mina had passed beyond his sight. "Come on," he said uneasily. "Let's keep moving. The sooner we're out of this place, the better."

Galdar pondered this. Samuval was right, of course. In the military one obeyed orders. A soldier didn't get to vote on whether or not he'd like to storm a city, whether or not he'd like to face a barrage of arrows or have a cauldron of hot boiling oil poured on his head. A soldier did what he was told to do without question. Galdar knew that, and he accepted that. Why was this any different?

Galdar didn't know. Couldn't answer.

21

An Unexpected Visitor

Palin looked up from the book he had been studying and rubbed his watery eyes and the back of his neck. His vision, once so clear and keen, had deteriorated with age. He could still see well at a distance, but he was forced to read through spectacles that magnified the text or—in their absence—(he was forever misplacing them)—he had to read with his head bent close to the page. Slamming shut the book in frustration, he shoved it across the stone table, there to reside with the other books that had been of no help.

Palin glanced with little hope at the other books he had found upon the shelves and had yet to read. He had chosen these simply because he recognized his uncle's handwriting on the covers and because they pertained to magical artifacts. He had no reason to suppose they referred specifically to the Device of Time Journeying.

To be truthful, he found them depressing. Their references to magic and the gods of magic filled him with memories, longings, desires. This room where he sat—his uncle's laboratory—was the same, depressing.

He thought back to his conversation with Dalamar yesterday, the day the kender had been discovered missing, the day Palin had insisted on entering his uncle's old laboratory, searching through Raistlin's books on magic in hopes of finding useful information on the Device of Time Journeying.

"I know that the Wizards' Council ordered Raistlin's laboratory shut," Palin said as they wended their way up the treacherous stairs that spiraled around the dark heart of the Tower of High Sorcery—a misnomer now, if ever there was one. "But they are gone, as the magic is gone. I doubt they'll come looking for us."

Dalamar glanced at him, seemed amused. "What a fool you are, Majere. Did you really think I would let rules laid down by Par-Salian stop me from entering? I broke the seal to the laboratory long ago."

"Why?"

"Can't you guess?" Dalamar asked caustically.

"You were hoping to find the magic."

"I thought . . . well, it doesn't matter what I thought." Dalamar shrugged. "The Portal to the Abyss . . . the spellbooks . . . something might be left. Perhaps I was hoping that some of the *Shalafi*'s power might have lingered where he once walked. Or maybe I was hoping I would find the gods. . . ."

Dalamar spoke softly, gazing into the darkness, into the emptiness. "My mind was fevered. I wasn't well. Instead of the gods, I found death. I found necromancy. Or perhaps it found me."

They climbed the stairs, stood before the door that held so many memories. The door that had once looked so imposing, so forbidding, seemed now small and shabby. Palin reminded himself that many, many years had passed since he had last seen it.

"The undead that once guarded it are gone now," Dalamar remarked. "There is no longer any need for them."

"What of the Portal to the Abyss?" Palin asked.

"It leads to nowhere and to nothing," Dalamar answered.

"My uncle's spellbooks?"

"Jenna could fetch a high price for them at that shop of hers, but only as antiques, curiosities." Dalamar broke the wizard-lock. "I wouldn't have even locked the door if it hadn't been for the kender."

"Aren't you coming?" Palin asked.

Dalamar refused. "Hopeless as it may seem, I'm going to continue to search for the kender."

"He's been missing a day and a night. If Tas were here, he certainly could not go that long without popping up to annoy one of us. Face it, Dalamar, he has managed to escape."

"I have ringed this Tower round with magic," Dalamar stated grimly. "The kender could not have escaped."

"Famous last words," Palin remarked.

Palin felt a thrill of awe and excitement as he entered the laboratory that had been his Uncle Raistlin's, the place where his uncle had worked some of his most powerful and awful magic. Those feelings soon evaporated, to be replaced by the sadness and disappointment experienced by those of us who return to the home of our childhood to find that it is smaller than we remembered and that the current owners have let it fall into neglect.

The fabled stone table, a table so large a minotaur could lie down full length upon it, was dusty and covered in mouse dung. Jars that had once held the experiments of Raistlin's attempts to create life still stood upon the shelves, their contents dead and desiccated. The fabled spellbooks belonging not only to Raistlin Majere but to the archmage Fistandantilus, lay scattered about in disarray, their spines rotting, their pages grimy and covered in cobwebs.

Palin rose to stretch the kinks from his legs. Lifting the lamp that lighted his work, he walked to the very back of the lab to the Portal to the Abyss.

The dread Portal, created by the mages of Krynn to allow those with faith and courage and powerful magicks to enter the dark realm of Queen Takhisis. Raistlin Majere had done that, to his great cost. So potent was the evil of the Portal that Dalamar, as Master of the Tower, had sealed up the laboratory and everything inside.

The cloth that had once covered the Portal was rotted away, fell in rags about it. The carved heads of the five dragons that had glowed radiantly in homage to the Queen of Darkness were dark. Cobwebs covered their eyes, spiders crawled into their mouths. Once they had given the impression of silently screaming. Now they appeared to be gasping for air. Palin looked past the heads, looked inside the Portal.

Where once had been eternity was now only an empty room, not very large, covered with dust, populated by spiders.

Hearing the rustling of robes on the stairs leading to the laboratory, Palin hastily left the Portal. He returned to his seat, pretended to be absorbed in once more studying the ancient spellbooks.

"The kender has escaped," Dalamar reported, shoving open the door.

Taking one look at the elf's cold and angry expression, Palin bit his tongue on the "I told you so."

"I cast a spell that would reveal to me the presence of any living creature in the building," Dalamar continued. "The spell located you and myriad rodents but no kender."

"How did he get out?" Palin asked.

"Come with me to the library, and I will show you."

Palin was not sorry to leave the laboratory. He brought the books he had not yet read with him. He did not plan on coming back. He was sorry he had ever returned.

"Shortsighted of me, no doubt, but it never occurred to me to spellbind the chimney!" Dalamar stated. Bending down to peer into the fireplace, he made an irritated gesture. "Look, you can see a great quantity of soot in the grate, as well as several bits of broken stone that appear to have been dislodged. The chimney is narrow, and the climb long and arduous, but that would only encourage a kender, not stop him. Once he was outside, he could shinny down a tree trunk and so make his way into Nightlund."

"Nightlund is filled with the dead—" Palin began.

"An added inducement for a kender," Dalamar interjected dryly.

"It's my fault. I should have been keeping an eye on him. But, to be honest, I did not think there was any possible way he could escape."

"It's just like the perversity of the little beasts," said Dalamar. "When you *want* to lose one, you can't possibly. The one time we actually want to keep one, we can't hang onto him. No telling where he has gone. He could be halfway to Flotsam by now."

"The dead—"

"They would not bother him. It's magic they are after."

"To give to you" Palin said bitterly.

"Only a pittance. What they do with the rest of it, I haven't been able to discover. I can almost see it out there, like a vast ocean, yet I receive but a trickle, barely enough to slake my thirst. Never enough to satisfy it. At first, when the Shadow Sorcerer led me to discover necromancy, I was given all I wanted. My power was immense. I thought to increase that power by removing to this location. I discovered, too late, that I had walked into my own prison cell.

"Then I heard from Jenna that you had come across the magical Device of Time Journeying. For the first time in years, I felt hope. At last, this would offer a way out."

"For you," Palin said coldly.

"For all of us!" Dalamar returned with a flash of his dark eyes. "Yet what do I find? You have broken it. Not only that, but you managed to scatter pieces of it throughout the Citadel of Light!"

"Better than Beryl having it!"

"Perhaps she has it already. Perhaps she had brains enough to gather up the bits and pieces—"

"She would not be able to put it back together. I'm not even sure *we* could put it back together." Palin gestured toward the books piled up on the desk. "I can find no reference to what to do if the artifact breaks."

"Because it was never meant to break. Its maker had no notion of the dead feeding off it. How could he? Such a thing never happened in the Krynn of the gods. The Krynn we knew."

"Why have the dead begun feeding now?" Palin wondered. "Why not five years ago or ten? The wild magic worked for me once, just as necromancy worked for you and healing worked for Goldmoon and the Mystics. The dead never interfered with us before."

"The wisest among us never really knew what happened to the souls of the dead," Dalamar said, musing. "We knew that some of the dead remained on this plane, those who had ties to this world, like your uncle, or those who were cursed to remain here. The god Chemosh ruled over these unquiet spirits. What of the rest? Where did they go? Because none ever returned to tell us, we never found out."

"The clerics of Paladine taught that the blessed spirits departed this stage of life to travel on to the next," Palin said. "That is what my father and mother believed. Yet—"

He glanced out the window, hopeful—and fearful—of seeing his father's spirit among those unhappy ghosts.

"I will tell you what I think," said Dalamar. "Mind you, this is only what I think, not what I know. If the dead were once allowed to depart, they are not being allowed to leave now. The night of the storm . . . Did you mark that terrible storm?"

"Yes," said Palin. "It was no ordinary storm. It was fraught with magic."

"There was a voice in the storm," Dalamar said. "A voice that boomed in the thunder and cracked in the lightning. Almost I could hear it and understand it. Almost, but not quite. The voice sent out a call that night, and it was then the dead began to congregate in Nightlund in force. I watched them from my window, flowing from all directions, an immense river of souls. They have been summoned here for a purpose. As to what the purpose is—"

"Hail the Tower!" a voice called out from below the laboratory window. Simultaneously, a battering knock sounded on the Tower door.

Astounded, Palin and Dalamar stared at one another.

"Who can that be?" Palin asked, but at the very moment he spoke the words, he saw that he was talking to himself.

Dalamar's body stood before him, but that body might have been a wax dummy on exhibit at some traveling fair. The eyes were open, stared straight at Palin, but they did not see him. The body breathed, but that was all it did.

Before Palin could react, Dalamar's eyes blinked. Life and light and intelligence returned.

"What is it?" Palin demanded.

"Two Knights of Neraka, as they are calling themselves these days. One is a minotaur, and the other is very strange."

As he talked, Dalamar began half-leading, half-dragging Palin across the room. Reaching a far wall, he pressed on a stone in certain way. Part of the wall slid aside, revealing a narrow opening and a staircase.

"They must not find you here!" Dalamar said, shoving Palin inside.

Palin had come to the same conclusion himself. "How did they travel through the forest? How did they find the Tower—"

"No time! Down those stairs!" Dalamar hissed. "They lead to a chamber located in the library. There is an opening in the wall. You'll be able to hear and to see. Go quickly! They will start to get suspicious."

The pounding on the door and the shouting had increased.

"The wizard Dalamar!" the deep voice of the minotaur rumbled. "We have come a long distance to talk to you!"

Palin ducked inside. Dalamar pressed his hand against the panel, and the wall slid noiselessly in place, leaving Palin in complete darkness.

He took a moment to calm himself after the alarm and the flurry, put a hand against the cold stone. He tried casting a light spell, uncertain of his success. To his relief, the spell worked perfectly. A flame like the flame of a candle burned in the palm of his hand.

Palin traversed the stairs quietly and swiftly, keeping one hand against the wall to steady his steps, the other lifted to light his way. The staircase spiraled down at such a steep angle that rounding the last turn in the stair, he came up against a blank wall with a suddenness that nearly caused him to bash his head against the stones.

He searched for the opening Dalamar had promised him but found nothing. The stones were set solidly in place. There was no chink or crack in the mortar. He might have feared that Dalamar had used this ruse to imprison him except that he could hear voices growing steadily louder.

Palin reached out his hand, began to touch each of the stones. The first several were solid—cold, hard, rough. He moved higher. Reaching over his head, he tried to touch one of the stones and saw his hand pass right through.

"Of course," he said to himself. "Dalamar is taller than I am by a head and shoulders. I should have made allowances."

The illusion of stone dispelled, Palin looked through it directly into the library. From his vantage point, he could see the desk, see the person seated at the desk, and observe any visitors. He could hear every word as clearly as if he were in the room, and he had to fight against an uneasy impression that those inside the library could see him as clearly as he could see them.

Perhaps the apprentice Dalamar had once hidden himself to spy upon Raistlin Majere, his *Shalafi*. The notion provided Palin some amusement, as he settled himself to watch—a rather uncomfortable proceeding, since he had to stand as tall as possible and stretch his neck to look through the opening in the stone wall. Recalling the fact that Raistlin had been aware that his apprentice had been spying on him did little to add to Palin's sense of wellbeing. He reminded himself that he had been in this very library and had undoubtedly looked at this very wall without any notion that a small portion was not real.

The door opened. Dalamar ushered his visitors inside. One was a minotaur—hulkish and brutish with that gleam of intelligence in the animal eyes that was both disconcerting and dangerous. The other Dark Knight was, as Dalamar had said, "very strange."

"Why . . ." Palin whispered, shocked as he watched her walk into Dalamar's library, her armor gleaming in the light of the fire. "I know her! Or rather, I knew her. Mina!"

The girl entered the room and looked about her with what Palin at first took for childlike wonder. She looked at the shelves of books, the ornately carved and beautiful desk, the dusty velvet curtains, the frayed silk rugs of elven make that covered the stone floor. He knew teenage girls—he'd had them as pupils in his school—and expected the usual squeals at the sight of the more grisly objects, such as the skull of a baaz draconian. (Raistlin had once engaged on a study of these creatures, perhaps with the intent of recreating them himself. The full skeleton could be found in the old laboratory, along with some of the internal organs, kept in a solution in a jar.)

Mina remained silent and apparently unimpressed by anything she saw, including Dalamar.

She shifted her gaze around the room, taking in everything. She turned her face toward Palin. Eyes that were the color of amber focused on the place in the wall behind which he was hiding. Palin had the impression that they saw through the illusion, saw him as plainly as if he were standing in the room. He felt this so acutely that he recoiled, glanced about him to ascertain his route of escape, for he was certain that her next move would be to point him out, demand his capture.

The eyes fixed on him, absorbed him. The liquid amber surrounded him, solidified, passed on to continue the investigation of the room. She said nothing, made no mention of him, and Palin's fast-beating heart began to return to some semblance of normal.

Of course, she had not seen him. He berated himself. How could she? He thought back to the last time he had seen her, an orphan in the Citadel of Light. She had been a scrawny little girl with skinned knees and a mass of glorious red hair. Now she was a slender young woman, the red hair cut off, playing at dress-up in a Knight's armor. Yet she had a look on her face that was certainly not childlike. Resolute, purposeful, confident—all that and something more. Exalted . . .

"You are the wizard Dalamar," Mina said, turning the amber eyes on him. "I was told I would find you here."

"I am Dalamar, the Master of the Tower. I would be considerably interested to know who told you where to find me," said Dalamar, folding his hands in the sleeves of his robes and giving a graceful bow.

"The Master of the Tower . . ." Mina repeated softly with a half-smile, as if she knew the truth of the matter. "As to how I found you, the dead told me."

"Indeed?" Dalamar seemed to find this troubling. He tried to evade her eyes, slid out from beneath the amber gaze. "Who might you be, Lady Knight, that you are on such intimate terms with the dead?"

"I am Mina," she said. She raised the amber eyes, and this time she caught him. She gestured. "This is my second-in-command, Galdar."

The minotaur gave an abrupt nod of his horned head. He was not comfortable in the Tower. He kept glancing about darkly as if he expected something to spring out and attack at any moment. He was not worried about himself, however. His sole concern appeared to be for Mina. He was protective to the point of worship, adoration.

Palin was overcome by curiosity. Dalamar was wary.

"I am interested to know how you made your way unscathed through Nightlund, Lady Mina," Dalamar said. He sat down in the chair behind his desk, perhaps trying to break that entrancing gaze. "Will you be seated?"

"Thank you, no," Mina replied and continued to stand. She now gazed down upon him, putting Dalamar at an unexpected disadvantage. "Why does my being in Nightlund astonish you, Wizard?"

Dalamar shifted in his chair, not willing to stand up, for that would make him appear vacillating and weak, yet not enjoying being looked down upon.

"I am a necromancer. I sense magic about you," he said.

312

"The dead drain magic, they feed off it. I am surprised that you were not mobbed."

"That which you sense about me is not magic," Mina replied, and her voice was unusually low and mature for one her age. "You feel the power of the God I serve, the One God. As to the dead, they do not touch me. The One God rules the dead. They see in me the One God, and they bow down before me."

Dalamar's lip twitched.

"It is true!" Galdar stated, growling in anger. "I saw it myself! Mina comes to lead—"

"—my army into Nightlund," Mina concluded. Resting her hand upon the minotaur's arm, she commanded silence.

"Lead your army against what?" Dalamar asked sarcastically. "The dead?"

"Against the living," Mina replied. "We plan to seize control of Solamnia."

"You must have a large army, Lady Knight," Dalamar said. "You must have brought along every soldier in the Dark Knighthood."

"My army is small," Mina admitted. "I was required to leave troops behind to guard Silvanesti, which fell to our might not long ago—"

"Silvanesti . . . fallen . . ." Dalamar was livid. He stared at her. "I don't believe it!"

Mina shrugged. "Your belief or disbelief is all one to me. Besides, what do you care? Your people cast you out, or so I have heard tell. I mentioned that only in passing. I have come to ask a favor of you, Master of the Tower."

Dalamar was shaken to the core of his being. Palin saw that despite claiming not to believe her, the dark elf realized she spoke the truth. It was impossible to hear that calm, resolute, confident voice and not believe whatever she said.

Dalamar struggled to regain at least outward control of himself. He would have liked to have asked questions, demanded answers, but he could not quite see how to do this without revealing an uncharacteristic concern. Dalamar's love for his people was a love that he constantly denied and in that denial constantly reaffirmed.

"You have heard correctly," he said with a tight smile. "They cast me out. What favor can I do for you, Lady Mina?"

"I have arranged to meet someone here," she began.

"Here? In the Tower?" Dalamar was astonished beyond words. "Out of the question. I am not running an inn, Lady Mina."

"I realize that, Wizard Dalamar," Mina replied, and her tone was gentle. "I realize that what I am asking will be an imposition, an inconvenience to you, an interruption to your studies. Rest assured that I would not ask this of you, but that there are certain requirements that must be met as to the location of this meeting. The Tower of High Sorcery fulfills all those requirements. Indeed, it is the only place on Krynn that fulfills the requirements. The meeting must take place here."

"I am to have no say in this? What are these requirements of which you speak?" Dalamar demanded, frowning.

"I am not permitted to reveal them. Not yet. As to your say in this, what you do or say matters not at all. The One God has decided this will be, and therefore this will be."

Dalamar's dark eyes flickered. His face smoothed.

"Your guest is welcome in the Tower, Lady. In order to make the guest's stay comfortable, it would help if I knew something about this person . . . male or female? A name, perhaps?"

"Thank you, Wizard," Mina said, and turned away.

"When will the guest arrive?" Dalamar pursued. "How will I know that the person who comes is the person you expect?"

"You will know," Mina replied. "We will leave now, Galdar."

The minotaur had already crossed the room and was reaching for the door handle.

"There is a favor you could do for me in return, Lady," Dalamar said mildly.

Mina glanced back. "What is that, Wizard?"

"A kender I was using in an important experiment has escaped," Dalamar said, his tone casual, as if kender were like caged mice and were found or lost on a routine basis. "His loss would be of no importance to me, but the experiment was. I would like very much to recover him, and it occurs to me that perhaps, if you are bringing an army into Nightlund, you might come upon him. If you do, I would appreciate his return. He calls himself Tasslehoff," Dalamar added with an offhanded and charming smile, "as so many of them do these days."

"Tasslehoff!" Mina's attention was caught directly. A crease marred her forehead. "The Tasslehoff who carried with him the magical Device of Time Journeying? You had him here? You had him and the device, and you *lost* him?"

Dalamar stared, confounded. The elven wizard was older by hundreds of years than this girl. He had been deemed one of the great mages of his or any time. Though he worked in magic's shadows, he had gained the respect, if not the love, of those who worked in the light. Mina's amber-eyed gaze pinned the powerful wizard to the chair. Dalamar wriggled beneath her gaze, struggled, but she had caught him and held him fast.

Two bright spots of color stained Dalamar's pale cheeks. The elf's slender fingers nervously stroked a bit of carving on the desk, an oak leaf. The too-thin fingers traced its shape over and over until Palin longed to rush from his hiding place and seize that nervous hand to make it stop.

"Where is the device?" Mina demanded, advancing on

him until she stood at his desk, gazing down at him. "Did he have it with him? Do you have it here?"

Dalamar had reached his limit. He rose from his chair, looked down at her, looked down the length of his aquiline nose, looked down from his greater height, looked down from the confidence of his own power.

"What business can this possibly be of yours, Lady Mina?"

"Not *my* business," Mina said, not at all intimidated. Indeed, it was Dalamar who seemed to shrink as she spoke. "The business of the One God. All that happens in this world is the business of the One God. The One God sees into your heart and into your mind and your soul, Wizard. Though you may hide the truth from my mortal eyes, you cannot hide the truth from the One God. We will search for this kender, and if we find him we will do with him what needs to be done."

She turned again and walked away calm, unruffled.

Dalamar remained standing at his desk, the hand that had nervously traced the oak leaf clenched tightly in a fist that he concealed beneath his robes.

Arriving at the door, Mina turned around. Her gaze passed over Dalamar, another insect in her display case, and fixed on Palin. In vain he told himself she could not see him. She caught him, held him.

"You believe the artifact was lost in the Citadel of Light. It was not. It came back to the kender. He has it in his possession. That is why he ran away."

Palin doused the magical light. In the darkness, he could see nothing but those amber eyes, hear nothing but her voice. He remained there so long that Dalamar came searching for him. The elf's footsteps were soft upon the stone stairs, and Palin did not hear him until he sensed movement. He looked up in alarm, found Dalamar standing in front of him.

"What are you still doing here? Are you all right? I thought for certain something had happened to you," Dalamar said, irritated.

"Something did happen to me," Palin returned. "*She* happened to me. She saw me. She looked straight at me. The last words she spoke were to me!"

"Impossible," Dalamar said. "No eyes, not even amber eyes, can see through solid stone *and* magic."

Palin shook his head, unconvinced. "She spoke to me."

He expected a sarcastic rejoinder from Dalamar, but the dark elf was in no mood to banter, apparently, for he climbed the stairs leading back to the laboratory in silence.

"I know that girl, Dalamar," Palin said.

Dalamar halted on the staircase, turned to stare. "How?"

"I haven't seen her in a long time. Not since she ran away. She was an orphan. A fisherman found her washed upon the shore of Schallsea Isle. He brought her to the Citadel of Light, to the orphans' home. She became a favorite of Goldmoon's, almost a daughter to her. Three years ago she ran away. She was fourteen. Goldmoon was devastated. Mina had a good home. She was loved, pampered. She seemed happy, except I never knew a child to ask so many questions. None of us could understand why she ran off. And now . . . a Dark Knight. Goldmoon will be heartbroken."

"That is very odd," Dalamar said thoughtfully, and they resumed their climb. "So she was raised by Goldmoon. . . ."

"Do you suppose what she said about Tas and the device was true?" Palin asked, as they emerged from the hidden stairwell.

"Of course, it was true," Dalamar replied. He walked over to the window, stared down into the cypress trees below. "That explains why the kender ran away. He feared we would find it."

"We would have, if we had bothered to think through this rationally, instead of haring off in a panic. What ninnies

317

we are! The device will always return to the one who owns it. Even in pieces, it will always return."

Palin was frustrated. He felt the urgent need to do something, yet there was nothing he could do.

"You could search for him, Dalamar. Your spirit can walk this world, at least—"

"And do what?" Dalamar demanded. "If I did find him—which would be a miracle to surpass all miracles— I could do nothing except frighten him into burrowing deeper into whatever hole he's dug."

Dalamar had been staring out the window. He stiffened. His body went rigid.

"What is it?" Palin asked, alarmed. "What's wrong?"

Dalamar made no answer, except to point out the window.

Mina walked through the forest, trod upon the brown pine needles.

The dead gathered around her. The dead bowed to her.

22

Reunion of Old Friends

kender is never out of sorts for long, not even
after encountering his own ghost. True, the sight
had been a considerable shock, and Tasslehoff
still experienced unpleasant qualms whenever he thought
about it, but he knew how to handle a qualm. You held
your breath and drank five sips of water, and the qualm
would go away. This done, his next decision was that he
had to leave this terrible place where ghosts went around
giving one qualms. He had to leave it, leave it fast, and
never, never come back.

Moss and his father proved to be of little help, since as
far as Tas could see, moss had the bad habit of growing on
all sides of rocks and trees, with apparently no regard for
the fact that someone might be trying to use it to find north.
Tasslehoff decided to turn instead to the time-honored
techniques that have been developed by kender over
centuries of Wanderlust, techniques guaranteed to find
one's self after losing one's self. The best known and most
favored of these involves the use of the body compass.

The theory behind the body compass is as follows. It is well-known that the body is made up of various elements, among these being iron. The reason that we know the body has iron in it is because we can taste the iron in our blood. Therefore, it stands to reason that the iron in our blood will be drawn to the north, just as the iron needle on the compass is drawn to the north. (Kender go so far to state that we would, all of us, be congregated at the north end of the world if we let our blood have its way. We fight a constant battle with our blood, otherwise we would all collect at the top of the world, thereby causing it to tip over.)

In order to make the body compass work, you must shut your eyes, so as not to confuse things, extend the right arm with the index finger pointing, then spin around three times to the left. When you stop, open your eyes, and you will discover that you are facing north.

Kender who use this technique almost never arrive at where they're going, but they will tell you that they always arrive at where they need to be. Thus it was that Tasslehoff wandered about in the forests of Nightlund for a good many hours (he was *not* lost), without finding either Solanthus or the way out, and he was just about to try the body compass one last time when he heard voices, real, live voices, not the tickling whispers of the poor souls.

Tasslehoff's natural instinct was to introduce himself to the voices, who were perhaps lost, and offer to show them which way was north. However, at this juncture, he heard yet another voice. This voice was inside his head and belonged to Tanis Half-Elven. Tasslehoff often heard Tanis's voice on occasions such as this, reminding him to stop and think if what he was doing was "conducive to self-preservation." Sometimes Tas listened to Tanis's voice in his head, and sometimes he did not, which was pretty much how their relationship had worked when Tanis had been alive.

This time, Tasslehoff recalled that he was running away from Dalamar and Palin, both of whom wanted to murder him, and that they might either be out hunting for him themselves or they might have sent out minions. Wizards, Tas recalled, were forever sending out minions. Tas wasn't sure what a minion was—he thought it some sort of small fish—but he decided that it would be conducive to his self-preservation if he climbed a tree and hid in the branches.

Tasslehoff climbed nimbly and swiftly and was soon settled comfortably high up amidst the pine needles. The three voices, with bodies attached, walked right underneath him.

Seeing that they were Knights of Takhisis or Neraka or whatever it was they were calling themselves these days, Tas congratulated himself on having listened to Tanis. An entire army, Knights and foot soldiers, marched beneath Tas's tree. They marched swiftly and did not appear to be in very good spirits. Some darted nervous glances left and right, as if searching for something, while others traveled with eyes facing forward, fearful that if they looked they might find it. There was little talking in the ranks. If they did speak, they kept their voices low. The tail end of the line of soldiers was just moving underneath Tasslehoff's tree, and he was just congratulating himself on having successfully avoided detection when the front of the line came to a halt, which meant the back of the line had to come to a halt, too.

The soldiers stopped, standing beneath Tas. They breathed heavily and looked tired to the point of dropping, but when the word came down the line that there was to be a fifteen-minute rest, none of them looked happy. A few squatted down on the ground, but they did not leave the trail, they did not throw off their packs.

"Let's get on with it, I say," said one. "I don't want to spend another night in this death's den."

"You're right, there," said another. "Let's march on Solanthus. This minute. I'd welcome a fight with an enemy who's got flesh and blood in him."

"Two hundred of us, and we're going to take Solanthus," said a third. "Rot! If there were two hundred thousand we couldn't take that city, even with the help of the One God. It's got walls the size of Mt. Nevermind. Infernal devices, too, or so I've heard. Giant ballista that can shoot dragons out of the skies."

"Like you said we'd never take the elf city," said one of his comrades irritably. "Remember, boys? 'It'll take two hundred thousand of us to whip those pointy-ears.' "

The others laughed, but it was nervous laughter, and no one laughed too long or too loudly.

"We're off again," said one, rising to his feet.

The others stood up, moved back into formation. Those in front turned to say something to those in back.

"Keep watch for the kender. Pass it on." The word came down the line. "Keep watch for the kender."

The soldiers in back waited impatiently for those in front to start moving. Finally, with a sluggish lurch, the line of men began to advance, and they were soon lost to Tasslehoff's eyes and ears.

" 'Keep watch for the kender,' " Tas repeated. "Hah! Those must be Dalamar's minions. I was wrong about the fish part. I'll just wait here until I'm sure they're gone. I wonder who this One God is? It must very dull, to have only one god. Unless, of course, it was Fizban, but then there probably wouldn't be any world, because he'd keep misplacing it, just like he misplaces his hat.

"Uh, oh!" The kender gave a stifled groan, noting that the troops were heading in the identical direction his finger had pointed. "They're going north. That means I have to go some other direction. The opposite direction, in fact."

Which was how Tasslehoff came at last to find his way out of Nightlund and on the road leading to Solanthus—proving yet again that the kender body compass works.

Arriving at the great walled fortress city of Solanthus, Tasslehoff walked around the walls until he came to the front entrance. There he stopped to rest himself a bit and to watch with interest the crowds of people coming and going. Those entering the city stood in a long line that moved very slowly. People stood in the road, fanning themselves and talking to their neighbors. Farmers dozed on their carts, their horses knowing enough to move forward as the line inched along. Soldiers posted outside the walls kept watch to make certain that the line continued to move, that no one grew impatient and attempted to shove his way to the front. No one seemed too upset by the delay but appeared to expect it and to take in stride.

Every person who entered the city was being questioned by the guards. Pouches were searched. Wagons were searched. If the wagon carried goods, the goods were examined by the guards, who loosened bags, pried up the tops of crates, and poked pitchforks into loads of hay. Once he was familiar with the rules, fully intending to comply with them, Tasslehoff took his place at the very end of the line.

"Hullo, how are you?" he said to a large matronly woman carrying an enormous basket of apples, who was gossiping with another large woman, carrying a basket of eggs. "My name is Tasslehoff Burrfoot. My, this is a long line. Is there any other way in?"

The two turned around to look at him. Both scowled at him fiercely, and one actually shook her fist at him.

"Keep away from me, you little vermin. You're wasting your time. Kender aren't allowed inside the city."

"What a very unfriendly place," Tasslehoff observed and walked off.

He did not go far, however, but sat down in the shade of a tree near the front entrance to enjoy his apple. As he ate, he observed that while no kender could be seen entering the city, two were seen leaving it, accompanied by city guards.

Tas waited until the kender had picked themselves up, dusted themselves off, and gathered up their pouches. Then he began to wave and shout. Pleased as always to see a fellow kender, the two came running over to greet him.

"Leafwort Thumbfloggin," said one, extending his hand.

"Merribell Hartshorn," said the other, extending her hand.

"Tasslehoff Burrfoot," said Tas.

"No, really?" said Merribell, highly pleased. "Why I met you just last week. You don't look the same though. Are you doing something different with your hair?"

"What have you got in your pouches?" asked Leafwort.

In the ensuing excitement of answering that interesting question, followed by Tas's asking them what they had in their pouches and a general round of pouch-dumping and object-trading, Tas explained that he wasn't one of the innumerable Tasslehoffs wandering about Ansalon, he was the original. He was particularly proud to show off the pieces of the Device of Time Journeying, complete with the story of how he and Caramon had used it to travel back to the past and how it had taken him inadvertently to the Abyss and how it had brought him forward to a future that wasn't this future but some other.

The two kender were impressed and quite happy to trade their most valuable objects for pieces of the device. Tas watched the pieces vanish into their pouches without much hope that they would stay there. Still it was worth a shot. Finally, when everything had been traded that could possibly be traded and all the stories told that could possibly be told, he told them why he was in Solanthus.

"I'm on a quest," Tas announced, and the other two kender appeared quite respectful. "I'm searching for a Solamnic Knight."

"You've come to the right place," said Leafwort, jerking a thumb behind him at the city walls. "There're more Knights in there than you can shake a stick at."

"What do you plan on doing once you've got one?" Merribell wondered. "They don't look like they'd be much fun to me."

"I'm searching for a specific Knight," Tas explained. "I had him once, you see, but I lost him, and I was hoping he might have come here, this being a place where Knights tend to congregate, or so I've heard. He's about so high"— Tas jumped to his feet, stood on his tiptoes and raised his arm—"and he's extremely ugly, even for a human, and he has hair the color of Tika's corn bread muffins."

The two kender shook their heads. They'd seen lots of Knights—they described several—but Tas didn't have any use for them.

"I have to find my own," he said, squatting down comfortably again. "He and I are great friends. I guess I'll just go look for myself. These ladies told me— I say, would anyone care for an apple? Anyhow two ladies told me that kender aren't allowed inside Solanthus."

"That's not true. They're really quite fond of kender in Solanthus," Merribell assured him.

"They just have to say that to keep up appearances," added Leafwort.

"They don't put kender in jail in Solanthus," Merribell continued enthusiastically. "Imagine that! The moment they catch—er—find you, they give you an armed escort through the town—"

"—so that you can see all the sights—"

"—and they throw you out the front gate. Just like a regular person."

Tasslehoff agreed that Solanthus sounded like a wonderful place. All he had to do was to find a way inside. His new friends provided him with several entrances that were not known to the general public, adding that it was best to have an alternate route in case the first he tried happened to have been shut down by the guards.

Bidding good-bye to his new friends, Tas went off to try his luck. The number-two location worked extraordinarily well (we have been asked not to reveal it) and after only an hour's work, Tasslehoff entered the city of Solanthus. He was hot and sweaty, grimy and torn, but all his pouches were intact and that, of course, was of paramount importance.

Fascinated by the immensity of the city, as well as by the large numbers of people, he wandered the streets until his feet were sore and the apples he'd had for lunch were just a distant memory. He saw lots of Knights, but none who resembled Gerard. Tas might have stopped to question a few, but he was afraid that they might treat him in the friendly fashion the other two kender had described, and while he would have liked to have been shown the sights of the city by armed guards and nothing would have made him happier than to be tossed bodily out the front gate, he was forced to put aside such pleasures in the more serious pursuit of his quest.

It was about sunset when Tas began to grow seriously annoyed with Gerard. Having decided that the Knight should be in Solanthus, the fact that he was not where he was supposed to be was highly provoking. Tired of tramping up and down the streets in search of him, weary of dodging city guards (fun at the beginning but old after awhile), Tas decided grumpily that he would sit down and let Gerard find *him* for a change. Tas planted himself in the shadows of a large statue near a fountain close to the main entrance on the main street, figuring that he would watch everyone coming in and out and that Gerard would be bound to find him eventually.

He was sitting with his chin in hand, trying to decide which inn he was going favor with his presence for dinner when he saw someone he knew enter the front gate. It wasn't Gerard, but someone even better. Tasslehoff jumped to his feet with a glad cry.

"Goldmoon!" he shouted, waving.

Respectful of Goldmoon's white robes that marked her a Mystic of the Citadel of Light, one of the city guards was providing her a personal escort into the city. He pointed in a certain direction. She nodded and thanked him. He touched his forehead to her, then returned to his duties. A small and dust-covered figure trotted along at Goldmoon's heels, hard-pressed to keep up with her long strides. Tas didn't pay much attention to this other person. He was so glad and so thankful to see Goldmoon that he didn't notice anyone else, and he forgot all about Gerard. If anyone could save him from Dalamar and Palin, it was Goldmoon.

Tas raced across the crowded highway. Bumping into people, and nimbly avoiding the long arm and grasping hands of the law, Tasslehoff was about to greet Goldmoon with his usual hug when he stopped short.

She was Goldmoon, but she wasn't. She was still in the youthful body that had been so detestable to her. She was still beautiful, with her shining silver-gold hair and her lovely eyes, but the hair was straggly and uncombed, and the eyes had a vague and distant look about them, as if she wasn't seeing anything close to her but was staring at something very far away. Her white robes were mud-stained, the hem frayed. She seemed tired to the point of falling, but she walked on determinedly, using a wooden staff to aid her steps. The small, dusty person kept up with her.

"Goldmoon?" Tasslehoff said, uncertain.

She did not pause, but she did glance down at him. "Hello, Tas," she said in a sort of distracted way and continued on.

Just that. Hello, Tas. Not, My gosh, I'm glad to see you, where have you been all this time, Tas? Just, Hello, Tas.

The small and dusty person *was* surprised to see him, however. Also very pleased.

"Burrfoot!"

"Conundrum!" Tas cried, at last recognizing the gnome through the dust.

The two shook hands.

"What are you doing here?" Tas asked. "The last time I saw you, you were mapping the Hedge Maze at the Citadel of Light. By the way, the last time I saw the Hedge Maze it was on fire."

Tasslehoff realized too late that he shouldn't have sprung such terrible news on the gnome in so sudden a manner.

"Fire!" Conundrum gasped. "My life quest! On fire!"

Stricken to the heart, he collapsed against the side of a building, clutching his breast and gulping for breath. Tas paused to fan the gasping gnome with his hat, still keeping one eye on Goldmoon. Not noticing the gnome's distress, she kept on walking. When Conundrum showed signs of recovering, Tas grasped his arm and pulled him along down the street after her.

"Just think," Tas said soothingly, aiding the gnome's staggering steps, "when they start to rebuild, they'll come to you because you've got the only map."

"That's right!" Conundrum exclaimed on thinking this over. He perked up considerably. "You're absolutely right." He would have halted on the spot to drag the map out of his knapsack, but Tas said hurriedly that they didn't have time, they had to keep up with Goldmoon.

"How do you two come to be here in Solanthus, anyway?" Tasslehoff asked, to distract the gnome from thoughts of the blazing Hedge Maze.

Conundrum regaled Tas with the doleful tale of the wreck of the *Indestructible*, how he and Goldmoon had been cast up on strange shores, and how they had been walking ever since.

"You will not believe this," Conundrum said, lowering his voice to a fearful whisper, "but she is following *ghosts!*"

"Really?" said Tasslehoff. "I just left a forest filled with ghosts."

"Not you, too!" The gnome regarded Tas in disgust.

"I'm quite experienced around the undead," Tas said with a careless air. "Skeletal warriors, disembodied hands, chain-rattling ghouls . . . Never a problem for the experienced traveler. I have the Kender Spoon of Turning given to me by my Uncle Trapspringer. If you'd like to see it—"

He began to rummage in his pouch but stopped abruptly when he came across the bits and pieces of the Device of Time Journeying.

"Personally, I think the woman's mad, unhinged, loony, deranged, bricks missing, spilt marbles, that sort of thing," Conundrum was saying in low and solemn tones.

"Yes, I suspect you're right," said Tas, glancing at Goldmoon, sighing. "She certainly doesn't act like the Goldmoon I once knew. *That* Goldmoon was pleased to see a kender. *That* Goldmoon wouldn't have let evil wizards send a kender off to be squashed by a giant." Tas patted Conundrum's arm. "It's awfully good of you to stick with her, look out for her."

"I have to be honest with you," said Conundrum, "I wouldn't do it except for the money. Look at this, will you?"

329

Glancing around to make certain no pickpockets were lurking about, the gnome pulled from the very bottom of his knapsack a large purse that was bulging with coins. Tasslehoff expressed his admiration and reach out to take a look at the pouch. Conundrum cracked the kender's hand across the knuckles and stuffed the purse back in his sack.

"And don't you touch it!" the gnome warned with a scowl.

"I don't think much of money," Tas said, rubbing his bruised knuckles. "It's heavy to carry around, and what's the good of it? I have all these apples with me. Now, no one's going to clonk me over the head for these apples, but if I had a coin to buy the apples, they'd hit me over the head to steal the coin, and so it's much better to have the apples. Don't you agree?"

"Why are you talking about apples?" Conundrum shouted, waving his hands in the air. "What have apples got to do with anything? Or spoons for that matter?"

"You started it," Tas advised him. Knowing gnomes and how excitable they were, he decided it would be polite to change the subject. "How did you come by all that money anyway?"

"People give it to her," Conundrum replied, shifting the hand-waving in Goldmoon's general direction. "Wherever we go, people give her money or a bed for the night or food or wine. They're extremely kind to her. They're kind to me, too. No one's ever been kind to me before," the gnome added wistfully. "People always say nasty, stupid things to me like, 'Is it supposed to smoke like that?' and 'Who's going to pay for all the damage?' but when I'm with Goldmoon, people say kind things to me. They give *me* food and cold ale and a bed for the night and money. She doesn't want the money. She gives it to me. I'm keeping it, too." Conundrum looked quite fierce. "The repairs to *Indestructible* are going to cost a bundle. I think it was insured for liability only and not collision—"

Tas had a feeling the subject was veering off into a boring area, so he interrupted. "By the way, where are we going?"

"Something to do with Knights," Conundrum replied. "Live knights, I hope, although I wouldn't bet on it. You can't believe how sick I am of hearing about dead people all the time."

"Knights!" Tasslehoff cried joyfully. "I'm here for the same thing!"

At this juncture, Goldmoon halted. She looked up one street and down another and appeared to be lost. Tasslehoff left the gnome, who was still muttering to himself about insurance, and hastened over to see if Goldmoon required help.

Goldmoon ignored Tas and instead stopped a woman who, to judge by her tabard marked with a red rose, was a Solamnic Knight. The woman gave her directions and then asked what brought Goldmoon to Solanthus.

"I am Goldmoon, a Mystic of the Citadel of Light," she said, introducing herself. "I hope to be able to speak before the Knights' Council."

"I am Lady Odila, Knight of the Rose," the woman replied and bowed respectfully. "We have heard of Goldmoon of the Citadel of Light. A most highly revered woman. You must be her daughter."

Goldmoon looked suddenly very worn and weary, as if she had heard this many times before now.

"Yes," she said with a sigh. "I am her daughter."

Lady Odila bowed low again. "Welcome to Solanthus, Daughter of Goldmoon. The Knights' Council has many urgent matters before it, but they are always glad to hear from one of the Mystics of the Citadel of Light, particularly after the terrible news we received of the attack on the citadel."

"What attack?" Goldmoon went exceedingly pale, so pale that Tasslehoff took hold of her hand and gave a sympathetic squeeze.

"I can tell you—" Tas began.

"Merciful goodness, it's a kender," said Lady Odila in the same tone as she might have said, "Merciful goodness, it's a bugbear." The Knight detached Tasslehoff's hand, placed herself in between Tas and Goldmoon. "Don't worry, Healer. I'll deal with it. Guard! Another of the little beasts has broken in. Remove it—"

"I am *not* a little beast!" Tasslehoff stated indignantly. "I'm with Goldmoon . . . her daughter, that is. I'm a friend of her mother's."

"And I'm her business manager," said Conundrum, bustling up importantly. "If you'd care to contribute money—"

"What attack?" Goldmoon demanded desperately. "Is this true, Tas? When did it happen?"

"It all started when— Excuse me, but I'm talking to Goldmoon!" Tas said, wriggling in the grip of the City Guard.

"Please, leave him alone. He *is* with me," Goldmoon pleaded. "I take full responsibility."

The guard looked dubious, but he could not very well go against the express wishes of one of the revered Mystics of the citadel. He looked to Lady Odila, who shrugged and said in an undertone, "Don't worry. I will see to it that he is removed before nightfall."

Tas, meanwhile, was telling his tale.

"It all started when I went to Palin's room because I had decided that I would be noble and go back in time and let the giant squish me, only I've changed my mind about that now, Goldmoon. You see, I thought about it and—"

"Tas!" Goldmoon said sharply, giving him a little shake. "The attack!"

"Oh, right. Well, Palin and I were talking this over and I looked out the window and saw a big dragon flying toward the citadel."

"What dragon?" Goldmoon pressed her hand against her heart.

"Beryl. The same dragon who put the curse on me," Tasslehoff stated. "I know because I went squirmy and shivery all over, even my stomach. So did Palin. We tried to use the Device of Time Journeying to escape, but Palin broke it. By that time Beryl was there, and a lot of other dragons and draconians were jumping out of the skies, and people were running around screaming. Like that time in Tarsis. Do you remember that? When the red dragons attacked us, and the building fell on top of me, and we lost Tanis and Raistlin?"

"My people!" Goldmoon whispered, half-suffocated. She swayed unsteadily on her feet. "What about my people?"

"Healer, please, sit down," Lady Odila said gently. Putting her arms around Goldmoon, she led her to a low wall that encircled a splashing fountain.

"Can this be true?" Goldmoon asked the Knight.

"I am sorry to say that, strange as it may seem, the kender's tale is a true one. We received reports from our garrison stationed on Schallsea Isle that the Citadel was attacked by Beryl and her dragons. They did an immense amount of destruction, but most of the people were able to escape safely into the hills."

"Thank the One God," Goldmoon murmured.

"What, Healer?" Lady Odila asked, perplexed. "What did you say?"

"I'm not certain," Goldmoon faltered. "What *did* I say?"

"You said, 'Thank the One God.' We have heard of no god coming to Krynn." Lady Odila looked intrigued. "What do you mean?"

"I wish I knew," said Goldmoon softly. Her gaze grew abstracted. "I don't know why I said that. . . ."

"I escaped, too," Tas exclaimed loudly. "Along with Palin. It was quite exciting. Palin threw the pieces of the device at the draconians, and it made some truly spectacular magic, and we ran up the Silver Stair in the smoke of the burning Hedge Maze—"

At this further reminder of his life quest going up in smoke, Conundrum began to wheeze and sat down heavily beside Goldmoon.

"—and Dalamar saved us!" Tas announced. "One minute we were on the very edge of the Silver Stair, and then *whoosh!* we were in the Tower of High Sorcery in Palanthas, only it isn't anymore. In Palanthas. It's still a Tower of High Sorcery—"

"What a little liar you are," said Lady Odila. She sounded almost respectful, so Tas chose to take this as a compliment.

"Thank you," he said modestly, "but I'm not making this up. I really did find Dalamar and the Tower. I understand it's been lost for quite a while."

"I left them to face the danger alone," Goldmoon was saying distractedly, paying no attention to Tas. "I left my people to face the dragons alone, and yet what could I do? The voices of the dead called to me. . . . I had to follow!"

"Do you hear her?" asked Conundrum, prodding the Knight with his finger. "Ghosts. Ghouls. That's who she's talking to, you know. Mad. Quite mad." He rattled the money pouch. "If you'd like to make a donation . . . it's tax-deductible—"

Lady Odila regarded them as if they were all suitable candidates for a donation, but seeing Goldmoon's fatigue and distress, the Knight's expression softened. She put her arm around Goldmoon's thin shoulders.

"You have had a shock, Healer. You have traveled far, by the sounds of it, and in strange company. Come with me. I will take you to Starmaster Mikelis."

"Yes, I know him! Although," Goldmoon added, sighing deeply, "he will not know me."

Lady Odila rose to lead Goldmoon away. Tas and Conundrum rose, too, following right behind. Hearing their footsteps, the Knight turned around. She had that look on her face that Knights get when they are about to summon the City Guard and have someone dragged off to jail. Guessing that the someone might be him, Tasslehoff thought fast.

"Say, Lady Odila!" he said. "Do you know a Knight named Gerard uth Mondar? Because I'm looking for him."

The Lady Knight, who had indeed been about to shout for the guard, shut her mouth on the words and stared at him.

"What did you say?"

"Gerard uth Mondar. Do you know him?" Tas asked.

"Maybe I do. Excuse me a moment, Healer. This won't take long." Lady Odila squatted down in front of Tas, to look him in the eye. "Describe him to me."

"He has hair the color of Tika's corn bread and a face that looks ugly at first, until you get to know him, then for some reason, it doesn't seem all that ugly anymore, especially when he's rescuing you from Dark Knights. He has eyes that are—"

"Blue as cornflowers," said Lady Odila. "Corn bread and cornflowers. Yes, that pretty much describes him. How do you know him?"

"He's a great friend," said Tas. "We traveled to Qualinesti together—"

"Ah, so *that's* where he came from." Lady Odila regarded Tas intently, then she said, "Your friend Gerard is here in Solanthus. He is being brought up before the Knights' Council. They suspect him of espionage."

"Oh, dear! I'm sorry to hear he's sick," said Tas. "Where is he? I'm sure he'll be glad to see me."

"Actually such a meeting might prove extremely interesting," the lady returned. "Bring these two along, Guard. I suppose the gnome is in on this plot, too?"

"Oh, yes," said Tasslehoff, taking firm hold of Conundrum's hand. "He keeps the money."

"Don't mention the money!" Conundrum snapped, clutching his robes.

"Obviously some sort of mix-up," Tasslehoff whispered. "Don't worry, Conundrum. I'll fix everything."

Knowing that *I'll fix everything* has been emblazoned in the annals of Krynnish history as the last words many associates of kender ever hear, the gnome was not comforted.

23

Council of the Knights of Solamnia

Goldmoon was weary from her long journey, weary as if her body were the frail and elderly one that was rightfully her own, not this strange, youthful, strong body. She had come to use the body as she used the wooden staff, to take her to wherever strange destiny called. The body carried her long distances every day without tiring. It ate and drank. It was young and beautiful. People were entranced by it and were glad to help her. Farmers gave her lodging in their humble cottages and eased her weary way by providing rides in their farm carts. Noble lords and ladies took her into their castles and sent her forth on her journey in their fine carriages. Thus, because of the body, she had traveled to Solanthus far more swiftly than she had dared hope.

Goldmoon believed her beauty and youth charmed them, but in this she was wrong. The farmers and the noble lords saw first that she was beautiful, but then they looked into her eyes. They saw there a sorrow and a seeking that touched them deeply, touched the peasant who shared a loaf of bread with her and received her grateful thanks with bowed head, touched the wealthy lady who kissed her and asked for her blessing. They saw in Goldmoon's sorrow their own fears and anxieties. They saw in her seeking their own questing for something more, something better, something in which to believe.

Lady Odila, noting Goldmoon's pallor and her faltering steps, took her directly to the hall where the Knights' Council convened and found her a small, comfortable room in the main chamber with a warm fire. The Knight ordered servants to bring water for washing away the stains of the road, and food and drink. After assuring herself that she could do nothing more to make Goldmoon comfortable, Lady Odila departed. She sent a runner to the Temple of the Mystics with word of Goldmoon's arrival, while she herself saw to the disposition of her prisoners, Tasslehoff and Conundrum.

Goldmoon ate and drank without tasting the food or knowing that she had consumed it. The body demanded fuel to keep going, and she was forced to accede to its demands. She had to keep going, to follow the river of the dead, who called to her and swept her along in their chill, dread current. She sought among the ghostly faces that pressed around her for some among them that she knew: Riverwind, Tika, Caramon, her own beloved daughter . . . all the old friends who had departed this world, leaving her behind. She could not find them, but that was not surprising, for the numbers of the dead were like the drops in a river, bewildering, overwhelming.

The body was hale and strong, but she was tired, so very tired. She thought of herself as a candle flame burning inside an ornate lantern. The flame burned low, the wax had all melted, the wick was down to the last tiny portion. What she could not see was that as the flame dwindled, her light burned ever brighter.

The One God. Goldmoon did not remember having spoken of the One God. She had not said anything, but she had dreamed about the One God. Dreamed often, the same dream, over and over so that her sleep was almost as wearying as her waking hours.

In the dream, Goldmoon was once again in the Temple of the Gods in the ancient city of Xak Tsaroth. She held in her hands the blue crystal staff. Before her was the statue of the blessed Mishakal, goddess of healing. The statue's hand was curled as if to hold a staff, yet no staff was there. As Goldmoon had done once, so long ago, she gave the magical staff to the statue. That time, the statue had accepted it, and Goldmoon had come to understand the love the gods bore their children. In the dream, though, when she tried to give the staff to the goddess, the crystal staff shattered, cutting her hands that were soon covered in blood. Her joy changed to terror.

The dream ended with Goldmoon waking, trembling and confused.

She pondered the portent of this dream. First she thought it might mean one thing, then another. She dwelled on it until the images began to wheel in her mind, one chasing the other, like a snake swallowing its own tail. Shutting her eyes, she pressed her hands against them, trying to banish the wheel.

"Daughter of Goldmoon?" came a concerned voice.

She dropped her hands, startled, and looked into the kindly, anxious face of Starmaster Mikelis. She had met him before. He had studied at the Citadel of Light, where he had been an excellent student, a capable and gentle healer. A Solamnic by birth, he had returned to Solanthus and was now head of the Temple of Light in that city. Often they had spent hours talking together, and she sighed to see that he did not recognize her.

339

"I am sorry," he said gently. "I did not mean to frighten you, Daughter. I would not have entered without knocking, but Lady Odila said she feared you might be unwell, and she hoped you might be sleeping. Yet I am glad to see that you have eaten and drunk with good appetite."

He looked with some perplexity at the numerous plates and a basket that had been filled with bread. The strange body had eaten a dinner that would have fed two, and there was not a crumb left.

"Thank you, Starmaster," Goldmoon said. "You did not frighten me. I have traveled a long distance, and I am fatigued. I am distraught over this news that the citadel was attacked. I did not know. It was the first I had heard—"

"Some were killed," Mikelis said, taking a seat beside her. "We grieve for them and trust that their spirits wing their way from this world to the next. Daughter," he asked in sudden alarm, "are you ill? Is there something I can do?"

Goldmoon had started at this statement about the spirits and, shuddering, glanced around. Ghosts filled the room, some watching her, some roving about restlessly, some seeking to touch her, others paying no attention to her. They never stayed long. They were forced to keep moving, to join the river that flowed steadily north.

"No," she said confusedly. "It's this terrible news. . . ."

She knew better than to try to explain. Mikelis was a good man, a dedicated man, but he would not understand that the spirits could never wing their way anywhere, that they were trapped, prisoners.

"I regret to say," he added, "that we have received no news of your mother. We take this as a hopeful sign that Goldmoon was not injured in the attack."

"She was not," said Goldmoon briskly. Better to end this and tell the truth. She did not have much time. The river drew her onward. "Goldmoon was not hurt in the attack because she wasn't there. She fled. She left her people to face the dragons without her."

Starmaster Mikelis looked troubled. "Daughter, do not speak so disrespectfully of your mother."

"I know that she fled," Goldmoon continued relentlessly. "I am *not* Goldmoon's daughter, as you well know, Starmaster. You know that I have only two daughters, one of whom is . . . dead. *I* am Goldmoon. I have come to Solanthus to tell my story before the Knights' Council, to see if they can help me and also to give them a warning. Surely," she added, "you have heard rumors of my 'miraculous' transformation."

Starmaster Mikelis was clearly uncomfortable. He was obviously trying not to stare, yet he could not take his eyes from her. He looked at her, then looked quickly away, only to gaze back at her in bewilderment.

"Some of our young Mystics made a pilgrimage to the citadel not long ago," he conceded. "They returned with the tale that you had been the recipient of a miracle, that you had been given back your youth. I confess that I thought this an overabundance of youthful exuberance." He halted, now openly staring. "Can it be you, First Master? Forgive me," he added awkwardly, "but we have received reports that the Dark Knights have infiltrated the Orders of the Mystics. . . ."

"Do you remember the night we sat beneath the stars, Starmaster, and spoke of the gods you had known in your youth and how, even as a small boy, you felt drawn to be a cleric of Paladine?"

"First Master!" Mikelis cried. Taking hold of her hands, he pressed them to his lips. "This is truly you, and it is truly a miracle."

"No, it is not," said Goldmoon tiredly. "It is me, but it is not me. It is not a miracle, it is a curse. I don't expect you to understand. How could I, when I don't understand? I know that the Knights honor and revere you. I sent for you to ask you a favor. I must speak before the Knights' Council, and I cannot wait until next week or next month or whenever it is they might make room for me on their schedule. Can you gain me entry to see them now, this day?"

"I can!" Mikelis returned, smiling. "I am not the only Mystic they revere. When they hear that First Master Goldmoon is present, they will be only too glad to give you audience. The council has adjourned but only for supper. They are holding a special session to consider the fate of a spy, but that should not take long. Once that sordid business is concluded, you will come as a ray of light to the darkness."

"I fear that I come only to deepen the darkness, but that will be as it may." Goldmoon rose to her feet, gripping the wooden staff. "Take me to the council room."

"But, Master," Mikelis protested, rising in his turn, "the Knights will still be at table. They may be there some time. And there is this matter of the spy. You should remain here where you are comfortable—"

"I am never comfortable," she said, her voice crisp with anger and impatience, "so it does not matter whether I remain here or sit in a drafty chamber. I must speak before the council this day. Who knows but that this business with the spy might drag on, and they would send me word that I should return tomorrow."

"Master, I assure you—"

"No! I do *not* intend to be put off until tomorrow or whenever it may suit them. If I am present in the room, they cannot very well refuse to listen to me. And, you will make no mention to them of this so-called miracle."

"Certainly, Master, if that is what you wish," Mikelis said.

He looked and sounded hurt. He was disappointed in her. Here was a miracle, right before his eyes, and she would not permit him to glory in it.

In my hands, the blue crystal staff shattered.

She accompanied Starmaster Mikelis to the council chamber, where he persuaded the guards to permit her entry. Once they were inside, he started to ask if she was comfortable—she saw the words form on his lips—but he stammered and, with a stumbling apology, said that he would go to apprise the Lord Knight that she was here. Goldmoon took a seat in the large, echoing chamber decorated with roses. Their perfume scented the air.

She waited alone in the darkness, for the room faced away from the afternoon sunlight and the candles that lit it had been put out upon the Knights' departure. The servants offered to bring light, but Goldmoon preferred to sit in the darkness.

At the same moment Goldmoon was being led to the council chamber, Gerard was being escorted by Lady Odila from his prison cell to the meeting of the Knights' Council. He had not been treated harshly, not by the standards of the Dark Knights of Neraka. He had not been tied to the rack nor hung by his thumbs. He had been brought before the inquisitor and badgered with questions for days, the same questions, over and over, the man tossing them out at random, jumping forward in time, leapfrogging back, always hoping to catch him in a lie.

Gerard was faced with a choice. Either he could tell his story from beginning to end, starting with a time-traveling dead kender and ending with his inadvertently switching sides to become aide-de-camp to Marshal Medan, one of the most notorious of the Dark Knights of Neraka. Or he could state over and over that he was a Solamnic Knight who had been sent on a secret mission by Lord Warren and that he had a perfectly logical, reasonable and innocent explanation for why he came to be riding a blue dragon and wearing the leathers of a Dark Knight dragonrider, all of which he would explain in full before the Knights' Council.

Not, admittedly, the best of choices. Gerard had decided on the latter.

At length, after many weary hours of badgering, the inquisitor reported to his superiors that the prisoner was sticking by his story and that he would speak only to the Knights' Council. The inquisitor had also added that, in his opinion, the prisoner was either telling the truth, or he was one of the most cunning and clever spies of this age. Whichever was true, he should be brought before the Knights' Council and questioned.

As Lady Odila accompanied Gerard to the hall, she disconcerted him by staring quite often at his hair, which was probably standing straight up, since it would do nothing else.

"It's yellow," he said at last, put out. "And it needs trimming. I don't usually—"

"Tika's corn bread," said Lady Odila, her green-eyed gaze on his hair. "You have hair as yellow as Tika's corn bread."

"How do you know Tika?" Gerard demanded, astonished.

"How do *you* know Tika?" she returned.

"She was the proprietor of the Inn of the Last Home in Solace, where I was posted, as I stated, if you're trying to test me—"

"Ah," said Lady Odila. "That Tika."

"Where did you— Who said—"

Lady Odila, a thoughtful expression on her face, shook her head, refused to answer any of his questions. She held his arm in a pincerlike grip—she had uncommonly large, strong hands—and was absentmindedly urging him forward at her own long-strided pace, taking no notice that he was hampered by the manacles and chains on his ankles and was forced to keep up with her by means of a painful, hobbled trot.

He saw no reason to call her attention to this fact. He had no intention of saying anything further to this baffling female, who would only make a jest or a riddle of his words. He was going before the Knights' Council, appearing before lords who would hear him without prejudice. He had decided on which parts of his story he would tell without qualification and which he would keep to himself (such as the time-traveling dead kender). His tale, although strange, was believable.

They arrived at the Hall of Knights, the oldest building in Solanthus, dating back to the city's founding by, so legend had it, a son of the founder of the Knighthood, Vinus Solamnus. Made of granite faced with marble, the Hall of Knights had originally been a simple structure, resembling a block house. Additional levels had been added down through the ages—wings and towers and spires—so that now the simple block house had been transformed into a complex of buildings, surrounding an inner courtyard. A school had been established, instructing aspiring Knights not only in the art of warfare, but also the study of the Measure and how its laws were to be interpreted, for these Knights would spend only a small portion of their time fighting. Noble lords, they were leaders in their communities and would be expected to hear pleas, render judgment. Although the vast complex of structures had long outgrown the term "hall," the Knights continued to refer to it as that, in deference to the past.

Once, temples to Paladine and Kiri-Jolith, a god particularly honored by the Knights, had been a part of the complex. After the departure of the gods, the Knights had politely permitted the priests to remain, but—their power of prayer gone—the priests had felt useless and uncomfortable. The temples held such sorrowful memories that they had departed. The temples remained open. They had become a favorite place for Knights to go to study or to spend evenings in long philosophical discussions. The temples had a peace about them that was conducive to thought, or so it was said. Many of the younger students found them a curiosity.

Gerard had himself never visited Solanthus, but he had heard his father describe it, and recalling his father's descriptions, he tried to figure out which buildings were which. He knew the Great Hall, of course, with its sharply pointed roof and flying buttresses and ornate stonework.

Odila led him inside the Great Hall. He caught a glimpse of the enormous chamber, where town meetings were held. Odila escorted him up a winding stone stairway and down a long, echoing corridor. The corridor was lit with oil lamps mounted on tall, heavy pedestals carved from stone to resemble maidens holding lamps in their outstretched hands. The sculptures were extraordinary— each maiden was different, having been modeled from real life—but Gerard was so absorbed in his thoughts that he paid them scant attention.

The council, made up of three Knights, the heads of the three Orders of the Knighthood—Knights of the Sword, Knights of the Rose, Knights of the Crown—was just convening. The Knights stood together at the end of the hallway, apart from the noble lords and ladies and a few common folk who had come to witness the proceedings and who were now filing quietly into the chamber. A Knights' Council was a solemn procedure. Few spoke, or if they did, they kept their voices low. Lady Odila brought her prisoner to a halt and, leaving him in the care of guards, went to inform the herald the prisoner was present.

When those seated in the gallery had all entered, the Lord Knights walked into the room, preceded by several squires carrying the emblem of the Knights of Solamnia with its sword, rose, and kingfisher. Next came the flag of the city of Solanthus, and after that the banners of the Lord Knights who sat upon the council.

While waiting for them to take their places, Gerard scanned the crowd, searching for someone who might know either him or his father. He saw no signs of anyone he recognized, and his heart sank.

"There *is* someone here who claims to know you," said Lady Odila, returning. She had seen his scrutiny of the assembly, guessed what he was doing.

"There is?" he asked, relieved. "Who is it? Perhaps Lord Jeffrey of Lynchburg or perhaps Lord Grantus?"

Lady Odila shook her head, her mouth twitched. "No, no. None of those. Not a Knight at all, in fact. He's going to be called to testify on your behalf. Please accept my condolences."

"What—" Gerard began angrily, but she cut him off.

"Oh, and in case you were concerned about your blue dragon, you will be pleased to know that he has thus far escaped our attempts to slay him. We discovered the cave empty, but we know he is still in the vicinity. We have received reports of livestock disappearing."

Gerard knew that he should be on the Knights' side in this contest, but he found himself rooting for Razor, who had been a loyal and gallant mount. He was touched by the fact that the dragon was risking his own life to remain in the area, even though Razor must realize by now that something unfortunate had happened to Gerard.

"Bring forth the prisoner," cried the bailiff.

Lady Odila reached to take hold of Gerard, to lead him into the hall.

"I am sorry you must be manacled," she said to him quietly, "but that is the law."

He looked at her in astonishment. He could not, for the life of him, figure her out. Giving her a grudging nod, he evaded her grip and walked past her. He might have to enter the council room clanking and shackled, but he would enter on his own, carrying himself proudly, with his head high.

He hobbled into the room to the whispers and murmurs of those seated in the gallery. The Lord Knights sat behind a long wooden table placed at the front of the chamber. Gerard knew the custom. He had attended Knights' Councils as a spectator before, and he advanced to the center of the room, to make his obeisance to the three who would be sitting in judgment upon him. The Lord Knights watched him with grave countenances, but he guessed by their approving looks and nods that he was creating a favorable impression. He rose from his bow and was turning to take his place at the dock when he heard a voice that dashed all his hopes and expectations and caused him to think that he might as well call for the executioner and save everyone the trouble.

"Gerard!" cried the voice. "Over here, Gerard! It's me! Tasslehoff! Tasslehoff Burrfoot!"

The spectators were located at the far end of the large, rectangular room. The Lord Knights were seated at the front. The dock, holding the prisoners and their guards, was to their left. On the right, against the wall, were chairs for those who had business before the Knights' Council, petitions to present, or testimony to offer.

Goldmoon rested in one of these chairs. She had waited two hours for the council to convene. She had slept some during that time, her sleep disturbed as usual by the spinning wheel of whirling, multicolored forms and images. She woke when she heard the people filing in to take their seats at the gallery. They looked at her strangely, some staring, others painfully careful to avoid doing so. When the Lord Knights entered, each bowed low before her. One knelt to ask for her blessing.

Goldmoon understood by this that Starmaster Mikelis had spread the word of the miracle of her renewed youth.

At first she was annoyed and even angry with the Starmaster for having told people when she had specifically requested him not to do so. On reflection, she admitted that she was being unreasonable. He would have to offer some explanation for her altered appearance, and he had saved her the weary work of having to describe yet again what had happened to her, to relive the night of that terrible transformation. She accepted the Knights' homage and reverence with patience. The dead flitted around her, as well, but then the dead were always around her.

Starmaster Mikelis returned to sit protectively beside her, watching over her with a mixture of awe and pity and perplexity. Obviously he could not understand why she was not running through the streets displaying the wondrous gift she had been granted. None of them understood. They mistook her patience for humility, and they honored her for that, but they resented her for it as well. She had been given this great gift, a gift every one of them would have been glad to receive. The least she could do was enjoy it.

The Knights' Council convened with the ritual formalities the Solamnics love. Such formalities grace every important epoch in a Solamnic's life, from birth to death, and no function is considered to have truly happened without innumerable solemn pronouncements and readings and quotations from the Measure.

Goldmoon sank back against the wall, closed her eyes, and fell asleep. The trial of some Knight began, but Goldmoon was not consciously aware of it. The droning voices were an undercurrent to her dreams, and in her dreams she was back in Tarsis. The city was being attacked by an immense flight of dragons. She cowered in terror as the shadows of their many-colored wings turned bright day into darkest night. Tasslehoff was calling her name. He was telling her something, something important. . . .

"Tas!" she cried, sitting bolt upright. "Tas, fetch Tanis! I must speak to him—"

She blinked and looked around her in confusion.

"Goldmoon, First Master," Mikelis was saying softly, as he chafed her hands soothingly. "You were dreaming."

"Yes," she murmured, "I was dreaming. . . ."

She tried to recall the dream, for she had discovered something important, and she had been going to tell Tanis. But of course, Tanis was not there. None of them were there. She was alone, and she could not remember what it was she had been dreaming about.

Everyone in the hall was staring at her. Her outburst had interrupted the proceedings. Starmaster Mikelis made a sign that all was well. The Lord Knights turned their attention to the case at hand, calling forth the prisoner Knight to take his place before them.

Goldmoon's gaze roamed aimlessly about the room, watching the restless dead rove among the living. The voices of the Lord Knights droned, and she paid no attention to them until they called upon Tasslehoff to give testimony. He stood in the dock, a shabby and diminutive figure among the tall, splendidly accoutered guards.

Never daunted or intimidated by any show of either ceremony or force, the kender gave the Lord Knights an account of his arrival in Solace and told what had happened to him after that.

Goldmoon had heard this story before in the Citadel of Light. She recalled Tasslehoff talking about a Solamnic Knight who had accompanied him to Qualinesti in search of Palin. Listening to the kender, Goldmoon realized that the Knight on trial was the very Knight who

350

had discovered the kender in the Tomb of the Last Heroes, the Knight who had been present at Caramon's death, who had stayed behind to fight the Dark Knights so that Palin could escape Qualinesti. The Knight who had forged the first link in a long chain of events.

She looked with interest now at the Knight. He had entered the room with an air of grim and injured dignity, but now that the kender began to defend him, he stood in a state of dejection. He slumped in the dock, his hands dangling before him, his head bowed, as if his fate had already been determined and he were being led to the block. Tasslehoff, needless to say, was enjoying himself.

"You state, kender, that you have attended a Knights' Council prior to this one," said Lord Ulrich, Knight of the Sword, who was apparently endeavoring to impress upon the kender the gravity of the situation.

"Oh, yes," Tas answered. "Sturm Brightblade's."

"I beg your pardon," said Lord Ulrich in bemused tones.

"Sturm Brightblade," said Tas, raising his voice. "You've heard of Sturm? One of the Heroes of the Lance. Like myself." Tasslehoff placed his hand modestly on his chest. Seeing the Knights regarding him with blank stares, he determined it was time to elaborate. "While I wasn't at the High Clerist's Tower when Sir Derek tried to have Sturm thrown out of the Knighthood for cowardice, I heard all about it from my friend Flint Fireforge when I came later, after I broke the dragon orb at the Council of Whitestone. The elves and the Knights were arguing about who should have the dragon orb—"

Lord Tasgall, Knight of the Rose, and head of the council, interrupted. "We are familiar with the story, kender. You could not possibly have been there, so dispense with your lies. Now, please tell us again how it was that you came to be in the tomb—"

"Oh, but he *was* there, my lords," said Goldmoon, rising to her feet. "If you know your history as you claim, then you know that Tasslehoff Burrfoot was at the Council of Whitestone and that he did break the dragon orb."

"I am aware that the heroic kender Tasslehoff Burrfoot did these things, Master," said Lord Tasgall, speaking to her in respectful, gentle tones. "Perhaps your confusion arises from the fact that this kender calls himself Tasslehoff Burrfoot, undoubtedly in honor of the heroic kender who bore the original name."

"I am *not* confused," Goldmoon stated sharply. "The so-called miracle that transformed my body did not affect my mind. I knew the kender you refer to. I knew him then, and I know him now. Haven't you been listening to his story?" she demanded impatiently.

The Knights stared at her. Gerard lifted his head, a flush of hope reddening his face.

"Are you saying that you affirm his story, First Master?" Lord Nigel, Knight of the Crown, asked, frowning.

"I do," said Goldmoon. "Palin Majere and Tasslehoff Burrfoot traveled to the Citadel of Light to meet me there. I recognized Tasslehoff. He is not an easy person to forget. Palin told me that Tasslehoff was in possession of a magical artifact that permitted him to travel through time. Tasslehoff came to the Tomb of the Last Heroes the night of the terrible storm. It was a night for miracles," she added with a touch of bitter irony.

"This kender"—Lord Tasgall glanced at Tas uncertainly—"claims that the Knight here on trial escorted him to Qualinesti, where they met Palin Majere at the home of Laurana, wife of the late Lord Tanis Half-Elven."

"Tasslehoff told me the same story, my lords. I have no reason to doubt it. If you mistrust his story or if you question my word, I suggest that there is an easy way to prove it. Contact Lord Warren in Solace and ask him."

"Of course, we do not question your word, First Master," the Lord Knight said, looking embarrassed.

"But you should, my lords," Lady Odila said. Rising to her feet, she faced Goldmoon. "How do we know you are what you claim to be? Your word alone. Why should we believe you?"

"You shouldn't," said Goldmoon. "You should question, Daughter. You should always question. Only by asking are we answered."

"My lords!" Starmaster Mikelis was shocked. "The First Master and I are old friends. I can testify that she is indeed Goldmoon, First Master of the Citadel of Light."

"Tell me what you are thinking, Daughter," Goldmoon said, ignoring the Starmaster. Her gaze fixed upon Lady Odila as if they were the only two in the room. "Speak your heart. Ask your question."

"Very well, I will do so." Lady Odila turned to face the Knights' Council. "My lords, the First Master Goldmoon is more than ninety years old! This woman is young, beautiful, strong. How is it possible, in the absence of the gods, that such miracles happen?"

"Yes, that is the question," Goldmoon said and sank back down in her chair.

"Do you have an answer, First Master?" asked Lord Tasgall.

Goldmoon looked at him steadily. "No, my lord, I do not. Except to say that, in the absence of the gods, what has happened to me is not possible."

The spectators began to whisper among themselves. The Knights exchanged doubtful glances. Starmaster Mikelis stared at her in helpless, baffled confusion. The Knight, Gerard, put his head in his hands.

Tasslehoff bounced to his feet. "I have the answer," he offered, but was quickly settled—and muffled—by the bailiff.

"*I* have something to say," said Conundrum in his thin and nasaly tones. He slid off his chair, nervously plucking at his beard.

Lord Tasgall gave the gnome gracious permission to speak. Solamnics have always felt a certain affinity for the gnomes.

"I just wanted to say that I had never seen any of these people before in my entire life until just a few weeks ago when this kender sabotaged my attempts to map the Hedge Maze and this human female stole my submersible. I have started a legal defense fund. If anyone would care to contribute?"

Conundrum glanced around hopefully. No one did, and so he sat back down. Lord Tasgall appeared considerably taken aback, but he nodded and indicated that the gnome's testimony was to be recorded.

"The Knight Gerard uth Mondar has already spoken in his own defense," said Lord Tasgall. "We have heard the testimony of the kender who claims to be Tasslehoff Burrfoot and that of Lady Odila Windlass and the . . . um . . . First Master. We will now withdraw to consider all of the testimony."

Everyone stood. The Knights withdrew. After they had departed, some people returned to their seats, but most hastened out of the room and into the corridor, where they discussed the matter in excited tones that could be heard clearly by those still inside the chamber.

Goldmoon rested her head against the wall and closed her eyes. She wanted nothing now but to be in a room by herself away from all this noise and commotion and confusion.

Feeling a touch on her hand, she saw Lady Odila standing before her.

"Why did you want me to ask that about the gods, First Master?" Lady Odila asked.

"Because it needed asking, Daughter," Goldmoon replied.

"Are you claiming there is a god?" Lady Odila frowned. "You spoke of a one—"

Goldmoon took hold of the woman's hand, wrapped her fingers around it, pressed it firmly. "I am saying to open your heart, Daughter. Open it to the world."

Lady Odila smiled wryly. "I opened my heart once, First Master. Someone came in and ransacked the place."

"So now you lock it with a quick wit and a glib tongue. Gerard uth Mondar is telling the truth, Lady Odila. Oh, they will send messengers to Solace and his homeland to verify his story, but you know as well as I do that this could take weeks. This will be too late. You believe him, don't you?"

"Corn bread and cornflowers," Lady Odila said, glancing at the prisoner as he stood patiently, but wearily, in the dock. She looked back at Goldmoon. "Maybe I do, and maybe I don't. Still, as you say, only by asking are we answered. I will do what I can to either prove or disprove his claim."

The Knights returned. Goldmoon heard them speak their ruling, but their voices were distant, came to her from across a vast river.

"We have determined that we cannot pronounce judgment on the critical issues raised in the case until we have spoken to additional witnesses. Therefore we are sending messengers to the Citadel of Light and to Lord Warren in Solace. In the meantime, we will make inquiries throughout Solanthus to see if someone here knows the defendant's family and can verify this man's identity."

Goldmoon barely heard what was said. She had only a brief time left in this world, she felt. The youthful body could no longer contain the soul that yearned to be free of the burden of flesh and of feeling. She was living moment to moment. Heartbeat to heartbeat. Each beat grew a little weaker than the one before. Yet, there was something she still must do. Somewhere she still must go.

"In the meantime," Lord Tasgall was saying, concluding the proceedings, "the prisoner Gerard uth Mondar, the kender who goes by the name of Tasslehoff Burrfoot, and the gnome Conundrum are to be held in confinement. This council is adjourned—"

"My lords, I will speak!" Gerard cried, shaking loose the bailiff who was attempting to stop him. "Do what you will with me. Believe my story or not, as you see fit." He raised his voice to overcome the lord's repeated commands for him to be silent. "Please, I beg of you! Send aid and succor to the elves of Qualinesti. Do not allow the dragon Beryl to exterminate them with impunity. If you have no care for the elves as fellow beings, then at least you must see that once Beryl has destroyed the elves, she will next turn her attention northward to Solamnia—"

The bailiff summoned assistance. Several guards finally subdued Gerard. Lady Odila watched, said nothing, but glanced again at Goldmoon. She appeared to be asleep, her head slumped forward on her chest, her hands resting in her lap, much as an elderly woman might doze by the fire or in the warm sunshine, oblivious to what is now, dreaming of what will be.

"She *is* Goldmoon," Lady Odila murmured.

When order was restored, Lord Tasgall continued speaking. "The First Master is to be given into the care of Starmaster Mikelis. We ask that she not leave the city of Solanthus until such time as the messengers return."

"I will be honored if you would be a guest in my home, First Master," said Starmaster Mikelis, giving her a gentle shake.

"Thank you," said Goldmoon, waking suddenly. "But I will not be staying long."

The Starmaster blinked. "Forgive me, First Master, but you heard what the Knights said—"

Goldmoon had not in fact heard a word the Knights had said. She paid no heed to the living and no heed to the dead who came clustering around her.

"I am very tired," she told them all and, grasping her staff, she walked out the door.

24

Preparing for the End

Ever since their king had told them of their danger, the people of Qualinesti had been making preparations to stand against the dragon and her armies that were drawing near the elven capital. Beryl focused all her strength and her attention on capturing the elven city that had graced the world for so many years and on making that city her own. Soon humans would be moving into elven homes, chopping down the elves' beloved forests for lumber, turning hogs loose to forage in elven rose gardens.

The refugees were gone now. They had been evacuated through the dwarven tunnels, they had fled through the forests. With the refugees gone, those elves who had volunteered to remain behind to fight the dragon began to concentrate on the city's defenses. They were under no illusions. They knew that this was a battle they could win only by a miracle. At best, they were fighting a rearguard action. Every few hours they delayed the enemies' advance meant their families and friends were another few miles closer to safety. They had heard the news that the shield had fallen, and they spoke of the beauty of Silvanesti, of how their cousins would welcome the refugees, take them into their hearts and their houses. They spoke of the healing of the old wounds, of the future reunification of the elven kingdoms.

Their king, Gilthas, encouraged their hopes and their beliefs. Marshal Medan wondered when the young man found time to sleep. Gilthas was everywhere, it seemed. One moment he was underground, working alongside the dwarves and their burrowing worms, the next he was helping to set fire to a bridge across the White-rage River. The next time the Marshal saw the king, Gilthas was again in the underground tunnels, where most of the elves now lived. Down in these tunnels, built by the dwarves, the elves worked day and night forging and mending weapons and armor and braiding rope, miles and miles of thin, strong rope that would be needed to carry out the king's plan to destroy the dragon.

Every bit of cloth that could be spared had been given over to the production of the rope, from baby clothes to bridal gowns to shrouds. The elves took silken sheets from their beds, took woolen blankets from cribs, took tapestries that had hung for centuries in the Tower of the Sun. They tore them up without a second thought.

The work proceeded day and night. When one person grew too weary to continue braiding or cutting, when someone's hands grew too stiff or blistered, another would take over. After dark, the coils of rope that had been made during that day were smuggled out of the tunnels to be stowed away inside elven homes, inns, taverns, shops and warehouses. Elven mages went from place to place, placing enchantments on the rope. Sometimes the erratic magic worked, other times it did not. If one mage failed, another would come back and try later.

Above ground, the Dark Knights carried out the orders they had been given to rid the city of Qualinost of its inhabitants. They dragged elves out of their homes, beat them, and hauled them off to the prison camps that had been established outside the city. The soldiers threw furniture into the street, set homes ablaze, looted, and pillaged.

Beryl's spies, flying overhead, saw all this and reported back to Beryl that her orders were being faithfully followed. The spies did not know that the elves who huddled in terror in the prison camp by day were released by night, dispatched to different homes, there to be "arrested" again in the morning. If the spies had been careful observers, they might have noted that the furniture that was tossed in the streets blocked major thoroughfares and that the houses that were set ablaze were also strategically located throughout the elven city to impede the advance of troops.

The one person Medan had not seen during this busy time was Laurana. Since the day the Queen Mother had assisted him so ably in fooling Beryl's pet draconian, Medan had been occupied with planning the city's defenses and innumerable other tasks, and he knew that she must be busy, too. She was packing up her household and that of the king's, preparatory to traveling south, although, from what he had seen, she had little left to pack. She had given all her clothes except those on her back to be cut up for rope—even her wedding gown.

She had brought the gown herself, Medan heard, and when the elves had protested and told her she must keep that, if nothing else, she had taken up a pair of shears and cut the beautiful, silken fabric into strips with her own hands. All the while she told stories of her wedding to Tanis Half-Elven, making them laugh at the antics of the kender, Tasslehoff Burrfoot, who had wandered off with the wedding rings and been found upon the verge of trading them to a street urchin for a jar of tadpoles, and how Caramon Majere, the best man, had been so flustered that when he rose to make the toast, he forgot Tanis's name.

Marshal Medan went to look at that particular coil of rope. He held the strand made up of the glistening silk that was the color of hyacinths in his hand and thought to himself that this length of rope needed no additional magical enchantment of strength, for it had been braided not with cord but with love.

The Marshal was himself extremely busy. He was able to snatch only a few hours of sleep every night, and these he forced himself to take, knowing well that he could not operate efficiently without them. He could have taken time to visit the Queen Mother, but he chose not to do so. Their former relationship—that of respectful enemies—had changed. Each knew, when they parted after that last meeting, that they would not be the same to each other as they had been in the past.

Medan felt a sense of loss. He was under no illusions. He had no right to her love. He was not ashamed of his past. He was a soldier, and he had done what a soldier must do, but that meant that he had the blood of her people on his hands and that therefore he could not touch her without staining her with that blood. He would never do that. Yet he sensed that they could not meet comfortably as old friends. Too much had happened between them for that. Their next meeting must be awkward and unhappy for both of them. He would bid her farewell, wish her luck in her journey south. When she was gone and he would never see her again, he would prepare himself to die as he had always known he would die—as a soldier, doing his duty.

At the precise moment when Gerard was eloquently but futilely pleading the cause of the elves before the

Knights' Council in Solanthus, Marshal Medan was in the palace, making preparations to hold a final meeting of officers and commanders. He had invited the dwarf thane, Tarn Bellowsgranite; King Gilthas and his wife, the Lioness; and the elven commanders.

Medan had informed the king that tomorrow would be the last day the royal family could leave the city with any hope of escaping the enemy armies. He was concerned that the king had lingered too long as it was, but Gilthas had refused to leave earlier. This night, Medan would tell Laurana good-bye. Their farewells would be easier for both of them if they could do so when there were other people about.

"The meeting will begin at moonrise," Medan told Planchet, who would be carrying the messages to the elven commanders. "We will hold it in my garden."

His excuse was that the elves in attendance would not be comfortable in the thick-walled, stifling headquarters, but, in reality, he wanted a chance to show off his garden and to enjoy it himself for what would probably be the last time.

Naming off those who were to come, he said, almost offhandedly, "the Queen Mother—"

"No," said Gilthas.

The king had been pacing up and down the room, his head bowed, his hands clasped behind his back, so lost in meditation that Medan had not thought the king was paying any attention to him and was considerably startled when he spoke.

"I beg your pardon, Your Majesty?" Medan said.

Gilthas ceased pacing and came over to the desk that was now covered with large maps of the city of Qualinost and its environs.

"You will not tell my mother of this meeting," said Gilthas.

"This meeting is one of vital importance, Your Majesty," the Marshal argued. "We will be finalizing our plans for the city's defense and for your safe evacuation. Your mother is knowledgeable in such matters, and—"

"Yes," Gilthas interrupted, his voice grave. "She is knowledgeable. That is the very reason I do not want her to attend. Don't you understand, Marshal?" he added, bending over the desk, gazing intently into Medan's eyes. "If we invite her to this council of war, she will think we expect her to contribute that knowledge, to take part . . . "

He did not finish the sentence. He straightened abruptly, ran a hand through his hair, and stared unseeing out the window. The setting sun slanted through the crystal panes, shone full on the young king. Medan gazed at him expectantly, waiting for him to finish his sentence. He noted how the tension of the past few weeks had aged the young man. Gone was the languid poet, gazing listlessly around the dance floor. True, that mask had been put on to deceive the king's enemies. But they had been deceived because part of the mask was made of flesh and blood.

Gilthas was a gifted poet, a man of dreams, a man who taught himself to live much of his life internally, because he had come to believe he could not trust anyone. The face he showed the world—the face of the confident, strong and courageous king—was as much a mask as the other. Behind the mask was a man tormented by self-doubt, uncertainty, fear. He concealed it masterfully, but the sunlight on his face revealed the gray smudges beneath the eyes; the taut, tight-lipped smile that was no smile; the eyes that looked inward into shadows, not outward into sunlight.

He must be very like his father, Medan thought. It was too bad his father was not here to counsel him now, to put his hand upon his shoulder and assure him that his feelings were not a symptom of weakness, that they did him no discredit. Far from it, they would make him a better leader, a better king. Medan might have said these words himself, but he knew that coming from him they would be resented. Gilthas turned away from the window, and the moment passed.

"I understand," said Medan, when it became apparent from the uncomfortable silence that the king did not intend to finish his sentence, a sentence that presented a new and astonishing possibility to the Marshal. He had assumed Laurana intended to leave Qualinost. Perhaps he had assumed wrongly. "Very well. Planchet, we will say nothing about this meeting to the Queen Mother."

The moon rose and shone pale and sickly in the sky. Medan had never much liked this strange moon. Compared to the argent brilliance of Solinari or the red flame of Lunitari, this moon looked forlorn and meek. He could almost imagine it apologizing to the stars every time it appeared, as if ashamed to take its place among them. It did its duty now, and shed light enough that he did not have to bring the harsh glare of torches or lamps into his garden, lights that might reveal to any watcher flying overhead that there was a meeting in progress.

The elves expressed their admiration for his garden. Indeed, they were amazed that a human could create such beauty, and their amazement gave Medan as much satisfaction as their praise, for it meant the praise was genuine. His garden had never looked so hauntingly beautiful as it did by moonlight this night. Even the dwarf, who viewed plants as nothing more than food for cattle, looked about the garden with not quite a bored air and termed it "pretty," although he sneezed violently immediately afterward and constantly rubbed his itching nose throughout the meeting.

The Lioness was the first to give her report. She had nothing to say about the garden. She was cool, business-minded, obviously intending to end this quickly. She indicated where the enemy army was located, pointing to a map that had been spread out on a table near the fishpond.

"Our forces did what they could to slow the enemy's advance, but we were stinging flies to this behemoth. We annoyed him, we irritated him, we drew blood. We could impede him, but we could not stop him. We could slay a hundred men, and that was nothing but an irritant to him. Therefore, I ordered my people to pull back. We are now assisting the refugees."

Medan approved. "You will provide escort for the royal family. Of which you yourself are one," he added with a polite smile.

The Lioness did not return his smile. She had spent long years fighting him. She did not trust him, and for that he could not fault her. He did not trust her either. He had the feeling that if it had not been for Gilthas's intervention, the Marshal would have found the Lioness's knife sticking out of his ribcage.

Gilthas looked grim as he always did when his own departure was mentioned. Medan sympathized with the young king, understood how he felt. Most of the elves understood the reason for his departure. There were those who did not understand, who whispered that the elven king was abandoning Qualinost in its hour of need, leaving his people to die that he might live. Medan did not envy the young man the life that lay ahead of him: the life of the refugee, the life of the exile.

"I will personally escort His Majesty out through the tunnels," Bellowsgranite stated. "Then those of my people who have volunteered will remain in the tunnels beneath the city, ready to assist the battle. When the armies of darkness march into Qualinost"—the dwarf grinned broadly—"they will find more than woodchucks rising up out of holes to meet them."

As if to emphasize his words, the ground shook slightly beneath their feet, a sign that the giant dirt-devouring worms were at work.

"You and those coming with you must be in the tunnels first thing in the morning, Your Majesty," the Thane added. "We dare not wait longer."

"We will be there," said Gilthas, and he sighed and stared down at his hands, clasped tightly on the top of the table.

Medan cleared his throat and continued. "Speaking to the defense of the city of Qualinost: The spies sent to infiltrate Beryl's army report no change in her plan of attack. She will first order in the lesser dragons to scout the city, make certain all is well, and intimidate with their dragon-fear any who may remain." The Marshal permitted himself a grim smile. "When Beryl has been assured that the city is deserted and her precious hide will be safe, she herself will enter Qualinost as leader of her armies.

Medan pointed to the map. "The city of Qualinost is protected from attack by a natural moat—the two arms of the White-rage River that encircle the city. We've received reports that Beryl's armies are already gathering along the banks of these streams. We have cut the bridges, but the water level is low this time of year and they will be able to ford the streams here, here, and here." He indicated three areas. "The crossing will slow them, for they will be forced to move through water that is swift-flowing and waist deep in some places. Our troops will be posted here and here and here"—more reference to the map—"with orders to allow a substantial number of troops to cross before they attack."

He looked around at the officers. "We must emphasize to the troops that they wait for the signal before they attack.

We want the enemy forces split, with half on one side of the stream and half on the other. We want to create panic and disruption, so that those who are trying to cross are bottled up by those fighting for their lives on the bank. Elven archers stationed here and here will decimate their ranks with arrow fire. The dwarven army, under the leadership of the Thane's cousin"—Medan bowed to the dwarf—"will hit them here, drive them back into the water. The other elven forces will be posted here on the hillside to harry their flanks. Is this plan understood? Satisfactory to everyone?"

They had gone over this several times before. Everyone nodded.

"Finally, at our last meeting, we discussed sending for the Gray Robes who are stationed on the western border of Qualinesti and asking them for their assistance. It was decided that we would not seek their services, the feeling being that these gray-robed wizards cannot be trusted, a feeling in which I most heartily concurred. As it has turned out, it was well we did not count on them. It seems they have vanished. Not only have they disappeared without a trace, but the entire Forest of Wayreth has disappeared. I received a report that a strike force of draconians, one of Beryl's crack units, who had been diverted south with orders to slaughter the refugees, entered the forest and has not come out. We have heard nothing more of them, nor, I think, are we likely to.

"I suggest that we raise our glasses in a toast to the Master of the Tower of Wayreth."

Medan lifted a glass of elven wine from one of his last bottles. He was damned if he was going to leave any to be gulped by goblins. All shared in the toast, taking comfort in the fact that, for a change, a powerful force was on their side, mysterious and vagarious as it might be.

"I hear the sounds of laughter. I come upon you at a good time, it seems," said Laurana.

Medan had posted guards at the entrance, but he had given orders that if the Queen Mother arrived, she was to be admitted. He rose to do her honor, as did all of those present. The Lioness greeted her mother by marriage with an affectionate kiss. Gilthas kissed his mother, but he cast a rebuking glance at Medan.

"I took it upon myself to invite your honored mother," said the Marshal, bowing to the king. "I know that I went against Your Majesty's express wishes, but considering the extreme gravity of the situation, I deemed it best to exert my authority as military leader. As you yourself said, Your Majesty, the Queen Mother is knowledgeable in such matters."

"Please, be seated," said Laurana, taking a chair beside the Marshal, a chair he had made certain was left vacant. "I am sorry to be late, but an idea came to me, and I wanted time to think it through before I mentioned it. Tell me what I have missed."

He related the details of the meeting up to now, not knowing what he was saying, repeating by rote. Like his garden, Laurana was hauntingly beautiful that night. The moonlight stole away all color, so that the golden hair was silver, her skin white, her eyes luminous, her gown gray. She might have been a spirit, a spirit of his garden, for the scent of jasmine clung to her. He etched this image of her in his mind, planned to carry this image of her into death's realm, where, he hoped, it would serve to light the unending darkness.

The meeting continued. He asked for reports from the elven commanders. They reported that all was ready or nearly so. They needed more rope, but more rope was forthcoming, for those making it had not ceased their work, nor would they until the very final moments. The barricades were in place, trenches dug, traps set. The archers had been given their unusual assignment, and although they had found their work strange and difficult at first, they had soon accustomed themselves to the requirements and needed nothing but the signal to attack.

"It is imperative . . . imperative"—Medan repeated that firmly—"that no elf be seen by the dragon walking the streets. Beryl must think that the city has been cleared, that all the elves have either fled or are being held captive. The Knights will patrol the streets openly, accompanied by those elves disguised as Knights to fill out our ranks. Tomorrow night, once I have been assured the royal family is safely on their way"—he looked at the king as he spoke and received Gilthas's reluctant nod—"I will send a messenger to Beryl and tell her that the city of Qualinost surrenders to her might and that we have met all her demands. I will take my position at the top of the Tower of the Sun, and it is then that—"

"I beg your pardon, Marshal Medan," Laurana interrupted, "but you have not met the dragon's demands."

Medan had guessed this was coming. He knew by Gilthas's stiff rigidity and his sudden pallor that he had guessed it, as well.

"I beg *your* pardon, Madam," said Medan politely, "but I can think of nothing I have left undone."

"The dragon demanded that the members of the royal family be handed over to her. I believe that I was among those she specifically named."

"To my deep regret," said the Marshal with a wry smile, "the members of the royal family managed to escape. They are at this moment being pursued, and I am certain that they will be captured—"

Laurana was shaking her head. "That will not do, Marshal Medan. Beryl is no fool. She will be suspicious. All our carefully laid plans would be for naught."

"I will stay," said Gilthas firmly. "It is what I want to do anyhow. With myself as the Marshal's prisoner, standing with him on the tower, the dragon will have no suspicions. She will be eager to take me captive. You, Mother, will lead the people in exile. You will deal with the Silvanesti. You are the diplomat. The people trust you."

"The people trust their king," said Laurana quietly.

"Mother . . . " Gilthas's voice was agonized, pleading. "Mother, you cannot do this!"

"My son, you are king of the Qualinesti. You do not belong to me anymore. You do not belong to yourself. You belong to them."

Reaching across the table, Laurana took hold of her son's hand. "I understand how hard it is to accept the responsibility for thousands of lives. I know what you face. You will have to tell those who come to you for answers that all you have are questions. You will have to tell the despairing that you have hope, when despair is heavy in your own heart. You will bid the terrified to have courage when inside you are shivering with fear. It would take great courage to face the dragon, my son, and I admire and honor you for showing that courage, but such courage is paltry compared to the courage that will be required of you to lead your people into the future, a future of uncertainty and danger."

"What if I can't, Mother?" Gilthas had forgotten anyone else was there. These two spoke only to each other. "What if I fail them?"

"You will fail, my son. You will fail time and again. I failed those who followed me when I put my own wants over their needs. Your father failed his friends when he abandoned them while he pursued his love for the Dragon Highlord Kitiara."

Laurana smiled tremulously. Her eyes shimmered with tears. "You are the child of imperfect parents, my son. You will stumble and fall to your knees and lie bruised in the dust, as we did. You will only truly fail if you remain lying in the dust. If you regain your feet and continue, you will make of that failure a success."

Gilthas said nothing for long moments. He held fast to his mother's hand. Laurana held his hand, knowing that when she let go, she would let go of her son forever.

"I will not fail you, Mother," Gilthas said softly. He raised her hand to his lips, kissed it reverently. "I will not fail the memory of my father." Releasing her hand, he rose to his feet. "I will see you in the morning, Mother. Before I depart." He spoke the words without faltering.

"Yes, Gilthas," she said. "I will be waiting."

He nodded. The farewell they spoke then would last for all eternity. Blessed, heart-wrenching, those words were words to be spoken in private.

"If that is all, Marshal Medan," Gilthas said, keeping his eyes averted, "I have a great deal to do yet this night."

"I understand, Your Majesty," said the Marshal. "We have only small matters of no importance to clear up now. I thank you for coming."

"Small matters of no importance," Gilthas murmured. He looked back at his mother. He knew very well what they would be discussing. He drew in a deep breath. "Then I bid you good night, Marshal, and good luck to you and to all of you."

Medan rose to his feet. Lifting his glass of elven wine, he raised it. "I give you His Majesty, the King."

The elves raised their voices in unison. Bellowsgranite shouted out the toast in a hearty bellow that made the Marshal cringe and glance swiftly into the sky, hoping that none of Beryl's spies were in earshot.

Laurana raised her glass and pledged her son, her voice soft with love and pride.

Gilthas, overcome, gave a brief nod. He could not trust himself to speak. His wife put her arm around him. Planchet walked behind him. The king had no other guard.

He had taken only a few steps when he looked back over his shoulder. His eyes sought out the Marshal.

Medan read the silent message and, excusing himself, accompanied the king through the darkened house. Gilthas said no word until he reached the door. Halting, he turned to face the Marshal.

"You know what my mother plans, Marshal Medan."

"I think I do, Your Majesty."

"Do you agree with her that such a sacrifice on her part is necessary?" Gilthas demanded, almost angrily. "Will you permit her to go through with this?"

"Your Majesty," the Marshal replied gravely, "you know your mother. Do you think there is any possible way to stop her?"

Gilthas stared at him, then he began to laugh. When the laughter came perilously close to tears, he fell silent until he could regain mastery over himself.

He drew in a deep breath, looked at the Marshal. "There is a chance that we will defeat Beryl, perhaps even destroy her. A chance that her armies will be stopped, forced to retreat. There is that chance, isn't there, Marshal?"

Medan hesitated, not wanting to offer hope where, in his opinion, there was none. Yet, which of them knew what the future would hold?

"There is an old Solamnic adage, Your Majesty, which I could quote just now, an adage that says there is about as much chance of that happening as of the moons falling out of the sky." Medan smiled. "As Your Majesty knows, the moons *did* fall out of the sky, so I will only tell you that, yes, there is a chance. There is always a chance."

"Believe it or not, Marshal Medan, you cheer me," Gilthas said. He held out his hand. "I regret that we have been enemies."

Medan took the king's hand, rested his other hand over it. He knew the fear that was in Gilthas's heart, and the Marshal honored him for not speaking it aloud, for not demeaning Laurana's sacrifice.

"Please rest assured, Your Majesty, that the Queen Mother will be a sacred trust for me," said Medan. "The most sacred of my life. I vow to you on my admiration and regard for her that I will be true to that trust to my last breath."

"Thank you, Marshal," Gilthas said softly. "Thank you."

Their handshake was brief, and the king departed. Medan stood a moment in the doorway, watching Gilthas walk down the path that gleamed silver-gray in the moonlight. The future the Marshal faced was grim and bleak. He could count the remaining days of his life upon the fingers of one hand. Yet, he thought, he would not trade it for the future faced by that young man.

Yes, Gilthas would live, but his life would never be his own. If he had no care for his people, it would be different. But he did care, and the caring would kill him.

25

Alone Together

After a few more questions and some desultory discussion, the commanders departed. Medan and Laurana said nothing to each other, but between them words were no longer needed. She remained when the others had gone, and the two of them were alone together.

Alone together. Medan pondered that phrase. It was all two people could ever be to each other, he supposed. Alone. Together. For the dreams and secrets of our heart may be spoken, but words are poor handmaidens. Words can never fully say what we want them to say, for they fumble, stammer, and break the best porcelain. The best one can hope for is to find along the way someone to share the path, content to walk in silence, for the heart communes best when it does not try to speak.

The two sat in the garden beneath the moon that was strange and pale, as if it were the ghost of a moon.

"Beryl will come to Qualinost now," said the Marshal with satisfaction. "She will not pass up the opportunity to see you—the Golden General who defeated Queen

Takhisis—shrink in terror before her bloated majesty. We will give Beryl what she wants. We will put on an excellent show."

"Indeed we will," said Laurana. "I have some ideas on that score, Marshal Medan. I spoke to you of them earlier in the evening." She cast a regretful look around the garden. "As beautiful as this place is, it seems a shame to leave it, yet what I have to show you should best be viewed under the cover of darkness. Will you accompany me back to Qualinost, Marshal?"

"I am yours to command, Madam," he replied. "The road is long and might be dangerous. Who knows if Beryl has assassins lurking about? We should ride, if that will be suitable to you."

They rode through the moonlit night. Their talk was of dragons.

"It is said of the Golden General that she was never daunted by dragonfear," Medan said, regarding Laurana admiringly. She sat a horse superbly, although she claimed it had been years since she last rode one.

Laurana laughed ruefully, shook her head. "Those who claimed that never knew me. The dragonfear was horrible. It never went away."

"Then how did you function?" he asked. "For certainly you fought dragons, and you fought them well."

"I was so afraid that the fear became a living part of me," Laurana replied, speaking softly, looking not at him, but into the night. "I could feel its pulse and beat inside me as if I had grown a terrible kind of heart, a heart that did not quite fit in my chest, for it always seemed to cut off my breathing."

She was silent a moment, communing with voices from the past. He no longer heard the voices from his past, but he remembered how they haunted a man or a woman, and he remained silent.

"I thought at first I could not continue on. I was too frightened, but then a wise man—his name was Elistan—taught me that I should not fear death. Death is inevitable, a part of life. It comes to all of us—humans, elves, even dragons. We defeat death by living, by doing something with our lives that will last beyond the grave. What I fear is fear, Marshal. I have never rid myself of that. I fight it constantly."

They rode in silence, alone together. Then she said, "I want to thank you, Marshal, for paying me the compliment of not trying to dissuade me from this course of action."

He bowed his head in acknowledgment but remained silent. She had more to say. She was thinking how to say it.

"I will use this opportunity to make reparation," she continued, speaking now not to him alone but to those voices in the past. "I was their general, their leader. I left them. Abandoned them. The War of the Lance was at a critical stage. The soldiers looked to me for guidance, and I let them down."

"You were faced with a choice between love and duty, and you chose love. A choice I, too, have made," he said with a glance at the aspen trees through which they rode.

"No, Marshal," she returned, "you choose duty. Duty to that which you love. There is a difference."

"At the beginning, perhaps," he said. "Not at the end."

She looked over at him and smiled.

They were nearing Qualinost. The city was empty, appeared abandoned. Medan drew up his horse. "Where are we bound, Madam? We should not ride openly through the streets. We might be seen."

"We are going to the Tower of the Sun," she said. "The implements of my plan are to be found inside. You look dubious, Marshal. Trust me." She regarded him with a mischievous smile, as he assisted her to dismount. "I cannot promise to make the moon fall from the sky. But I can give you the gift of a star."

The streets of Qualinost were empty, deserted. The two kept to the deep shadows, for they could feel the presence of watchers in the skies though they could not see them. Dragons would be difficult to see in the moonlight through the predawn mists that rose from the river, wound lovingly among the boles of the aspen trees.

The early morning was silent, eerily silent. The animals had gone to ground, the birds huddled hushed in the trees. The smell of burning, the smell of the dragon, the smell of death was in the air, and all creatures fled its coming.

"All those with sense," Medan said to himself. "Then there are the rest of us."

So deep was the silence that he thought if he listened closely he could hear the heartbeats of those hiding within the houses. Hearts that beat steadily, hearts that beat fast, hearts that trembled with fear. He could imagine lovers and friends sitting in the darkness in the silence, hands clasped, their touch conveying the words they could not speak and must be inadequate anyway.

They reached the Tower of the Sun just as the moon was dropping down from the sky. Located on the far eastern border of Qualinost, the tower graced the tallest hill. It provided a spectacular view of the city. The tower was made of burnished gold that shone as brilliantly as another sun when morning's first rays struck it, setting it aflame with warmth and life and the joy of a new day. So bright was the light that it dazzled the eyes. Approaching the tower in the daytime, Medan had often been forced to look away, lest it blind him.

At night, the tower reflected the stars, so that it was difficult to distinguish the tower—a myriad stars floating on its surface—from the night sky that was its backdrop.

They entered the tower through an entry hall whose doors were never locked and walked from there into the main chamber. Laurana had brought with her a small lantern to light their way. Torchlight would be too bright, too noticeable to anyone outside.

Medan had been inside the tower before for various ceremonies. Its beauty never failed to impress him. The tower rose hundreds of feet into the air with one central spire and two smaller ones jutting out to the sides. A person standing on the floor could see straight up to the top, to a wondrous mosaic. Windows placed in a spiral pattern in the tower's walls were positioned to capture the sunlight and reflect it downward upon the rostrum that stood in the center of the main chamber.

It was too dark for him to see the mosaic that portrayed the sky by day and the sky by night. Thus symbolically had the Qualinesti portrayed their relationship with their cousins, the Silvanesti. The creator of the mosaic had been optimistic, separating the two by a rainbow. He would have done better to separate them by jagged lightning.

"Perhaps this is the reason," Laurana said softly, looking upward to the mosaic not yet illuminated by the sunlight but hidden in darkness and in shadow. "Perhaps the sacrifice of my people is necessary for a new beginning—a beginning in which our two sundered people are finally one."

Medan could have told her that the reasons for the destruction of Qualinost had nothing to do with new beginnings. The reasons were evil and hideous, embedded in a dragon's hatred for all that she admired, the need to tear down that which she could never build and destroy that which she most desired to possess.

He kept his thoughts to himself. If her idea brought Laurana peace, he was more than willing to let her believe it. And, maybe, after all, their thoughts were but two sides to the same coin. Her side the light, his side the dark.

Leaving the main chamber, Laurana led the Marshal up one flight of stairs and onto a balcony that overlooked the main chamber. Doors made of silver and of gold lined the circular hallway. Laurana counted the doors as she went. When she came to the seventh door, counting from either direction, she drew a key from a blue velvet bag attached to her wrist. The key was also made of silver and of gold. The seventh door was decorated with an image of an aspen tree, its arms extended upward to the sun. Medan could see no lock.

"I know what is in this room," Medan said. "The Royal Treasury." He placed his hand over hers, stopped her from continuing. "Are you certain you want to reveal this to me, Madam? In there are secrets the elves have kept for a thousand years. Perhaps it would not be wise to betray them, even now."

"We would be like the miser in the story who hordes his money against the bad times and starves to death in the process. You would have me keep locked up that which well might save us?" Laurana asked.

"I honor you for your trust in me, Madam," said the Marshal, bowing.

Laurana counted seven tree limbs up from the bottom branch, counted seven leaves upon the trees and touched her key to the seventh leaf.

The door did not open. It vanished.

Medan stared into a vast hall that held the wealth of the elven kingdom of Qualinost. As Laurana lifted the lantern, the sight was more dazzling to the eyes than the sunlight striking the tower. Chests of steel coins, golden coins, and silver covered the floor. Weapons of fabulous make and design lined the walls. Casks of gems and pearls stood on the floor. The royal jewels— crowns and scepters and diadems, cloaks heavy with rubies and diamonds and emeralds—were displayed on velvet stands.

"Don't move, Marshal," Laurana warned him.

Medan had no intention of moving. He stood frozen inside the door. He gazed around and was angry. Coldly furious, he turned to Laurana.

"You speak of misers, Madam," he said, gesturing. "You have wealth enough here to buy the swords of every mercenary in Ansalon, and you horde gold while you spend the lives of your people!"

"Once, long ago, in the days of Kith-Kanan, such wealth was ours," said Laurana. "This is only its memory."

The moment she said the word, he understood. He saw through the illusion to the reality.

A large hole gaped at his feet. A single spiral staircase carved of stone led straight down into blackness. Anyone who did not know the secrets of that room would take no more than two steps across that illusory floor before plunging to his death.

Their only light was the single ray shining from the small lantern. By its steady and unwavering light, Medan followed Laurana down the stairs. At the bottom lay the true wealth of the elven kingdom of Qualinost: a single chest with a few bags of steel coins. Several empty chests, whose lids stood open, the homes of spiders and mice. Weapons had once been displayed on the walls, but these had long since been removed. All except one. Hanging on the wall was a footman's lance. The beam of light from her lantern struck it, caused it to shine silver as once had shone the silver moon of Solinari.

"A dragonlance," said Marshal Medan, his voice tinged with awe. "I have never seen one before, yet I would know it anywhere."

Laurana looked up at the lance with quiet pride. "I want you to have it, Marshal Medan." She glanced back at him. "Do you now understand what I have in mind?"

"Perhaps I do," he said slowly. He could not take his rapt gaze from the dragonlance. "Perhaps I am starting to."

"I wish I could tell you it had some heroic history," she said, "but if it does, we do not know it. The lance was given to Tanis shortly after we were married. A woman brought it to him. She said they had found it among her husband's possessions after his death. He had taken loving care of it, and he'd left a note saying that he wanted it given to someone who would understand. She knew he had fought in the war, but he never spoke of his deeds. He would say that he had done his duty, as did many others. He'd done nothing special."

"Yet, as I recall, only renowned and proven warriors were granted the honor of carrying the dragonlance," said Medan.

"I knew him, you see, Marshal. I remembered him. Oh, not him personally. But I remembered all those who gave up so much to join our cause and who were never honored with songs or immortalized with tombs or statues. They went back to their lives as butchers, seamstresses, farmers, or shepherds. What they did they did for no other reason than because they felt it was their duty. I thought it appropriate we should use this lance.

"As to the other weapons that were stored here, I sent many of them with those who departed Qualinost. I gave many more to those who remain to fight. In this casket"— Laurana ran her hand over a box carved plainly and simply of rosewood—"are the truly valuable jewels of antiquity. They will remain here, for they represent the past and its glory. Should a time come in the future when we are at peace, they will be recovered. If the time should come when no one lives who remembers us, perhaps these will be discovered and bring back the dreams of the elves to the world."

She turned from the rosewood casket, rested her hand on a tree limb. Odd, he thought, that a tree limb should be lying in the room. Kneeling beside it, she reached down

381

and removed a piece of wood that was all but invisible in the center of the tree limb. Now Medan could see that the limb had been split lengthwise to form a case. Laurana lifted the lid.

Inside lay a sword. The weapon was enormous—a two-handed broadsword—and it would require two immensely large and strong hands to wield it. The blade was of shining steel, perfectly kept, with no spot of rust anywhere, no notches or scratches. The sword was plainly made, with none of the fancy ornamentation that sends the amateur into raptures but that veterans abhor. The sword had only a single decoration. Set into the pommel was a lustrous star sapphire, as big as a man's clenched fist.

The sword was lovely, a thing of deadly beauty. Medan reached out his hand in longing, then paused.

"Take it, Marshal," said Laurana. "The sword is yours."

Medan grasped the hilt, lifted the sword from its tree-limb case. He swung it gently, tested the balance. The sword might have been made for him. He was surprised to find that, although it appeared heavy, it was so well designed that he could wield it with ease.

"The sword's name is the Lost Star," said Laurana. "It was made for the elven paladin, Kalith Rian, who led the elves in the battle against Takhisis in the First Dragon War."

"How did the sword come by the name?" Medan asked.

"Legend has it that when the smith brought the sword to Kalith Rian, he told the elf lord this tale. While he was forging the sword, the smith saw a star flash across the heavens. The next morning, when he came to finish his work, he found this star sapphire lying amid the embers of his forge fire. He took it as a sign from the gods and placed the jewel in the sword's pommel. Rian named the sword the Lost Star. He slew the great red dragon Firefang with this sword, his final battle, for he himself was slain in the fight. The sword is said to be magical."

Medan frowned and handed the sword back hilt-first to Laurana. "I thank you, Madam, but I would much prefer to take my chances with an ordinary sword made of ordinary steel. I have no use for a sword that suddenly starts to sing an elven ditty in the midst of battle or one that transforms both me and it into a matched pair of serpents. Such occurrences tend to distract me."

"The sword will not start to sing, Marshal, I assure you," Laurana said with a ripple of laughter. "Hear me out before you refuse. It is said that those who look into the Lost Star when it is shining cannot look away, nor can they do anything else but stare at the jewel."

"That is even worse," he returned impatiently. "I become enamored of my own sword."

"Not you, Marshal. The dragon. And although I give the dragonlance to you, you will not wield the lance. I will."

"I see." Medan was thoughtful. He continued holding the sword, regarded it with new respect.

"This night as I was walking to the meeting in the darkness, I remembered this sword and its story, and I realized how it might be of use to us."

"Of use! This could make all the difference!" Medan exclaimed.

He took down the dragonlance from the wall and regarded it with interest, held it with respect. He was a tall man, yet the lance topped him by two feet. "I see one difficulty. This lance will be difficult to hide from Beryl. From what I recall, dragons are sensitive to the lance's magic."

"We will not hide it from her," Laurana replied. "As you say, she would sense its magic. We will keep it in the open, where she may see it plainly."

"Madam?" Medan was incredulous.

"Your gift to your overlord, Marshal. A powerful magical artifact from the Fourth Age."

383

Medan bowed. "I honor the wisdom of the Golden General."

"You will parade me, your hostage, before the dragon on top of the Tower of the Sun, as arranged. You will exhibit the dragonlance and offer that to her as a gift. If she tries to take hold of the lance—"

"She will," Medan interjected grimly. "She thirsts for magic as a drunkard his liquor."

"When she takes the lance," Laurana continued, "the lance—an artifact of light—will send a paralyzing shock through her. You will lift the sword and hold it before her eyes. Enthralled by the sword, she will be unable to defend herself. While the dragon stares mesmerized at the sword, I will take the lance and thrust it through the jaw and into her throat. I have some skill in the use of the lance," she added with quaint modesty.

Medan was approving, enthusiastic. "Your plan is an excellent one, General, and insures our success. I believe that, after all, I may yet live to walk my garden again."

"I hope so, Marshal," Laurana said, extending her hand to him. "I would miss my best enemy."

"And I mine," he replied, taking her hand and kissing it respectfully.

They climbed the stairs, leaving the treasure chamber to illusion. As they reached the door, Laurana turned and threw the velvet bag containing the key inside the room. They heard it strike the floor with a faint, muffled clink.

"My son now has the only key," she said softly.

26

Penalty for Betrayal

The dragon Khellendros, whose common name among the lesser creatures of Krynn was Skie, had his current lair near the top of one of the smaller peaks of the Vingaard Mountains. Unlike the other dragon overlords, Malystryx and Sable, Skie had numerous lairs, all of them magnificent, none of them his home.

He was an enormous blue dragon, the largest of his kind by many times, an aberration of a blue dragon. Whereas most blues averaged forty feet in length, Skie had grown over the years until he was three hundred feet long from massive head to thrashing tail. He was not the same shade of blue as the other dragons of his type. Once his scales had gleamed sapphire. Over the past few years, however, the rich blue of his scales had faded, leaving him a dreary blue, as if he had acquired a fine coating of gray dust. He was aware that this color shift caused considerable comment among the smaller blues who served him. He knew they considered him a mutation, a freak, and although they deferred to him, deep inside they considered themselves better dragons because of it.

He didn't care what they thought. He didn't care where he lived, so long as it wasn't where he was. Restless, restive, he would move from one vast, serpentine tunnel gouged through the very heart of some immense mountain to another on a whim, never remaining long in any of them.

A puny human might wander the wondrous labyrinths for a year and never find the ending. The blue's vast wealth was stashed in these lairs. Tribute came to him in a never-ending flood. Skie was overlord of the rich lord-city of Palanthas.

Skie cared nothing for the wealth. What need had he of steel coins? All the treasure chests of all the world overflowing with steel, gold, silver, and jewels could not buy him what he wanted. Even his own magical power—although it was inexplicably waning, it was still formidable—could not gain him his one desire.

Weaker dragons, such as the blue dragon Smalt, Skie's new lieutenant, might revel in such wealth and be glad to spend their paltry, pitiful lives in its gain. Skie had no care for the money. He never looked at it, he refused to listen to reports of it. He roamed the halls of his castle cavern until he could no longer stand the sight of them. Then he flew off to another lair, entered that one, only to soon sicken of it as well.

Skie had changed lairs four times since the night of the storm, the magical storm that had swept over Ansalon. He had heard a voice in that storm, a voice that he had recognized. He had not heard it since that night, and he searched for it, searched in anger. He had been tricked, betrayed, and he blamed the Speaker in the Storm for that betrayal. He made no secret of his rage. He spoke of it constantly to his minions, knowing that it would reach the right ears, trusting that someone would come to placate him.

"She had better placate me," Skie rumbled to Smalt. "She had better give me what I want. Thus far I have held my hand as I agreed. Thus far I have let her play her little game of conquest. I have not yet been recompensed, however, and I grow weary of waiting. If she does not give me what is my due, what I have been promised, I will end this little game of hers, break the board, and smash the pieces, be they pawn or Dark Knight."

Skie was kept apprised of Mina's movements. Some of his own subject blues had been among those who traveled to Silvanost to carry Mina and her forces into Nightlund. He was not surprised, therefore, when Smalt arrived to say that Mina wanted to arrange a meeting.

"How did she speak of me?" Skie demanded. "What did she say?"

"She spoke of you with great respect, O Storm Over Ansalon," Smalt replied. "She asks that you be the one to name the time and place for the meeting. She will come to you at your convenience, although it means leaving her army at a critical moment. Nevertheless, Mina deems this meeting with you important. She values you as an ally and is sorry to hear that you are in any way displeased or dissatisfied with the current arrangements. She is certain it is all a misunderstanding that can be smoothed over when the two of you come together."

Skie grunted, a sound that shook his enormous body— he was many times larger than the small blue dragon with the glistening sapphire scales who crouched humbly before him, wings drooping, tail curled submissively.

"In other words, you have fallen under her spell, Smalt, as they all do. Do not bother to deny it."

"I do not deny it, O Storm Over Ansalon," Smalt returned and there was an unusually defiant gleam in the blue's eyes. "She has conquered Silvanost. The wicked elves have fallen as grain to her scythe. Lord Targonne attempted to have her killed and instead was slain by her hand. She is now leader of the Dark Knights of Neraka. Her troops are in Nightlund where she works on plans to lay siege to Solanthus—"

"Solanthus?" Skie growled.

Smalt's tail twitched nervously. He saw that he was in possession of news his master had not yet heard, and when a master is all knowing, to know something ahead of the master is never good.

"Undoubtedly she plans to discuss this with you first," Smalt faltered, "which is another reason why she is coming to meet with you, O Storm Over—"

"Oh, shut up and stop blathering, Smalt!" Skie snarled. "Get out."

"The meeting?" Smalt ventured.

"Tell her to meet me here at the eastern opening of this lair," Skie said glumly. "She may come to me whenever it suits her. Now leave me in peace."

Smalt was only too happy to do as he had been ordered.

Skie didn't give a damn about Solanthus. He had to do some hard thinking even to recall where the blasted city was located, and when he remembered, he thought his forces had already conquered Solanthus—he had a vague recollection of it. Perhaps that was some other city of humans. He didn't know, and he didn't care, or at least he hadn't cared until just now. Attacking Solanthus without asking his permission was another example of Mina's disdain for him, her lack of respect. This was a deliberate affront. She was showing him he was expendable, of no more use.

Skie was angered now, angry and, in spite of himself, afraid. He knew her of old, knew her vengeance, knew her wrath. It had never been turned on him. He had been a favorite. But then he had made a mistake. And now he was being made to pay.

His fear increased his anger. He had chosen the entrance of his lair as the meeting place because he could keep watch on all around him. He had no intention of being caught deep underground, trapped and ambushed. Once Smalt had departed, Skie paced about his lair and waited.

The blind beggar had reached his destination. He cast about with his staff until he located a large rock, sat down to rest himself and to consider what to do next. Since he could not see, he could not tell by sight exactly where he was. He knew from asking questions of people on the road that he was in Solamnia, somewhere in the foothills of the Vingaard Mountains. He had no real need to know his precise location, however, for he was not following a map. He was following his senses, and they had led him to this place. The fact that he knew the name of the place served merely to confirm in his mind what his soul already understood.

The silver dragon Mirror had traveled an immense distance in human form since the night of the magical storm—the storm that had wounded and scarred him, knocked him from the skies over Neraka, sent him plunging to the rocks below. Lying there, dazed and blind and bleeding, he had heard an immortal voice singing the Song of Death and he had been awed and appalled.

He had wandered aimlessly for a time, searching for and then finding Mina. He spoke with her. She was the one who sang the Song of Death.

The voice in the storm had been a summons. The voice had spoken the truth to him and, when he had refused to accept the truth, the Bringer of the Storm had punished him. Robbed of his sight, Mirror realized that he might be the only one in the world to see truly. He had recognized the voice, but he did not understand how it could be or why. So he had embarked on a quest to find out. In order to travel, he had been forced to take human form, because a blind dragon dare not fly, whereas a blind human can walk.

Trapped in this frail body, Mirror was helpless to act. He was frustrated in his search for answers, for the voice spoke to him constantly, taunted him, fed his fear, singing to him of the terrible events happening in the world: the fall of Silvanesti, the peril of Qualinost, the destruction of the Citadel of Light, the gathering of the dead in Nightlund. This was his punishment. Although he could not see, he was made to see all too clearly those he loved dying. He saw them stretch out their hands to him for help, and he was powerless to save them.

The voice sought to make despair his guide, and it had almost succeeded. He stumbled along the dark path, tapping out his way with his stick, and when he came to places where he cast about him with the stick and felt nothing ahead, he sometimes wondered if it would not be easier to keep walking, to fall off the edge of the precipice into the eternal silence that would close his ears to the voice, the darkness of death that could not be more dark than that in which he lived.

His search for others of his kind who had heard the voice, who might have heard the ancient words and understood them, had failed. He could find no other silver dragons. They had fled, disappeared. That gave him some indication that he had not been alone in recognizing the voice, but that was not much help if he were alone in the world—a blind dragon in human form—unable to do anything. In the moment of his despair Mirror formed a desperate resolution. One dragon would know the truth and might share it. But he was not a friend. He was a longtime enemy.

Skie, the immense blue dragon, had not arrived on Krynn as a stranger, as had Malys and the others. He had been in the world for years. True, Skie had changed much following the Chaos War. He had grown larger than any blue dragon was ever meant to grow. He had conquered Palanthas—the Dark Knights ruled that wealthy land in his name. He had gained the grudging respect of the great red Malystryx and her green cousin Beryl. Although rumor had it that he had turned upon his own kind and devoured them, as had Malys and Beryl, Mirror—for one—had not believed it.

Mirror would stake his life on that belief.

The silver dragon left Solace seeking Skie, tracking his enemy using the eyes of his soul to find the trail. His trek had led him here, to the foot of one of the blue dragon's mountain lairs. Mirror could not see the lair, but he could hear the enormous blue dragon roaming inside. He could feel the ground shake with every step Skie took, the mountains tremble as he lashed his tail. Mirror could smell the ozone of the blue's breath, feel the electricity tingle in the air.

Mirror rested for several hours, and when he felt his strength return, he began to climb. A dragon himself, he knew that Skie would have opened up many entrances to his lair. Mirror had only to find one of them.

Skie regarded the slight human female standing before him with barely concealed contempt. He had fostered a secret hope that in this female commander of armies he would find, once again, his lost Kitiara. He had relinquished that hope almost immediately. Here was no hot blood, no passion. Here was no love of battle for the sake of the challenge and the thrill of outwitting death. This female was as different from Kitiara as the ice floe differs from the frothing, crashing waves driven by the storm.

Skie might have been tempted to tell this girl to go away and send some responsible adult to deal with him, but he knew from the reports of his agents that she had flummoxed the Solamnics at Sanction, brought down the shield over Silvanost, and been the death of Lord Targonne—gone and quite easily forgotten.

She stood before him unafraid, even unimpressed, though he could have cracked the lithe, frail body with the flick of a claw. He had teeth that were bigger than this human.

"So you are the Healer, the Bringer of Death, the Conqueror of Elves," he grunted.

"No," she said. "I am Mina."

As she spoke, she lifted her gaze to meet his. He looked into the amber eyes and saw himself inside them. He saw himself small, shrunken, a lizard of a dragon. The sight was disquieting, made him ill at ease. He rumbled deep in his massive throat and arched his great neck and shifted the immense bulk of his body so that the mountain shook, and he felt reassured in his might and his strength. Still, in the amber eyes, he was very small.

"The One Who Heals, the One Who Brings Death, the One Who Conquers is the One God," Mina continued. "The One God I serve. The One God we both serve."

"Indeed I have served," Skie said, glowering. "I have served faithfully and well. I was promised my reward."

"You were given it. You were permitted to enter the Gray to search for her. If you have failed in your search, that is not the fault of the One God." Mina shrugged and slightly smiled. "You give up too easily, Skie. The Gray is a vast plane. You could not possibly have looked everywhere. After all, you did sense her spirit—"

"Did I?" Skie lowered his head so that his eyes could look directly into the amber eyes. He hoped to see himself grow large, but he failed. He was frustrated now, as well as angry. "Or was it a trick? A trick to get rid of me. A trick to cheat me of what I have earned."

He thrust forth his great head near her, exhaled a frustrated, sulfurous breath. "Two centuries ago, I was taken from my home world and brought in secret to the world known as Krynn. In return for my services it was promised that I would one day be granted the rulership of this world. I obeyed the commands given me. I traveled the Portals. I scouted out locations. I made all ready. I now claim the right to rule a world—this world. I could have done so thirty-eight years ago, but I was told that now was not the time.

"Then came the great red Malys and my cousins, and again I demanded my right to assert my authority. I could have stopped them, then. I could have cowed them, made them bow before me. Again, I was told, it is not the time. Now Beryl and Malystryx have grown in power that they gained by killing dragons of my own kin—"

"Not your kin," Mina corrected gently.

"My kin!" Skie thundered, his anger swelling to rage. Still, in the amber eyes, he remained small. "For over two hundred years I lived among blue dragons and fought alongside them. They are more my kin than those great bloated wyrms. Now the wyrms divide up the choicest parts between them. They extend their control. Be damned to the pact that was made. I—I am shunted off to the Gray on some wild kender chase.

"I say I was tricked!" the blue snarled. "I say I was deluded. Kitiara is not in the Gray. She was never in the Gray. I was sent there so that another could rule in my stead. Who is that other? You, girl? Or will it be Malys? Has another pact been made? A secret pact? That is why I came back—long before I was expected, seemingly, for I hear you are to now march upon Solanthus."

Mina was silent, considering.

Skie shifted his great bulk, lashed his tail so that it thumped against the walls of his lair, sending tremors through the mountain. Though the ground quaked beneath her feet, the human remained complacent. She gazed steadily at the dragon.

"The One God owes you nothing."

Skie drew in a seething breath. Lightning crackled between his teeth, sparked, and smoldered. The air was charged. Mina's cropped red hair rippled like that of a stalking panther. Ignoring his display of anger, she continued speaking, her voice calm.

"You abrogated your right to rule when you forgot your duties and forsook your oath of allegiance to the One to whom you owed everything, choosing instead to bestow your love and loyalty on a mortal. You rule the world!" Mina regarded the dragon with scorn and cool contempt. "You are not fit to rule a dung heap! Your services are no longer needed. Another has been chosen to rule. Your followers will serve me as they once served you. As to your precious Kitiara, you will never find her. She has passed far beyond your reach. But then, you knew that, didn't you, Skie?"

Mina's eyes fixed on him, unblinking. He found himself caught in them. He tried to look away, to break free, but he was held fast, the amber hardening around him.

"You refused to admit it," she went on, relentless, her voice digging deep beneath his scales. "Go back to the Gray, Skie. Go there to seek Kitiara. You can return anytime you want. You know that, don't you? The Gray is in your mind, Skie. You *were* deluded, but not by the One God. You deluded yourself."

Skie would send his answer to the One God—a charred lump. He unleashed his lethal breath, spat a gout of lightning at the girl. The bolt struck Mina on her black breastplate, over her heart. The fragile body crumpled to the cavern floor, frail limbs curled, contorted as those of a dead spider. She did not move.

Skie watched, cautious, wary. He did not trust her or the one she served. It had been too easy.

Mina lifted her head. A bolt of light flashed from her amber eyes and struck Skie in the center of his forehead.

The lightning burned his scales, jolted through his body. His heart clamored painfully in his chest, its rhythm knocked wildly askew. He could not breathe. Mist, gray mist, swirled before his eyes. His head sank to the stone floor of his lair. His eyes closed upon the gray mist that he knew so well. The gray mist where he heard Kitiara's voice calling to him. The gray mist that was empty . . .

Mina stood up. She had taken no hurt, seemingly, for her body was whole, her armor unblemished. She remained in the cave for several moments, watching the dragon, imprisoning his image behind her long lashes. Then she turned on her heel and walked from his lair.

The blind beggar remained crouched in the darkness of his hiding place while he tried to understand what had happened. He had arrived in Skie's lair at about the same time as Mina, only Mirror had come in by one of the back entrances, not by the front. His astonishment on hearing and recognizing Mina's voice had been immense. The last time he had seen her, he had met her on the road leading to Silvanost. Though he could not see her with his eyes, he had been able to see her through her voice. He had heard stories about her all along his road, and he had marveled that the orphan child he had known at the Citadel of Light, the child who had disappeared so mysteriously, had returned even more mysteriously. She had recognized him, known him for the silver dragon who had once guarded the citadel.

His astonishment at seeing her here, speaking to Skie, was not so great as his astonishment at their conversation.

He was starting to understand, starting to find answers to his questions, but those answers were too astounding for him yet to comprehend them fully.

The silver dragon felt the Blue's fury building. Mirror trembled for Mina, not so much for her sake as for the sake of the orphan child she had been. Mirror would have to be the one to return to tell Goldmoon the horrible fate of the child she had once so loved. He heard the cracking of the lightning, bent beneath the shock wave of the thunder.

But it was not Mina who cried out in agony. The voice of pain was Skie's. Now the great blue dragon was quiet, except for a low, piteous moan.

Footsteps—booted, human footsteps—echoed in the lair and faded away.

Mirror felt more than heard the irregular thumping of Skie's heart, felt it pulse through the cavern so that it jarred his body. The giant heart was slowing. Mirror heard the soft moan of anger and despair.

Even a blind dragon was more at home in these twisting corridors than a human—sighted or not. A dragon could find his way through them faster. Mirror had once, long ago, been larger than the Blue. That had changed. Skie had grown enormous, and now Mirror knew the reason why. Skie was not of Krynn.

Transforming himself into his true dragon form, Mirror was able to move without hindrance through the corridors of Skie's lair. The silver dragon glided along the passage, his wings folded tightly at his side, reaching out with his senses as a sightless human gropes with his hands. Sound and smell and a knowledge of how dragons build their lairs guided him, leading him in the direction of that last tortured cry of shock and pain.

Mirror advanced cautiously. There were other blue dragons in the vicinity of the lair. Mirror could hear their voices, though they were faint, and he could not understand what they said. He could smell their scent, a mixture of dragon and thunder, and he feared one or more of them might return to see what had befallen their leader. If the blues discovered Mirror, the blind silver would not stand a chance in battle against them.

The voices of the blue dragons died away. He heard the flapping of their wings. The lair stank of blue dragon, but instinct told Mirror the others were gone. They had left Skie to die. The other blues had deserted him to follow Mina.

Mirror was not surprised, nor did he blame them. He recalled vividly his own meeting with her. She had offered to heal him, and he had been tempted, sorely tempted, to let her. He had wished not so much that she would restore his sight but that she would restore to him something he had lost with the departure of the gods. He had found it, to his dismay. He had refused to allow her near him. The darkness that surrounded her was far deeper than the darkness that enveloped him.

Mirror reached the lair where Skie lay, gasping and choking. The Blue's immense tail twitched, back and forth, thumping the walls spasmodically. His body jerked, scraping against the floor, his wings flapped, his head thrashed. His claws scrabbled against the rock.

Mirror might be able to heal the body of the Blue, but that would avail Mirror little if he could not heal Skie's mind. Loyalty to Kitiara had turned to love, a hopeless love that had darkened to an obsession that had been fed and fostered so long as it served a useful purpose. When the purpose was complete, the obsession became a handy weapon.

It would be an act of mercy to let the tormented Skie die. Mirror could not afford to be merciful. He needed answers. He needed to know if what he feared was true.

Crouching in the cavern beside the body of his dying enemy, Mirror lifted his silver wings, spread them over Skie, and began to speak in the ancient language of the dragons.

27

The City Slumbers

itting in the dark on the wooden plank that was his bed in the cell, listening to his fourth Uncle Trapspringer tale in an hour, Gerard wondered if strangling a kender was punishable by death or if it would be considered a meritorious act, worthy of commendation.

" . . . Uncle Trapspringer traveled to Flotsam in company with five other kender, a gnome, and a gully dwarf, whose name I can't remember. I think it was Phudge. No, that was a gully dwarf I met once. Rolf? Well, maybe. Anyway, let's say it was Rolf. Not that it matters because Uncle Trapspringer never saw the gully dwarf again. To go on with the story, Uncle Trapspringer had come across this pouch of steel coins. He couldn't remember where, he thought maybe someone had dropped it. If so, no one had come to claim it from him, so he decided that since possession is nine-tenths of a cat's lives he would spend some of the steel on magic artifacts, rings, charms, and a potion or two. Uncle Trapspringer was exceedingly fond of magic. He used

399

to have a saying that you never knew when a good potion would come in handy, you just had to remember to hold your nose when you drank it. He went to this mage-ware shop, but the moment he walked in the door the most marvelous thing happened. The owner of the mage-ware shop happened to be a wizard, and the wizard told Uncle Trapspringer that not far from Flotsam was a cave where a black dragon lived, and the dragon had the most amazing collection of magical objects anywhere on Krynn, and the wizard just couldn't take Uncle Trapspringer's money when, with a little effort, Uncle Trapspringer could kill the black dragon and have all the magical objects he wanted. Now, Uncle Trapspringer thought this was an excellent idea. He asked directions to the cave, which the wizard most obligingly gave him, and he—"

"Shut up!" said Gerard through clenched teeth.

"I beg your pardon?" said Tasslehoff. "Did you say something?"

"I said 'shut up.' I'm trying to sleep."

"But I'm just coming to the good part. Where Uncle Trapspringer and the five other kender go to the cave and—"

"If you don't be quiet, I will come over there and quiet you," said Gerard in a tone that meant it. He rolled over on his side.

"Sleep is really a waste of time, if you ask me—"

"No one did. Be quiet."

"I—"

"Quiet."

He heard the sound of a small kender body squirming about on a hard wooden plank—the bed opposite where Gerard lay. In order to torture him, they had locked him in the same cell as the kender and had put the gnome in the next cell over.

" 'Thieves will fall out,' " the warden had remarked.

Gerard had never hated anyone in his life so much as he hated this warden.

The gnome, Conundrum, had spent a good twenty minutes yammering about writs and warrants and *Kleinhoffel* vs. *Mencklewink* and a good deal about someone named Miranda, until he had eventually talked himself into a stupor. At least Gerard supposed that was what had happened. There had been a gargle and a thump from the direction of the gnome's cell and then blessed silence.

Gerard had just been drifting off himself when Tasslehoff—who had fallen asleep the moment the gnome had opened his mouth—awakened the moment the gnome was quiet and launched into Uncle Trapspringer.

Gerard had put up with it for a long time, mostly due to the fact that the kender's stories had a numbing effect on him, rather like repeatedly hitting his head against a stone wall. Frustrated, angry—angry at the Knights, angry at himself, angry at fate that had forced him into this untenable position—he lay on the hard plank, unable to go back to sleep, and worried about what was happening in Qualinesti. He wondered what Medan and Laurana must think of him. He should have returned by now, and he feared they must have decided he was a coward who, when faced with battle, had run away.

As to his predicament here, the Lord Knight had said he would send a messenger to Lord Warren, but the gods knew how long that would take. Could they even find Lord Warren? He might have pulled out of Solace. Or he might be fighting for his life against Beryl. The Lord Knights said they would inquire around Solanthus to find someone who knew his family, but Gerard gave that long odds. First someone would actually have to inquire and in his cynical and pessimistic mood, he doubted if the Knights would trouble themselves. Second, if someone did know his father, that person might not know Gerard. In the past ten years, Gerard had done what he could to avoid going back home.

Gerard tossed and turned and, as one is prone to do during a restless, sleepless night, he let his fears and his worries grow completely out of proportion. The kender's voice had been a welcome distraction from his dark thoughts, but now it had turned into the constant and annoying drip of rain through a hole in the roof. Having fretted himself into exhaustion, Gerard turned his face to the wall. He ignored the kender's pathetic wrigglings and squirmings, intended, no doubt, to make him— Gerard—feel guilty and ask for another story.

He was floating on sleep's surface when he heard, or imagined he heard, someone singing a lullaby.

> Sleep, love; forever sleep.
> Your soul the night will keep.
> Embrace the darkness deep.
> Sleep, love; forever sleep.

The song was restful, soothing. Relaxing beneath the song's influence, Gerard was sinking beneath peaceful waves when a voice came out of the darkness, a woman's voice.

"Sir Knight?" the woman called.

Gerard woke, his heart pounding. He lay still. His first thought was that it was Lady Odila, come to torment him some more. He knew better almost at once, however. The voice had a different note, a more musical quality, and the accent was not Solamnic. Furthermore Lady Odila would have never referred to him as "Sir Knight."

Warm, yellow light chased away the darkness. He rolled over on his side so that he could see who it was who came to him in the middle of the night in prison.

He couldn't find her at first. The woman had paused at the bottom of the stairs to hear a reply, and the wall of the stairwell shielded her from his sight. The light she held wavered a moment, then began to move. The woman rounded the corner and he could see her clearly. White robes shimmered yellow-white in the candlelight. Her hair was spun silver and gold.

"Sir Knight?" she called again, looking searchingly about.

"Goldmoon!" cried out Tasslehoff. He waved his hand. "Over here!"

"Is that you, Tas? Keep your voice down. I'm looking for the Knight, Sir Gerard—"

"I am here, First Master," Gerard said.

Sliding off the plank, bewildered, he crossed the cell to stand near the iron bars, so that she could see him. The kender reached the bars in a single convulsive leap, thrust both arms out between the bars and most of his face. The gnome was awake, too, picking himself up off the floor. Conundrum looked groggy, bleary-eyed, and extremely suspicious.

Goldmoon held in her hand a long, white taper. Lifting the light close to Gerard's face, she studied him long and searchingly.

"Tasslehoff," she said, turning to the kender, "is this the Knight of Solamnia you told me about, the same Knight who took you to see Palin in Qualinesti?"

"Oh, yes, this is the same Knight, Goldmoon," said Tasslehoff.

Gerard flushed. "I know that you find this impossible to credit, First Master. But in this instance, the kender is telling the truth. The fact that I was found wearing the emblem of a Dark Knight—"

"Please say nothing more, Sir Knight," Goldmoon interrupted abruptly. "I do believe Tas. I know him. I have

403

known him for many years. He told me that you were gallant and brave and that you were a good friend to him."

Gerard's flush deepened. Tas's "good friend" had been wondering, only moments earlier, how he might dispose of the kender's body.

"The best friend," Tasslehoff was saying. "The best friend I have in all the world. That's why I came looking for him. Now we've found each other, and we're locked up together, just like old times. I was telling Gerard all about Uncle Trapspringer—"

"Where am I?" the gnome asked suddenly. "Who are all of you?"

"First Master, I must explain—" Gerard began.

Goldmoon raised her hand, a commanding gesture that silenced all of them, including Tasslehoff. "I do not need explanations." Her eyes were again intent upon Gerard. "You flew here on a blue dragon."

"Yes, First Master. As I was about to tell you, I had no choice—"

"Yes, yes. It makes no difference. Haste is what counts. The Lady Knight said the dragon was still in the area, that they had searched for it but could not find it, yet they knew it was near. Is that true?"

"I . . . I have no way of knowing, First Master." Gerard was mystified. At first he thought she had come to accuse him, then maybe to pray for him or whatever Mystics did. Now he did know what she wanted. "I suppose it might be. The blue dragon promised to wait for me to return. I had planned to deliver my message to the Knights' Council, then fly back to Qualinesti, to do what I could to assist the elves in their battle."

"Take me there, Sir Knight."

Gerard stared at her blankly.

"I must go there," she continued, and her voice sounded frantic. "Don't you understand? I must find a way to go there, and you and your dragon will carry me. Tas, you remember how to get back, don't you?"

"To Qualinesti?" Tas said, excited. "Sure, I know the way! I have all these maps—"

"*Not* Qualinesti," Goldmoon said. "The Tower of High Sorcery. Dalamar's Tower in Nightlund. You said you were there, Tas. You will show me the way."

"First Master," Gerard faltered, "I am a prisoner. You heard the charges against me. I cannot go anywhere."

Goldmoon wrapped her hand around one of the bars of the cell. She tightened her grip until the knuckles on that hand grew as white as bare bone. "The warden sleeps under the enchantment I cast upon him. He will not stop me. No one will stop me. I must go to the Tower. I must speak with Dalamar and Palin. I could walk, and I will walk, if I have to, but the dragon is faster. You will take me, won't you, Sir Gerard?"

Goldmoon had been the ruler of her people. All her life, she had been a leader. She was accustomed to command and to being obeyed. Her beauty moved him. Her sorrow touched him. Beyond that, she offered him his freedom. Freedom to return to Qualinesti, to join the battle there, to live or die with those he had come to care for.

"The key to the cell is on the ring the warden carries—" he began.

"I have no need of it," Goldmoon said.

She closed her hand over the iron bars. The iron began to dissolve, melting like the wax of her candle. A hole formed in the center as the iron bars drooped, curled over.

Gerard stared. "How . . ." His voice was a hoarse croak.

"Hurry," Goldmoon said.

He did not move but continued to stare at her.

"I don't know how," she said and a note of desperation made her voice tremble. "I don't know how I have the power to do what I do. I don't know where I heard the words to the song of enchantment I sang. I know only that whatever I want I am given."

"Ah, now I remember who this woman is!" Conundrum heaved a sigh. "Dead people."

Gerard didn't understand, but then this was nothing new. He had not understood much of anything that had happened to him in the past month.

"Why start now?" Gerard muttered, as he stepped through the bars. He wondered where they had stashed his sword.

"Come along, Tas," Goldmoon said sternly. "This is no time to play games."

Instead of leaping joyously to freedom, the kender had suddenly and inexplicably retreated to the very farthest corner of the cell.

"Thank you for thinking of me, Goldmoon," Tasslehoff said, settling himself in the corner, "and thank you for melting the bars of the cell. That was wonderful and something you don't see everyday. Ordinarily I'd be glad to go with you, but it would be rude to leave my good friend Conundrum here. He's the best friend I have in all the world—"

Making a sound expressive of exasperation, Goldmoon touched the bars of the gnome's cell. The bars dissolved, as had the others. Conundrum climbed out the hole. Brow furrowed, he squatted with his hands on his knees, and began scraping up the iron meltings, muttering to himself something about smelting.

"I'll bring the gnome, Tas," Goldmoon said impatiently. "Now come out of there at once."

"We had better hurry, First Master," Gerard warned. He would have been quite happy to leave both gnome and kender behind. "The jailer's relief arrives two hours past midnight—"

"He will not come this night," Goldmoon said. "He will sleep past his time. But you are right. We must make haste, for I am called. Tas, come out of that cell this minute."

"Don't make me, Goldmoon!" Tasslehoff begged in pitiful tones. "Don't make me go back to the Tower. You don't know what they want to do to me. Dalamar and Palin mean to murder me."

"Don't be silly. Palin would never—" Goldmoon paused. Her severe expression softened. "Ah, I understand. I had forgotten. The Device of Time Journeying."

Tasslehoff nodded.

"I thought it was broken," he said. "Palin threw parts of it at the draconians, and it exploded, and I figured that's one thing I don't have to worry about anymore."

He gave a mournful sigh. "Then I reached into my pocket, and there it was. Still in pieces, but all the pieces were back in my pocket. I've thrown them away, time and again. I even tried giving them away, but they keep coming back to me. Even broken, they keep coming back." Tas looked at Goldmoon pleadingly. "If I go back to the Tower, they'll find it, and they'll fix it, and I'll have to be stepped on by a giant, and I'll die. I don't want to die, Goldmoon! I don't want to! Please don't make me."

Gerard almost suggested to Goldmoon that he hit the kender on the jaw and haul him out bodily, but on second thought, he kept silent. The kender looked so completely and utterly miserable that Gerard found himself feeling sorry for him. Goldmoon entered the cell and sat next to the kender.

"Tas," Goldmoon said gently, reaching out her hand and stroking back a lock of hair that had escaped his top-knot and was straggling over his face, "I can't promise you that this will have a good and happy ending. Right now, to me it seems that it must end very badly. I have been following a river of souls, Tas. They gather at Night-lund. They do not go there of their own free will. They are prisoners, Tas. They are under some sort of terrible con-straint. Caramon is with them, and Tika, Riverwind, and my daughter; perhaps all those we love. I want to find out why. I want to find out what is happening. You tell me that Dalamar is in Nightlund. I must see him, Tas. I must speak to him. Perhaps he is the cause. . . ."

Tasslehoff shook his head. "I don't think so. Dala-mar's a prisoner, too, at least that's what he told Palin." The kender hung his head and plucked nervously at his shirt front. "There's something else, Goldmoon. Some-thing I haven't told anyone. Something that happened to me in Nightlund."

"What is it, Tas?" Goldmoon looked concerned.

The kender had lost his jaunty gaiety. He was droop-ing and wan and shivering—shivering with fright. Gerard was amazed. He had often felt that a really good scare would be beneficial for a kender, would teach the rattle-brained little imps that life was not picnics by the tomb and taunting sheriffs and swiping gewgaws. Life was earnest and hard, and it was meant to be taken seriously. Now, seeing Tas dejected and fearful, Gerard looked away. He didn't know why, but he had the feeling that he had lost something, that he and the world had both lost something.

"Goldmoon," said Tas in an awful whisper, "I saw myself in that wood."

"What do you mean, Tas?" she asked gently.

"I saw my own ghost!" Tas said, and he shuddered. "It wasn't at all exciting. Not like I thought seeing one's own ghost would be. I was lost and alone, and I was searching for someone or something. It may sound funny, I know, but I always thought that after I died, I'd meet up with Flint somewhere. Maybe we'd go off adventuring together, or maybe we'd just rest, and I'd tell him stories. But I wasn't adventuring. I was just alone . . . and lost . . . and unhappy."

He looked up at her, and Gerard was startled to see the track of a single tear trickle down through the grime on the kender's cheek.

"I don't want to be dead like that, Goldmoon. That's why I can't go back."

"Don't you see, Tas?" Goldmoon said. "That's why you *have* to go back. I can't explain it, but I am certain that what you and I have both seen is wrong. Life on this world is meant to be a way-stop on a longer journey. Our souls are supposed to move on to the next plane, to continue learning and growing. Perhaps we may linger, wait to join loved ones, as my dear Riverwind waits for me and somewhere, perhaps, Flint waits for you. But none of us can leave, apparently. You and I together must try to free these prisoner souls who are locked in the cell of the world as surely as you were locked in this cell. The only way we can do that is to go back to Nightlund. The heart of the mystery lies there."

She held out her hand to Tasslehoff. "Will you come?"

"You won't let them send me back?" he bargained, hesitating.

"I promise that the decision to go back or not will be yours," she said. "I won't let them send you back against your will."

"Very well," Tas said, standing up and dusting himself off and glancing about to see that he had all his pouches. "I'll take you to the Tower, Goldmoon. It just so happens that I have an extremely reliable body compass. . . ."

At this juncture, Conundrum, who had finished scraping up the melted iron, began to discourse on such things as compasses and binnacles and lodestones and his great-great-uncle's theory on why north could be found in the north and not in the south, a theory that had proved to be quite controversial and was still being argued to this day.

Goldmoon paid no attention to the gnome's expostulations or Tasslehoff's desultory replies. She was imbued with a fixed purpose, and she went forward to achieve it. Unafraid, calm, and composed, she led them up the stairs, past the slumbering warden slumped over his desk, and out of the prison.

They hastened through Solanthus, a city of sleep and silence and half-light, for the sky was pearl gray with the coming of dawn. The gnome wound down like a spent spring. Tasslehoff was uncharacteristically quiet. Their footfalls made no sound. They might have been ghosts themselves as they roamed the empty streets. They saw no one, and no one saw them. They encountered no patrols. They met no farmer coming to market, no carousers stumbling home from the taverns. No dog barked, no baby cried.

Gerard had a strange impression of Goldmoon passing over the city streets, her cloak billowing out behind her, blanketing the city, closing eyes that were starting to open, lulling those who were waking back into sweet slumber.

They left Solanthus by the front gate, where no one was awake to stop them.

28

Overslept

Lady Odila woke to find the sun blazing in her eyes. She sat straight up in bed, irritated and annoyed. She was not generally a late sleeper; her usual time to rise being shortly before the gray light of dawn filtered through her window. She hated sleeping late. She was dull and listless, and her head ached. She felt as if she had spent the night carousing. True, after the Knights' Council, she had gone to the Dog and Duck, a tavern favored by members of the Knighthood, but not to drink. She had done what she had promised the First Master she would do: She had asked around to see if anyone knew or had ever met Gerard uth Mondar.

None of the Knights had, but one knew of someone who came from that part of Ansalon or thereabouts and another thought perhaps his wife's seamstress had a brother who had been a sailor and might have worked for Gerard's father. Not very satisfactory. Odila had lifted a mug of hard cider with her comrades and then gone to her bed.

411

She muttered imprecations to herself as she dressed, tugging on the padded leather tunic, linen shirt, and woolen socks she wore beneath her armor. She had intended to rise early to lead a patrol in search of the blue dragon, hoping to catch the beast while it was out hunting in the cool mists of early morning before it disappeared into its lair to sleep through the sunny part of the day. So much for that idea. Still, they might catch the beast napping.

Sliding the tunic, embroidered with the kingfisher and rose of the Solamnic Knighthood, over her head, Odila buckled on her sword, locked her door, and hurriedly left her quarters. She lived on the upper floor of a former inn that had been turned over to the Knighthood to house those who served in Solanthus. Clattering down the stairs, she noted that her fellow Knights appeared to be moving as slowly as she was this morning. She nearly collided with Sir Alfric, who was supposed to be in charge of the changing of the guard at the city's front gate and who would be late for his duty. Carrying his shirt and his sword belt in one hand, his helm in the other, he came dashing out of his room.

"And a good morning to you, too, my lord," said Odila, with a pointed stare at the front of his breeches.

Flushing deeply, Sir Alfric hastily laced himself into proper decorum and then fled out the door.

Chuckling at her jest, thankful she was not in for his reprimand, Odila walked briskly to the armorer. She had taken her breastplate to the armory yesterday to mend a torn leather strap and a bent buckle. They had promised to have it mended by this morning. Everyone she met looked sleepy and bedraggled or annoyed and put out. She passed by the man who was the relief for the night warden. The man was yawning and stumbling over his feet in his haste to report for work.

Had everyone in Solanthus overslept?

Odila pondered this disturbing question. What had seemed an odd and annoying occurrence was now starting to take on sinister significance. She had no reason to think this unusual bout of slothfulness on the part of Solanthus's inhabitants had anything to do with the prisoners, but, just to make certain, she altered her direction, headed for the prison.

She arrived to find everything peaceful. To be sure, the warden was sprawled over his desk, snoring blissfully, but the keys still hung from their hook on the wall. She woke the sleeping warden with a sharp rap of her knuckles on his bald pate. He sat straight up, wincing and blinking at her in confusion. While the warden rubbed his head, she made the rounds to find that the prison's inmates were all slumbering soundly in their cells. The prison had never been so quiet.

Relieved, Odila decided she would check on Gerard while she was here, to let him know that she knew people who might be able to swear to his identity. She walked down the stairs, rounded the corner and stopped and stared in amazement. Shaking her head, she turned on her heel and walked slowly up the stairs.

"And I had just decided he was telling the truth," she said to herself. "That will teach me to admire cornflower-blue eyes. Men! Born liars, every one of them.

"Sound the alarm!" she ordered the sleep-befuddled warden. "Turn out the guard. The prisoners have escaped."

She paused a moment, wondering what to do. First disappointed, she was now angry. She had trusted him, the absent gods knew why, and he had betrayed her. Not the first time this had happened to her, but she intended it should be the last. Turning, she headed for the stables. She knew where Gerard and his friends had gone, where they must go. He would head for his dragon.

When she reached the stables, she checked to see if any horses were missing. None were, and so she assumed that the Knight must be on foot. She was relieved. The gnome and kender, with their short legs, would slow him down.

Mounting her horse, she galloped through the streets of Solanthus that were slowly coming to life, as if the entire city was suffering from the ill effects of a wild drinking bout.

She passed through the numerous gates, pausing only long enough to determine if the guards had seen anything of the prisoners in the night. They hadn't, but then, by the looks of them, they hadn't seen anything except the insides of their eyelids. She arrived at the final gate to find Starmaster Mikelis there, as well.

The guards were red in the face, chagrined. Their superior was speaking to Mikelis.

"—caught sleeping on duty," he was saying irately.

Odila reigned in her horse. "What is the matter, Starmaster?" she asked.

Absorbed in his own troubles, he did not recognize her from the trial. "The First Master has gone missing. She did not sleep in her bed last night—"

"She was the *only* one in Solanthus who did not sleep, apparently," Lady Odila returned with a shrug. "Perhaps she went to visit a friend."

The Starmaster was shaking his head. "No, I have looked everywhere, spoken to everyone. No one has seen her since she left the Knights' Council."

Odila paused, considered this. "The Knights' Council. Where the First Master spoke in defense of Gerard uth Mondar. It might interest you to know, Starmaster, that last night the prisoner escaped from his cell."

The Starmaster looked shocked. "Surely, Lady Knight, you're not suggesting—"

"He had help," Odila said, frowning, "help that could have come only from someone who has mystical powers."

"I don't believe it!" Starmaster Mikelis cried heatedly. "First Master Goldmoon would never—"

Odila didn't wait to hear anymore about First Master Goldmoon. Spurring her horse to a gallop, she rode out of the gate and down the main road. As she rode, she tried to sort all this out. She had believed Gerard's story—strange and bizarre though it might be. She had been impressed by his eloquent plea at the end of the trial, a plea not for himself but for the elves of Qualinesti. She had been deeply impressed by the First Master, and that was odd, considering that Lady Odila did not put much stock in miracles of the heart or whatever it was clerics were peddling these days. She even believed the kender, and it was at that point that she wondered if she was running a fever.

Odila had ridden about two miles from the city when she saw a rider approaching her. He was riding fast, bent over his steed, kicking his horse in the flanks to urge it to even greater speed. Spittle whipped from the horse's mouth as it thundered past Odila. She recognized by his garb that the man was a scout and concluded that the news he brought must be urgent, judging from the breakneck pace he set. She was curious but continued on her way. Whatever news he brought, it would keep until she returned.

She had ridden another two miles when she heard the first horn call.

Odila reigned in her steed, turned in the saddle, stared back in consternation at the walls of the city. Horns and now drums were sounding the call to arms. An enemy had been sighted, approaching the city in force. To the west, a large cloud of dust obscured the horizon line. Odila stared at the dust cloud intently, trying to see what caused it, but she was too far away. She sat for a moment, irresolute. The horns called her back to duty behind the city walls. Her own sense of duty called her to continue on, to recapture the escaped prisoner.

Or, at least, to have a talk with him.

Odila cast a final glance at the dust cloud, noted that it appeared to be drawing nearer. She increased her speed down the road.

She kept close watch along the side of the highway, hoping to find the location where the group had left the road to go in search of their dragon. A few more miles brought her to the spot. She was surprised and oddly pleased to find that they had not even bothered to hide their tracks. An escaping felon—a cunning and hardened criminal—would have worked to throw pursuers off his trail. The party had cut a wide swath in the waving prairie grass. Here and there small excursions slanted off to the side as if someone—probably the kender—had wandered off, only to be hauled back.

Odila turned her horse's head and began following the clearly marked path. As she rode farther, drawing nearer to the stream, she came upon more evidence that she was on the right trail, sighting various objects that must have tumbled out of the kender's pouches: a bent spoon, a shining piece of mica, a silver ring, a tankard with Lord Tasgall's crest. She was among the trees now, riding along the bank of the stream where she had first caught Gerard.

The ground was damp from the morning mists, and she could see footprints: one pair of large booted feet, one pair of smaller feet wearing boots with soft soles, one pair of small kender feet—they were in front—and another pair of small feet straggling behind. Those must belong to the gnome.

Odila came to a place where three of them had halted and one had gone on ahead—the Knight, of course, going to seek out the dragon. She could see some signs that the kender had started to go with the Knight but had apparently been ordered back, because the small footprints, toes dragging, reversed themselves. She could see where the Knight had returned and the rest had gone forward with him.

Dismounting, Odila left her horse by the side of the river with a command to remain there until summoned. She proceeded forward on foot, moving silently, but with as much haste as she could. The footprints were fresh. The ground was just now starting to dry with the morning sun. She had no fear that she would be too late. She had kept watch on the skies to catch sight of a blue dragon, but she had seen no sign of one.

It would take some time, she reasoned, for the Knight to persuade a blue dragon—known to be extremely proud and wholly dedicated to the cause of evil—to carry a kender, a gnome, *and* a Mystic of the Citadel of Light. For that matter, Odila could not imagine the First Master, who had long ago risked her life to battle blue dragons and all they stood for, agreeing to come near a blue dragon, much less ride on one.

"Curiouser and curiouser," Odila said to herself.

The horn calls were distant, but she could still hear them. The city's bells were ringing now, too, warning the farmers and shepherds and those who lived outside the city to leave their homes and seek the safety of the city's walls. Odila strained her ears, focused on one sound, a sound apart from the horn calls and the wild clamoring of the bells. Voices.

Odila crept forward, listening. She recognized Gerard's voice and Goldmoon's. She loosened her sword in its sheath. Her plan was to rush in, knock down Gerard before he could react, and hold him hostage in order to prevent the dragon from attacking. Of course, depending on the relationship between dragon and Knight, the blue might well attack her with no regard for what happened to its master. That was a risk Odila was prepared to take. She was sick and tired of being lied to. Here was one man who was going to tell her the truth or die in the process.

Odila recognized this cavern. She had come across it in her earlier attempts to capture the dragon. She and her patrol had searched the cave but had found no trace of the beast. He must have moved here afterward, she concluded, venturing forward. Concentrating on her footing, taking care that she did not crack a stick beneath her boot, or tread on a pile of rustling leaves, she listened intently to what the voices were saying.

"Razor will carry you into Nightlund, First Master." Gerard was speaking, his voice low and deferential, respectful. "If, as the kender claims, the Tower of High Sorcery is located there, the dragon will find it. You need *not* rely on the kender's directions. But I beg you to reconsider, First Master." His voice grew more earnest, his tone more intense. "Nightlund has an evil reputation that, from all I have heard, is well deserved."

A pause, then, "Very well, First Master, if you are committed to this action—"

"I am, Sir Knight." Goldmoon's voice, clear and resolute, echoed in the cave.

Gerard spoke again. "Caramon's dying request was for me to take Tasslehoff to Dalamar. Perhaps I should reconsider and travel with you." He sounded reluctant. "Yet, you hear the horns. Solanthus is under attack. I should be back there. . . ."

"I know what Caramon intended, Sir Gerard," said Goldmoon, "and why he made that request. You have done more than enough to fulfill his last wishes. I absolve you of the responsibility. Your life and that of the kender have been intertwined, but the threads are now untangled.

You are right to return to defend Solanthus. I will go forth on my own. What have you told the dragon about me?"

"I told Razor that you are a dark mystic, traveling in disguise. You have brought the kender because he claims to have found a way inside the Tower. The gnome is an accomplice of the kender who will not be separated from him. Razor believed me. Of course, he believed me." Gerard was bitter. "Everyone believes the lies I tell. No one believes the truth. What sort of strange, twisted world do we inhabit?"

He sighed heavily.

"You have the letter from King Gilthas," Goldmoon said. "They must believe that."

"Must they? You give them too much credit. You should make haste, First Master." Gerard paused, arguing with himself. "Yet, the more I think about it, the more I am loath to allow you to enter Nightlund alone—"

"I need no protection," Goldmoon assured him, her voice softening. "Nor do I think there is any protection you could offer me. Whoever summons me will see to it that I arrive safely at my destination. Do not lose faith in the truth, Sir Gerard," she added gently, "and do not fear the truth, no matter how awful it may seem."

Odila stood irresolute outside the cave, pondering what to do. Gerard had a chance to escape, and he was not taking it. He was planning to return to defend Solanthus. *Everyone believes the lies I tell. No one believes the truth.*

Drawing her sword, gripping the hilt tightly in her hand, Odila left the cover of the trees and walked boldly into the mouth of the cave. Gerard stood with his back to her, gazing into the darkness beyond. He wore the leathers of a dragonrider, the only clothes he had, the same that he'd worn in prison. He had recovered his sword and sword belt. In his hand he held the leather headgear of a dragonrider. He was alone.

Hearing Odila's footsteps, Gerard glanced around. He sighted her, rolled his eyes, shook his head.

"You!" he muttered. "All I need." He looked away into the darkness.

Odila thrust the tip of her sword into the back of his neck. She noted, as she did so, that he'd made a hasty job of putting on his leathers. Either that or he'd dressed in the dark. The tunic was on backward.

"You are my prisoner," she said, her voice harsh. "Make no move. Do not try to call out to the dragon. One word and I will—"

"You'll what?" Gerard demanded.

Whipping around, he shoved aside her sword with his hand and strode past her, out of the cave.

"Make haste, Lady, if you're coming," he said brusquely. "Or we will arrive back in Solanthus after the battle has ended."

Odila smiled, but only when his back was turned and he couldn't see her. Rearranging her face to look stern and severe, she hurried after him.

"Wait a minute!" she said. "Where do you think you are going?"

"Back to Solanthus," he said coolly. "Don't you hear the horns? The city is under attack."

"You are my prisoner—"

"Fine, I'm your prisoner," he said. Turning, he handed her his sword. "Where is your horse? I don't suppose you brought another one for me to ride. No, of course not. That would have required forethought, and you have all the brains of a newt. As I recall, however, your horse is a sturdy animal. The distance back to Solanthus is not far. He can carry us both."

Odila accepted the sword, used the hilt to rub her cheek. "Where did the Mystic go? And the others? The kender and the gnome. Your . . . um . . . accomplices."

"In there," Gerard said, waving his hand in the direction of the cave. "The dragon is in there, too, at the far end. They plan to wait until nightfall before they leave. Feel free to go back to confront the dragon. Especially since you brought only one horse."

Odila pressed her lips tightly together to keep from laughing.

"You really intend to go back to Solanthus?" she demanded, frowning darkly.

"I really do, Lady Knight."

"Then I guess you'll need this," she said and tossed him his sword.

He was so startled, he fumbled, nearly dropped it.

Odila walked past, giving him a wink and sly look from out the corner of her eye. "My horse can carry both of us, Cornbread. As you yourself said, we'd best hurry. Oh, and you better close your mouth. You might swallow a fly."

Gerard stared, dumbfounded, then sprang after her.

"You believe me?"

"*Now* I do," she said pointedly. "I don't want to hurt your feelings, Cornbread, but you're not clever enough to have put on an act like the one I just witnessed. Besides"— she sighed deeply—"your story is such a muddle, what with young ninety-year-old crones, a dead living kender, *and* a gnome. One has to believe it. No one could make up something like that." She looked at him over her shoulder. "So you really do have a letter from the elf king?"

"Would you like to see it?" he asked with a grudging smile.

Odila shook her head. "Not me. To be honest, I didn't even know the elves had a king. Nor do I much care. But it's good that someone does, I guess. What sort of a fighter are you, Cornbread? You don't look to have much in the way of muscle." She glanced disdainfully at his arms. "Maybe you're the small, wiry type."

"If Lord Tasgall will even let me fight," Gerard muttered. "I will offer my parole that I will not try to escape. If they will not accept it, I will do what I can to assist with the wounded or put out fires or however else I may serve—"

"I think they'll believe you," she said. "As I said, a story with a kender *and* a gnome . . ."

They reached the place where Odila had left her horse. Odila swung herself up into the saddle. She looked at Gerard, who looked up at her. He truly had the most startling blue eyes. She had never seen eyes that color before, never seen eyes of such clarity and brilliance. She reached out her hand to him.

Gerard grabbed hold, and she pulled him up to sit uncomfortably on the horse's rump behind her. Clucking her tongue, she commanded the horse forward.

"You had better put your arms around my waist, Cornbread," she said, "so that you don't fall off."

Gerard clasped his arms around her midriff, holding her firmly, sliding forward on the horse's rump so that he was pressed against her.

"Nothing personal, Lady Odila," he said.

"Ah, me," she returned with a gushy sigh. "And here I was going to go choose my wedding dress."

"Don't you ever take anything seriously, Lady?" Gerard asked, nettled.

"Not much," Odila answered, turning to grin at him. "Why should I, Cornbread?"

"My name is Gerard."

"I know," she replied.

"Then why don't you call me that?"

She shrugged. "The other suits you, that's all."

"I think it's because calling me by my name makes me a person, not a joke. I despise women, and I have the feeling you don't think much of men. We've both been hurt. Maybe both of us fear life more than we fear death. We can discuss that later over a cold pitcher of ale. But for now let's agree on this much: You will call me Gerard. Or Sir Gerard, if you prefer."

Odila thought she should have an answer to this, but she couldn't come up with one readily, one that was funny, at least. She urged her horse to a gallop.

"Stop!" Gerard said suddenly. "I thought I saw something."

Odila reined in the horse. The animal stood panting, flanks heaving. They had emerged from the tree line along the stream bank, were heading out into the open. The road lay before them, dipped down into a shallow depression before rising again to enter the city. She saw now what Gerard had seen. What she should have seen if she hadn't been so damn preoccupied with blue eyes.

Riders. Riders on horses. Hundreds of riders pouring across the plains, coming from the west. They rode in formation. Their flags fluttered in the wind. Sunlight gleamed off spear tips and flashed off steel helms.

"An army of Dark Knights," said Odila.

"And they are between us and the city," said Gerard.

29

Captor Captive

uick, before they see us!" said Gerard. "Turn this beast's head around. We can hide in the cave—"

"Hide!" Odila repeated, casting him a shocked glance over her shoulder. Then she grinned. "I like you, Corn—" She paused, then said, with a wry smile, "Sir Gerard. Any other Knight would have insisted we rush into battle." Sitting up straight and tall, she placed her hand on her sword hilt and declaimed, "I will stand and fight though the odds are a hundred to one. My honor is my life."

She turned her horse's head, began to ride back toward the cave.

Now it was Gerard who looked shocked. "Don't you believe that?"

"What good is your honor going to do you when you're dead? What good will it do anyone? I'll tell you what, Sir Gerard" she continued, "they'll make a song for you. Some damn stupid song they'll sing in the taverns, and all the fat shopkeepers will get misty-eyed and slobber in their beer about the brave Knight who fought odds of six hundred to one. But you know who *won't* be singing? Those Knights inside Solanthus. Our comrades. Our friends. The Knights who aren't going to have a chance to fight a glorious battle in the name of honor. Those Knights who have to fight to stay alive to protect people who have put their trust in them.

"So maybe our swords are only two swords, and two swords won't make a difference. What if every one of those Solamnic Knights in Solanthus decided to ride out onto the battlefield and challenge six hundred of the enemy to glorious combat? What would happen to the peasants who fled to the Knights for safety? Will the peasants die gloriously, or will they be spitted on the end of some soldier's spear? What will happen to the fat shopkeepers? Will they die gloriously, or will they be forced to watch while enemy soldiers rape their wives and daughters and burn their shops to the ground. The way I see it, Sir Gerard, we took an oath to protect these people. We didn't take an oath to die gloriously and selfishly in some hopeless, inane contest.

"The main objective of the enemy is to kill you. Every day you remain alive you defeat their main objective. Every day you stay alive you win and they lose—even if it's only skulking about, hiding in a cave until you can find a way to return to your comrades to fight alongside them. That, to me, is honor."

Odila paused for breath. Her body trembled with the intensity of her feeling.

"I never thought of it like that," Gerard admitted, regarding her in admiration. "I guess there is something you take seriously, after all, Lady Odila. Unfortunately, it all appears to have been for nothing." He raised his arm, pointed past her shoulder. "They've sent outriders to guard the flanks. They've seen us."

A group of horsemen, who had been patrolling the edge of the tree line, rode into view about a half mile away. The horse and riders standing alone amidst the prairie grass had been easily spotted. The patrol wheeled as one and was now galloping toward them to investigate.

"I have an idea. Unbuckle your sword belt and give it to me," Gerard said.

"What—" Frowning, Odila glanced around to see him pulling the leather helm over his head. "Oh!" Realizing what he meant to do, she began to unbuckle her sword. "You know, Sir Gerard, this ruse might work better if you weren't wearing your tunic backside-front. Hurry, shift it before they get a good look at us!"

Cursing, Gerard pulled his arms out of the sleeves and wriggled the tunic around until the emblem of the Dark Knights of Neraka was in the front.

"No, don't turn around," he ordered her. "Just do it. Be quick. Before they can get a good look at us."

Odila unbuckled her sword belt and slipped it into his hands. He thrust her sword, belt and all, inside his own swordbelt, then pulled on his helm. He did not fear he would be recognized, but the helm was excellent for concealing facial expressions.

"Hand me the reins and put your hands behind your back."

Odila did as he ordered. "You've no idea how exciting I find this, Sir Gerard," she murmured, breathing heavily.

"Oh, shut up," he muttered, fumbling with the knot. "Take *this* seriously, at least."

The patrol was drawing near. He could see details now, and he noted with astonishment that the leader was a minotaur. Gerard's hopes that they might get out of this alive increased. He had never met or even seen a minotaur before, but he had heard that they were thick-skulled and dim-witted. The remainder of the patrol were Knights of Neraka, experienced cavalrymen, judging by their skill in handling their mounts.

The enemy patrol galloped across the prairie, their horses sending up clouds of dust from the dry grass. A single gesture from the minotaur, who rode in the lead, sent the other members of the patrol out in a wide circle, surrounding Gerard and Odila.

Gerard had thought about riding forward to meet them but decided this might seem suspicious. He was a Dark Knight of Neraka near an enemy stronghold, encumbered with a prisoner, and he had good reason to react as warily to them as they did to him.

The minotaur raised his hand in salute. Gerard returned the salute, thanking whoever might be listening for his training under Marshal Medan. He sat his horse in silence, waited for the minotaur, who was his superior, to speak. Odila's cheeks were flushed. She glared at them all in stony silence. Gerard only hoped that silence would continue.

The minotaur eyed Gerard closely. The minotaur's eyes were not the dull eyes of a beast but were bright with intelligence.

"What is your name, your rank, and your commanding officer?" the minotaur demanded. His voice was gruff and growling, but Gerard had no difficulty understanding him.

"I am Gerard uth Mondar, aide to Marshal Medan."

He gave his real name because if, by some wild chance, they checked with Marshal Medan, he would recognize Gerard's name and know how to respond. He added the number of the unit serving in Qualinesti but nothing more. Like any good Knight of Neraka, he was suspicious of his comrades. He would answer only what he was asked, volunteering nothing.

The minotaur frowned. "You are a long way from home, dragonrider. What brings you this far north?"

"I was en route to Jelek on Marshal Medan's blue dragon with an urgent message from Marshal Medan to Lord of the Night Targonne," Gerard replied glibly.

"You are still a long way from home," the minotaur stated, the bestial eyes narrowing. "Jelek is a long way east of here."

"Yes, sir," said Gerard. "We flew into a storm and were blown off course. The dragon thought he could make it, but we were hit by a sudden gust of wind that flipped us over. I almost fell from the saddle, and the dragon tore a shoulder muscle. He continued to fly as long as he could, but it proved much too painful. We had no idea where we were. We thought we were near Neraka, but then we saw the towers of a city. Having grown up near here, I recognized Solanthus. At about the same time, we saw your army advancing on the city. Fearing to be noticed by the cursed Solamnics, the dragon landed in this forest and located a cave where he could rest and heal his shoulder.

"This Solamnic"—Gerard gave Odila a rough poke in the back—"saw us land. She tracked us to the cave. We fought, and I disarmed and captured her."

The minotaur looked with interest at Odila. "Is she from Solanthus?"

"She will not talk, sir, but I have no doubt that she is and can provide details about the number of troops stationed inside the city, its fortifications, and other information that will be of interest to your commander. Now, Talon Leader," Gerard added, "I would like to know your name and the name of your commander."

This was bold, but he felt that he'd been interrogated enough, and to continue meekly answering questions without asking a few of his own would look out of character.

The minotaur's eyes flashed, and for a moment, Gerard thought he had overplayed his part. Then the minotaur answered. "My name is Galdar. Our commander is Mina."

He spoke the odd name with a mixture of reverence and respect that Gerard found disconcerting. "What is the message you were carrying to Jelek?"

"My message is to Lord Targonne," Gerard replied and at the word *message*, his heart upended and slid down his gullet.

He remembered, suddenly, that he was carrying on his person a message that was not from Marshal Medan, but from Gilthas, king of the Qualinesti; a letter that would ruin him if it fell into the hands of the Dark Knights. Gerard could not believe his ill luck. The day when the letter might have done him some good, he'd left it with the dragon. The day when the letter could do him irreparable harm, it was tucked in his belt. What had he done in his lifetime to so outrage Fate?

"Lord Targonne is dead," responded the minotaur. "Mina is now Lord of the Night. I am her second-in-command. You may deliver the message to me, and I will relay it to her."

Gerard was not unduly surprised to hear that Targonne was dead. Promotion up the ranks of the Dark Knights often took place at night in the dark with a knife thrust to the ribs. This Mina had presumably taken command. He wrested his mind from dwelling on that blasted incriminating letter to dealing with the new turn of events. He could give his false message to this minotaur and be done with it. Then what would happen? They would take Odila from him and haul her off to be tortured while he would be thanked for his service and dismissed to return to his dragon.

"I was told to deliver the message to the Lord of the Night," returned Gerard stubbornly, playing the quintessential commander's aide—officious and self-important. "If that is not Lord Targonne, then my orders require me to deliver it to the person who has taken his place."

"As you will." The minotaur was in a hurry. He had more important things to do than bandy words with a marshal's aide. Galdar jerked a thumb in the direction of the dust cloud. "They'll be raising the command tent now. You'll find Mina there, directing the siege. I'll send a man with you to guide you."

"There is really no need, sir—" Gerard began, but the minotaur ignored him.

"As to your prisoner," the minotaur continued, "you can turn her over to the interrogator. He'll be setting up shop somewhere near the blacksmith's forge."

An image of red hot pokers and flesh-ripping iron tongs came unpleasantly to mind. The minotaur ordered one of his Knights to accompany them. Gerard would have liked to have dispensed with the company, but he didn't dare argue. Saluting the minotaur, Gerard urged the horse forward. For a moment he feared that the animal, feeling an unfamiliar hand on the reins, would balk, but Odila gave a slight kick with her heels, and the horse started moving. The minotaur stared intently at Gerard, during which the sweat trickled down the front of Gerard's breast. Then the minotaur wheeled his horse and galloped off. He and the rest of the patrol were soon lost to sight, entering the tree line. Gerard pulled up and peered back in the direction of the river.

"What is it?" their Dark Knight escort demanded.

"I'm concerned about my dragon," Gerard said. "Razor belongs to the Marshal. They've been comrades for years. It would mean my head if anything happened to the beast." He turned back to face the Knight. "I'd like to go check on the dragon, let Razor know what's going on."

"My orders are to take you to Mina," said the Knight.

"You don't have to come," said Gerard shortly. "Look, you don't seem to understand. Razor must have heard the horn calls. He's a blue. You know how blues are. They can *smell* battle. He probably thinks that the cursed Solamnics have turned out the city to search for him. If he feels threatened, he might mistakenly attack your army—"

"My orders are to take you to Mina," the Knight repeated with dull-witted stubbornness. "When you have reported to her, you can return to the dragon. You need not be concerned about the beast. He will not attack us. Mina wouldn't let him. As to his wounds, Mina will heal him, and you both will be able to return to Qualinesti."

The Knight rode on, heading for the main body of the army. Gerard muttered imprecations at the Knight from the safety of the helm, but he had no choice except to ride after him.

"I'm sorry," he said under cover of the horse's hoofbeats. "I thought sure he'd fall for it. He gets rid of us, gets out of patrol duty, does what he wants for an hour or two, then reports back." Gerard shook his head. "Just my luck that I have to run into the only reliable Dark Knight who ever lived."

"You tried," said Odila and by twisting her hands, she managed to give him a pat on his knee. "You did the best you could."

Their guide rode on ahead, eager to do his duty. Annoyed that they weren't moving faster, he gestured with his arm for them to hasten their pace. Gerard ignored the Knight. He was thinking about what the minotaur had said, about the Dark Knights laying siege to Solanthus. If that was the case, he might well be riding into an army of ten thousand or more.

"What did you mean when you said I hated men?" Odila asked.

Jolted out of his thoughts, Gerard had no idea what she was talking about, and he said so.

"You said that you despised women and that I hated men. What did you mean?"

"When did I say that?"

"When we were talking about what to call you. You said that both of us feared life more than we did death."

Gerard felt his skin burn and was glad he was wearing the helm to cover his face. "I don't remember. Sometimes I say things without thinking—"

"I had the feeling you'd been thinking about this for a long time," Odila interrupted.

"Yes, well, maybe." Gerard was uncomfortable. He hadn't meant to lay himself wide open, and he certainly didn't want to talk to her about what was inside. "Don't you have other things to worry about?" he demanded irritably.

"Like having red-hot needles jabbed beneath my fingernails?" she asked coolly. "Or my joints dislocated on the rack? I have plenty to worry about. I'd rather talk about this."

Gerard fell silent a moment, then he said, awkwardly, "I'm not sure what I meant. Maybe it's just the fact that you don't seem to have much use for men. Not just me. That's understandable. But I saw how you reacted to the other Knights during the council meeting and to the warden and—"

"*How* do I react?" she demanded, shifting in the saddle to look back at him. "What's the matter with the way I react?"

"Don't turn around!" Gerard snapped. "You're my prisoner, remember? We're not supposed to be having a cozy chat."

She sniffed. "For your information, I adore men. I just happen to think they're all cheats and scoundrels and liars. Part of their charm."

Gerard opened his mouth to reply to this when the Knight escort dashed back toward them at a gallop.

"Blast!" Gerard muttered. "What does this great idiot want now?"

"You are dawdling," said the Knight accusingly. "Make haste. I must return to my duties."

"I've lost a dragon to injury," Gerard returned. "I don't plan to lose a horse."

There was no help for it, however. This Knight was apparently going to stick to them like a bloodsucking tick. Gerard increased the pace.

As they entered the outskirts of the camp, they saw the army that was beginning to dig in for the siege. The soldiers were setting up camp well outside the range of arrows from the city walls. A few Solanthus archers tried their luck, but their arrows fell well short, and eventually the firing ceased. Probably their officers told them to quit being fools and save their arrows.

No one in the enemy camp paid the archers any attention, beyond glancing now and then at the walls that were lined with soldiers. The glances were furtive and were often followed by an exchange of words with a comrade, both of whom would raise their eyebrows, shake their heads and return to work quickly before an officer noticed. The soldiers did not appear frightened at the daunting sight of the walled city, merely bemused.

Gerard indulged his curiosity, looked about intently. He was not part of this army and so his curiosity would appear justified.

He turned to his guide. "When do the rest of the troops arrive?"

The Knight's voice was calm, but Gerard noted that the man's eyes flickered behind his helm. "Reinforcements are on the way."

"A great number, I suppose," Gerard said.

"A vast number," said the Knight. "More than you can imagine."

"They're nearby?"

The Knight eyed Gerard narrowly. "Why do you want to know? What is it to you?"

Gerard shrugged. "I thought I might lend my sword to the cause, that's all."

"What did you say?" the Knight demanded.

Gerard raised his voice to be heard above the din of hammers pounding, officers shouting orders, and the general tumult that went along with setting up a field camp.

"Solanthus is the most well-fortified city on the continent. The mightiest siege engines on Krynn couldn't make a dent in those walls. There must be five thousand troops ready to defend the city. What do you have here? A few hundred? Of course, you're expecting reinforcements. It doesn't take a genius to figure that out."

The Knight shook his head. Rising in his stirrups, he pointed. "There is Mina's command tent. You can see the flag. I will leave you to find your own way."

"Wait a minute," Gerard shouted after the Knight. "I want to deliver my prisoner safely to the interrogator. There'll be a reward in this for me. I don't want her dragged off and lynched!"

The Knight cast him a scornful glance. "You are not in Neraka, sir," he said disdainfully and rode off.

Gerard dismounted, began leading the horse through the ordered confusion. The soldiers were working swiftly and with a will. The officers gave direction, but they were not haranguing, not threatening. No whips urged the men to work faster and smarter. Morale appeared high. The soldiers were laughing and joking with each other and singing songs to help ease their labor. Yet, all they had to do was to look up on the city walls to see ten times more than their own number.

"This is a joke," said Odila, keeping her voice low. They were surrounded by the enemy, and although the din was deafening, someone might overhear. "They have no army of reinforcements nearby. Our patrols go out daily. They would have seen such a massive buildup of troops."

"Apparently, they didn't," Gerard returned. "Solanthus was caught with its pants down."

Gerard kept his hand on his sword hilt, ready to fight should anyone decide to take it into his head to have a little fun with the Solamnic prisoner. The soldiers glanced at them with interest as they passed. A few halted to jeer at the Solamnic, but their officers quickly ordered the men back to work.

You're not in Neraka, the Knight had said. Gerard was impressed, also uneasy. This was not a mercenary army that fought for loot, for gain. This was a seasoned army, a disciplined army, one dedicated to its cause, whatever that cause might be.

The flag that fluttered on the spear driven into the ground beside the command was not really a flag, nothing more than a dirty scarf that looked as if it had been dipped in blood.

Two Knights posted guard outside the command tent that had been the first tent raised. Other tents were now going up around it. An officer stood in front of the tent, speaking with another Neraka Knight. The officer was an archer by his dress and the fact that he wore an enormous longbow slung over one shoulder. The Knight had his back to Gerard. He could not see the face. Judging by his slight build, this Knight was no more than a youth, eighteen, if that. He wondered if he was some Knight's son dressed up in his father's armor.

The archer spotted Gerard and Odila first. The archer's gaze was keen and appraising. He said something to the Knight, who turned to look at them. Gerard saw with a shock that the Knight was not a youth, as he had supposed, but a girl. A sheen of red hair, closely cropped, covered her head. Her eyes caught and held both of them in an amber gaze. He had never seen such extraordinary eyes. He felt uncomfortable under their scrutiny, as if he were a child again and she had caught him in some crime, perhaps stealing apples or teasing his little sister. She forgave him his offense because he did not know better. He was just a child. She might punish him, but the punishment would help him understand how to do right in the future.

Gerard was thankful for the helm, for he could avert his gaze and she wouldn't know it. But even as he tried, he couldn't keep his eyes from her. He stared at her, enthralled.

Pretty was not the word to describe her, nor beautiful. Her face was marked by its equanimity, its purity of thought. No line of doubt marred her smooth forehead. Her eyes were clear and saw far beyond what his eyes saw. Here was a person who would change the world for good or for evil. He recognized in that calm equanimity, Mina, commander of this army, whose name had been spoken with reverence and respect.

Gerard saluted.

"You are not one of my Knights, sir," Mina said. "I like to see faces. Remove your helm."

Gerard wondered how she knew he wasn't one of her Knights. No badge or emblem marked him as having come from Qualinesti, Sanction, or any other part of Ansalon. He removed his helm reluctantly, not because he thought she might recognize him, but because he had enjoyed its meager protection, shielded him from the intense scrutiny of her amber eyes.

He gave his name and related his story that had the advantage of being true for the most part. He spoke confidently enough, but the parts where he was forced to twist the truth or embellish it proved difficult. He had the strange feeling that she knew far more about him than he knew about himself.

"What is Marshal Medan's message?" Mina asked.

"Are you the new Lord of the Night, Lady?" Gerard asked. The question seemed expected of him, but he was uncomfortable. "Forgive me, but I was told that my message was to be delivered to the Lord of the Night."

"Such titles hold no meaning for the One God," she answered. "I am Mina, a servant of the One. You may deliver your message to me or not, as you choose."

Gerard stared, baffled and uncertain. He dared not look at Odila, although he wondered what she was thinking, how she was reacting. He had no idea what to do and realized that no matter what he did, he risked looking foolish. For some reason, he did not want to look foolish in those amber eyes.

"I choose to deliver my message to Mina," he said and was surprised to hear that same note of respect in his voice. "My message is this: Qualinesti is coming under attack from the green dragon Beryl. She has ordered Marshal Medan to destroy the city of Qualinost and threatens that if he does not, she will do so herself. She has ordered him to exterminate the elves."

Mina said nothing, indicated by a slight nod that she was listening and understood.

Gerard drew in a breath and continued. "Marshal Medan respectfully reminds the Lord of the Night that this attack on Qualinesti breaks the pact between the dragons. The Marshal fears that should Malys hear of it, all-out war will erupt among the dragons, a war that is likely to devastate much of Ansalon. Marshal Medan does not consider himself under the orders of Beryl. He is a loyal Knight of Neraka and therefore he requests orders from his superior, the Lord of the Night, on how to proceed. Marshal Medan also respectfully reminds his lordship that a city in ruins is worth very little and that dead elves pay no tribute."

Mina smiled slightly. The smile warmed the amber eyes, and they seemed to flow over Gerard like honey. "Lord Targonne would have been deeply moved by that sentiment. The *late* Lord Targonne."

"I am sorry to hear of his death." Gerard glanced somewhat helplessly at the archer, who was grinning at him as if he knew exactly what Gerard was thinking and feeling.

"Targonne is with the One God," Mina replied, her tone solemn and earnest. "He made mistakes, but he understands now and repents."

Gerard was thoroughly astounded by this. He had no idea what to say. Who was this One God, anyway? He dared not ask, thinking that as a Dark Knight, he might be supposed to know.

"I've heard of this One God," Odila said in dire tones. She ignored Gerard, who pinched her calf to warn her to keep her mouth shut. "Someone else spoke of a One God. One of those false Mystics from the Citadel of Light. Blasphemy! I tell you. All know that the gods are gone."

Mina lifted the amber eyes, fixed them on Odila.

"The gods may be gone to you, Solamnic," Mina said, "but not to me. Release the Knight's bindings. Let her dismount. Don't worry. She will not try to escape. After all, where could she go?"

Gerard did as he was told, helped Odila from the horse. "Are you trying to get us both killed?" he demanded under his breath as he undid the knot of the leather thong around her wrists. "This is no time to be discussing theology!"

"It got my hands untied, didn't it?" Odila returned, glancing at him from beneath her long lashes.

He gave her a rough shove toward Mina. Odila stumbled but caught herself and stood in front of the girl, who reached only to Odila's shoulder.

"There are no gods for anyone," Odila repeated with typical Solamnic stubbornness. "For you or me."

Gerard wondered what she had in mind. No way to tell. He would have to stay alert, be ready to pick up on her plan.

Mina was not angry or even annoyed. She regarded Odila with patience, rather like a parent watching a spoiled child throwing a temper tantrum. Mina reached out her hand.

"Take hold," she said to Odila.

Odila regarded her in blank astonishment.

"Take hold of my hand," Mina repeated, as if the child was rather a slow child.

"Do as she says, cursed Solamnic," Gerard ordered.

Odila cast him a glance. Whatever she had hoped would happen, this wasn't it. Gerard inwardly sighed, shook his head. Odila looked back at Mina and seemed on the point of refusing. Then her hand extended, reached out to Mina. Odila looked at the hand in amazement, as if the hand were acting of its own accord, against her will.

"What sorcery is this?" she cried, and she was in earnest. "What are you doing to me?"

"I am doing nothing," Mina said softly. "The part of you that seeks nourishment for your soul reaches out to me."

Mina took hold of Odila's hand in her own.

Odila gasped, as if in pain. She tried to break the hold, but could not, though Mina was not exerting any force that Gerard could see. Tears sprang to Odila's eyes, she bit her lip. Her arm shook, her body trembled. She gulped and seemed to try to bear the pain, but the next moment she sank to her knees. The tears spilled over, coursed down her cheeks. She bowed her head.

Mina moved close to Odila. She stroked Odila's long black hair.

"Now you see," said Mina softly. "Now you understand."

"No!" Odila cried in a choked voice. "No, I don't believe it."

"You do believe," Mina said. She put her hand beneath Odila's chin, lifted her head so that Odila was forced to look into the amber eyes. "I do not lie to you. You are lying to yourself. When you are dead, you will go to the One God, and there will be no more lies."

Odila stared at her wildly.

Gerard shuddered, chilled to the core of his being.

The archer leaned forward, said something to Mina. She listened and nodded.

"Captain Samuval says that you can undoubtedly provide us with valuable information about the defenses of Solanthus." Mina smiled, shrugged. "I do not require such information, but the captain believes that he does. Therefore you will be questioned first, before you are put to death."

"I won't tell you anything," Odila said thickly.

Mina regarded her with sorrow. "No, I don't suppose you will. Your suffering will be wasted, for, I assure you, you could not tell me anything that I do not already know. I do this only to humor Captain Samuval."

Bending down, Mina kissed Odila on the forehead. "I commend your soul to the One God," Mina said, and straightening, she turned to Gerard.

"I thank you for delivering your message. I would not advise you to return to Qualinost. Beryl would not permit you to enter that city. She launches her attack tomorrow at dawn. As for Marshal Medan, he is a traitor. He has fallen in love with the elves and their ways. His love finds shape and form in the Queen Mother, Lauralanthalasa. He has not evacuated the city as he was ordered. Qualinost is filled with elven soldiers, prepared to give their lives in defense of their city. The king, Gilthas, has laid a trap for Beryl and her armies—a cunning trap, I must admit."

Gerard gaped. His jaws went slack. His mouth hung open. He thought he should defend Medan, then knew he shouldn't, for doing so might implicate him. Or perhaps she already knew Gerard wasn't what he appeared and nothing that he did or didn't do would make any difference. He managed, at last, to ask the one thing that he had to know.

"Has Beryl . . . been warned?" Gerard's mouth was dry. He could barely speak the words.

"The dragon is in the keeping of the One God, as are we all," Mina replied.

She turned away. Waiting officers moved forward to claim Mina's attention, badgered her with questions. She walked off to listen to them, answer them. Gerard was dismissed.

Odila stood up, staggering, and would have fallen if Gerard had not stepped forward and, under the guise of seizing her arm, supported her. He wondered, at that, who was leaning on whom. He was in need of some sort of support himself. Sweating profusely, he felt wrung out.

"I can't answer you," Captain Samuval said, although Gerard had not asked a question. The captain walked over to converse. "Is what Mina said about Medan true? Is he a traitor?"

"I don't . . . I don't . . ." Gerard's voice failed him. He was tired of lying, and it seemed pointless anyway. The battle for Qualinost would be held tomorrow at dawn, if he believed her, and he believed her, although he had no idea how or why. He shook his head wearily. "I guess it doesn't matter. Not now."

"We'd be glad if you joined our ranks," Captain Samuval offered. "Here, I'll show you where to take your prisoner. The interrogator's setting up, but he should be in business by tomorrow morning. We could use another sword." He glanced at the city, whose walls were dark with soldiers. "How many troops do you reckon are in there?"

"A lot," Gerard said with emphasis.

"Yes, I suppose you're right." Captain Samuval rubbed his grizzled chin. "I'll wager she knows, eh?" He jerked a thumb at Odila, who walked as if in a daze, hardly seeming to notice where she was going, hardly seeming to care.

"I don't know if she does or not," Gerard said glumly. "She hasn't said anything to me about it, and she won't say anything to that torturer of yours. She's stubborn, that one. Where do I put her? I'll be thankful to be rid of her."

Captain Samuval led Gerard to a tent that was close to where the blacksmith and his assistants were setting up his portable forge. Pausing at the smith's, Captain Samuval appropriated a pair of leg irons and manacles, assisted Gerard in attaching them to Odila's legs and wrists. He handed Gerard the key.

"She's your prisoner," he said.

Gerard thanked him, tucked the key into his boot.

The tent had no bedding, but the captain brought water and food for the prisoner. Odila refused to eat, but she drank some water and managed to sound grudgingly grateful for the attention. She lay down on the tent floor, her eyes wide open and staring.

Gerard left her, went outside, wondering what he was going to do now. He decided the best thing he could do was to eat. He had not realized how hungry he was until he saw the bread and dried meat in the captain's hand.

"I'll take that food," Gerard said, "since she doesn't want it."

Samuval handed it over. "No mess tent as yet, but there's more where this came from. I was headed that way myself. You want to join me?"

"No," said Gerard. "Thanks, but I'll keep an eye on her."

"She's not going anywhere," said the captain, amused.

"Still, she's my responsibility."

"Suit yourself," said Captain Samuval and strode off. He had sighted a friend apparently, for he began waving his hand. Gerard saw the minotaur who had been leading the patrol waving back.

Gerard squatted down outside the prison tent. He ate the meal without tasting it. Realizing that he'd left the waterskin inside with Odila, he entered the tent to retrieve it. He moved quietly, thinking she might be asleep.

She had not stirred since he had left her, except that now her eyes were closed. He was reaching quietly for the waterskin, when she spoke.

"I'm not asleep," she said.

"You should try to rest," he returned. "Nothing to do now except to wait for nightfall. I have the key to the leg irons. I'll try to find you some armor or a soldier's tunic—"

She shifted her gaze from him, looked away.

Gerard had to ask. "What did you see, Odila? What did you see when she touched you?"

Odila closed her eyes, shivered.

"I saw the mind of God!"

30

The War of Souls Begins

aldar walked through the slumbering camp, yawning so wide he heard a distinct crack. A sharp pain in his jaw made him wince. Resolving not to do that again, he rubbed his jaw and continued on. The night was bright. The moon, within a sliver of being full, was large, lumpish, and vacuous. Galdar had the impression that it was a doltish moon. He'd never liked it much, but it would serve its purpose, if all went according to plan. Mina's plan. Mina's strange, bizarre plan. Galdar yawned again, but this time he took care not to crack his jaw.

The guards in front of Mina's tent recognized him—easy to spot the only minotaur in the entire army. They saluted and looked at him expectantly.

Her tent was dark. Not surprising, considering it was nearly dawn. He was loath to wake her, for she had been up before the sunrise the day before and had gone to bed well after midnight. He hesitated. After all, there wasn't anything she could do that he hadn't already done. Still, he felt she should know.

He thrust aside the flap and entered the command tent.

"What is it, Galdar?" she asked.

He was never certain if she was awake before he entered or if she woke on hearing him enter. Either way, she was always alert, responsive.

"The prisoner has escaped, Mina. The female Solamnic Knight. We can't find her captor, either. We believe they were in this together."

She slept in her clothes, woolen hose, and tunic. Her armor and her morning star stood at the foot of the bed. He could see her face, pale white, colder, more awful than the gibbous moon.

She evinced no surprise.

"Did you know of this, Mina? Did someone else come to tell you?" Galdar frowned. "I gave orders you were not to be disturbed."

"Yet now you disturb me, Galdar." Mina smiled.

"Only because all our efforts to find the Solamnic and this traitor Knight have failed."

"They are back in Solanthus now," Mina replied. Her eyes had no color in the darkness. He felt more comfortable with her in the darkness. He could not see himself in the amber. "They have been greeted as heroes. Both of them."

"How can you take this so calmly, Mina?" Galdar demanded. "They have been in our camp. They have tallied our numbers. They know how few of us there are."

"They can see that from the walls, Galdar."

"Not clearly," he argued. He had been opposed to this wild scheme from the beginning. "We have done what we could to deceive them. Put up empty tents, kept the men milling about so that they could not be easily counted. Our efforts have gone for naught."

Mina propped herself up on one elbow. "You remember that you wanted to poison their water supply, Galdar?"

"Yes," he said dourly.

"I counseled against it, for then the city would be useless to us."

He snorted. The city was useless to them right now and would remain so, for all he could see.

"You have no faith, Galdar," Mina said sadly.

Galdar sighed. His hand stole to his right arm, rubbed it involuntarily. It always seemed to ache now, as with rheumatism.

"I try, Mina. I truly do. I thought I had settled my doubts back in Silvanost, but now . . . I do not like our new allies, Mina," he stated abruptly. "And I am not alone."

"I understand," Mina said. "That is why I have been patient with you and with the others. Your eyes are clouded by fear, but the time will come when you will see clearly. Your eyes will be the only eyes that see clearly."

She smiled at her own jest.

Galdar did not smile. This was no laughing matter, as far as he was concerned.

She looked at him and very slightly shook her head. "As to the Solamnic, I have sent her into the city carrying a poison more destructive than the nightshade you wanted to dump in the city well."

He waited, suppressing a yawn. He had no idea what she was talking about. All he could think of was that it had all been for nothing. Hours of lost sleep sending out search parties, ransacking the camp, all for nothing.

"I have sent them the knowledge that there is a god," Mina continued, "and that the One God fights on our side."

Their escape had been ridiculously easy. So easy, Gerard would have said that it had been facilitated, if he could have thought of one single reason why the enemy would want them to return to Solanthus in possession of damning information about the enemy army camped outside their walls.

The only really tense moments came at Solanthus's outer gate, when there was some question as to whether or not the sentries were going to shoot them full of arrows. Gerard blessed Odila's strident voice and mocking tone, for she was immediately recognized and, on her word, they were both allowed admittance.

After that came hours of questioning from the officers of the Knighthood. The sun was rising now, and they were still at it.

Gerard had not had much sleep the night before. The day's strain and tension and the night's adventure had left him completely worn out. He'd told them everything he had seen or heard twice and was propping his eyelids open with his fingers when Odila's next words caused a minor explosion that jolted him into full wakefulness.

"I saw the mind of God," she said.

Gerard groaned and slumped back in his chair. He'd tried to warn her to keep quiet on that score, but, as usual, she had not listened to him. He'd been hoping for his bed, even if it was back in his cell, whose cool, quiet, and kenderless darkness was now strongly appealing. Now they were going to be here the rest of the day.

"What do you mean, exactly, Lady Odila?" Lord Tasgall asked carefully. He was thirty years Gerard's senior. His hair was iron gray and worn long, and he had the traditional mustaches of the Solamnic Knight. Unlike some Rose Knights Gerard had met, Lord Tasgall was not, as someone once disparagingly phrased it, a "solemnic" Knight. Although his face was suitably grave on this serious occasion, laugh lines around the mouth and eyes testified that he had a sense of humor. Obviously respected by those under his command, Lord Tasgall appeared to be a sensible, wise leader of men.

"The girl called Mina touched my hand, and I saw . . . eternity. There's no other way to describe it." Odila spoke in low tones, halting, obviously uncomfortable. "I saw a mind. A mind that could encompass the night sky and make it seem small and confining. A mind that could count the stars and know their exact number. A mind that is as small as a grain of sand and as large as the ocean. I saw the mind, and at first I knew joy, because I was not alone in the universe, and then I knew fear, terrible fear, because I was rebellious and disobedient and the mind was displeased. Unless I submitted, the mind would become angrier still. I . . . I could not understand. I did not understand. I still don't understand."

Odila looked helplessly at the Lord Knights as if expecting answers.

"What you saw must have been a trick, an illusion," Lord Ulrich replied soothingly. He was a Sword Knight, only a few years older than Gerard. Lord Ulrich was on the pudgy side, with a choleric face that indicated a love of spirits, perhaps more than was entirely good for him. He had a bright eye and a red nose and a broad smile. "We all know that the dark Mystics cause members of the Knighthood to experience false visions. Isn't that true, Starmaster Mikelis?"

The Starmaster nodded, agreed almost absently. The Mystic looked worn and haggard. He had spent the night searching for Goldmoon and had been amazed and bewildered when Gerard told him that she had left on the back of a blue dragon, flying to Nightlund in search of the wizard Dalamar.

"Alas," the Starmaster had said sadly. "She is mad. Quite mad. The miracle of her returned youth has overthrown her mentally. A lesson to us, I suppose, to be content with what we are."

Gerard would have been inclined to think so himself, except that her actions last night had been those of a sane person who is in command of the situation. He made no comment, kept his thoughts to himself. He had come to feel a great admiration and reverence for Goldmoon, although he had known her only one night. He wanted to keep the memory of their time together secret, sacred. Gerard closed his eyes.

The next moment, Odila elbowed him. Gerard jerked awake, sat up straight, blinking his eyes and wondering uneasily if anyone had noticed him napping.

"I tend to agree with Lord Ulrich," Lord Tasgáll was saying. "What you saw, Lady Odila—or thought you saw—was not a miracle, but a trick of a dark mystic."

Odila was shaking her head, but she held her tongue, for which miracle Gerard was grateful.

"I realize we could debate the subject for days or even weeks and never reach a satisfactory conclusion," Lord Tasgall added. "However, we have much more serious matters that require our immediate attention. I also realize that you are both probably very tired after your ordeal." He smiled at Gerard, who flushed deeply and squirmed uncomfortably in his chair. "First, there is the matter of Sir Gerard uth Mondar. I will now see the letter from the elf king, Sir Knight."

Gerard produced the letter, somewhat crumpled, but quite legible.

"I am not familiar with the elf king's signature," said Lord Tasgall, reading the letter, "but I recognize the royal seal of Qualinesti. Alas," he added quietly, "I fear there is little we can do to help them in their hour of need."

Gerard bowed his head. He might have argued, but the presence of enemy troops camped outside Solanthus would render any argument he might make ineffective.

"He may have a letter from an elf," said Lord Nigel, Knight of the Crown, "but he was still apprehended in company with a dragon of evil. I cannot easily reconcile the two."

Lord Nigel was in his forties, one of those people who do not want to make a decision until he has ruminated on it long and hard and looked at every fact three times over from all possible angles.

"I believe his story," said Odila in her forthright manner. "I saw him and heard him in the cave with the First Master. He had the chance to leave, and he didn't take it. He heard the horns, knew we were under attack, and came back to help defend the city."

"Or betray it," said Lord Nigel, glowering.

"Gerard told me that if you would not let him wear his sword, as a true Knight, he would do anything he could to help, from fighting fires to tending the wounded," Odila returned heatedly. "His quick thinking saved both our lives. He should be honored, not castigated."

"I agree," said Lord Tasgall. "I think we are all in agreement?" He looked at the other two. Lord Ulrich nodded at once and gave Gerard a grin and a wink. Lord Nigel frowned, but he had great respect for Lord Tasgall and so agreed to abide by his ruling.

Lord Tasgall smiled. "Sir Gerard uth Mondar, all charges against you are formally dropped. I regret that we have no time to publicly clear your name, but I will issue an edict to the effect that all may know of your innocence."

Odila rewarded Gerard with a grin and kicked his leg underneath the table, reminding him that he owed her one. This matter now dispensed with, the Knights could turn their attention to the problem of the enemy.

Despite the information they had received about the ridiculously small numbers of the enemy army currently besieging their city, the Solamnics did not take the situation lightly. Not after what Gerard told them about the expected reinforcements.

"Perhaps she means an enemy army marching out of Palanthas, my lord," Gerard suggested deferentially.

"No," said Lord Tasgall, shaking his head. "We have spies in Palanthas. They would have reported any massive troop movement, and there has been none. We have scouts watching the roads, and they have seen nothing."

"Begging your pardon, my lord," said Gerard, "but you didn't see this army coming."

"There was sorcery at work," said Lord Nigel grimly. "A magical sleep affected everyone in the city and its environs. The patrols reported that they were overcome with this fey sleep that affected man and beast alike. We thought the sleep had been cast upon us by the First Master Goldmoon, but Starmaster Mikelis has assured us that she could not possibly cast such a powerful spell."

He looked uneasily at Odila. Her words about the mind of God had brought a disquieting notion. "He tells us that no mortal could. Yet, we all slept."

I did not sleep, Gerard thought. Neither did the kender or the gnome. Goldmoon caused the iron bars to melt as if they were wax. What was it she said? *I don't know how I have the power to do what I do. I know only that whatever I want I am given.*

Who is the giver? Gerard glanced at Odila, troubled. None of the other Knights spoke. They were all sharing the same unwelcome thoughts, and no one wanted to give them voice. To go there was to walk the edge of a precipice blindfolded.

"Sir Gerard, Lady Odila, I thank you for your patience," Lord Tasgall said, rising to his feet. "We have information enough on which to act. If we have further need of you, we will summon you."

They were being dismissed. Gerard rose, saluted, thanked each Knight in turn. Odila waited for him, walked out with him. Looking back, Gerard saw the Knights already deep in discussion.

"It's not as if they have much choice," Odila said, shaking her head. "We can't just sit here and wait for them to bring in reinforcements. We'll have to attack."

"Damn strange way to run a siege," Gerard reflected. "I could understand it, their leader being hardly out of her baby clothes, but that captain looked to me to be a savvy officer. Why do they go along with her?"

"Perhaps she has touched their minds, as well," Odila muttered.

"What?" Gerard asked. She had spoken so softly he didn't think he'd heard right.

She shook her head glumly, and kept walking. "Never mind. It was a stupid thought."

"We'll be riding to battle soon," Gerard predicted, hoping to cheer her up.

"It can't be too soon for me. I'd like to meet that red-haired vixen with a sword in my hand. What about a drink?" she asked abruptly. "Or two or six or thirty?"

An odd tone in her voice caused Gerard to look at her sharply.

"What?" she demanded, defensive. "I want to drink that blasted God out of my mind, that's all. Come on. I'll buy."

"Not for me," he said. "I'm for my bed. Sleep. You should be, too."

"I don't know how you expect me to sleep with those eyes staring at me. Go to bed, then, if you're so tired."

He started to ask, "What eyes?" but Odila walked off, heading for a tavern whose signboard was a picture of a hunting dog holding a limp duck in its mouth.

Too exhausted to care, Gerard headed for a well-earned rest.

Gerard slept through the daylight and far into the night. He woke to the sounds of someone pounding on the door.

"Turn out! Turn out!" a voice called softly. "Muster in the courtyard in one hour. No lights, and keep the noise down."

Gerard sat up. The room was bright, but it was the white, eerie brightness of moonlight, not sunlight. Outside his door came the muffled sounds of Knights, their pages, squires, and servants up and about. So it was to be an attack by night. A surprise attack.

No noise. No lights. No drums calling the troops to muster. Nothing to give away the fact that the army of Solanthus was preparing to ride out and break the siege. Gerard approved. An excellent idea. They would catch the enemy asleep. With luck, perhaps they'd catch them sleeping off a night of carousing.

He had gone to bed in his clothes, so he had no need to dress, only to pull on his boots. Hastening down stairs crowded with servants and squires dashing about on errands for their masters, he shoved his way through the mob, pausing only to ask directions to the armory.

The streets were eerily silent, for most of the city was deep in slumber. Gerard found the armorer and his assistants scantily clad, for they had been yanked out of their beds at a moment's notice. The armorer was distraught that he could not outfit Gerard in proper Solamnic armor. There was no time to make any.

"Just give me the stuff you use in training," Gerard said.

The armorer was appalled. He couldn't think of sending a Knight to battle in armor that was dented, ill fitting, and scratched. Gerard would look like a scarecrow. Gerard didn't care. He was riding to his first battle, and he would have gone stark naked and not minded. He had his sword, the sword given to him by Marshal Medan, and that was what counted. The armorer protested, but Gerard was firm, and eventually the man brought what was required. His assistants—two pimple-faced, thirteen-year-old boys—

were wild with excitement and bemoaned the fact that they could not ride out to fight. They acted as Gerard's squires.

He went from the armory to the stables where grooms were frantically saddling horses, trying to quiet the animals, excited by the unusual commotion. The stable master eyed Gerard dubiously in his borrowed armor, but Gerard gave the man to know in no uncertain terms that he intended to steal a horse if he wasn't provided one. The stable master still might not have gone along with Gerard's demand, but Lord Ulrich entered at that moment, and although he laughed uproariously at the sight of Gerard's shabby accouterments, he vouchsafed Gerard's credentials, giving orders that he was to be treated with the consideration due a Knight.

The stable master didn't go quite that far, but he did provide Gerard with a horse. The beast looked more suited to drawing a wagon than carrying a Knight. Gerard could only hope that it would head for the field of battle and not start morning milk deliveries.

His arguings and persuadings appeared to Gerard to take forever, and he was in a fever of impatience, afraid he would miss the battle. As it was he was already ahead of most of the other Knights. By the time he arrived in the courtyard, the foot soldiers were forming ranks. Well trained, they moved into position quickly, obeying soft-spoken commands. They had muffled the jingling of their chain mail with strips of cloth, and woe betide the spearman who dropped his spear with an awful rattle onto the cobblestones. Hissing curses, the officers pounced on the offender, promising all sorts of dire punishments.

The Knights began to assemble. They, too, had wrapped parts of their armor in cloth to reduce the noise. Squires stood by the side of each horse, ready to hand up weapon and shield and helm. The standard-bearers took their places. The officers took their places. Except for the normal sounds of the City Guard making their accustomed rounds, the remainder of the city was quiet. No one was shouting out, demanding to know what was going on. No crowds of gawkers had gathered. Gerard admired both the efficiency of the Knights' officers and the loyalty and common sense of the citizenry. Word must have been passed from household to household, warning everyone to stay indoors and douse their lights. The marvel was that everyone was obeying.

The Knights and soldiers—five thousand strong— were ready to march. Here and there the silence was broken by the muffled whinny of an excited steed, a nervous cough from one of the foot soldiers, or the rattle of a Knight putting on his helm.

Gerard sought out Odila. A Knight of the Crown, she took her place riding among the front ranks. She was accoutered in armor similar to that of the other Knights, but he picked her out immediately by the two long black braids that trailed down from the gleaming silver helm and her laughter that rang out for a brief moment, then was suitably stifled.

"Bless the woman, she'd clown at her own funeral," he said, laughing, and then, realizing the ill omen of his remark, he wished uneasily he hadn't made it.

Lord Tasgall, Knight of the Rose, rode at the head among his command staff, a white scarf fluttering from his hand. He raised it high, so that everyone could see, then let it fall. The officers started their men marching, the Knights rode forward. Gerard took his place in the very last ranks among the youngsters newly knighted. He didn't mind. He could have walked with the foot soldiers and wouldn't have minded. The army of Solanthus moved out with a shuffling, scraping sound like some huge wingless, moon-glittering dragon sliding over the ground. The inner gates, whose hinges had been well greased, were silently shoved open by silent men.

A series of bridges allowed access over the moat. After the last foot soldier had crossed the bridges, they were drawn up. The gates were closed and barred, the murder holes manned.

The army marched on to the outer gates that pierced the thick curtain wall surrounding the city. The hinges on these gates had also been well oiled. Gerard, riding underneath the walls, saw archers crouching down among the shadows of the crenellations to avoid being seen. He trusted the archers would have nothing to do this night. The Solamnic army should be able to wipe out the army of the Dark Knights almost before they knew what hit them. Still, the Lord Knights were wise to take no chances.

Once the foot soldiers and Knights were outside the last gate, and that gate had been shut, barred, and manned, the Lord Knight paused, looked back to see his command solid behind him. He raised another white scarf, let this one fall.

The Knights broke the silence. Lifting their voices in a song that was old when Huma was a boy, they urged their horses into a thundering gallop. The song sent the blood coursing through Gerard's veins. He found himself singing lustily, shouting whatever came to mind in the parts where he didn't remember the words. The order to the cavalry had been to split the ranks, to send half the Knights charging to the east, the other half to the west. The plan was to encircle the slumbering camp, drive the inhabitants into the center, where they would be attacked by the foot soldiers, who were to charge straight on down the center.

Gerard kept his eyes fixed on the enemy encampment. He expected, at the sound of thundering hooves, to see the camp roused. He expected torches to flare, sentries to cry out the alarm, officers to shout, and men to race for their weapons.

Strangely, the camp remained quiet. No sentry shouted a warning and, now that Gerard looked, he couldn't see a picket line. No movement, no sound came from the camp, and it began to look as if the camp had been abandoned in the night. But why would an army of several hundred troops walk off and leave tents and supplies behind?

Had the girl realized she'd bitten off more than she could chew? Had she decided to slink off in the night, save her own skin and that of her men? Thinking back to her, to her supreme faith in the One God, Gerard doubted it.

The Solamnic Knights continued their charge, sweeping around both sides of the camp in a great widening circle. They continued to sing, but the song had lost its charm, could not dispel the uneasiness creeping into their hearts. The silence was uncanny, and they didn't like it. They smelled a trap.

Lord Tasgall, leading the charge, was presented with a problem. Did he proceed as planned? How was he to react to this new and unexpected situation? A veteran of many campaigns, Lord Tasgall was well aware that the best-laid strategy never survives contact with the enemy. In this instance, however, the problem appeared to be the absence of contact with the enemy. Tasgall figured the girl had simply come to her senses and departed. If so, he and his forces had lost nothing but a few hours sleep. Lord Tasgall could not count on this, however. Quite possibly it was a trap. Better to error on the side of caution. Changing strategies now would only throw everyone into confusion. The Lord Knight would carry out his plan, but he did raise his hand to slow the progression of the cavalry, so that they were not riding heedlessly into whatever might await them.

He might have spared himself the trouble. The Knights were not prepared for what awaited them. They could never have been prepared for it.

Another song lifted into the air, a song that was a minor to their major, a song that ran counterpoint to theirs. One person sang the song, and Gerard, who had heard her voice, recognized Mina.

MARIONETTE

In bygone times and warmer climes
    You Marionettes played.
Now restless, silent in a box,
    Your scattered limbs are splayed.
Come feel the tug of dancing strings.
    Your dust responds on shivering wings.
        The Master Puppeteer now sings!
Rise up from where you're laid.

The Master calls you from the dark.
    Your bones respond in haste.
Come act the part of living souls.
    Their glory once more taste.
Connect again with warmer days,
    And hearken to your former ways.
        Out of that darkness you will raise
Up from your place of waste!
Now dance, you spirits gone before
    The surging blood of old.
You sundered souls from times of yore
    Play at a life once bold!
The Master heaves on strings of woe.
    Torn from the dark your bones must go
        To act once more that all may know
The Master's tale is told!

Soldiers on the right flanks began to shout and point. Gerard turned to look to see what was happening.

A thick fog rolled out of the west. The strange fog advanced swiftly, roiling over the grass, obliterating all it touched, blotted out the stars, swallowed the moon. Those watching it could see nothing within the fog, nothing behind it. Reaching the city's western walls, the fog boiled over them. The towers on the west side of Solanthus vanished from sight as thoroughly as if they had never been built. Faint cries came from that part of the city, but they were muffled, and no one could make out what was going on.

Watching the advance of this strange and unnatural fog, Lord Tasgall halted the charge and, with a wave of his hand, summoned his officers to him. Lord Ulrich and Lord Nigel left the ranks and galloped forward. Gerard edged near enough to overhear what they were saying.

"There is sorcery at work here." Lord Tasgall's voice was grim. "We've been duped. Lured out of the city. I say we sound the retreat."

"My lord," protested Lord Ulrich, chuckling, "it is a heavy dew, nothing more."

"Heavy dew!" repeated Lord Tasgall, with a snort of disgust. "Herald, sound the retreat!"

The herald lifted his horn to his lips, gave the signal to retreat. The Knights reacted with discipline, did not give way to panic. Rounding their horses, they began to ride in column toward the city. The foot soldiers wheeled about, headed in orderly march back to the walls. The Knights advanced to cover the footmen's retreat. The archers were now visible on the walls, arrows nocked.

Yet Gerard could see—everyone could see—that no matter how fast they moved, the strange fog would engulf them before the closest soldier could reach the safety of the sheltering walls. The fog slid over the ground with the rapidity of a cavalry charging at full gallop. Gerard stared at the fog as it drew nearer. Stared at it, blinked, rubbed his eyes. He must be seeing things.

This was not fog. This was not a "heavy dew." These were Mina's reinforcements.

An army of souls.

An army of conscripts, for the souls of the dead were trapped in the world, unable to depart. As each soul left its body that had bound it to this world, it knew an instant's elation and exultation and freedom. That feeling was quashed almost immediately. An Immortal Being seized the spirit of the dead and gave it to know an immense hunger, a hunger for magic.

"Bring me the magic, and you will be free," was the promise. A promise not kept. The hunger could never be satiated. The hunger grew in proportion to what it fed on. Those souls struggling to free themselves found there was nowhere to go.

Nowhere to go until they received the summons.

A voice, a human voice, a mortal voice, Mina's voice called to them. "Fight for the One God, and you will be rewarded. Serve the One God, and you will be free."

Desperate, suffering unending torments, the souls obeyed. They formed no ranks for their numbers were too great. The soul of the goblin, its hideous visage recreated from the soul's memory of its mortal shell, barred teeth of mist, grappled for a sword of gossamer and answered the call. The soul of a Solamnic Knight that had long ago lost all notions of honor and loyalty answered the call. The souls of goblin and Knight walked side by side and knew not what they attacked or what they fought. Their only thought was to please the Voice and, by pleasing, escape.

A fog it seemed at first to the mortals who faced it, but Mina called upon the One God to open mortal eyes to see what previously had been kept from their sight. The living were constrained to look upon the dead.

The fog had eyes and mouths. Hands reached out from the fog. Voices whispered from the fog that was not fog at all but a myriad souls, each holding a memory of what it had been, a memory traced in the ethers with the magical phosphoresence of moonlight and foxfire. The face of each soul bore the horror of its existence, an existence that knew no rest, knew only endless seeking and the hopeless desolation of not ever finding.

The souls held weapons, but the weapons were mist and moonglow and could not kill or maim. The souls wielded a single weapon, a most horrible weapon. Despair.

At the sight of the army of trapped souls, the foot soldiers threw down their weapons, heedless to the furious shouts of their officers. The knights guarding their flanks looked at the dead and shuddered in horror. Their instinct was to do the same as the soldiers, to give way to the feelings of terror and panic. Discipline held them for the moment, discipline and pride, but when each turned to look at the other, uncertain what to do, each saw his own fear reflected back to him in the faces of his comrades.

The ghostly army entered the enemy camp. The souls flitted restlessly among the tents and the wagons. Gerard heard the panicked neighing of horses and now, at last, sounds of movement from the camp—calls of officers, the clash of steel. Then all sound was swallowed up by the souls, as if jealous of sounds their dead mouths could not make. The enemy camp vanished from sight. The army of souls flowed toward the city of Solanthus.

Thousands of mouths cried out in silent torment, their whispered shouts a chill wind that froze the blood of the living. Thousands and thousands of dead hands reached out to grasp what they could never hold. Thousands upon thousands of dead feet marched across the ground and bent not a single blade of grass.

Officers fell prey to the same terror as their men, gave up trying to keep their men in order. The foot soldiers broke ranks and ran, panic-stricken, for the walls, the faster shoving aside or knocking down the slower in order to reach safety.

The walls afforded no sanctuary. A moat is no deterrent to those who are already dead, they have no fear of drowning. Arrows cannot halt the advance of those who have no flesh to pierce. The ghostly legions slid beneath the wicked points of the portcullis and swarmed over the closed gates, flitted through the murder holes and glided through the arrow slits.

Behind the army of souls came an army of the living. Soldiers of Mina's command had kept hidden inside their tents, waiting for the army of souls to advance, to terrify the enemy and drive him into panicked chaos. Under cover of this dread army, Mina's soldiers emerged from their tents and raced to battle. Their orders were to attack the Solamnic Knights when they were out in the open, isolated, cut-off, a prey to horror.

Gerard tried to halt the soldiers' flight as they trampled each other, fought to escape the ghost army. He rode after the men, yelling for them to stand their ground, but they ignored him, kept running. Everything disappeared. The souls of the dead surrounded him. Their incorporeal forms shimmered with an incandescent whiteness that outlined hands and arms, feet and fingers, clothing and armor, weapons or other objects that had been familiar to them in life. They closed in on him, and his horse screamed in terror. Rearing back on its hind legs, the horse dumped Gerard on the ground and dashed off, vanishing into a swirling fog of grasping, ghostly hands.

Gerard scrambled to his feet. He drew his sword out of instinct, for what was he going to kill? He had never been so terrified. The touch of the souls was like cold mist. He could not count the number of dead that encircled him. One, a hundred, twelve hundred. The souls were intertwined, one with another. Impossible to tell where one ended and another began. They flitted in and out of his vision so that he grew dizzy and confused watching them.

They did not threaten or attack him, not even those who might have done so in life. An enormous hobgoblin reached out hairy hands, which were suddenly the hands of a beautiful young elven woman, who became a fisherman, who shriveled into a frightened, whimpering dwarf child. The faces of the dead filled Gerard with a nameless horror, for he saw in all of them the misery and hopelessness of the prisoner who lies forgotten in the dungeon that is the grave.

The sight was so awful that Gerard feared he might go mad. He tried to remember the direction to take to reach Solanthus, where he could at least feel the touch of a warm hand as opposed to the caress of the dead, but the fall from the horse had disoriented him. He listened for sounds that might give him some indication which way to go. As in a fog, all sound was distorted. He heard steel clash and cries of pain and guessed that somewhere men fought the living, not the dead. But whether the sounds of battle came from in front of him or behind, he could not tell.

Then he heard a voice speaking coldly and dispassionately. "Here's another one."

Two soldiers, living men, wearing the emblem of Neraka, rushed at him, the ghostly figures parting like white silken scarves cut through by a cleaver. The soldiers fell on Gerard, attacking without skill, slashing and beating at him with their swords, hoping to over-whelm him with brute force before he could recover from his panicked horror. What they had not counted on was the fact that Gerard was so relieved to see a flesh-and-blood foe, one that could be punched and kicked and bloodied, that he defended himself with spirit.

He disarmed one man, sent his sword flying, and drove his fist into the jaw of the other. The two did not stick around to continue the fight. Finding their foe stronger than they had hoped, they ran off, leaving Gerard to his dread jailers, the souls of the dead.

Gerard's hand clenched spasmodically around his sword's hilt. Fearing another ambush, he looked constantly over his shoulder, afraid to stay where he was, more afraid to move. The souls watched him, surrounded him.

A horn call split the air like a scythe. The call came from within the city, sounding the retreat. The call was frantic and short-lived, ending in midnote, but it gave Gerard a sense of where he must go. He had to overcome his instincts, for the last time he'd seen the city walls, they were behind him. The horn call came from in front. He walked forward, slowly, unwilling to touch the souls, though he need not have worried, for though some reached out their hands to him with what seemed pitiful supplication and others reached out their hands in what seemed murderous intent, they were powerless to affect him, other than by the horror and fear they inspired. Still, that was bad enough.

When the sight became too awful for him to bear, he involuntarily shut his eyes, hoping to find some relief, but that proved even more harrowing, for then he could feel the touch of the ghostly fingers and hear the whis-pers of ghostly voices.

By this time the foot soldiers had reached the enormous iron gate that pierced the curtain wall. The panic-stricken men beat on the gate, shouted for it to open. The gate remained closed and barred against them. Angry and terrified, they cried out for their comrades within the city to open the gate and let them enter. The soldiers began to shove on the gate and shake it, cursing those within.

White light flared. A blast shook the ground, as a section of the wall near the gate exploded. Huge chunks of broken stone rained down on the soldiers massed in front of the closed gate. Hundreds died, crushed to death beneath the rubble. Those who survived lay pinned in the wreckage, begging for help, but no help came. From inside the city, the gates remained locked and barred. The enemy began to pour through the breech.

Hearing the blast, Gerard peered ahead, trying to see what had happened. The souls swirled around him, flitted past him, and he saw only white faces and grasping hands. Desperate, he plunged into the wavering figures, slashing at them wildly with his sword. He might have tried to skewer quicksilver, for the dead slid away from him, only to gather around him ever more thickly.

Realizing what he was doing, Gerard halted, tried to regain control of himself. He was sweating and shivering. The thought of his momentary madness appalled him. Feeling as if he were being smothered, he removed his helm and drew in several deep breaths. Now that he was calm, he could hear voices—living voices—and the sound of ringing steel. He paused another moment to orient himself and replace his helm, leaving the visor raised in order to hear and see better. As he ran toward the sound, the dead snatched at him with their chill hands. He had the skin-crawling sensation he was running through enormous cobwebs.

He came upon six enemy soldiers, who were very much alive, fighting a knight on horseback. He could not see the knight's face beneath the helm, but he saw two long black braids whipping around the knight's shoulders. The soldiers surrounded Odila, tried to drag her from her horse. She struck at them with her sword, kicked at them, fended off their blows with her shield. All the while, she kept the horse under control.

Gerard attacked the enemy from behind, taking them by surprise. He ran his sword through one. Yanking his weapon free of the corpse, Gerard elbowed another in the ribs. Doubling him over, he smashed his nose with a thrust of a knee.

Odila brought her sword down on a man's skull with such force that it split his helm and cleaved through his skull, splattering Gerard with blood and brains and bits of bone. He wiped the blood from his eyes and turned to a soldier who had hold of the horse's bridle, was trying to haul the animal down to the ground. Gerard slashed at the man's hands as Odila bashed another with her shield and struck again with her sword. Another man ducked beneath the horse's belly, came up behind Gerard. Before Gerard could turn from one foe to defend himself against the new one, the soldier struck Gerard a savage blow to the side of the head.

Gerard's helm saved him from a killing stroke. The blade glanced off the metal and cut open Gerard's cheek. He felt no pain and knew he'd been hit only because he could taste the warm blood that flooded his mouth. The man caught hold of Gerard's sword hand in a clench of iron, began trying to break his fingers to force him to drop his weapon. Gerard struck the man in the face, breaking his nose. Still the man hung on, grappled with Gerard. Flinging the man backward, Gerard kicked him in the gut, sent the man sprawling. Gerard moved to finish him, but the man scrambled to his feet and ran. Gerard was too exhausted to pursue him.

Gerard stood gasping for breath. His head hurt now, hurt abominably. Holding a sword was painful, and he shifted the weapon to his left hand, although what he would do with it there was open to question, since he'd never attained the skill to fight with both hands. He could at least use it as a club, he supposed.

Odila's armor was dented and blood-covered. He could not tell if she was hurt, and he lacked the breath to ask. She sat on her horse, looking around her, sword poised, waiting for the next assault.

Gerard realized suddenly that he could see trees silhouetted against the stars. He could see other knights, some mounted, some standing on the ground, some kneeling, some fallen. He could see stars, he could see the walls of Solanthus, gleaming white in the bright moonlight, with one terrible exception. An enormous section of wall was missing, a section near the gate. A huge pile of blasted rock lay in front.

"What happened?" Odila gasped, snatching off her helm to see better. "Who did this? Why did the gates not open? Who barred them?" She stared at the walls that were silent and empty. "Where are our archers? Why have they left their posts?"

In an answer that seemed almost personal, so nearly did it coincide with Odila's question, a lone figure came to stand atop the city's outer walls above the gates that had had remained closed and barred against their own defenders.

The dead soldiers of Solanthus lay stacked in front of the city gate, an offering before an enormous altar. An offering to the girl Mina, whose black armor was sleek in the moonlight.

"Knights of Solamnia. Citizens of Solanthus." Mina addressed them, her voice ringing so that none on that bloody field had to strain to hear. "Through the might of the One God, the city of Solanthus has fallen. I hereby claim the city of Solanthus in the name of the One God."

Hoarse cries of shocked anger and disbelief rose from the battlefield. Lord Tasgall spurred his horse forward. His armor was dark with blood, his right arm hung limply, uselessly at his side.

"I do not believe you!" he shouted. "Perhaps you have won the outer walls, but you cannot fool me into thinking you have conquered the entire city!"

Archers appeared on the walls, archers wearing the emblems of Neraka. Arrows landed all around him; stuck, quivering, in the ground at his feet.

"Look to the heavens," said Mina.

Reluctantly, Lord Tasgall raised his head, his gaze searching the skies. He did not have to search long to see defeat.

Black wings slid over the stars, blotting them from view. Black wings sliced across the face of the moon. Dragons wheeled in the air, flying in low victorious circles over the city of Solanthus.

Dragonfear, awful and debilitating, shook Lord Tasgall and all the Solamnic Knights, caused more than one to quail and fling up his arm in terror or grip his weapon with hands that sweat and trembled.

No arrows from Solanthus fired at the dragons. No machines spewed forth flaming oil. One horn call alone had sounded the alarm at the start of battle, and that had been silenced in death.

Mina had spoken truly. The battle was over. While the Solamnic Knights had been held hostage by the dead and ambushed by the living, Mina and the remainder of her forces had flown on dragonback unimpeded into a city that had been emptied of most of its defenders.

"Knights of Solamnia," Mina continued, "you have witnessed the power of the One God, who rules the living and the dead. Go forth and carry word of the One God's return into the world with you. I have given the dragons orders not to attack you. You are free to leave. Go where you will." She waved her hand in a graceful, magnanimous gesture. "Even to Sanction. For that is where the gaze of the One God turns next. Tell the defenders of Sanction of the wonders you have seen this night. Tell them to fear the One God."

The Lord Knight sat unmoving in his saddle. He was in shock, stunned and overwhelmed by this unexpected turn of events. Other Knights rode or walked or limped to stand at his side. They gathered around him. Judging by their raised voices, some were demanding that they ride to the attack.

Gerard snorted in derision. Let them, he thought. Let this horde of dragons come down and snap off their fool heads. Idiots like that don't deserve to live and should certainly never father progeny. One had only to look up into the sky to see that there was nothing left for the Solamnic Knighthood in Solanthus.

Mina spoke one last time. "The night wanes. The dawn approaches. You have one hour to depart in safety. Any who remain within sight of the city walls by this day's dawning will be slain." Her voice grew gentle. "Have no fear for your dead. They will be honored, for they now serve the One God."

The bluster and the fury of the defeated Knights soon blew out. Those few foot soldiers who had escaped alive began to straggle off across the fields, many looking backward over their shoulders as if they could not believe what had happened and must constantly assure themselves by staring at the gruesome sight of their comrades crushed to death beneath the rubble of the once-mighty city.

The Knights managed to salvage what dignity they had left and returned to the field to pick up their fallen.

They would not leave their dead behind, no matter what Mina or the One God promised. Lord Tasgall remained seated on his horse. He had removed his helm to wipe away the sweat. His face was grim and fixed, his complexion as white as that of the ghosts.

Gerard could not look at him, could not bear to see such suffering. He turned away.

Odila had not joined the rest of the Knights. She had not appeared even to see what was transpiring. She sat her horse, staring at the wall where the girl Mina had been standing.

Gerard had planned to go assist the other Knights with the wounded and dead, but he didn't like the expression on Odila's face. He grasped hold of her boot, jogged her foot to gain her attention.

She looked down at him and didn't seem to recognize him.

"The One God," Odila said. "The girl speaks the truth. A god has returned to the world. What can mortals do against such power?"

Gerard looked up to where the dragons danced in the heavens, flying triumphant amidst ragged wispy clouds that were not clouds, but the souls of the dead, still lingering.

"We do what she told us to do," Gerard said flatly, glancing back at the walls of the fallen city. He saw the minotaur standing there, watching the Solamnic Knights' retreat. "We ride to Sanction. We warn them of what is coming."

31

The Red Rose

In the dark hours before the dawn, on the day the dragon Beryl had appointed for the destruction of Qualinost, Marshal Medan took his breakfast in his garden. He ate well, for he would need the reserves of energy food provided later in the day. He had known men unable to swallow a mouthful before a fight or those who ate and then disgorged the contents of their stomachs shortly after. He had disciplined himself long ago to eat a large meal before a campaign and even to enjoy it.

He was able to accomplish this by focusing on each single minute as it happened, looking neither ahead to what must come or behind to what might have been. He had made his peace with the past last night before he slept—another discipline. As to what brief future might remain to him, he put his trust in himself. He knew his limits; he knew his strengths. He knew and trusted his comrades.

He dipped the last of the season's strawberries in the last of his elven wine. He ate olive bread and soft white cheese. The bread was hard and a week old, for the bakery fires had not been lighted these many days, the bakers either having left Qualinost or gone into hiding, working toward this day. Still, he relished the taste. He had always enjoyed olive bread. The cheese, spread on the bread, was excellent. A simple pleasure, one he would miss in death.

Medan did not believe in life beyond the grave. No rational mind could, as far as he was concerned. Death was oblivion. Each night's short sleep prepares us for the final night's long one. Yet he thought that even in oblivion, he would miss his garden and the soft cheese on the fragrant bread, he would miss moonlight shining on golden hair. He finished the cheese, scattered bread crumbs to the fish. He sat for another hour alone in the garden, listening to the sparrow sing her mournful song. His eyes misted for a moment, but that was for the birdsong that would for him be silenced, and for the beauty of the late-blooming flowers that he also would miss. When his eyes misted, he knew it was time to depart.

The Dark Knight Dumat was on hand to assist Medan into his armor. The Marshal would not wear full plate this day. Beryl would notice and find it suspicious. The elves had been killed, driven out, vanquished. The elven capital city was being delivered to her without a fight. Her Marshal was here to greet her in triumph. What use did he have for armor? Besides that, Medan needed to be free to move swiftly, and he was not going to be encumbered by heavy plate or chain mail. He wore his ceremonial armor—the highly polished breastplate with the lily and the skull, and his helm—but he dispensed with all the rest.

Dumat helped fasten the long, flowing cloak around Medan's shoulders. The cloak was made of wool that had been dipped in black dye and then in purple. Trimmed in gold braid, the cloak reached to the floor and weighed nearly as much as a chain-mail shirt. Medan despised it, never wore it except on those days when he had to make a show for the Senate. Today, though, the cloak would come in handy, for it covered a multitude of sins. Once he was attired, he experimented with the cloak to make certain it would perform as required.

Dumat assisted him to arrange the folds so that cloak fell over his left shoulder, concealing beneath those folds the sword he wore on his left hip. The sword he wore now was not the magical sword, not the Lost Star. For now, his customary sword would serve his purpose. He had to remember to make certain he held fast the cloak's edge with his left hand, so that the wind created by the dragon's fanning wings would not cause it to billow out. He practiced several times, while Dumat watched with a critical eye.

"Will it work, do you think?" the Marshal asked.

"Yes, my lord," Dumat replied. "If Beryl does catch a glimpse of steel, she will think it is only your sword, such as you always wear."

"Excellent." Medan let fall the cloak. He unbuckled his sword from its belt, started to set it aside. Then, thinking better of it, he handed the weapon to Dumat. "May it serve you well as it has served me."

Dumat rarely smiled, and he did not smile then. He removed his own sword—that was regulation issue—and buckled on the Marshal's, with its fine, tempered steel blade. He made no show of gratitude, other than a muttered thanks, but Medan saw that his gift had pleased and touched the soldier.

"You had better leave now," Medan said. "You have a long ride back to Qualinost and much to do this morning before the appointed time."

Dumat started to salute, but the Marshal extended his hand. Dumat hesitated, then grasped Medan's hand, shook it heartily in silence. Dumat took his leave. Mounting his horse, he headed at a gallop back to Qualinost.

Medan went over the plan again in his mind, checking and rechecking to see if he had missed anything. He was satisfied. No plan was perfect, of course, and events rarely went as one hoped, but he was confident he and Laurana had anticipated most contingencies. He shut his house and locked it up. He wondered, idly, if he would be returning to unlock it or if they would carry his body back here to bury him in his garden as he had requested. In the afterdays when the elves came back to their homeland, would anyone live in this house? Would anyone remember?

"The house of the hated Marshal Medan," he said to himself with half a smile. "Perhaps they'll burn it to the ground. Humans would."

But elves were not like humans. Elves did not take satisfaction in such petty revenge, knowing that it would serve no purpose. Besides, they would not want to harm the garden. He could count on that.

He had one more task to perform before he left. He searched the garden until he found two perfect roses— one red, one white. He plucked them both and stripped the white one of its thorns. He placed the red rose, thorns and all, beneath his armor, against his breast.

The white rose in hand, he left his garden without a backward look. What need? He carried the sight and the fragrance in his mind, and he hoped, if death took him, that his last thought would wend its way back here, live forever in beauty and peace and solitude.

In her house, Laurana was doing much the same thing as the Marshal, with a few exceptions. She had managed to swallow only a few mouthfuls of food before putting aside the plate. She drank a glass of wine to give her heart, then retired to her room.

She had no one to assist her to dress and arm herself, for she had sent her maidservants away to safety in the south. They had gone reluctantly, separating from their mistress with tears. Now, only Kelevandros remained with her. She had urged him to leave, as well, but he had refused, and she had not pressed him. He wanted to stay, he said, to redeem his family's honor that had been besmirched by the treachery of his brother.

Laurana understood, but she was almost sorry he had done so. He was the perfect servant, anticipating her wants and needs, unobtrusive, a hard and diligent worker. But he no longer laughed or sang as he went about his tasks. He was quiet, distant, his thoughts turned inward, rebuffing any offers of sympathy.

Laurana wrapped around her waist the leather skirt that had been designed for her years ago when she was the Golden General. She had just enough feminine vanity to note that the skirt was a little tighter on her than it had been in her youth and just enough sense of the absurd to smile at herself for minding. The leather skirt was slit up the side for ease of movement and served well as protective armor whether standing or riding. When this was done, she started to summon Kelevandros, but he had been waiting outside and entered the room as his name formed on her lips.

Without speaking, he fastened on her the breastplate, blue with golden trim, she had worn those long years ago, then she draped a cloak around her shoulders. The cloak was oversized. She had made it specially for this occasion, working on it day and night so it would be ready in time. The cloak was white, of finely carded wool, and was fastened in the front by seven golden clasps. Slits had been placed in the side for her arms. She studied herself critically in the looking glass, moving, walking, standing still, making certain that no hint of leather or glint of metal gave her away. She had to look the part of the victim, not the predator.

Because the cloak restricted the movement of her arms, Kelevandros brushed and arranged her long hair around her shoulders. Marshal Medan had wanted her to wear her helm, arguing that she would need its protection. Laurana had refused. The helm would look out of place. The dragon would be suspicious.

"After all," she had said to him, half-teasing, wholly serious, "if she attacks, I don't suppose a helmet will make much difference."

Silver chimes rang outside the house.

"Marshal Medan is here," Laurana said. "It is time."

Lifting her gaze, she saw that Kelevandros's face had gone pale. His jaw tightened, his lips pressed tight. He looked at her, pleading.

"I must do this, Kelevandros," Laurana said, laying her hand gently on his arm. "The chance is a slim one, but it is our only hope."

He lowered his gaze, bowed his head.

"You should leave now," Laurana continued. "It is time you took your place in the tower."

"Yes, Madam," Kelevandros said in the same empty, toneless voice he had used since the day of his brother's death.

"Remember your instructions. When I say the words, *Ara Qualinesti* you will light the signal arrow and shoot it into the air. Fire it out over Qualinost, so that those watching for it can see it."

"Yes, Madam." Kelevandros bowed silently and

turned to leave. "If you do not mind, I will depart through the garden."

"Kelevandros," Laurana said, halting him. "I am sorry. Truly sorry."

"Why should you be sorry, Madam?" he asked, not turning, keeping his back to her. "My brother tried to murder you. What he did was not your fault."

"I think perhaps it was," Laurana said, faltering. "If I had known how unhappy he was . . . If I had taken time to find out . . . If I had not assumed that . . . that . . ."

"That we were happy to have been born into servitude?" Kelevandros finished her sentence for her. "No, it never occurs to anyone, does it?" He looked at her with a strange smile. "It will from now on. The old ways end here. Whatever happens this day, the lives of the elves will never be the same. We can never go back to what we were. Perhaps we will all know, before the end, what it means to be born a slave. Even you, Madam. Even your son."

Bowing, Kelevandros picked up his bow and a quiver of arrows and started to take his leave. He was almost out the door when he turned to face her, yet he did not look at her.

"Oddly enough, Madam," he said, his voice rough, his eyes downcast. "I was happy here."

With another bow, he left.

"Was that Kelevandros I saw skulking through the garden?" Medan asked when Laurana opened the door to him. He looked at her intently.

"Yes," she said, glancing in that direction, though she could not see him for the thick foliage. "He has gone to take his place in the tower."

"You look troubled. Has he said or done something to upset you?"

"If he did, I must make allowances. He has not been himself since his brother's death. His grief overwhelms him."

"His grief is wasted," said the Marshal. "That wretched brother of his was not worth a snivel, let alone a tear."

"Perhaps," Laurana said, unconvinced. "And yet . . ." She paused, perplexed, and shook her head.

Medan regarded her earnestly. "You have only to say the word, Madam, and I will see to it that you escape safely from Qualinost this instant. You will be reunited with your son—"

"No, I thank you, Marshal," Laurana answered calmly, looking up at him. "Kelevandros must wrestle with his own demons, as I have wrestled with mine. I am resolved in this. I will do my part. You need me, I think, sir," she added with a hint of mischief, "unless you plan to dress up in one of my gowns and wear a blonde wig."

"I have no doubt that even Beryl, dense as she is, would see through that disguise," said Medan dryly. He was pleased to see Laurana smile. Another memory for him to keep. He handed her the white rose. "I brought this for you, Madam. From my garden. The roses will be lovely in Qualinost this fall."

"Yes," said Laurana, accepting the rose. Her hand trembled slightly. "They will be lovely."

"You will see them. If I die this day, you will tend my garden for me. Do you promise?"

"It is bad luck to speak of death before the battle, Marshal," Laurana warned, partly in jest, wholly in earnest. "Our plan will work. The dragon will be defeated and her army demoralized."

"I am a soldier. Death is in my contract. But you—"

"Marshal," Laurana interrupted with a smile, "every contract ever written ends in death."

"Not yours," he said softly. "Not so long as I am alive to prevent it."

They stood a moment in silence. He watched her, watched the moonlight gently touch her hair as he longed to touch it. She kept her gaze fixed upon the rose.

"The parting with your son Gilthas was difficult?" he asked at last.

She replied with a soft sigh. "Not in the way you imagine. Gilthas did not try to dissuade me from my chosen path. Nor did he try to free himself from walking his. We did not spend our last hours in fruitless argument, as I had feared. We remembered the past and talked of what he will do in the future. He has many hopes and dreams. They will serve to ease his journey over the dark, perilous road he must travel to reach that future. Even if we win this day, as Kelevandros said, the lives of the elves will never be the same. We can never go back to what we were." She was pensive, introspective.

In his heart Medan applauded Gilthas. The Marshal guessed how difficult it must have been for the young man to leave his mother to face the dragon while he departed safely out of harm's way. Gilthas had been wise enough to realize that attempting to dissuade her from her chosen course would have accomplished nothing and left him with only bitter recriminations. Gilthas would need all the wisdom he possessed to face what lay ahead of him. Medan knew the peril better than Laurana, for he had received reports of what was happening in Silvanesti. He said nothing to her, not wanting to worry her. Time enough to face that crisis when they had disposed of this one.

"If you are ready, Madam, we should leave now," he told her. "We'll steal through the city while night's shadows yet linger and enter the tower with the dawn."

"I am ready," Laurana said. She did not look behind her. As they walked down the path that led through the late-blooming lilacs, she said to him, "I want to thank you, Marshal, on behalf of the elven people, for what you do for us this day. Your courage will be long remembered and long honored among us."

Medan was embarrassed. "Perhaps it is not so much what I do this day, Madam," he said quietly, "as what I try to undo. Rest assured I will not fail you or your people."

"*Our* people, Marshal Medan," said Laurana. "Our people."

Her words were meant kindly, but they pierced his heart. He deserved the punishment, and he bore it in silence, unflinching, as a soldier. Thus he bore unflinching the sting of the rose's thorns against his breast.

Muffled sounds could be heard coming from the houses of the elves as Medan and Laurana passed swiftly through the streets on their way to the tower. Although no elf showed his face, the time for skulking in silence was gone. There were sounds of heavy objects being hauled up stairs, the rustlings of tree branches as the archers took their places. They heard orders given in calm voices both in Common and Elvish. Near the tower, they actually caught a glimpse of Dumat adding the finishing touches to a web of tree branches he had constructed over the roof of his house. Chosen to watch for Kelevandros's signal, Dumat would give the signal to the elves for the attack. He saluted the Marshal and bowed to the Queen Mother, then continued on about his work.

The morning sun rose, and by the time they reached the tower, the sun shone bright. Shading his eyes, Medan blessed the day for its clear visibility, although he caught himself thinking that his garden would have welcomed rain. He put the thought aside with a smile and concentrated on the task ahead.

The bright light streamed in through the myriad windows, sent rainbows dancing in dazzling array around the tower's interior, and lit the mosaic on the ceiling: the day and the night, separated by hope.

Laurana had locked away the sword and the dragonlance in one of the tower's many rooms. While she retrieved them, Medan looked out one of the windows, watching the preparations as Qualinost made ready for war. Like its Queen Mother, the city was transforming itself from lovely and demure maid into doughty warrior.

Laurana handed Medan the sword, Lost Star. He gravely saluted her with the sword, then buckled it around his waist. She helped him arrange the folds of the cloak to conceal it. Stepping back, she eyed him critically and pronounced his disguise successful. No gleam of metal could be seen.

"We climb this staircase." Laurana indicated a circular stair. "It leads to the balcony at the top of the tower. The climb is a long one, I fear, but there will be time to rest—"

Sudden night, strange and awful as that of an eclipse, quenched the sunlight. Medan hastened to look out the window, well knowing, yet dreading what he would see.

The sky was dark with dragons.

"Very little time, I fear," Medan said calmly, taking the dragonlance from her hand and shaking his head when she started to try to retrieve it. "The great green bitch has launched her attack early. No surprise there. We must make haste."

Opening the door, they began to climb the stairs that wound around and around a hollow shaft, a vortex of stone. A railing made of gold and of silver, twined together, spiraled upward. Formed in an imitation of a vine of ivy, the railing did not appear to have been built into the stone but seemed to have grown around it.

"Our people are ready," Laurana said. "When Kelevandros gives the signal, they will strike."

"I hope we can count on him to carry out his part," the Marshal said. "He has, as you say, been acting strange of late."

"I trust him," Laurana replied. "Look." She pointed at narrow booted footprints in the thick dust on the stairs. "He is here already, waiting for us."

They climbed as rapidly as possible, yet they dared not move too swiftly, lest they lose their strength before they had reached the top. "I am thankful . . . I did not wear full plate armor," the Marshal stated with what breath he had left. As it was, he had only reached what Laurana told him was the halfway mark and he was gasping for breath, his legs burned.

"I used to race . . . my brothers and Tanis up these stairs . . . when I was a girl," Laurana said, pressing her hand over her side to ease a jabbing pain. "We had better rest . . . a moment, or we're not going to make it."

She sank down on the staircase, wincing at the pain. Medan remained standing, staring out the window. He drew in deep breaths, flexed his legs to ease the cramped muscles.

"What can you see?" Laurana asked tensely. "What is happening?"

"Nothing yet," he reported. "Those are Beryl's minions in the skies. Probably scouting the city, making certain it is deserted. Beryl is a coward at heart. Without her magic, she feels naked, vulnerable. She won't come near Qualinost until she is assured nothing will harm her."

"When will her soldiers enter the city?"

Medan turned from the window to look down at her. "Afterward. The commanders won't send in the men until the dragons are gone. The dragonfear unsettles the troops, makes them difficult to manage. When the dragons are finished leveling the place, the soldiers will arrive. To 'mop up.' "

Laurana laughed shakily. "I hope they will not find much to 'mop.' "

"If all goes as planned," said Medan, returning her smile, "the floor will be wiped clean."

"Ready?" she asked.

"Ready," he replied and gallantly extended his hand to help her to her feet.

The stairs brought them to the top of the tower, to an entrance to a small alcove with an arched ceiling. Those passing through the alcove walked out onto a balcony that overlooked all of the city of Qualinost. The Speaker of the Suns and the clerics of Paladine had been accustomed to come to the top of the tower on holidays and feast days, to thank Paladine—or Eli, as the elves knew him—for his many blessings, the most glorious of which was the sun that gave life and light to all. That custom had ended after the Chaos War, and now no one came up here. What was the use?

Paladine was gone. The sun was a strange sun, and though it gave light and life, it seemed to do so grudgingly, not gloriously. The elves might have kept up the old tradition simply because it was tradition. Their Speaker, Solostaran, had kept up the custom during the years after the Cataclysm, when Paladine had not heeded their prayers. The young king, Gilthas, had not been able to make the arduous climb, however. He had pleaded ill health, and so the elves had abandoned tradition. The real reason Gilthas did not want to climb to the top of the Tower of the Sun was that he did not want to look out over a city that was captive, a city in chains.

"When Qualinost is no longer held in thrall," Gilthas had promised his mother during their last night together, "I will come back, and no matter if I am so old that my bones creak and I have lost every tooth in my head, I will run up those stairs like a child at play, for at the top I will look out over a country and a people who are free."

Laurana thought of him as she set her foot gratefully upon the last stair. She could see her son, young and strong—for he would be young and strong, not old and decrepit—bounding up the stairs joylessly to look out upon a land bathed in blessed sunlight.

She looked out the open archway leading to the balcony and saw only darkness. The wings of Beryl's subject dragons cut off the sunlight. The first tremors of dragonfear caused her throat to constrict, her palms to sweat, her hand involuntarily to tighten its grip around the slender railing. She had felt such fear before, and as had told Marshal Medan, she knew how to combat it. She walked across the landing, faced her enemy squarely, stared at the dragons long and hard until she had mentally conquered them. The fear did not leave her. It would always be there, but she was the master. The fear was under her control.

This settled, she looked around to find Kelevandros. She had expected to find him waiting for them on the landing, and she felt a twinge of worry that she did not see him. She had forgotten the effects of dragonfear, however. Perhaps he had been overcome by it and run away.

No, that could not have happened. There was only one way down. He would have passed them on the stairs.

Perhaps he had gone out on the balcony.

She was about to go in search of him when she heard the Marshal's footsteps behind her, heard him heave a great sigh of relief at finally reaching the top of the stairs. She turned to face him, to tell him that she could not find Kelevandros, when she saw Kelevandros emerging from the shadows of the arched entryway.

I must have walked right past him, she realized. Caught by the dragonfear, she had never noticed him.

He stood crouched in the shadows, paralyzed, seeming unable to move.

"Kelevandros," Laurana said to the young elf in concern, "what you are feeling is the dragonfear—"

Marshal Medan rested the dragonlance against the wall. "And to think," he said, sucking in air, "we still have to make the climb down."

Kelevandros gave a convulsive leap. Steel flashed in his hand.

Laurana shouted a warning and lunged to stop him, but she was too late.

Kelevandros stabbed through the cloak the Marshal wore, aiming to strike beneath his upraised arm that had been holding the dragonlance, strike a part of the body the armor could not protect. The elf buried his knife to the hilt in Medan's ribcage, then jerked the knife free. His hand and the blade were stained with blood.

Medan gave a pain-filled cry. His body stiffened. He pressed his hand to his side and stumbled forward, fell to the floor on one knee.

"Ah!" He gasped for breath and found none. The blade had punctured his lung. "Ah!"

"Kelevandros . . ." Laurana whispered, overcome by shock. "What have you done?"

He had been staring at the Marshal, but now he turned his gaze to her. His eyes were wild and fevered, his face livid. He held up his hand to ward her off, raised the knife.

"Don't come near me, Madam!" he cried.

"Kelevandros," Laurana asked helplessly, "why? He was going to help us—"

"He killed my brother," Kelevandros gasped, his pallid lips quivering. "Killed him years ago with his filthy money and his foul promises. He used him, and all the while he despised him. Not dead yet, are you, you bastard?"

Kelevandros lunged to stab the Marshal again.

Swiftly, Laurana interposed her body between the elf and the human. For a moment she thought Kelevandros, in his rage, was going to stab her.

Laurana faced him, unafraid. Her death didn't matter. She would die now or later. Their plan lay in ruins.

"What have you done, Kelevandros?" she repeated sadly. "You have doomed us."

He glared at her. Froth bubbled on his lips. He raised the knife, but not to stab. With a wrenching sob, he threw the knife at the wall. She heard it hit with a clang.

"We were already doomed, Madam," he said, choking.

He fled the chamber, running blindly. Either he could not see where he was going or he did not care, for he crashed headlong into the railing of silver- and gold-twined ivy. The ancient railing shuddered, then gave way under the young elf's weight. Kelevandros plunged over the edge of the staircase. He made no attempt to catch himself. He fell to the floor below without a cry.

Laurana pressed her hands over her mouth and closed her eyes, aghast at the horror of the young elf's death. She stood shivering, trying desperately to banish the sickening feeling of numbness that paralyzed her.

"I won't give up," she said to herself. "I won't . . . Too much depends . . ."

"Madam . . ." Medan's voice was weak.

He lay on the floor, his hand still pressed against his side, as if he could halt the flow of blood that was draining away his life. His face was ashen, his lips gray.

Tears dimming her eyes, Laurana sank down on her knees beside him and began frantically to thrust aside the folds of the bloody cloak to find the wound, to see if there was anything she could do to stop the bleeding.

Medan caught her hand, held it fast, and shook his head.

"You weep for me," he said softly, astonished.

Laurana could not reply. Her tears fell on his face.

He smiled and made a move as if he would kiss her hand, but he lacked the strength. His grip on her hand tightened. He struggled to speak through the tremors of pain that shook his body.

"You must go now," he told her, using his remaining strength to force out each word. "Take the sword . . . and the lance. You are in command, Laurana."

Laurana shivered. *You are in command, Laurana.* The words had a familiar sound, harkened back to another time of darkness and death. She could not think why that should be so or where she had heard them before. She shook her head.

"No," she said brokenly. "I can't. . . ."

"The Golden General," Medan whispered. "I would have liked to have seen her. . . ."

He gave a sigh. The bloodstained hand loosed its grip, dropped limply to the floor. His eyes continued to look fixedly at her, and although no life was in them, she saw his faith in her, steadfast, unwavering.

He meant what he had said. She was in command. Except it was not his voice speaking those words. Another voice . . . far away.

You can command, Laurana. Farewell, elfmaid. Your light will shine in this world . . . It is time for mine to darken.

"No, Sturm, I can't do this," she cried wretchedly. "I am alone!"

As Sturm had been alone, standing by himself at the top of another tower in the bright sunshine of a new day. He had faced certain death, and he had not faltered.

Laurana wept for him. She wept for Medan and for Kelevandros. She wept for the hatred that had destroyed them both and would keep on destroying until someone somewhere had the courage to love. She wept for herself, for her weakness. When she had no more tears left, she lifted her head. She was calm now, in command of herself.

"Sturm Brightblade." Laurana clasped her hands together, praying to him, since there was no one else to hear her prayer. "True friend. I need your strength. I need your courage. Be with me, that I may save my people."

Laurana wiped away her tears. With hands that were firm and did not tremble, she closed the Marshal's eyes and kissed his cold forehead.

"You had the courage to love," she said to him softly. "That will be your salvation and my own."

Sunlight lit the alcove, gleamed on the dragonlance that stood against the wall, glistened in the splatters of blood on the floor. Laurana glanced out through the arched entrance to the blue sky, the empty blue sky. The minion dragons had departed. She did not rejoice. Their departure meant that Beryl was coming.

She thought despairingly of the plan she and the Marshal had made, then resolutely thrust aside both the thought and the despair. Kelevandros's bow and the pitch-covered signal arrow, his flint and tinderbox lay abandoned in the alcove where he had dropped them. She had no one to fire the signal arrow. She could not do it herself, not do that and face the dragon. She had no way now to send word to Dumat, who would be watching for the flare to give his order.

"No matter," she said to herself. "He will know when it is time. They will all know."

She unbuckled the sword belt from around the Marshal's waist. Trying to move hurriedly with fingers that were stiff and shaking, she fastened the belt with the heavy sword around her own waist and arranged the folds of her cloak over the sword. Her white cloak was stained red with the Marshal's blood. Nothing she could do about that. She would have to find some way to explain it to the dragon, explain not only the blood but why she was here atop the tower, a hostage without a captor. Beryl would be suspicious. She would be a fool not to be, and the dragon was no fool.

This is hopeless. There is no chance, Laurana told herself. She heard Beryl approaching, heard the creaking of enormous wings that obliterated the sun. Darkness descended. The air was tainted with the smell of the dragon's poisonous breath.

The dragonfear overwhelmed Laurana. She began to tremble, her hands were numb with cold. The Marshal was wrong. She couldn't do this. . . .

A ray of sunlight escaped from beneath the dragon's wings and shone bright on the dragonlance. The lance blazed with silver flame.

Moved by the beauty, Laurana remembered those who had wielded the lances so long ago. She remembered standing over Sturm's body, the lance in hand, defiantly facing his killer. She had been afraid then, too.

Laurana reached out her hand to touch the lance. She did not intend to take it with her. The lance was eight feet long. She could not hide it from the dragon. She wanted only to touch it, for memory's sake and in memory of Sturm.

Perhaps at this moment Sturm was with her. Perhaps the courage of those who wielded the lance was a part of the lance and now flowed through the metal and into her. Perhaps her own courage, the courage of the Golden General, the courage that had always been there, flowed from her into the dragonlance. All she knew was that when she touched the lance, her plan came to her. She knew what she would do.

Resolute, Laurana took hold of the dragonlance and carried it with her into the sunlight.

32

Lost Star

Once, she had thought dragons beautiful.

The enemy dragons of Queen Takhisis. Beautiful they were, and deadly. The red dragons, whose scales flashed fire in the sunlight and whose breath was flame. The blue dragons with their swift and graceful flight, wheeling among the clouds, drifting with the thermals. White dragons, cold and glittering, and black dragons, shining, sinuous, and green dragons, emerald death. She feared them and hated them and loathed them, yet she never killed one but that she did not feel a flashing pang of remorse to see such a magnificent creature fall mortally wounded from the skies.

This dragon was not beautiful. Beryl was ugly, fat, and bloated—hideous. Her wings could barely support her hulking body. Her head was misshapen, the forehead jutting out over the eyes that were flat and opaque. Her lower jaw was underslung, the teeth snaggled and rotting. Her scales were not the shining green of emeralds but the green of putrid flesh, of maggot-ridden meat. Her eyes did not gleam with intelligence but flickered with the feeble flame of greed and low cunning. It was then Laurana knew with certainty that this dragon was not of Krynn. Beryl was not a dragon who had been touched by the minds of the gods. She worshiped nothing except her own brutish desire, reverenced nothing but herself.

The shadow of Beryl's wings slid over Qualinost, covering the city in darkness. Laurana stood proudly on the balcony, looked out over the city, and saw that the darkness could not wither the aspen trees or cause the roses to wilt. That might come later, but for now the elven people and the elven homeland stood defiant.

"We will rid the world of one monster, at least," Laurana said softly, as the first blast of wind from the dragon's wings tore at her hair. "You were wrong, Kelevandros. This hour is not our doom. This hour is our glory."

Beryl flew ponderously toward her, jaws gaping in a slavering grin of triumph. The dragonfear rolled off the dragon in waves but no longer affected Laurana. She had known the fear of a god. This mortal monster held no terror for her, no matter how hideous its visage.

The balcony of the Tower of the Sun was rimmed by a wall of burnished gold that came to her waist. The wall was thick and solid, for it had been shaped by ancient elven wizards from the bones of the tower itself. Flowing out from the tower, the balcony wrapped protectively around the people standing behind it. The balcony was large enough to hold a delegation of elves. A single elf standing alone in the center looked very small—almost lost. There should have been two people on the balcony. That had been the plan. Beryl would expect two: Marshal Medan and his prisoner, the Queen Mother.

Nothing Laurana could say or do, no lie she could tell, would alleviate Beryl's suspicions. Talk would only give the dragon time to think and to react.

Beryl's red gleaming eyes swept over the balcony. She was close enough now that she could see, and what she saw was apparently not sitting well with her, for the eyes swept back and forth several times. The lumpish forehead wrinkled, the wicked red eyes narrowed. The fanged mouth widened in a knowing sneer, as if she had foreseen something like this would happen.

That didn't matter now. Nothing mattered now except that this day the elves of Qualinesti and those who were their friends and allies would expend their last breaths to destroy this loathsome beast.

Laurana reached to the clasp of the white cloak and unfastened it. The cloak came off in her hands and fell to the balcony floor. Laurana's armor, the armor of the Golden General, shone in the sunlight. The wind of the dragon's wings blew back her hair that streamed out behind her, a gilded banner.

Beryl was perilously close to the tower now. A few more ungainly flaps of her wings would bring her hulking head so close to Laurana that she might have reached out to touch it. Laurana gagged on the fumes of the dragon's deadly, noxious gaseous breath. She choked, feared she must lose consciousness. The wind—a chill wind with a tinge of thunder in it—shifted directions to blow from the north, blow away the fumes.

Laurana grasped the hilt of the sword, Lost Star, clasped her hand around it. She drew the sword. The blade flashed in the sunlight, the jewel sparkled.

Beryl saw the sword in the hands of the lone elf woman and found the sight diverting. The dragon's jaws creaked apart in what might have been a horrible laugh, but then she sensed the magic. The red eyes flared, and a drool of saliva dribbled from between the fangs. The cruel eyes shifted to the dragonlance, a flame of argent in the sunlight. Beryl's eyes widened. She sucked in a breath of awe and desire.

The fabled dragonlance—bane of dragons. Forged by Theros Ironfeld of the Silver Arm, using the blessed Hammar of Kharas, the lances had the power to pierce a dragon's scales, penetrate through sinew, tissue, flesh, and bone. Dragons native to this wretched world spoke of the lance with fear and awe. Beryl had laughed in disdain. But she had been curious, eager to see one and, because the lances were magic, eager to possess one.

A magic sword, a magic lance, an elf queen, an elf city—rich reward for this day's work.

Clasping the sword beneath the hilt, Laurana walked to the very edge of the balcony and held the Lost Star high. She raised her voice and sang out in a rousing paean of defiance and pride.

Soliasi Arath!

Far below the balcony of the Tower of the Sun, Dumat crouched in the shadows of the rooftop of an elven house. Concealed by the camouflaging branches of the aspen trees, twenty elves watched him, awaiting the signal. At Dumat's side was his elven wife, Ailea, ready to translate should he need to give orders. Dumat spoke some Elvish, but when he did, Ailea always laughed at his accent. She had told him once it was like hearing a horse speak Elvish. He smiled at her, and she smiled at him, both confident, both ready. They had said their good-byes last night.

From his vantage point, Dumat could see the balcony of the tower. He could not gaze at the sunlit building too long, The light gleaming off the sides, made his eyes water. He looked, then, blinking, looked away, then looked again, waiting for Marshal Medan and Laurana to appear. The advent of the flight of minion dragons overhead had shaken Dumat, caused him momentarily to lose sight of the tower as the dragonfear cast a dimness over his eyesight and sent tremors through his body.

The elves on the roof were affected as well, but they, like Dumat, clenched their teeth on the fear. No one cried out, no one panicked. When Dumat was able to see again, he could see the tower clearly now. The shadow of the dragons' wings blotted out the sunlight.

The balcony was empty. No sign of Laurana or the Marshal.

Dumat began to worry. He did not know why, could not explain it. The instinct of a veteran soldier, perhaps. Something had gone wrong. Dumat considered for a brief moment making a dash for the tower, to see if there was anything he could do, but rejected the idea almost immediately. His orders were to remain here and wait for the signal. He would obey those orders.

The minion dragons departed and, like Laurana, Dumat realized that this was not a good sign. Beryl would be on her way. He tensed, staring at the tower that once again gleamed blindingly in the sunlight. He dared not look away for fear he might miss the signal, and he was forced to blink almost constantly to clear the tears from his eyes. When he saw Laurana, he let out a grateful whistle and watched for the Marshal.

Medan did not come.

Dumat gave the Marshal a count of ten, then a count of ten again, then gave up. He had known the truth before he started counting. Laurana would have never appeared on that balcony alone if Medan had been alive and able to stand beside her. Dumat said farewell to the Marshal, a soldier's farewell, brief and silent, but heartfelt. He crouched and waited, watching for the signal flare.

Those were the orders. Dumat and the rest of the elves and the few Dark Knights and dwarves who made up

Qualinost's defense force were to watch for the flaming arrow and then launch the attack. Greatly daring, he lifted his head above the branches in order to gain a better view. Ailea pinched his leg to force him to duck back down, but he ignored her. He had to see.

Beryl came in sight, flying toward the tower. Dragon-fear washed off her in great, billowing waves, but the fact that she had sent her followers first worked to her disadvantage. Those who were going to succumb to dragon-fear had already done so and were recovering. Those who had not were not going to start now. Beryl's cunning eyes roved here and darted there, not trusting to Medan's reports the city was abandoned.

Search all you want, you great bitch, Dumat told her silently. You are here, you are right above us. There's no escape now.

Dumat ducked back down moments before the dragon's eyes might have seen him. Ailea gave him a look he knew well. It meant he was in for a scolding. He hoped against hope he'd live to receive it, but he wasn't counting on it. He stared back at the tower.

His eyesight was good, and he could see Laurana approach the edge of the balcony. He could not see her face, not from this distance—she was a small smear of white against the gold—but he could guess from the fact that she went to meet the dragon that she was not afraid.

"Good for you, Mum," he said quietly. "Good for you."

Beryl was close to the tower now. Dumat could see her underbelly and the underside of the wings, the hulking legs dangling beneath and the twitching tail. Her scaly hide was an evil green, mud-covered from her wallows.

When devising his plan, King Gilthas had first thought of trying to pierce her hide with arrows, but he had discarded the idea. Beryl's hide was thick, the scales strong. Arrows might bring her down but only if fired in massive numbers, and the elves did not have those numbers. Besides, she would expect such an attack and be prepared for it. They hoped she would not expect what she was about to get.

Dumat waited now only for the signal arrow that was to have been fired by the elf Kelevandros . . . Kelevandros . . . Dumat knew what had happened, knew it as well as if he had seen it himself. Kelevandros had avenged his brother. Medan was wounded . . . dead. Laurana was alone up there now. She had no one to fire the signal.

He saw her lift her arms.

The sun in this new sky might have seemed pale and strange to the people of Krynn, but perhaps they had managed to win its favor. As Dumat watched, the sun sent a ray of light, straight as an arrow to strike Laurana. In that moment, he thought she held a star.

White flame flared, a flame so brilliant and dazzling that Dumat had to squint his eyes against it and avert his gaze, as he might have done looking into the sun itself. This was the signal, he knew it more in his heart than his head.

With a wild shout, he reared up from among the tree branches and flung them aside. Around him, elves jumped to their feet, grabbed their slings and bows and took their places. Dumat looked to the other rooftops. He was not alone. He had no need to give another signal. Every one of the commanders had seen that flash of light and known it for what it was.

Dumat did not hear Laurana's shouted challenge because he was shouting a challenge of his own, as were the elves around him. Dumat gave the order, and the elves opened fire.

Soliasi Arath! Laurana shouted as she had shouted so many years before, challenging the dragons attacking the High Clerist's Tower to fly to their deaths. She held the sword with the Lost Star above her, held it with her left hand. If the jewel failed, if the legends were wrong, if the magic of the sword had dwindled as much of the magic in the world had dwindled during the Age of Mortals, their plans and hopes and dreams would end in death.

The sun pierced the jewel and the jewel burst in white fire. Laurana whispered a blessing on the soul of Kalith Rian and on the soul of that unknown elven smith who had found the lost star glittering in the ashes of the forge fire.

Beryl stared at the sword with intense longing, for its magic was powerful, and she wanted it desperately. The jewel in the hilt was the most fabulous she had ever seen. She could not take her eyes from it. She must have it. Malys had nothing this valuable in her treasure trove. Beryl could not take her eyes from it. . . .

Beryl was caught.

Laurana realized the spell had worked when she saw the glow of the jewel burn in the dragon's eyes, burn deep into the beast's brain. She held the sword steady, held it high.

Enthralled, Beryl hung almost motionless in the air above Qualinost, her wings fanning gently to keep her aloft, her rapt gaze fixed upon the Lost Star.

The sword was heavy, and Laurana held it in an awkward position in her left hand, but she dared not give way to weakness, dared not drop the sword. She feared even to move, afraid that she might break the spell. Once freed from the enchantment, Beryl would attack in a violent rage. Laurana knew a moment's despair as she waited in vain to hear some sign that the elves had launched the attack. Her plan had failed. Dumat was waiting for the signal arrow that would never come.

The cheering and shouted challenges rising up from the rooftops were sweeter than bards' songs to her, gave her tired arm muscles renewed strength. Elves appeared on the bridges that spanned the borders of Qualinost. Elves and Knights could be seen bursting out from the tree-branch rooftops, a blossom of deadly flowers. Ballistae that had been covered with vines were wheeled into position. The sling-throwers moved to the attack. A single shouted command begat hundreds of others. The elves launched the assault.

Spears fired from the ballistae streamed upward, flew in a graceful arc over Beryl's body. Trailing behind the spears were long lengths of rope—rope that had been formed of wedding gowns and baby clothes, cooks' aprons and senators' ceremonial robes. The hundreds of spears carried the ropes up and over Beryl. When the spears plummeted back down to the ground, the ropes settled over the dragon, falling across her body and her wings and her tail.

The sling-throwers launched their attack, sending lead missiles soaring into the air. Attached to the missiles were more ropes that sailed over the dragon. Reloaded, the ballistae fired again. The sling-throwers hurled their missiles again and yet again.

Elf wizards cast spells, not on the dragon, but on the ropes. They cast their spells not knowing if the erratic, wayward magic would work or not. They cast the spells more out of hope and despair than out of certainty. In some instances, the wizards cast spells as they had known them in the Fourth Age. In other instances they cast the spells of the wild magic of this new age. In all instances, the spells worked perfectly. The elf wizards were amazed—thrilled, but amazed.

Some spells strengthened the rope and made the cloth as strong as steel. Others caused the rope to burst into magical fire. The enchanted flames ran along the length of the cable, burning the dragon but not consuming the rope. Certain spells made the rope as sticky as cobweb. Adhering to the dragon's scales, the rope stuck fast. Still other spells caused the rope to loop and spiral as if it were alive. The living rope wrapped around and around the dragon's feet, trussed Beryl like a chicken going to market.

Now some of the elves dropped their weapons and grabbed hold of the ends of the ropes, waiting for the final command. More and more rope filled the air until Beryl looked like an enormous moth caught in a web spun by many thousands of spiders.

Beryl could do nothing. The dragon was aware of what was happening to her. Laurana looked directly into the reptilian eyes and saw first amusement at the feeble efforts of these puny beings to ensnare her, then annoyance, as Beryl realized her movements were becoming increasingly hampered by the ropes. The annoyance altered very rapidly to fury, when she realized she could do nothing to help herself. She could do nothing but stare at the jewel.

The dragon's body quivered in impotent rage. Saliva dripped from her jaws. Her neck muscles bulged and strained as she tried frantically to wrench her gaze from the jewel. Rope after rope fell over her body. Her wings were weighed down, her tail entangled. She could not move her hind feet. They were tied together. The horrid ropes were winding themselves around her forefeet. She could feel herself being hauled down out of the sky, and suddenly she was afraid. She was powerless to save herself.

It was at this moment, while Beryl was caught by the jewel and ensnared by the ropes, that Laurana had planned to attack with the dragonlance. She had intended to drive the lance into the dragon's throat, prevent her from breathing her deadly fumes. She was to have wielded the lance. Medan was to have wielded the sword, used it to slay the dragon.

A good plan, but Medan was dead. Laurana was alone. To wield the lance, she would have to drop the sword, free the dragon from the enchantment. This was the moment of peril.

Laurana began to edge backward, still holding the sword, still keeping it steady, though her tired arm muscles quivered with the strain. Step by step, she moved back to the wall where she had placed the dragonlance to have it ready within reach. She groped behind her with her right hand, feeling for the lance, for she did not dare take her eyes off Beryl. At first, Laurana could not find the lance, and fear seized her. Then her fingers touched the metal, warm in the sunshine. Her hand closed over it, and she sighed deeply.

Below Dumat was shrieking for those holding the ropes to pull hard. The elves and Knights who had been manning the ballistae and wielding the slings dropped their weapons and leaped to grab hold of the ropes, adding their weight to those already pulling. Slowly but inexorably, they began to drag the enmeshed dragon closer to the ground.

Laurana drew a deep breath, summoned all her strength. Silently speaking the name of Sturm, she sought inside herself for the courage and the will and the resolve that had been with him on the tower when death dived at him. Her one fear was that Beryl would attack her instantly upon being freed of the spell and breathe the deadly gas on her before Laurana could slay the dragon. If Beryl did that, if Laurana died before she could achieve her mission, the elves on the ground would die before they had accomplished their goal, for Beryl would breathe her poison on them, and they would fall where they stood.

Laurana had never felt so alone. There was no one to help her. Not Sturm, not Tanis, not the Marshal. Not the gods.

Yet at the end, we are all of us alone, she reminded herself. Those I have loved held my hand on the long journey, but when we came to the final parting, I released them, and they walked forward, leaving me behind. Now, it is my turn to walk forward. To walk alone.

Laurana lifted the sword with the Lost Star and flung it over the parapet. The spell was broken. Beryl's eyes blinked, then blazed with fury.

Beryl had two objectives. The first was to free herself from the infuriating snare. The second was to kill the elf who had tricked her, catching her in a magical trap that a hatchling might have had wit enough to avoid. Beryl could deal with one or the other. She was about to kill the elf, when a particularly violent pull of the ropes jerked her downward.

She heard laughter. The laughter came not from below her, not from the elves. The laughter came from the sky above.

Two of her minions, both reds, both dragons she had secretly suspected of plotting against her, wheeled among the clouds far, far above, and they were laughing. Beryl knew immediately the reds were laughing at her, watching and enjoying her humiliation.

She had never trusted them, these native dragons. She knew quite well they served her out of fear, not out of loyalty. Ascribing to them motives of treachery best suited to herself, Beryl concluded irrationally that the red dragons were in league with the elves. The reds were biding their time, waiting for her to become thoroughly ensnared, then they would close in for the kill.

Beryl dismissed Laurana from consideration. A lone

elf—what harm could she do compared to two treacherous red dragons?

As Medan had said, Beryl was a coward at heart. She had never been trapped like this, rendered helpless, and she was terrified. She must free herself from this net, must return to the skies. Only there, where she could wheel and dive and use her enormous weight and strength to her advantage, would she be safe from her foes. Once in the heavens, she could destroy these wretched elves with a single breath. Once in the heavens, she could deal with her traitor servants.

Anger burned inside her. Beryl struggled to rid herself of the entangling ropes that hampered her flight. Heaving her shoulders, she lifted her wings and thrashed her tail, attempting to snap the ropes. She clawed at them with her sharp talons and turned her head to snap at them with her teeth. She had thought to break the puny ropes easily, but she had not counted on the strength of the magic or the will of those who had twined their love for their people and their homeland into the ropes.

A few strands broke, but most held. Her wild lashing and gyrations caused some elves to lose their grips. Some were dragged off rooftops or slammed into buildings.

Beryl cast a glance at the red dragons, saw that they had flown closer. Fear evolved into panic. Maddened, Beryl sucked in a huge breath, intending to destroy these insects who had so humbled her. Out of the corner of her eye, she caught sight of a flash of silver. . . .

Laurana watched in awe and terror as Beryl fought frantically to free herself. The dragon's head thrashed wildly. She shrieked curses and snapped at the ropes with her teeth. Appalled by the ferocity of the beast's rage, Laurana could not move. She stood trembling, clutching the lance in sweating hands. Her glance slid to the doorway that led to the arched alcove beyond, led to safety.

Beryl drew in a huge breath, drew it into lungs that would breathe out death on Laurana's people. Seizing the dragonlance with both hands, Laurana cried *Quisalan elevas!* to Tanis and Sturm and those who had gone before her. "Our loves-bond eternal." Aiming the lance at Beryl's lashing head, Laurana lunged at the dragon.

The dragonlance gleamed silver in the light of the strange sun. Putting all the strength of her body and soul and heart into her effort, Laurana plunged the dragonlance into Beryl's skull.

Blood spurted out in a great torrent, splashing over Laurana. Though her hands were wet and slippery with the dragon's blood, she held desperately to the lance, shoving it deeper into the dragon's head, as deep as it would go.

Pain—burning, flaring pain—exploded in Beryl's brain, as if someone had bored a hole through the bone, let in the blazing sun to set her soul on fire. Beryl gagged on her own poison breath. Attempting to free herself from the horrible pain, she jerked her head.

The dragon's sudden, spasmodic movement lifted Laurana off the balcony. She hung suspended in the air, perilously close to the edge. Her hands lost their hold on the lance, and she fell to the balcony's floor, landing on her back. Bone snapped, pain flashed, but then, strangely, she could feel nothing. She tried to stand, but her limbs would not obey her brain's command. Unable to move, she stared into the dragon's gaping jaws.

Beryl's pain did not end. It grew worse. Half blinded by the blood that poured into her eyes, yet she could still see her attacker. She tried to breathe death on the elf woman, but the dragon failed, choked on her own poison.

Consumed by fear, maddened by pain, thinking only to avenge herself on the elf that had done her such terrible harm, Beryl brought her massive head crashing down on the Tower of the Sun.

The shadow of death fell over Laurana. She looked away from death, looked into the sun.

The strange sun, hanging in the sky. It seemed forlorn, bewildered . . . as though it were lost.

. . . a lost star . . .

Laurana closed her eyes against the darkening shadow. "Our loves-bond . . ."

Hanging onto one of the ropes, pulling with all his strength, Dumat was not able to see what had happened on the tower, but he knew by Beryl's fearful shriek and the fact that they were not all dead of poison gas that Laurana must have dealt a blow to the creature. Dragon's blood and saliva splashed on him and around him, a hideous shower. The dragon was hurt. Now was the time to take advantage of her weakness.

"Pull, damn you! Pull!" Dumat yelled hoarsely, his voice rasping, almost gone. "She's not finished! Not by a long shot!"

Elves and humans who felt their strength ebbing in the battle with the dragon rallied and flung themselves with renewed energy on the ropes. Blood, running from their hands where the skin had been peeled off, stained the ropes. The pain of the raw nerves was intense, and some cried out even as they continued to tug, while others gritted their teeth and pulled.

Dumat watched in shock as Beryl attacked the tower, bashed her head into the building. His heart ached for Laurana, who must be trapped up there, and he hoped for her sake that she was already dead. Beryl's head struck the balcony, tore it free of the tower. The balcony plunged to the ground. Those people standing beneath it stared up in terror. Some had wits enough to flee. Others, bound up in fear, were unable to move. The balcony struck with a horrific crash, taking out buildings and cracking the paving stones. Debris flew through the air, killing and maiming. Dust rose in an immense cloud and rolled over them.

Dumat, coughing, turned to Ailea, to say some word of comfort, for his wife would be grieving the Queen Mother's death. The words of comfort were never spoken. Ailea lay staring up at Dumat with eyes that could no longer see him. A rock shard had pierced her breast. She had not lived long enough to scream.

Dumat stared at the dragon. She was down at treetop level now. Her forefeet touched the ground. Grim and empty, he redoubled his efforts on the rope.

"Pull, damn you!" he shouted. "Pull!"

Beryl's mad assault on the tower managed to slay her attacker, but that was all she accomplished. She was at last able to draw breath again, though it was wheezing and shallow, but the blow had not dislodged the dragonlance, as she had dimly hoped would happen. Far from shaking loose the splinter, the blow seemed to have driven it still deeper into her head. Her world was burning pain, and all she wanted to do was end it.

Beryl thrashed about, trying to free herself from the ropes, trying to dislodge the lance. Her flailings knocked down buildings, toppling trees. Her tail smashed into Dumat's house. He held onto the rope until the last possible moment. When the dragon crushed the house to tinder, Dumat fell through the broken roof. The house fell down on top of him. Buried alive, Dumat lay trapped in the rubble, pinned beneath a heavy tree limb, unable to move. He tasted blood in his mouth. Looking through the tangle of broken and twisted limbs and leaves, he saw the dragon above him. She had freed her wings, though ropes still dangled from them. She struggled to gain altitude, to rise above treetop level. But for every rope that snapped, two ropes held. More ropes fell across her. Elves and humans had died, but more had survived, and they continued the fight.

"Pull, damn you!" Dumat whispered. "Pull!"

The elves saw the Queen Mother die, they saw their loved ones die. They saw the dragon destroy the Tower of the Sun, the symbol of elven pride and hope. They used the strength lent them by grief and anger to drag down the dragon, drag her from the skies.

Beryl fought to free herself from the ropes and the horrible pain, but the more she struggled, the more she tangled herself in the elven cobweb. Her thrashing limbs and head and tail, her flailing wings crushed buildings and snapped trees. She struggled furiously to free herself, for she knew that when she hit the ground, she was vulnerable. The elves would move in with spear and arrow and finish the kill.

The elves saw that Beryl was starting to weaken. Her flailing grew less violent, her thrashing less destructive.

The dragon was dying.

Certain of that now, the elves pulled with a will and finally succeeded. They dragged Beryl's hulking body to the ground.

She landed with a shattering crash that crushed buildings and all those who had not been able to scramble out of the way. The force of the impact sent tremors rippling through the ground, shook the dwarves who waited in the tunnels below, sent rock and dust down on their heads, caused them to look in consternation at the beams that shored up the walls, kept the tunnels from collapsing.

When the tremors ceased and the dust settled, the elves grabbed their spears, moved in for the kill. After they had destroyed the dragon, they would be ready to fight her army.

The elves began to speak of victory. Qualinost had been grievously hurt, many had died, but the elven nation would live. They would bury their dead and weep for them. They would sing songs, grand songs about the death of the dragon.

But Beryl was not dead. Not by a long shot, as Dumat had said. The dragonlance had caused her great pain and disordered her thinking, but now the pain was starting to lessen. Her panic subsided and gave way to a fury that was cold and calculating and dangerous, far more dangerous than her tumultuous flailing. Her troops were massing on the banks of the two streams—offshoots of the White-rage River—that surrounded and protected Qualinost. Her troops were even now preparing to cross those streams. The elves had taken out the bridges, but Beryl's soldiers had brought hundreds of rafts and temporary bridges to carry her army across the one-hundred-foot-wide ravines.

Soon her soldiers would overrun Qualinost, put the elves to the sword. Elf blood would flow through the streets, sweeter to Beryl than May wine. The advent of her troops caused Beryl one difficulty: She could not use her poison gas to kill the elves, not without killing her troops as well. This was only a minor inconvenience, nothing to be concerned about. She would simply kill elves by the tens and not by the hundreds.

Relaxing, Beryl feigned weakness, lay sprawled ignominiously on the ground. She took a grim satisfaction in feeling the trees—so beloved of the elves—smash to splinters beneath her crushing body. Blinking her eyes free of blood, Beryl could see the damage she had wrought upon the once-beautiful city, and the sight was a boost to her spirits. She had never hated anyone or anything—not even her cousin Malys—more than she now hated these elves.

The elves were creeping out of their rat holes, coming to stare at her. They held spears and bows with arrows pointed at her. Beryl scorned them. The spear had not been made that could stay her, not even the fabled dragonlance. Nor could the arrows that were to her the size of bee stingers. She could see the elves all around her, puny, witless creatures, staring at her with their little squint eyes, gibbering in their greasy language.

Let them gibber. They would have something to chatter about shortly, that much was certain.

The pain in her head continued to ease. Resting on the ground, Beryl took careful stock of the situation. She had flung off or dislodged some of the ropes, and she could feel others starting to loosen. The magic spells were waning. Soon Beryl would be free to kill elves, slaying them one by one, stomping on them and snapping them in two. Her army would join her, and between them not one elf would remain alive in the world. Not one.

The dragonlance continued to be an irritant. Every once in a while, molten hot pain shot through her head, increased her rage. She lay on the ground, the elves at eye level, peering at them through squinted lids. In the distance, she heard horn calls, the sounds of her army advancing. They must have seen her fall. Perhaps they thought her dead. Perhaps her commanders were already spending in their feeble brains the loot that they would have been forced to share with her. They were in for a surprise. They were all in for a grand surprise. . . .

Bellowing a roar of defiance and triumph, Beryl lifted her head. Her huge clawed talons dug into the ground. With one push, one massive thrust of her gigantic legs, Beryl heaved herself to her feet.

The dwarven tunnels, a labyrinthine honeycomb built beneath Qualinost, buckled and collapsed under the dragon's weight. The ground gave way.

Beryl's roar changed to a startled shriek. She fought to save herself, scrabbling with her feet, frantically beating her wings to lift herself from the ruin. But her wings were still entangled with rope, her feet could find no purchase. An Immortal Hand cracked the bones of the world, split the ground asunder. Beryl plunged into the gaping fissure.

Torvold Bellowsgranite, cousin to the Thane of Thorbardin and leader of the dwarven army that had come to Qualinost to fight the Dark Knights of Neraka, heard the battle being fought above him, if he could not see it. Torvald stood at the foot of a ladder that led up to the surface, about twenty feet above him. He waited for the signal that meant the invading army had started to ford the river. His own army, comprised of a thousand dwarves, would then swarm up out of this tunnel and others dug beneath the city, march to attack.

The tunnel was as dark as deepest night, for the digging worms and their glowing larva had been dispatched back to Thorbardin. The darkness and the confined space and smell of freshly turned earth and worm leavings didn't bother the dwarves, who found the darkness and the smell familiar, comfortable. They were eager to depart the tunnels, however; eager to face their enemies, to do battle, and they fingered their axes and spoke of the coming glories with grim anticipation.

When the dwarves felt the first shudderings of the ground beneath their feet, they gave a cheer that echoed up and down the tunnels, for they hoped that meant that the elven strategy was working. The dragon had been hauled out of the skies and was lying helpless on the ground, emeshed in magical rope from which she could not escape.

"What's going on?" Torvald bellowed up at the scout, who was hunkered down near the entrance, his head poking up through the branches of a lilac bush.

"They got her," was the scout's laconic answer. "She's not moving. She's a goner."

The dwarves cheered again. Torvald nodded and was about to give the order for his men to start to climb the ladder when a fierce roar proved the scout wrong. The ground shook beneath Torvald's feet, the tremor so severe that the beams shoring up the walls creaked ominously. Dirt rained down on their heads.

"What the—" Torvald started to holler at the scout, then changed his mind. He began to climb the ladder to see for himself.

Another quake rumbled through the ground. The tunnel's ceiling split wide open. Dazzling sunlight streamed down through the gaping hole, half-blinding the dwarves. The horrified Torvald saw the blazing red eye of the infuriated dragon glaring down at him, and then the beams holding up the tunnel's roof cracked, the ladder splintered. The eye vanished amidst a huge cloud of dust and debris. The roof of the tunnel collapsed.

The world fell on top of Torvald, knocking him from the ladder. The horrifying screams of his dying comrades rose above the rending bones of Krynn, the last sounds he heard as tons of rock smashed down on him, crushing his skull and shattering his chest.

Stone, long trusted by the dwarves to shelter and to guard them against their enemies, became their enemy. Their killer. Their tomb.

Rangold of Balifor, now forty years old, had been a mercenary since he was fourteen. He fought for one reason and one alone—plunder. He had no other loyalties, knew nothing of politics, would switch sides in the middle of battle if someone made it worth his while. He had joined Beryl's army because he had heard they were going to be march on Qualinost. He had long anticipated the looting and sacking of the elven city. A man of foresight, Rangold had brought with him several large burlap bags in which he intended to carry home his fortune.

Rangold stood on the riverbank, eating stale bread and munching on dried beef, waiting his turn to cross the river. The blasted elves had cut the bridges. The ropes dangled far above them, for the banks were steep, the river low this time of year. Their scouts kept watch but reported seeing no elves. The first units had started across, some carrying their packs over their heads, others carrying their weapons. Those who could not swim were clearly uncomfortable as they waded deeper and deeper into the water that swirled around them. The water was cold, but ran calmly this time of year. In the spring, fed by the melting snows, the river would have been impassable.

Occasionally a red dragon could be seen circling high above the army, keeping watch. The men did not like the red dragons, did not trust them, even though they were on the same side, and kept glancing upward, hoping that the beast would fly away. Rangold didn't care anything about dragons. He shivered when the dragonfear was on him, shrugged it off when it was past and continued to eat his food. The thought of slaughtering elves and stealing their riches gave a fine, sharp edge to this appetite.

His first twinge of unease came when the ground suddenly lurched beneath his feet, throwing Rangold off balance and causing him to drop his sandwich. A limb fell with a shattering crash. A tree toppled. The river water heaved and surged, splashing up onto the bank. Rangold clung to the tree and stared around, trying to figure out what was happening. Overhead, the red dragon spread her wings and flew low over the woods, shouting out what sounded like warnings, but no one could make out what she was screaming.

The tremors continued, grew more severe. An enormous cloud of debris roiled into the air, so thick that it obliterated the light of the sun. Those crossing the river lost their footing, tumbled into the water. Those on the bank began hollering and running this way and that in confusion and panic, as the ground continued to heave and buckle beneath their feet.

"What are your orders?" a captain shouted.

"Hold your ground," his superior, a Knight of Neraka, answered tersely.

"That's easier said than done," the captain returned angrily, staggering to keep his balance. "I think we should get the hell out of here!"

"You have your orders, Captain," the Knight shouted. "This will stop in a—"

With an ear-splitting crack, an enormous tree limb broke loose and fell with a thundering crash, burying the Knight and the captain beneath its branches. Cries and moans came from the wreckage, pleas for help, pleas that Rangold ignored. He didn't know what the rest of the army planned to do, and he didn't care. As the captain had suggested, Rangold was going to get the hell out of here.

He started to scramble up the bank, but at that moment he heard an ominous, rolling, thunderous rumble. Turning to find the source of the sound, he saw a horrifying sight. A wall of water, bubbling and foaming, rushed down on them. The quakes caused the banks of the White-rage River to crumble. Fissures split open the rock ravines through which the river ran. Freed of its confinement, driven into tumult by the repeated tremors, the river went on a wild rampage.

The water uprooted trees, tore huge chunks of rock from the cliff faces through which it thundered, carried the rock and debris before it.

Rangold stared, appalled, and then turned and began to run. Behind him, those trapped in the water shrieked for help, but the rising river swiftly drowned their cries, as it swept them downstream. Rangold tried to clamber up the bank, but the sides were steep and slippery. He knew a moment's horrible fear, and then the water crashed into him with a force that shattered his breastbone and stopped his heartbeat. His body, limp and bloody, became just one more bit of debris the river carried downstream.

Bellowing and shrieking in rage, Beryl sank deeper and deeper as the ground gave way. The earth cracked beneath her weight. The cracks spread and radiated outward. Buildings, trees and homes collapsed and slid into the widening fissures. The headquarters of the Knights of Neraka, that squat, ugly building, fell in upon itself with booming crash. Debris rained down upon the dragon, striking her in the head, puncturing her wings. The castle of the king, built of living aspen trees, was destroyed, the trees uprooted, limbs shattered, huge trunks twisted and snapped.

The elves of Qualinost, who had remained to defend their homeland, died in the rubble of the homes they had wrought with such care, died in the gardens they had loved. Though they knew death was imminent and that there was no escape, they continued to fight their enemy, stabbing at Beryl with spear and sword until the pavement split asunder, gave way beneath their feet. The elves died with hope, for though they had perished, they believed that their city would survive and rise again from the ruins.

It was well they died, before they knew the truth.

Beryl realized suddenly that she was not going to survive, that she could not escape. The knowledge bewildered her. This wasn't the way it was supposed to end. She—the mightiest force to have ever been seen on Krynn—was going to die an ignominious death in a hole in the ground. How could this have happened? What had gone wrong? She didn't understand. . . .

Boulders rained down on her, cracking her skull and breaking her spine. Splintered trees ripped holes in her wings, falling rocks snapped the tendons. Sharp, jagged stones slashed open her belly. Blood spurted from beneath her scales. Pain wrenched her and twisted, her and she screamed for death to come to release her. The monster who had slain so many moaned and writhed in agony as rocks and trees and crumbling buildings pummeled her. The immense, misshapen head sank lower and lower. The red eyes rolled back. The broken wings, the thrashing tail grew still. With a last sigh, a bitter curse, Beryl died.

Tremors shook the ground around the elven city as the Immortal Hand pounded on it with a fist of hatred. The earth quaked and shattered. Cracks widened, fissures split the bedrock on which Qualinost had been built. The red dragons, looking down from the skies, saw an enormous, gaping hole where once had stood a beautiful city. The reds had no love for elves, for they had been enemies since the beginning of time, but so terrible was this sight, expressive of awful power, that the reds could not rejoice. They looked down upon the ruin and bowed their heads in reverence and respect.

The tremors ceased. The ground settled, no longer heaved and quivered. The White-rage River overflowed its banks, poured into the immense chasm where once had stood the elven city of Qualinost. Long after the quakes stopped, the water continued to boil and bubble and surge and heave, wave after wave crashing upon the newly created banks. Gradually, the river grew calm. The water lapped tremulously at the new banks that now surrounded it, hugged them close, as if shocked by its own fury and bewildered by the destruction it had wrought.

Night came without starlight or moonlight, a shroud drawn over the dead who rested far beneath the dark, quivering water.

33

Nalis Aren

any miles away, Gilthas and his retinue parted with Tarn Bellowsgranite, the dwarven thane, then traveled south. They had ridden with what haste they could, the Lioness pushing them, for she feared that Beryl's army would split, send one force marching south to intercept the refugees while one force seized and held Qualinost. Despite her urging, their pace was slow, for their hearts were heavy and seemed to weigh them down. Whenever they came to the top of hill or ridge, Gilthas halted and turned in the saddle to stare at the horizon in some vain hope of seeing what was happening.

"We are too far away," his wife reminded him. "The trees block the view. I left runners, who will come after us swiftly to report. All will be well. We must move on, my love. We must move on."

They had stopped to rest and water their horses when they felt the ground shudder beneath their feet and heard a low rumble, as of a distant storm. The tremor

516

was mild, but it caused Gilthas's hand to shake so that he dropped the water skin he had been filling. He rose and looked to the north.

"What was that? Did you feel that?" he demanded.

"Yes, I felt it," said the Lioness, coming to stand beside him. Her gaze joined his, and she was troubled. "I don't know what that was."

"There are sometimes quakes in the mountains, Your Majesty," Planchet suggested.

"Not like that. I've never felt anything like that. Something has gone wrong. Something terrible has happened."

"We don't know that," the Lioness said. "Perhaps it was nothing but a tremor, as Planchet says. We should keep going—"

"No," said Gilthas. "I'm staying here to wait for the runners. I'm not leaving until I find out what has happened."

He walked away, heading for a rock promontory that thrust up out of the ground. The Lioness and Planchet exchanged glances.

"Go with him," the Lioness said softly.

Planchet nodded and hurried after Gilthas. The Lioness instructed her troops to set up camp. She looked often to the north, and when she did, she sighed softly and shook her head.

Gilthas climbed with fevered energy; Planchet had difficulty keeping up with his king. Reaching the top, Gilthas stood long moments, staring intently to the north.

"Is that smoke, do you think, Planchet?" he asked anxiously.

"A cloud, Your Majesty," Planchet replied.

Gilthas continued to stare until he was forced to lower his gaze, wipe his eyes.

"It's the sun," he muttered. "It's too bright."

"Yes, Your Majesty," said Planchet softly, looking away.

Imagining he could read the young king's thoughts, he added, "Your Majesty's decision to leave was the right—"

"I know, Planchet," Gilthas interrupted him. "I know my duty, and I will try to do it, as best as I am able. I wasn't thinking about that." He looked back to the north. "Our people have been forced to leave their ancient homeland. I was wondering what would happen to us if we could not go back."

"That will never come to pass, Your Majesty," said Planchet firmly.

"Why not?" Gilthas turned to look directly at him, curious to hear the answer.

Planchet was confounded. This was so simple, so elementary. "Qualinesti is ours, Your Majesty. The land belongs to the elves. It is ours by right."

Gilthas smiled sadly. "Some might say the only plot of land to which we mortals have an inherent right is the plot where we are finally laid to rest. Look down there. My dear wife paces like the giant cat for which she was named. She is nervous, worried. She does not want to stop. She wants to keep going. Why? Because our enemies pursue us. They hunt us—on our land."

"We will take it back—"

"Will we?" Gilthas asked quietly. "I wonder." He turned back to the north. "We are a people in exile. We have nowhere to go." He slightly turned his head. "I've heard the reports about Silvanesti, Planchet."

"Rumors, Your Majesty," Planchet returned, embarrassed and uncomfortable. "We cannot confirm them. We were going to tell you, but the Lioness said you were not to be troubled. Not until we knew something certain—"

"Certain." Gilthas shook his head. With the tip of his boot, he traced in the dust an outline of an oblong, six feet in length and three feet wide. "This is all that is certain, my friend."

"Your Majesty—" Planchet began, worried.

Gilthas turned to stare back to the north.

"Is that smoke, do you think?"

"Yes, Your Majesty," said Planchet. "That is smoke."

The runner caught up with them during the night. Accustomed to traveling under the cover of darkness, the Lioness and her rebel elves marked the trails as her Kagonesti ancestors had done long before her, using the petals of flowers that glowed in the darkness to indicate which fork to take, leaving glow worms trapped in bottles on a pile of rocks, or smearing a tree with phosphor. Thus the runner had been able to follow their trail even after night fell.

They had not lit a fire. The Lioness had counseled against it. They sat silently in the darkness, no one telling tales or singing a starsong, as they might have done in happier times.

Gilthas kept apart from the others, his thoughts straying back to his childhood as they had done often since his parting from his mother. He was remembering these times, thinking of his mother and his father, of their love and tender care for him, when he saw the guards jump to their feet. Their hands going to their swords, they ran to surround him.

Gilthas had not heard a sound, but that was not unusual. As his wife constantly teased him, he had "human ears." Sword drawn, Planchet came to stand by the side of his king. The Lioness remained in the center of the clearing, peering into the darkness. She whistled the notes of the song of the nightingale.

The answer came back. The Lioness whistled again. The elves relaxed, although they still kept up their guard. The runner entered the camp and, sighting the Lioness, approached her and began to speak to her in Kagonesti, the language of the Wilderelves.

Gilthas could speak some Kagonesti, but he could catch only fragments of the conversation, for the two kept their voices low, and the runner spoke too fast to be understood, his speech broken only by pauses for breath. Gilthas might have walked over and joined in the conversation, but he was suddenly unable to move. He could tell by the runner's tone that the news he was conveying was not good.

Then Gilthas saw his wife do something she had never before done. She fell to her knees and bowed her head. Her mane of hair covered her face like a veil of mourning. She lifted her hand to her eyes, and Gilthas saw that she wept.

Planchet gripped Gilthas's arm, but the king shook him off. Gilthas walked forward on feet that were numb. He could not feel the ground beneath them, and he stumbled once but caught himself. Hearing him approaching, the Lioness regained control of herself. Scrambling to rise, she hastened to meet him. She clasped his hands in hers. Her hands were as cold as death, and Gilthas shivered.

"What is it?" he demanded in a voice he did not recognize. "Tell me! My mother—" He could not speak it.

"Your mother is dead," the Lioness said softly, her voice trembling and husky with her tears.

Gilthas sighed deeply, but his grief was his own. He was king. He had his people to think about.

"What about the dragon?" he asked harshly. "What about Beryl?"

"Beryl is dead," the Lioness said. "There is more," she added quickly, when she saw Gilthas about to speak.

"The tremor we felt . . ." Her voice cracked. She moistened dry lips, then continued. "Something went wrong. Your mother fought alone. No one knows why or what happened. Beryl came and . . . your mother fought the dragon alone."

Gilthas lowered his head, unable to bear the pain.

"Laurana struck Beryl with the dragonlance but did not kill her. Furious, the dragon smashed the tower. . . . Your mother could not escape. . . . "

The Lioness was silent a moment, then went on. Her voice sounded dazed, as if she could not believe the words she was speaking. "The plan to snare the dragon worked. The people dragged her out of the skies. Your mother's attack kept Beryl from breathing her foul gas. The dragon was down on the ground, and it seemed she was dead. She was only shamming. Beryl heaved herself off the ground and was about to attack when the ground gave way beneath her."

Gilthas stared, appalled, unable to speak.

"The tunnels," said the Lioness, tears trailing down her cheeks. "The tunnels collapsed beneath the dragon. She fell in and . . . the city fell in on top of her."

Planchet gave a low cry. The elven guards, who had edged close to hear, gasped and cried out.

Gilthas could say nothing, could make no sound.

"Tell him," the Lioness ordered the runner in a choked voice, averting her face. "I can't."

The runner bowed to the king. The man's face was white. His eyes were wide. He was only now starting to recover his breath.

"Your Majesty," he said, speaking the Qualinesti tongue, "I grieve to tell you that the city of Qualinost is no more. Nothing remains."

"Survivors?" Gilthas asked without a voice.

"There could be no survivors, Your Majesty," the elf said. "Qualinost is now a lake. *Nalis Aren.* A lake of death."

Gilthas took his wife in his arms. She held him fast, murmuring incoherent words of comfort that could bring no comfort. Planchet wept openly, as did the elven guards, who began to whisper prayers for the spirits of the dead.

Bewildered, overwhelmed, unable to comprehend the enormity of the disaster, Gilthas held fast to his wife and stared out into the darkness that was a lake of death washing over him.

34

The Presence

The blue dragon circled over the treetops, searching for a place to land. The cypress trees grew thick, so thick that Razor talked of flying back to the east, to where grassy fields and low rolling hills provided more suitable sites. Goldmoon would not permit the dragon to turn back, however. She was nearing the end of her journey. Her strength waned with the passing seconds. Each beat of her heart was a little slower, a little weaker. What time she had left to her was precious, she could not waste a moment. Looking down from the dragon's back, she watched the river of souls flowing beneath her, and it seemed to her that she was not borne forward by the dragon's strong wings but by that mournful tide.

"There!" she said, pointing.

An outcropping of rock, gleaming chalk-white in the moonlight, thrust up from amid the cypress trees. The shape of the outcropping was strange. Seen from above, it had the look of a hand outstretched, palm upward, as if to receive something.

Razor regarded it intently and, after some thought, opined that he could land safely, although it would be their task to climb down the steep sides of the outcropping.

Goldmoon was not concerned. She had only to wade into the river to be carried to her destination.

Razor landed in the palm of the chalk-white hand, settling down as easily as possible, so as not to jar his passengers. Goldmoon dismounted, her strong youthful body carrying within it the faltering spirit.

She assisted Conundrum to slide down off the dragon's back. Her assistance was needed, for Razor rolled an eye, glared at the gnome balefully. Conundrum had spent the entire journey discoursing on the inefficiency of dragons for flight, the unreliability of scales and skin, bones and tendon. Steel and steam, said the gnome. Machines. That was the future. Razor flicked a wing, came very near knocking Conundrum off the cliff. The gnome, lost in a happy dream of hydraulics, never noticed.

Goldmoon looked up at Tasslehoff, who remained comfortably seated on the dragon's back.

"Here you are, Goldmoon," said Tas, waving his hand. "I hope you find whatever it is you're looking for. Well, come along, dragon. Let's get going. Can't waste time. We have cities to burn, maidens to devour, treasure to carry off. Good-bye, Goldmoon! Good-bye, Conund—"

Snapping his teeth, Razor arched his back, shook his mane. Tasslehoff's farewells were cut off in midsentence as the kender went flying heels over topknot, to land with uncomfortable finality on the rock.

"Bad enough I had to carry the little beast *this* far," Razor snarled. He shifted his gaze to Goldmoon. The dragon's red eye flickered. "You are not what the Knight Gerard claimed you to be, are you? You are not a dark mystic."

"No, I am not. But I thank you for bringing me to Nightlund," said Goldmoon absently. She was not afraid of the dragon's wrath. She felt a protective hand over her, as strong as the hand of rock that now supported her. No mortal being could harm her.

"I do not want your thanks," Razor returned. "Your thanks are nothing. I did this for her." His eyes clouded, his gaze lifted to the bright moon, the starlit heavens. "I hear her voice." He shifted the red eyes back to fix intently on Goldmoon. "You hear the voice, too, don't you? It speaks your name. Goldmoon, princess of the Qué-shu. You know the voice."

"I hear the voice," said Goldmoon, troubled. "But I do not know it. I do not recognize it."

"I do," said Razor restlessly. "I am called, and I will heed the call. But not without my master. We stand together, he and I."

The dragon spread his wings and soared off the rock, leaping straight up in order to clear the towering trees. He flew south, toward Qualinesti.

Tasslehoff picked himself up and collected all his pouches.

"I hope you know where we are, Burrfoot," said Conundrum in grim and accusing tones.

"No, I don't," said Tasslehoff cheerfully. "I don't recognize any of this." He added, with a heartfelt sigh of relief, "We're lost, Goldmoon. Most definitely lost."

"They know the way," said Goldmoon, looking down on the upturned faces of the dead.

Palin and Dalamar stood on the lowest floor of the Tower, staring intently into the darkness that lay thick and heavy beneath the cypress trees. Thick and heavy and empty. The roving, restless dead had vanished.

"We could leave now," Palin suggested.

He stood by the window, hands folded in his robes, for the Tower was chill and dank in the early morning and he was cold. Dalamar had mentioned something about mulled wine and a fire in the library, but although warmth for body and belly sounded good, neither man left to go in search of it.

"We could leave now, while the dead are not here to harass us. We could both leave."

"Yes," said Dalamar, standing, his hands in the sleeves of his robes, staring out the window. "We could leave." He cast a sidelong glance at Palin. "Or rather, you could leave, if you want. Search for the kender."

"You could leave, too," Palin returned. "Nothing's holding you here anymore." A sudden thought came to him. "Or perhaps since the dead have departed, so has your magic."

Dalamar smiled a dark smile. "You sound almost hopeful, Majere."

"You know I didn't mean it like that," Palin returned, nettled, although something deep inside him muttered that perhaps he had very much meant it like that.

Here am I, a middle-aged man, a spellcaster of considerable power and renown. I have not lost my abilities, as I had once feared. The dead have been stealing my magic. Yet, in the presence of Dalamar, I feel young and inferior and inadequate, as when I first came to the Tower to take my Test. Worse, perhaps, for youth by its nature is filled with confidence. I am constantly striving to prove my worth to Dalamar and always falling short of the mark.

And why should I? Palin demanded of himself. What does it matter what this dark elf thinks of me? Dalamar will never trust me, never respect me. Not because of anything I am, but because of what I am not. I am not my uncle. I am not Raistlin.

"I could leave, but I will not," Dalamar stated, his delicate brows drawing together as he continued to stare into the empty darkness. He shivered and withdrew more snuggly into his robes. "My thumbs prick. My hackles rise. There is a Presence here, Palin. I have felt it all this past night. A breath on the back of my neck. A whisper in my ear. The sound of distant laughter. An Immortal Presence, Majere."

Palin was uncomfortable. "That girl and her talk of her One God has gotten to you, my friend. That and an over-active imagination and the fact that you don't eat enough to keep my wife's canary bird alive."

Palin wished immediately he had not mentioned his wife, wished he had not thought about Usha. I should leave the Tower now if for no other reason than to return home. Usha will be worried about me. If she had heard of the attack on the Citadel of Light, perhaps she thinks I am dead.

"Let her think me dead," he said softly. "She will find more peace in the thought that I am dead than she knew when I was alive. If she thinks me dead, she will forgive me for hurting her. Her memories of me will be fond ones. . . ."

"Quit mumbling to yourself, Majere, and look outside. The dead have returned!"

Where before there had been stillness and quiet, the darkness was once again alive—alive with the dead. The restless spirits were back, roaming among the trees, prowling about the Tower, staring at it with eyes that were hungry and burning with desire.

Palin gave a sudden, hoarse cry and sprang to the window. He hit it with his hands so hard that he very nearly broke the glass.

"What?" Dalamar was alarmed. "What is it?"

"Laurana!" Palin gasped. He stared searchingly out into the shifting river of souls. "Laurana! I saw her! I swear! Look! Out there! No . . . She's gone. . . ."

Pushing away from the window, he walked resolutely toward the spellbound door.

Dalamar sprang after him, laid a wresting hand on his arm. "Majere, this is madness—"

Palin shook him off. "I'm going out there. I have to find her."

"No, Palin." Dalamar stood in front of him, grasped hold of him tightly, fingers digging into the flesh of Palin's arms. "You don't want to find her. Believe me, Majere. She won't be Laurana. She won't be the Laurana you knew. She'll be . . . like the others."

"My father wasn't!" Palin retorted angrily, struggling to free himself. Who would have thought the emaciated elf could be so strong? "He tried to warn me—"

"He wasn't, at first," Dalamar said. "But he is now. He can't help himself. I know. I've used them. They have served me for years."

He paused, still retaining his grip on Palin, watching him warily.

Palin shook off Dalamar's grip. "Let go of me. I'm not going anywhere." Rubbing his arms, he returned to stand staring out the window.

"Are you certain it was Laurana?" Dalamar asked after a moment's silence.

"I am not certain of anything anymore." Palin was chilled through, worried, frustrated. "So much for your blasted hackles—"

"—we've come to the wrong place," a high, shrill voice cried plaintively from out of the darkness. "You don't want to go there, Goldmoon. Trust me. I know my Towers of High Sorcery, and this is not the right one."

"I seek the wizard, Dalamar!" another voice called. "If he is within, let him please open the doors of the Tower to me."

"I don't know how or why," Palin exclaimed, peering

in astonishment through the glass, "but there's Tasslehoff, and he has brought Goldmoon with him."

"The other way round, from the sounds of it," Dalamar remarked, as he removed the magical spell from the door.

Tasslehoff continued to argue, as they stood outside the door of the Tower, that this was the wrong Tower. Goldmoon wanted Dalamar's Tower, the Tower of High Sorcery in Palanthas, and she could see quite obviously that this was not Palanthas. Therefore, she had the wrong Tower.

"You're not going to find anyone inside there," Tasslehoff was beginning to sound desperate. "You won't find Dalamar or Palin either, for that matter. Not that there's any reason to think Palin would be here," he added hastily. "I haven't seen Palin in the longest time. Not since Beryl attacked the Citadel of Light. He went one way, and I went another. He had the magical Device of Time Journeying with him, except that he lost it. He tossed bits of it at the draconians. The device is lost, destroyed. No sign of it anywhere. So don't go looking for it, because you won't find it—"

"Dalamar," came Goldmoon's voice. "Please let me in!"

"I keep telling you," Tasslehoff argued, "Dalamar's not— Oh, hullo, Dalamar." The kender tried very hard to sound astonished. "What are you doing here in this *strange* Tower?" Tasslehoff winked several times and motioned with his head at Goldmoon.

"Welcome, Goldmoon, Healer, Priestess of Mishakal," said Dalamar in gracious tones, using her old title. "I am honored by your visit."

Ushering her into his dwelling with elven courtesy, Dalamar whispered a soft aside, "Majere! Don't let the kender get away!"

Palin seized hold of Tasslehoff, who was hovering on the threshold. Palin was about to haul him bodily inside the Tower, when he was considerably disconcerted to find a gnome planted on the threshold, as well. The gnome had his hands shoved into his pockets and was looking about. Apparently, from his expression, he was not much liking what he saw.

"Eh?" said Palin, staring at the gnome. "Who are you?"

"Short version: Conundrum. I'm with her." The gnome pointed a grimy finger at Goldmoon. "She stole my submersible. Cost a lot of money, submersibles. And who's going to pay? That's what I want to know. Are you going to pay for it? Is that why we're here?"

Conundrum held up a small fist. "Cold, hard steel. That's what I want. No wizard stuff. Bat's eyes." The gnome sniffed disdainfully. "We've got a vault full of them. Once you've ruled out ball bearings, what good are they?"

Keeping a firm grip on Tasslehoff's collar, Palin dragged the kender, kicking and squirming, over the doorstoop. Conundrum followed on his own, his small, quick eyes taking in everything and dismissing it all out of hand.

Goldmoon said nothing in response to Dalamar's greeting. She barely looked at him or at Palin. Her gaze went around the Tower. She stared at the spiraling staircase that went up into darkness. She glanced around at the chamber in which they stood. She looked, and her eyes grew wide. Her face, already pale, went ashen.

"What is this I feel?" she asked, her voice low and filled with dread. "Who is here?"

Dalamar shot Palin a glance that said *I told you so.* Aloud, he replied, "Palin Majere and I are the only two here, Healer."

Goldmoon looked at Palin and seemed not to recognize him, for almost immediately her gaze went around him, past him, beyond him.

"No," she said softly. "There is someone else. I am meeting someone here."

Dalamar's dark eyes flashed. He silenced Palin's startled exclamation with a glance.

"The person you are expecting has not yet arrived. Will you wait in my library, Healer? The room is warm, and there is spiced wine and food."

"Food?" The gnome perked up, then was immediately cast back into gloom. "Not bat's brains, is it? Monkey toes? I won't eat wizard food. Ruins the digestion. Pork rinds and tarbean tea. That's more like it."

"It has been nice seeing you again, Palin, and you, too, Dalamar," Tasslehoff said, wriggling in Palin's grip, "and I wish I could stay for dinner, because the monkey toes sound delicious, but I have to be running along—"

"I will show you to the library in just a moment, Healer," Dalamar said, "but first I must settle our other guests. If you will excuse me—"

Goldmoon didn't appear to hear. She continued to stare around the Tower, searching for something or someone. The sight was unnerving.

Dalamar glided over to Palin, plucked at his sleeve. "Regarding Tas—"

"What regarding me?" Tas asked, eyeing Dalamar suspiciously.

"You recall what Mina said to you, Majere? About the device?"

"Who said?" Tas demanded. "Said what? What device?"

"Yes," said Palin. "I remember."

"Take him and the gnome to one of the student rooms in the north wing. The first one in the corridor will do. It is a room that has *no* fireplace," Dalamar added with grim emphasis. "Search the kender. When you find the device, for mercy's sake, keep it safe. Don't go tossing bits of it around. Oh, and you might want to remain hidden in that wing of the building. Our guest should not find you here."

"Why be so mysterious?" Palin asked, irritated by Dalamar's smug tone. "Why not just tell Goldmoon that the person coming to see her is her foster daughter, Mina?"

"You humans," Dalamar returned disparagingly. "So quick to blurt out everything you know. Elves have learned the power of secrets. We have learned the value of keeping secrets."

"But what can you hope to gain—"

Dalamar shrugged. "I don't know. Maybe something. Maybe nothing. You tell me that the two of them were once close. Much may come out of the shock of a sudden reunion, the shock of recognition. People say things they never intended in such circumstances, especially humans, who are so swayed by wayward emotions."

Palin's expression hardened. "I want to be there. Goldmoon may appear young, but that is only a façade. You speak glibly of the shock to her to see this child that she once dearly loved, but such a shock might be fatal."

Dalamar was shaking his head. "Too dangerous—"

"You can arrange it," Palin said firmly. "I know you have ways."

Dalamar hesitated, then said ungraciously, "Very well. If you insist. But the responsibility is entirely yours. Remember that this Mina saw you though you were hidden behind a wall. If you are discovered, I can do nothing to save you."

"I wouldn't expect you to," Palin returned crisply.

"Meet us in the library, then, once you have those two locked up tight." Dalamar jerked a thumb at the kender and the gnome.

The dark elf turned away, then, pausing, glanced back over his shoulder. "I suppose, by the way, Majere, that the significance of the gnome has occurred to you?"

"The gnome?" Palin was taken aback. "No. What—"

"Recall your uncle's history," Dalamar said and his voice was grim.

Returning to Goldmoon, he led her up the winding stairs. He was gracious and charming, as he could be when he wanted. Goldmoon followed where he led, moving as one who walks in sleep, with no conscious awareness of where she was or where she might be going. The youthful, beautiful body walked and took her with it.

"Significance of the gnome," Palin repeated in disgust. "Gnomes . . . my uncle's history . . . what does he mean? Always so damn mysterious . . ."

Muttering to himself, Palin hauled the reluctant Tasslehoff up the stairs. Palin paid no attention to the kender's pleadings and excuses and lies, some of them quite original. His attention was focused on the small and wizened gnome who was trudging up the stairs alongside, complaining the entire way about the pains in his legs and extolling the virtues of gnome-flingers over stairs.

Palin couldn't find any significance to the gnome whatsoever. Not unless Dalamar intended to install gnome-flingers.

He escorted the two to the room mentioned, pried Tas's fingers loose when the kender tried to cling to the doorjamb, and shoved him bodily inside. The gnome clumped in after, talking of building code violations and asking about yearly inspections. Casting a wizard-lock spell on the door to keep his reluctant guests inside, Palin turned to confront Tasslehoff.

"Now, about the Device of Time Journeying—"

"I haven't got it, Palin," Tas said quickly. "I swear by the beard of my Uncle Trapspringer. You threw all the pieces at the draconians. You know you did. They are scattered all over the Hedge Maze—"

"Hah!" the gnome shouted and went to stand in a corner with his head pressed against the wall.

Tas was going on at a desperate pace. "—the pieces of the device were scattered all over the Hedge Maze, along with pieces of the draconians."

"Tas," Palin interrupted sternly, mindful of the passing time and wanting to hasten this along. "You have the device. It came back to you. It must come back to you, even if it is in pieces. I thought I had destroyed it, but the device can't be destroyed, any more than it can be lost."

"Palin, I—" Tas began, his lip quivering.

Palin steeled himself, expecting more lies. "What is it, Tas?"

"Palin . . . I saw myself!" Tas blurted out.

"Tas, really—"

"I was dead, Palin!" Tas whispered. His normally ruddy face was pale. "I was dead and I . . . I didn't like it! It was horrid, Palin. I was cold, so very cold. And I was lost, and I was frightened. I've never been lost, and I've never been frightened. Not like that, anyway.

"Don't send me back to die, Palin," Tas begged. "Don't turn me into a . . . a dead thing! Please, Palin. Promise me you won't!" Tasslehoff clutched at him. "Promise me!"

Palin had never seen the kender so upset. The sight moved him almost to tears himself. He stood perplexed, wondering what to do, all the time absently smoothing Tasslehoff's hair in an effort to calm him.

What can I do? Palin asked himself helplessly. Tasslehoff *must* go back to die. I have no choice in the matter. The kender must return to his own time and die beneath the heel of Chaos. I cannot make the promise he asks of me. No matter how much I want to.

What Palin found perplexing was that Tasslehoff had seen his own ghost. Palin might have thought this a ruse, an attempt by the kender to distract Palin from finding the device. But while Palin knew that Tas would never hesitate to tell a lie—either out of self-interest or for its entertainment value—Palin was convinced that this was the truth. Palin had seen fear in the kender's eyes, an uncommon sight, and one that Palin found heart-wrenching.

At least this answered one nagging question: Had Tasslehoff truly died or had he just been roaming about the world for all those years? The fact that he had seen his own ghost proved the answer conclusively. Tasslehoff Burrfoot had died in the final battle against Chaos. He was dead. Or at least, he should be dead.

The gnome left his corner, walked up and poked Palin in the ribs. "Didn't somebody mention food?"

The significance of the gnome. What was the significance of this irritating gnome?

Disengaging Tas's clutching hands, Palin knelt down in front of Tas. "Look at me, Tas," he said. "Yes, that's it. Look at me and listen to what I am saying. I don't understand what is going on. I don't understand what is happening in the world and neither does Dalamar. But I know this. The only way we can find out what has gone wrong and maybe fix it is if you are honest with us."

"If I am honest," said Tas, wiping away his tears, "will you still send me back?"

"I am afraid I have to, Tas," Palin said reluctantly. "You must understand. I don't want to. I would do anything or give anything not to have to. You've seen the dead souls, Tas. You've seen for yourself that they are desperately unhappy. They aren't supposed to be here in the world. Something or someone is keeping them prisoner."

"You mean *I'm* not supposed to be here?" Tas asked. "Not the live me. The dead me?"

"I don't know for sure, Tas. No one does. But I don't think so. Don't you remember what Lady Crysania used to say—that death was not the end but the beginning of a whole new life? That we would join our loved ones who have passed beyond, and we would be together and make new friends—"

"I always thought I'd be with Flint," Tas said. "I know he misses me." He was quiet a moment, then said, "Well . . . if you think it will help . . ."

He unhooked the strap of his pouch and, before Palin could stop him, upended the bag, spilling its contents onto the floor.

Amid the birds' eggs and the chicken feathers and ink pots and jam jars and apple cores and what appeared to be a peg someone had been using for an artificial leg, the gears and jewels and wheels and chain of the Device of Time Journeying winked and sparkled in the candlelight.

"Why, what's this?" said the gnome, squatting down and sorting through the pile. "Cogs, a widget and a whatsit and a thingamajig. Technical terms, you know," he added, glancing at Tas and Palin to see if they were impressed. "Not understandable to the amateur. I'm not sure what it was." He gathered up the pieces one by one, eyeing each in turn. "But it doesn't appear to be in proper working order. That's not a guess, mind you. That's the opinion of a professional."

Making a tray of his robe, the gnome carried the pieces of the device to a table. Bringing out the remarkable knife that was also a screwdriver, he settled down to work.

"You, there, boy," he said, waving his hand at Palin. "Bring us some lunch. Sandwiches. And a pot of tarbean tea. Strong as you can make it. Going to be an all-nighter."

And, then, of course, Palin remembered the device's history. He understood the significance of the gnome.

Apparently, so did Tasslehoff, who was staring at Conundrum with a hopeless and woebegone expression.

"Where have you been, Majere?" Dalamar demanded, confronting Palin as he came through the library door. The dark elf was nervous, on edge. He'd obviously been pacing the floor. "You took long enough! Did you find the Device?"

"Yes, and so did the gnome." Palin looked intently at Dalamar. "His coming here—"

"—completes the circle," Dalamar finished.

Palin shook his head, unconvinced. He glanced around the room. "Where is Goldmoon?"

"She asked to be taken to the old laboratory. She said she was given to know that the meeting would be held there."

"The laboratory? Is that safe?"

Dalamar shrugged. "Unless she's afraid of dust bunnies. They're the only danger I can see."

"Once a chamber of mystery and power, the laboratory is now a repository of dust, the refuge of two impotent old men," Palin said bitterly.

"Speak for yourself." Dalamar laid a hand on Palin's arm. "And keep your voice down. Mina is here. We must go. Bring the light."

"Here? But how—"

"Apparently she has free run of my Tower."

"Aren't you going to be there with them?"

"No," said Dalamar shortly. "I was dismissed to go about my business. Are you coming or not?" he demanded impatiently. "There's nothing we can do, either of us. Goldmoon is on her own."

Still Palin hesitated, but then he decided that he might

best serve Goldmoon by keeping an eye on Dalamar. "Where are we going?"

"Through here," Dalamar said, halting Palin as he was continuing on down the stairs.

Making a turning, Dalamar passed his hand over the wall and whispered a word of magic. A single rune began to glow faintly on the stone. Dalamar put his hand over the rune, and a section of the wall slid to one side, revealing a staircase. As they entered, they could hear heavy footfalls echoing through the Tower. The minotaur, or so they guessed. The door slid shut after them, and they could hear nothing more.

"Where does this lead?" Palin whispered, holding up the lamp to illuminate the stairs.

"The Chamber of the Live Ones," Dalamar replied. "Hand me the lamp. I'll go first. I know the way." He descended the stairs rapidly, his robes fluttering around his ankles.

"I trust none of the 'Live Ones' are left alive," said Palin with a grimace, remembering what he had heard of some of his uncle's more gruesome experiments.

"No, they died a long time ago, poor wretches." Dalamar paused and looked up at Palin. His dark eyes glittered in the lamplight. "But the Chamber of Seeing remains."

"Ah!" Palin breathed, understanding.

When Raistlin Majere became Master of the Tower of High Sorcery of Palanthas, he also became a recluse. Rarely leaving his Tower, he spent his time concentrating on increasing his powers: magical, temporal, and political. In order to keep current on what was happening in the world, especially those events that might affect him, Raistlin used his magic to create a window onto the world. In the lowest regions of the Tower, he carved out a pool and filled it with enchanted water. Whoever looked into the pool could call to mind a location, and he would both see and hear what was transpiring in the location.

"Did you question the kender?" Dalamar asked, as they wound round and round down the hidden staircase.

"Yes. He has the device. He said something else that I found interesting, Dalamar"—Palin reached out his hand, touched the elf on the shoulder—"Tasslehoff saw his own ghost."

Dalamar swung the lamp around. "He did?" The elf was skeptical. "This isn't another of his swimming bird stories, is it?"

"No," said Palin. He could see again the fear and terror in the kender's bright eyes. "No, he was telling the truth. He's afraid, Dalamar. I've never see Tasslehoff afraid before."

"At least this proves he died," Dalamar said, offhandedly, and resumed his descent.

Palin sighed. "The gnome is trying to fix the device. That's what you meant, wasn't it? The significance of the gnome. A gnome fixed the device the last time it was broken. Gnimsh. The gnome my uncle murdered."

Dalamar said nothing. He continued hurrying down the stairs.

"Listen to me, Dalamar!" Palin said, moving so close to the elf that he had to be careful not to trip on the skirts of his robes. "How did the gnome come to be here? This is . . . this is not some simple coincidence, is it?"

"No," Dalamar murmured. "Not coincidence."

"Then what?" Palin demanded, exasperated.

Dalamar halted again, held up the light to illuminate Palin's face. He drew back, half-blinded.

"You don't understand?" Dalamar asked. "Not even now?"

"No," Palin retorted angrily. "And I don't think you do, either."

"Not entirely," Dalamar admitted. "Not entirely. This meeting should explain much, however."

Lowering the lamp, he turned back to the descent. He said nothing more, and neither did Palin, who had no intention of demeaning himself further by continuing to ask questions that would be answered only in riddles.

"I no longer keep the wizard-lock functional," Dalamar remarked. He gave the rune-covered door an impatient shove. "A waste of time and effort."

"You've obviously used this chamber once or twice yourself," Palin observed.

"Oh, yes," said Dalamar with a smile. "I keep close watch on all my friends."

He blew out the lamplight.

They stood on the edge of a pool of water that was as quiet and dark as the chamber in which they were standing. A jet of blue flame burned in the center of the pool. The flame gave no light. It seemed to exist in another place, another time, and at first Palin saw nothing except the reflection of the blue flame in the water. Then the two merged in his vision. The flame flared, and he could see the interior of the laboratory as clearly as if he had been inside.

Goldmoon stood by the long stone table. . . .

35

The One God

Goldmoon stood by the long stone table, staring down unseeing at several books that had been left lying about. She heard voices coming nearer. The voice of the person she was meeting, the person she had been summoned by the dead to meet.

Shivering, Goldmoon clasped her hands tightly around her arms. The Tower was cold with a chill that could never be warmed. A place of darkness, a place of sorrow, a place of overreaching ambition, a place of suffering and of death. Her destination. The culmination of her strange journey.

Dalamar had given her a lamp, but its feeble light could not banish the immense darkness. The glow of the lamplight did nothing more than keep her company. Yet, for that she was grateful, and she kept near the lamp. She did not regret sending Dalamar away. She had never liked, never trusted the dark elf. His sudden reappearance here in this forest of death only increased her suspicions of him. He used the dead. . . .

"But then," said Goldmoon softly, "so do I."

Amazing power . . . for a person. A mere mortal.

Goldmoon began to tremble. She had stood before in the presence of a god, and her soul remembered. But something about this was not right. . . .

The door opened, thrust aside by an impatient hand.

"I can see nothing in this wizard's murk," said a girl's voice, a child's voice whose melody sang through Goldmoon's dreams. "We need more light."

The light grew brighter gradually. Soft and warm, at first, the flames of a few dozen candles. The light grew brighter still, until it seemed that the limbs of the cypress trees had parted, the top of the Tower had been lifted, and sunlight poured down into the chamber.

A girl stood in the doorway. She was tall and well-muscled. She wore a chain-mail shirt, a black tunic and black hose and over that a black tabard decorated with a white death lily, the symbol of a Dark Knight. Her head was covered with a light down of red. Goldmoon would not have recognized her but for the amber eyes and the voice that sent a thrill through her body.

So terrible and wonderful was the shock that she caught hold of the table and leaned against it to support herself.

"Mina?" Goldmoon faltered, not daring to believe.

The girl's face was suddenly illuminated, as if she were the sun, and the sun shone from within.

"You . . . you are so beautiful, Mother," Mina said softly, awed. "You look just as I imagined."

Sinking to her knees, the girl extended her hands. "Come, kiss me, Mother," she cried, tears falling. "Kiss me as you used to. For I am Mina. Your Mina."

Bewildered, her heart made whole by joy and riven by a strange and terrible fear, Goldmoon could feel nothing except the wild and painful beating of her heart. Unable to take her eyes from Mina, she stumbled forward and fell to her knees before her. She clasped the sobbing girl in her arms.

"Mina," Goldmoon whispered, rocking her as she used to rock her when Mina woke crying in the night. "Mina. Child . . . why did you leave us, when we all loved you so much?"

Mina raised her tearstained face. The amber eyes gleamed. "I left for love of you, Mother. I left to seek what you wanted so desperately. And I found it, Mother! I found it for you.

"Dearest Mother." Mina took hold of Goldmoon's cold and trembling hands and pressed them to her lips. "All that I am and all that I have done, I have done for you."

"I . . . don't understand, child." Goldmoon kept hold of Mina's hands, but her eyes went to the dark armor. "You wear the symbol of evil, of darkness. . . . Where did you go? Where have you been? What has happened to you?"

Mina laughed. She glittered with happiness and excitement. "Where I went and where I have been is not important. What happened to me along the way—that is what you must hear.

"Do you remember, Mother, the stories you used to tell me? The story about how you traveled into darkness to search for the gods? How you found the gods and brought faith in the gods back to the people of the world?"

"Yes," said Goldmoon, but the word was a breath, not spoken. She had ceased trembling and begun to shiver.

"You told me the gods were gone, Mother," said Mina, her eyes shining like those of a child who has a delightful surprise. "You told me that because the gods were gone we had to rely on ourselves to find our way in the world. But I didn't believe that story, Mother.

"Oh"—Mina placed her hand over Goldmoon's mouth, silencing her—"I don't think you lied to me. You were mistaken, that was all. You see, I knew better. I knew there was a god, for I heard the voice of the god when I was little and our boat sank and I was cast alone into the sea. You found me on the shore, do you remember, Mother? But you never knew how I came to be there, because I promised I would never tell. The others drowned, but I was saved. The god held me and supported me and sang to me when I was afraid of the loneliness and dark.

"You said there were no gods, Mother, but I knew you were wrong. And so I did what you did. I went to find God and bring God back to you. And I've done that, Mother." Mina was flushed with joy and pride in her achievement. The amber eyes were radiant. "The miracle of the storm. That is the One God. The miracle of your youth and beauty. That is the One God, Mother."

"You asked for this," Goldmoon cried, lifting her hand to touch her face, the face that had always seemed strange to her. "This is not me. It is your vision of me. . . ."

"Of course, Mother." Mina laughed delightedly. "Aren't you pleased? I have so much to tell you that will please you. I've brought the miracle of healing back into the world with the power of the One God. With the blessing of the One, I felled the shield the elves had raised over Silvanesti, and I killed the treacherous dragon Cyan Bloodbane. Another truly monstrous green dragon, Beryl, is dead by the power of the One God. The elven nations, which were corrupt and faithless, have both been destroyed. In death, the elves will find redemption. Death will lead them to the One God."

"Ah, child!" Goldmoon gasped. Casting off Mina's hands, which had been wrapped tightly around her own, Goldmoon stared at her in horror. "I see blood on these hands. The blood of thousands! This god you have found is a terrible god. A god of darkness and evil!"

"The One God told me you would feel this way, Mother," Mina said patiently. "When the other gods departed and you thought you were left alone, you were angry and afraid. You felt betrayed, and that was only natural. For you *had* been betrayed." Mina's voice hardened. "The gods in which you had so misguidedly placed your faith fled in fear. . . ."

"No!" Goldmoon rose unsteadily to her feet. She fell back, away from Mina, held out her hand in warding. "No, child, I don't believe it. I won't listen you."

Mina followed after her, seized hold of Goldmoon's hand. "You will listen, Mother. You must so that you will understand. The gods fled in fear of Chaos. All except one. One god remained loyal to the people she had helped to create. One only had the courage to face the terror of the Father of All and of Nothing. The battle left her weak. Too weak for her to make manifest her presence in the world. Too weak to fight the strange dragons who came to take her place. But although she could not be with her people, she gave gifts to her people to help them. The magic that they call the wild magic. The power of healing that you know as the power of the heart. . . . Those were her gifts. Her gifts to you.

"There is her sign." Mina pointed to the heads of the five dragons that guarded the Portal.

Shuddering, Goldmoon turned. Dark and lifeless, the heads began to glow with an eerie radiance, one red, one blue, one green, one white, one black.

She moaned and averted her eyes.

"Mother," said Mina, gently rebuking, "the One God does not ask you for thanks for these past gifts. Rest assured, she has more gifts to bestow on her faithful in the future. But she does require service, Mother. She wants you to serve her and to love her, as she has served you and loved you. Do this, Mother. Kneel down and offer your prayers of faith and thanksgiving to the One True God. The One God who remained faithful to her creation."

"No! I don't believe what you are telling me!" Goldmoon said through lips so stiff she could barely cause them to form the words. "You have been deceived, child. I know this One God. I know her of old. I know her tricks and her lies and deceits."

Goldmoon looked back at the five-headed dragon, whose terrible radiance shone undimmed, for no other opposing force existed that could cloud it.

"I do not believe your lies, Takhisis!" Goldmoon cried defiantly. "I will never believe that the blessed Paladine and Mishakal left us to your mercy! You are what you have always been—a God of Evil who does not want worshipers but slaves. I will never bow down to you. I will never serve you."

Fire flared from the eyes of the five dragons. The fire was white hot, and Goldmoon withered in the terrible heat. Her body shrank and shriveled. Her strength ebbed, and she collapsed to the floor. Her hands shook with palsy. The skin stretched tight over tendon and bone. Her arms grew thin and splotched with age. Her face wrinkled. Her beautiful silver-gold hair was white and wispy. She was an old woman, her pulse feeble, her heartbeat slowing.

"See, Mother," Mina said and her voice was sorrowful and afraid, "see what will happen if you continue to deny the One God what is due her?"

Kneeling beside Goldmoon, Mina took hold of the old woman's palsied hands and pressed them again to her lips. "Please, Mother. I can restore your youth. I can bring back your beauty. You can begin life all over again. You will walk with me, and together we will rule the world in the name of the One God. All you have to do is to come to the One God in humility and ask this favor of her, and it will be done."

Goldmoon closed her eyes. Her lips did not move.

Mina bent close. "Mother," she begged, and she sounded fearful. "Mother, do this for me if not for yourself. Do this for love of me!"

"I pray," said Goldmoon. "I pray to Paladine and Mishakal that they forgive me for my lack of faith. I should have known the truth," she said softly, her voice weakening as she spoke the words with her dying breath, "I pray that Paladine will hear my words, and he will come . . . for love of Mina . . . For love of all. . . ."

Goldmoon sank, lifeless, to the floor.

"Mother," said Mina, as bewildered as a lost child, "I did this for you. . . ."

Epilogue

hat night, in the small port city of Dolphin View, in northern Abanasinia, a ship set sail across the Straits of Schallsea. The ship carried a single passenger, whose identity was known only to the captain. Heavily cloaked and hooded, the passenger boarded during the night, bringing with him nothing except his horse, a wild-eyed, short-tempered beast, who was housed below deck in a specially built stall.

The mysterious passenger was obviously a man of means, for he had hired the *Gull Wing* specially, and he had paid extra for his horse. The sailors, intensely curious about the passenger's identity, were envious of the cabin boy, who was granted permission to take the passenger his supper. They waited eagerly for the boy to return to tell them what he had seen and heard.

The cabin boy knocked on the door. No one answered and after a few more knocks, he trepidatiously tried the lock. The door opened.

A tall, slender man, wrapped in his cloak, stood staring

out the porthole at the vast and glittering sea. He did not turn around, even after the cabin boy mentioned dinner several times. Shrugging, the cabin boy was about to withdraw when the mysterious passenger spoke. He used Common, but with a heavy accent. His voice quivered with impatience.

"Tell the captain I want this ship to go faster. Do you hear? We must go faster."

In her mountain lair, surrounded by the skulls of the dragons she had slain, the great red dragon Malystryx dreamed of water, inky black water, rising up over her red legs, her belly, her massive red tail. Rising to cover her red wings, her back. Rising to her mane. Rising to cover her head, her mouth and nostrils. She could not breathe. She fought to lift herself above the water, but her legs were pinned. She could not free herself. Her lungs were bursting. Stars exploded before her eyes. She gasped, opened her mouth. The water poured in, and she was drowning. . . .

Malystryx woke, suddenly, glared around, angry and uneasy. She had been dreaming, and she never dreamed. Never before had any dream disturbed her rest. She had heard voices in her dream, mocking, goading, and she heard them still. The voices came from the skull totem, and they sang a song about sleep. Forever sleep.

Malystryx lifted her enormous head and stared hard at the skull totem, at the white skulls of blue dragons piled on top of the skulls of silver dragons; at the skulls of red dragons lying atop of the skulls of gold dragons.

From out the empty eye sockets of all the dead dragons, eyes, living eyes, stared back at Malystryx.

Sleep. Forever sleep.

In the Tower of High Sorcery, Galdar waited for Mina, but she didn't return. At last, worried about her, not trusting this place or the wizards who inhabitated it, he went in search of her.

He found her in the old laboratory.

Mina sat huddled on the floor beside the body of an old, old woman. Galdar approached, spoke to her. Mina did not look up. Bending down, Galdar saw that the old woman was dead.

Galdar lifted Mina, put his good strong right arm around her, and led her from the chamber.

The light of the dragons faded.

The laboratory was once more shrouded in darkness.

MARGARET WEIS
&
TRACY HICKMAN

The co-creators of the DRAGONLANCE® world return to the
epic tale that introduced Krynn to a generation of fans!

THE LOST CHRONICLES

VOLUME ONE
DRAGONS OF THE DWARVEN DEPTHS

As Tanis and Flint bargain for refuge in Thorbardin, Raistlin
and Caramon go to Neraka to search for one of the spellbooks of
Fistandantilus. The refugees in Thorbardin are trapped when the
draconian army marches, and Flint undertakes a quest to find the
Hammer of Kharas to free them all, while Sturm becomes a key of a
different sort.
Now Available in Paperback!

VOLUME TWO
DRAGONS OF THE HIGHLORD SKIES

Dragon Highlord Ariakas assigns the recovery of the dragon orb taken to
Ice Wall to Kitiara Uth-Matar, who is rising up the ranks of both the dark
forces and of Ariakas's esteem. Finding the orb proves easy, but getting
it from Laurana proves more difficult. Difficult enough to attract the
attention of Lord Soth.
Now Available in Hardcover!

VOLUME THREE
DRAGONS OF THE HOURGLASS MAGE

The wizard Raistlin Majere takes the black robes and travels to the
capital city of the evil empire, Neraka, to serve the Queen of Darkness.
July 2008

TRACY HICKMAN

PRESENTS

THE BRIDGES OF TIME

With the power of the Anvil of Time, the Journeyman can travel
the river of time as simply as walking upstream, visiting the
ancient past of Krynn with ease.

VOLUME ONE
THE SELLSWORD
Cam Banks

Vanderjack, a mercenary with a price on his head, agrees out of
desperation to retrieve a priceless treasure for a displaced noble. The
treasure is deep within enemy territory, and he must survive an army of
old foes, a chorus of unhappy ghosts, and the questionable assistance of
a mad gnome to find it.

April 2008

VOLUME TWO
THE SURVIVORS
Dan Willis

A goodhearted dwarf is warned of an apocalyptic flood by the god
Reorx, and he and his motley followers must decide whether the
warning is real—and then survive the disaster that sweeps
through their part of Krynn.

November 2008

JEAN RABE

THE STONETELLERS

"Jean Rabe is adept at weaving a web of deceit and lies, mixed with adventure, magic, and mystery."
—sffworld.com on *Betrayal*

Jean Rabe returns to the DRAGONLANCE® world with a tale of slavery, rebellion, and the struggle for freedom.

VOLUME ONE
THE REBELLION

After decades of service, nature has dealt the goblins a stroke of luck. Earthquakes strike the Dark Knights' camp and mines, crippling the Knights and giving the goblins their best chance to escape. But their freedom will not be easy to win.

August 2007

VOLUME TWO
DEATH MARCH

The escaped slaves—led by the hobgoblin Direfang—embark on a journey fraught with danger as they leave Neraka to cross the ocean and enter the Qualinesti Forest, where they believe themselves free. . . .

August 2008

VOLUME THREE
GOBLIN NATION

A goblin nation rises in the old forest, building fortresses and fighting to hold onto their new homeland, while the sorcerers among them search for powerful magic cradled far beneath the trees.

August 2009

RICHARD A. KNAAK

THE OGRE TITANS

The Grand Lord Golgren has been savagely crushing
all opposition to his control of the harsh ogre lands of
Kern and Blöde, first sweeping away rival chieftains, then
rebuilding the capital in his image. For this he has had to
deal with the ogre titans, dark, sorcerous giants who have
contempt for his leadership.

VOLUME ONE
THE BLACK TALON

Among the ogres, where every ritual demands blood and every ally can
become a deadly foe, Golgren seeks whatever advantage he can obtain,
even if it means a possible alliance with the Knights of Solamnia, a
questionable pact with a mysterious wizard, and trusting an elven slave
who might wish him dead.

December 2007

VOLUME TWO
THE FIRE ROSE

With his other enemies beginning to converge on him from all sides,
Golgren, now Grand Khan of all his kind, must battle with the
Ogre Titans for mastery of a mysterious artifact capable of ultimate
transformation and power.

December 2008

VOLUME THREE
THE GARGOYLE KING

Forced from the throne he has so coveted, Golgren makes a final
stand for control of the ogre lands against the Titans . . . against an
enemy as ancient and powerful as a god.

December 2009